Two Sides of Truth

K.S. Jones

WOLFPACK
PUBLISHING
— EST 2013 —

Two Sides of Truth
Paperback Edition
Copyright © 2022 K.S. Jones

Wolfpack Publishing
9850 S. Maryland Parkway, Suite A-5 #323
Las Vegas, Nevada 89183

wolfpackpublishing.com

This book is a work of fiction. Any references to historical events, real people or real places are used fictitiously. Other names, characters, places and events are products of the author's imagination, and any resemblance to actual events, places or persons, living or dead, is entirely coincidental.

All rights reserved. No part of this book may be reproduced by any means without the prior written consent of the publisher, other than brief quotes for reviews.

Paperback ISBN 978-1-63977-980-2
eBook ISBN 978-1-63977-979-6

Dedicated to Wanda Lillie Buckner O'Neal
I will forever be grateful for the stories that told the story.

TWO SIDES OF TRUTH

CHAPTER 1

ARKANSAS 1932

The town of Coaldale wound through the timbered valley like a black snake in the dark hole of an outhouse. Folks knew it was there by the grim feeling it posed, but the need to stay overpowered the urge to run.

I had lived my whole life in the low-lying basin between the Arkansas Western Railroad and the Poteau River—the only river in the state that flowed north. Fitting, I suppose. It seemed everything had turned around backward and was running the wrong way. I wasn't blaming God, though. A lot of trouble we caused ourselves.

Take my older brother, Henry, for instance. Making good decisions was out of his reach. But with my best friend, Leona, bound for California, he'd moved up a notch on my short list of friends. After school, I went looking for him and found him pitching pennies with Benny and the other boys behind Doc's office. When he saw the sorrowful look on my face, he'd gathered up his winnings and come without me having to ask.

Beneath the lopsided shadow of the chinquapin tree

between the jailhouse and the store, he waited with me. I killed time talking about the school lesson he had missed.

"Miss Stewart says the Panhandle folks can't even eat a meal of beans without the grit and dust wearin' their teeth away. Beans and mud. How can people live like that?"

But some days, a bad attitude just popped out of Henry. Mama said it's because he is itching to be a man. I think it's because he is tired of being nobody.

"Sooze, what makes you think we're any better off than those folks?" This being his last year of school, Henry talked like he knew something about everything. "We ain't got any dirt in our beans, and our lungs ain't filled with dust, but we ain't got much else neither."

Henry wore Daddy's brown hand-me-down overalls, and even though he'd rolled the hems twice, they still dragged the ground. He'd spent a lifetime telling me he was "only short for now," but he'd never grown much taller than my five-foot-five height, and that was a far shot shorter than Daddy. Using his fingers, he combed his reddish-brown hair back from his face, and with eyes as rich as pure honey, he stared at me.

"I'd suffer through a little dirt in my food if I could get me a T-bone and some potato pone, wouldn't you?" He pulled his lucky piece out of his hip pocket. It was nothing more than an old stag-handled knife handed down to him from our granddaddy, but he called it his good luck charm. Like an ear of corn, he held it to his lips, and with a chomp, chomp, chomp, he pretended to eat it. "Heck, Sooze, anything's better than poke salad and corn."

Henry always looked at the dark side of things, and I didn't want to encourage him, so I thought it best to ignore him. I circled the tree, kicking up dust off the bone-dry ground. Keeping one hand on the pine, I pushed my other inside my dress pocket, finding a new hole. It had worn clean through the pink, flowery patch I'd sewn onto my green dress, trying to hide a stain. Even though I'd mended it many times over, Mama said the dress still looked pretty on me. She said it matched my green eyes and rosy cheeks and made my blonde hair look like an angel's.

But it didn't matter to Henry whether I was paying attention to him or not. He just kept talking anyway.

"Shoot! At least those folks got automobiles, and here we are still with a horse and wagon! We're about as poor and backward as you get, Sooze."

"Life ain't all hard biscuits!" I stomped my foot. I didn't have the same outlook as Henry. "We got other things, you know?"

Our family still owned two cows, six prize hogs, almost three dozen chickens, and a field planted full of corn. And every night at supper, Daddy still bowed his head to thank the good Lord that hard times hadn't stripped us clean. I always listened to the tone of Daddy's voice, too, because Mama said you could hear defeat in a man's voice long before it settled in his brain, and I knew I hadn't heard it yet.

"So…" Henry's tone had a challenge. "Are you sayin' that I should be thankful for the piddlin' life I've got?" He shoved his lucky knife back into his pocket and straightened up as tall as he was, and then with pulled-back shoulders, he pushed out his chest like a mean old rooster. "Well, I'm *not* thankful. I'm meant for better things, Sooze!"

Henry had a way of flying off the handle but settling back quick. Soon his eyes flashed me an *I'm sorry* look. When his shoulders relaxed, he crooked his arm around my neck. Leaning in close to my ear, he whispered, "Now, don't go tellin' Daddy, not Mama neither, but me and Benny are headin' for Chicago the day after graduation." He grinned at me, and then he stepped back and held his arms wide, raising them high to the blue, cloudless sky. "Glory be, Sooze. I just can't hardly stand it! I want out of this little good-fer-nothin' town so bad my feet are itchin'." He began to march stiff-legged around the chinquapin. "I'm goin' places, Sis!"

I should have stopped his foolish talk right then, but the

automobile I'd been waiting for was driving up the blacktop road. Pointing, I said, "That's them, isn't it, Henry?"

Henry laid his freckled arm across the tops of my shoulders again and patted. "Settle down, Sis," he said, more like a friend than a brother. "It's them, sure enough. Leona'll be here before you know it."

I felt the choke in my voice. "And gone just as quick."

The black Model A rattled toward us. They had it packed to the brim inside and out with blankets and clothes, food and dishes, and it had every gasoline and water can that could be tied to its fenders and running boards strapped to it. On its rooftop lay a gray pinstripe bed mattress stacked with three wood-slatted egg crates, each holding zinc-topped canning jars. Their lids glinted in the fading sunlight. Ropes winding this way and that kept everything tied down.

The automobile rolled to a stop.

"Leona Gray!" I called through the open window. "What in the world am I supposed to do without my best friend?"

I dabbed my tears with a handkerchief as Leona got out of the automobile and came straight to me with a hug. Her fine, strawberry-blonde hair smelled like the lavender soap I'd made for her last Christmas.

"I can't believe we're movin' away." Leona's voice cracked. "And on your sixteenth birthday, too. What kind of gift is that?"

"It's the only thing you can do." Pressing the hankie to my nose, I pushed back a sniffle. "Your daddy was right about this awful time we're in. It'll eat you alive if you don't get out of its way."

"But what about you?" Leona asked. "Is your daddy still bent on stayin'? How are you gonna live, Sooze?"

Since the coal mine shut down, packed automobiles had been motoring out of Coaldale, leaving only dust behind.

"Daddy says we'll keep a watchful eye," I promised. "He says the shadow of the hawk ain't over us yet."

Other folks came from the blacksmith shop and the gas

station for their goodbyes. Even Uncle Ray and Aunt Lissie came with Arnold, and Uncle Will and Aunt Rose with Zane.

Sam Huckabee walked over with his daughters, Lauralee and Lillie, but Mrs. Huckabee stayed on the nearby steps of Huckabee's General Store, waving her farewell as her son, Owen, ignoring us all, swept their wide wooden porch. Just for a moment, I thought of David. Why hadn't he come, too? With my best friend moving away, I thought my boyfriend would be standing beside me. Some days it seemed I couldn't shake him loose with a stick, and then other days, when I expected him to be by my side, he'd be nowhere in sight.

"Maybe your folks will decide to come to California, too," Leona said. "Most have lost pert'near everything, Sooze. How long do you think your daddy can hold out?" She motioned toward the gathering of townsfolk. "Why, there's no more than sixteen or seventeen families left in Coaldale."

"It's surely dwindlin'," I agreed as I watched Daddy approach. He walked alongside Doc Farrell and Miss Stewart, the schoolteacher. They gathered at the packed automobile for their goodbyes, too.

When my gaze settled on Daddy, I realized how much these hard times had eaten away at him. He was still a handsome man, but almost overnight, it seemed his rusty-red colored hair had grayed, and deep furrows of wrinkles now creased his face. He was sunbaked and spent. Daddy had never been one to be defeated easily, so I feared times ahead might get harder.

"Good luck to you," Daddy said to Alvin Gray.

With a Second Reader in her hand, Miss Stewart handed it through the automobile's open window to Mrs. Gray, who held her bundled infant. Eight-year-old Dottie sat perched on a black box in the back seat.

"Make sure Dottie keeps up with her lessons," Miss Stewart told Leona's mother. "She especially likes to read

The Sparrow, and she does a fine job." She smiled and waved at curly-haired Dottie, who happily waved back.

"Thank you," Mrs. Gray said, taking the green-backed book.

"Oh, Sooze." Leona sank into a whine. "What if you lose everything before your daddy comes to his senses? How will you get to California then?"

I felt a swell of tears welling up inside me, but I didn't want Leona's last memory of me to be one of a blubbering crybaby, so I took stock of myself. "We'll make it fine," I said with as much confidence as I could push out of me. Then I pulled Leona close and hugged her tight. "You take care of yourself. Remember to write me once you settle."

"Come on, Leona!" Alvin Gray called out. "Let's get a move on! The promised land is a-waitin' for us."

Crawling into the back seat, my best friend in the whole world waved goodbye. As the Model A rattled away, Leona's face stared back with a look that said we were crazy to stay. I just stood there waving as they drove out of sight.

"Hey, Henry!" Benny Simmons shouted from where he stood across the street. His coal-black hair was slicked with oil, and the pocket of his red-and-black plaid shirt was torn and hanging half off. "Come huntin' with me?"

"Can't!" Henry called back. "It's Sooze birthday, and Ma's baked a cake!"

As if Daddy had been snakebit, he turned to Henry. "I told you to stay away from that boy. He's no good."

"Aww, Daddy, Benny's all right. He's just had hard times with his Ma workin' nights like she does. He ain't never had anyone around to raise him right like I did. He's had to learn things all on his own."

"We've all had hard times, Henry," Daddy told him, his tone low and serious. "But times aren't what dictates a man's worth, and that boy is just plain worthless."

"Henry!" Benny called louder, waving his hand in the air. "Get on over here!"

"He ain't got no other friends, Daddy. Let me talk to

him. I'll be right back." Henry trotted across the roadway until he was standing beside his friend. Handing Benny something from his pocket, Henry turned and trotted right back.

Ignoring all but me, Daddy wiped a lingering tear from under my eye. "Maybe some of that birthday cake Henry's been a-waitin' for will put a smile back on your face." After kissing me on the forehead, he said, "I'll bet your Mama has it frosted by now."

"I was hopin' she made it chocolate. Do you think she did?" I had a longing in my voice, but when Daddy lowered his head without answering, it reminded me how much a square of chocolate cost. Right away, I regretted my words.

"Come on, Henry," Daddy said without answering. "Let's get this birthday girl home."

Daddy hadn't told us he would be in town with the wagon, so I'd half expected Henry to ditch me after seeing Leona off, leaving me alone to walk the two miles back home. I was fine with it, especially with the spring day moving down into a somber blue sunset. I needed some quiet time to reminisce about Leona, and I wanted to be by myself to cry just a little, too. Besides, walking home through the wildflowers in Whitaker's Meadow was sure to cheer me up. They'd been growing like weeds for days, and I wanted to believe Leona would be looking at the same flowers all the way to California. The sight of them growing up through the cracked dirt gave me hope. No matter how hard the road, if you just kept pushing up, you'd find the light of day. But when I asked about walking home, Daddy wouldn't hear of it.

"Too close to sundown," he said. "Wolves and razorbacks will be out looking for food, and you don't need to be offerin' yourself up as dinner to any wild animal."

Usually, I'd argue or wouldn't pay no mind to the warning. I could outrun and out-climb most everything, but Daddy was right. Sundown in the spring was when wolves, wild pigs, and painter cats were more aggressive, trying to feed and protect their young. Daddy taught us to stay wary walking the narrow road to and from school this time of year because of it. Scrub grew so thick it was easy to get caught in its wiry limbs, and instead of us trapping the wild animals, it'd be like them trapping us. We'd be easy pickings for a meal. In some places, the tendrils knitted themselves so tight the tangles grew together like woven crop baskets turned upside down. The knotted mess was a perfect place to hide a litter, and stumbling across a den of wild animals was surely not as fun as finding a litter of kittens.

In the fall, I could count on bois d'arc trees for my defense. They dropped bumpy, green horse apples so hard and heavy even Frenchy, our mare, wouldn't eat them, but the fallen fruit sure came in handy for throwing when wild critters needed discouraging. Being springtime, the best throwing I could hope for was dirt clods or rocks, and they just didn't have the same impact as a horse apple.

As our wagon neared home, the road turned hardpan. I expected Daddy to bring up the land he wanted cleared or the new smokehouse he needed built. I wasn't keen on frittering away my next few weeks doing backbreaking work, but knowing how much Daddy depended on our help, I wasn't going to complain either.

About the time I thought he'd bring up the subject, he turned to me and instead said, "Sixteen! You've grown into a fine young lady, Sooze. Good cook and seamstress, too." It started me wondering whether Daddy had ever wished I'd been born a good, strong boy—worthy of working the farm right alongside him—instead of a girl. If he did, he never said so, but I always worked my hardest anyway, hoping he'd never regret me.

CHAPTER 2

West of Coaldale, just this side of Sugar Creek at the Oklahoma border, was our white clapboard house on eighty acres. After sundown, it came alive with the light of coal oil lamps. From a distance, it almost looked prosperous.

Folks got a good look at our farm from the hardpan road leading in, with their first sight being our weathered wood corncrib and big barn. Both stood on the south side of the house near a line of full-grown chinquapins. Our hog pen, chicken coop, and falling down smokehouse with its cattywampus roof were to the north. For privacy, the white-washed outhouse was back behind the house.

Pulling past the front porch, I knew Mama had our evening fire ablaze with pecan wood because a swirl of vanilla-scented smoke curled out of the chimney.

Daddy snapped the reins, urging Frenchy onward until the wagon neared the barn, then he pulled the straps taut before pushing the brake bar forward. Henry and me jumped to the ground.

"Henry," Daddy said. "Change out of your school clothes before doin' your chores, but don't you go runnin' off before puttin' Frenchy and the wagon up for the night."

"I know, Daddy," Henry groaned.

I was comforted by being home, smelling supper cooking, and seeing Mama's hand-painted *Welcome Home* plaque hanging on our plain, white walls. Alongside the plaque hung two framed photographs. One was a family portrait taken last year before Mama knew she was carrying baby Grace, and the other was a wedding photograph of Mama and Daddy done more than eighteen years before. The only other thing on our living room wall was a white oval Mama had embroidered with the words *Lord, Bless This House*. Our three books were on a shelf where our coal oil lamps sat: *The Holy Bible, Little Women,* and *Treasure Island*. It was hard to say which was my favorite—I'd read each one a half dozen times, but Meg's voice from *Little Women* stayed most in my head. Each time, when Meg looked down at her old dress and said, "It's so dreadful to be poor!" I'd feel the same, but then I'd remember Mama's lesson—money was just a means. It can't buy what we truly need. God gave us family as our most faithful companion and love as our most precious gift. When all else fails, it's only them we need.

Daddy and Granddaddy had built our house more than thirty years back after hacking out a clearing on this acreage. They'd built it with their own hands. That was when indoor plumbing was still a luxury, even to a rich man. A well and an outhouse were all anyone had, so the thought of building a room inside the house for a toilet was preposterous. No poles or lines for electricity either. Oil lamps were what they had. So, like lots of country folk, we still relied on lamps and an outhouse even though most townsfolk had modern indoor plumbing and electricity.

We used well water or rainwater collected in our two aluminum wash pots that Daddy used during hog killing to bathe. We'd take the water and heat it on our coal-burning cookstove, and then we'd pour it into our big, galvanized washtub and have a bath. But that was for Saturday only. The rest of the time, we just sponged off or, in Henry's case, just stank. He never was one for taking a bath. In fairness, though, during the summer and fall months after finishing his planting or harvesting, Henry would take off by himself with a bar of Mama's lye soap in his pocket. He'd jump in the water down at Sugar Creek and wash the sweat and dirt off his body. Then, even though he'd never admit it, he'd find a drink of corn whiskey before coming home to supper. I knew because the chore of doing the family's laundry was mine, and I often smelled the stinging scent of honeyed grain spilled on his clothes.

Every evening, fall, winter, or spring, we'd light a fire in the fireplace while our supper cooked on our coal-burning stove. Sometimes, when the cost of coal was too much for us, Daddy would send Henry into town to tote back a wagonful of coke, but that burned-up coal needed lots of extra wood before it'd start burning. I didn't mind stoking the stove for a coke-cooked meal, though, because it didn't burn with the same sulfurous tang. In the cold of winter, we'd keep the coal bin nearly full and leave the stove burning while the fireplace blazed to heat the house, but both would often go out in the middle of the night and leave us shivering.

With it being my special day, Mama sat me in the armchair next to the big rock fireplace and planted a kiss on my forehead. She went to the kitchen, and soon after, I heard the rattling of pots and pans. I knew she probably needed my help, but Mama had ordered me to sit, saying, "No one should have to cook their own birthday supper."

She'd told twelve-year-old Cora to rock baby Grace, which was supposed to be my job when Mama was cooking. Gently, Cora swung the pinewood cradle back and forth as Grace's wee newborn eyes opened and closed in quiet slumber.

After Henry finished his chores, he came in with an armload of pecan wood. He was stacking it inside our wood box when, with a *thud*, he dropped a log after a nubbin caught itself on his homemade knotted-rope handle.

"Quiet, or you'll wake the baby," I whispered. Henry nodded, but I kept talking anyway. "I told you the rope wasn't goin' to work when you put it on there. Why don't you just cut it off so's you can slide the wood in easier?"

"Can't," Henry said. "I lent my knife out." He knelt and commenced trying to untie the tightened knot with his hands.

It wasn't until then that I remembered his speech from earlier. *"Now don't you go tellin' Daddy, not Mama neither, but me and Benny are headed for Chicago..."* I opened my mouth to converse with him about it, but before a word came out, Mama walked past the kitchen doorway, headed for the table. She was carrying my cake. Behind her trailed Daddy, bringing bowls, forks, plates, and napkins.

"Where do you want these, Emma Jean?" Daddy asked her.

"Just put them here on the table."

I felt silly being so excited about my birthday, but I hurried to the kitchen table anyway. By the light of the coal oil lamp, I inspected the white layer cake.

"It's grand, Mama."

"Barely had enough sugar for the frosting, but it turned out." Mama glanced at Daddy and said, "We'll need sugar and a few other things from the store soon."

"That'll need to wait, Emma."

Mama nodded with understanding and then headed back to the cookstove.

Being just a little over five feet tall and weighing a sparrow-like ninety pounds, Mama didn't look like she'd given birth just a few weeks ago. Her stomach was flat as a washboard while her bosom had blossomed.

In honor of my birthday, Mama wore her best button-up white blouse, which she kept like new for special occasions. It was tucked into the waistband of her tan prairie skirt, and then she'd tied on her favorite brown-and-white apron. Her long hair, the muddled color of dishwater, was twisted into a bun and bobby-pinned to the back of her head. Having half-French, half-Cherokee blood swirling through her hill heritage, her smoky sage-green eyes had the power to soothe a crying child or heal a saddened heart. Although ours were the same color, she'd said my eyes still had a youthful twinkle. With her face thin and worn now, she hardly resembled that woman in the wedding photograph.

Using both hands, Mama picked up the cooking pot by its handle. The smell of chicken and dumplins with carrots and onions swirled out. As she carried it to the table, Daddy put our square board down so she could set the pot on top. Mama was always careful not to scorch the table. Daddy had spent weeks building it last summer from a fallen loblolly pine. "You got to value what you got, or you'll never have nothin'," she liked to say.

"Cora, if you got the baby to sleep, you and Henry need to come eat supper." Mama set a glass of water beside each plate.

As soon as we were seated, Daddy bowed his head. "Lord, thank you for this food, and thank you for keepin' us safe and together. Most of all, thank you for givin' us our sweet Sooze on this day sixteen years ago. Amen."

Once, I'd asked Mama why she'd given me such a funny name. She'd said her and Daddy had settled on the name Susanna before I was born, but soon as she saw me for the first time, she knew my name was Sooze instead, sort of like something belonging to a girl named Sue. "Sue's picked a flower," or "Sue's got the chickenpox," or "Sue's got that same readin' book with her again." But Mama says nothing ever really belongs to us except our beliefs, and she didn't want to mislead me, so instead of S-u-e, Mama taught me to spell my name S-o-o-z-e.

"Thank you, Daddy," I said after the prayer.

Crumbling leftover biscuits into the bowls, Mama ladled one full and handed it to Daddy and then another to Henry. Mama fed hardworking men first. As Henry shoveled a hot spoonful into his mouth, I asked, "Did you hear about Charley Ames?"

"Nope." With his mouth too full, creamy lines of broth ran down Henry's chin. He held his head up, mouth open to let the heat escape, and kept right on talking. "What's he up to?"

"His family is moving out," I told him, instinctively wiping my own chin as if it would clean up Henry's. "Charley came in after school while I was erasing the chalkboard and told Miss Stewart about his mama getting a letter from her cousin out in California. It said jobs were waitin' for them if they weren't making a livin' in Coaldale anymore."

"Hellfire, no one's makin' a livin' in Coaldale anymore," Henry answered.

"Henry!" Mama's tone was shaming. "They'll be no cursing inside this house. And wipe your chin so's you look like a human." She reached over, picked up his cloth napkin, and handed it to him.

"Sorry, Ma." Henry wiped his chin. "It just seems like everybody's leavin'. Why ain't we?"

"This is our home, Henry," Mama answered. "Where else would we go?"

"To Chicago!" His tone sizzled with excitement. "Or maybe California. There's food for the takin' out there. Jobs, too." He gulped water from his glass and then set it down hard on the table. This time he used the sleeve of his shirt to wipe his lips dry. "Jobs everywhere, Ma. Me and Daddy could both find work. We could be livin' the high life!"

Daddy had his head down, fiddling with his spoon. "You've got a job right here, Henry." With steam swirling out of his bowl, he kept stirring. "This farm is too much for one man. You're goin' to have your hands full right here, just like we planned, soon as you graduate. The crops and hogs need better tending, and you and me together can clear lots more land for planting. We can raise more hogs, too. If corn prices go up, we should be able to buy four or five more sows." With pride in his eyes, Daddy looked up. "And after watching you butcher hogs last December, I'd say you could make a fine living on hogs alone. You got a natural gift, son. We might make a go of this farm again."

"Henry's school comes first," Mama reminded.

"I know, Emma," Daddy said. "I said *after* the boy graduates. Besides," he said, grinning, "graduation is no more than a week away. Good thing, too. We need a new smokehouse built, and the garden needs planting."

With Henry quiet as a mouse, I said, "I can get the garden in the ground on Saturday, Daddy."

"Yeah." Daddy's voice stretched into a nod. "That'd be a big help, Sooze. Won't be as big of a garden this year, though. Only had enough cornmeal to trade for a few spoons of seed." He reached out and patted Mama's outstretched hand. "But your Mama's seedlings are growin' like weeds. They look good and strong this year."

"Snap beans, okra, and squash, too." Mama smiled with pride. "The pots are crowded, though. Sooze is right—we need to get them in the ground, and Saturday is as good a time as any since the frost has passed."

"What about onions and turnips?" Henry asked. "Melons, too. Ain't we plantin' any?"

"Your Uncle Ray's got those, son," Daddy told him. "With him livin' closer now, we'll be doin' some tradin' this season, and as much as he loves them okra, I figure we'll make out all right."

"Cora, can you help me on Saturday?" I tried to include my sister in most things so she could learn, but when I looked to her for an answer, I saw her eyes roll, and she gave a shrug. I didn't want to argue on my birthday, so I said, "If you got other chores, I can do it myself."

"This family works together for the good of us all," Daddy advised. Glancing at Cora, he said, "Cora can get up early to help, so's she can get her other chores done, too."

"Aww, Daddy," Cora said in a whine. "Zane promised to go fishin' with me on Saturday."

"Then maybe you'd better get up extra early." Daddy's voice was quiet but firm.

Cora dropped her spoon into her empty bowl. "I take care of the hen house all by myself. I don't never ask

Sooze for help. How come she's always askin' me to help her?"

With a turn toward Cora, Daddy stared with a look that made me cringe, but Mama took his focus right away by saying, "Don't back talk your daddy, or I'll help him cut a switch. Now clear the dinner bowls, Cora, and be careful carrying them to the sink." Mama's voice calmed as she reminded, "This china is the only thing Grandma Wanda left us. May God rest her soul. And I don't want any of them chipped or broken by your sassy attitude."

"I know, Ma." Cora gathered the dishes. "I'll be careful."

"Can we slice the cake, Mama?" I asked.

A low whistle came from Henry's lips. "I been a-waitin' for this cake all day."

"Me, too," Cora said on her way back to the table. "Should I bring the milk?" With a nod from Mama, she hurried back to the icebox and returned with the half-full bottle.

Mama stood and then sliced and served the first piece to me. "Here you go, birthday girl." Then she handed one to Daddy before serving the other slices.

"Have you talked to the Huckabee boy, Sooze?" Daddy asked me. "Are you still mulling over marryin' him?" He stretched, leaning back in his chair before patting his pooched-out belly. "Your mama and me had been married almost a year by the time she was sixteen."

But Mama had loved Daddy. She'd told me so time and time again. And fact was, true love felt like it'd been running from me my whole life, and I had no reason to believe I would ever find it. I knew admitting it wouldn't do no good.

"David's been gone a day or two," I said. "He didn't come to see Leona off today either. He must be in Waldron buying supplies for the store."

"Could be," Daddy agreed. "Huckabee's seems to be doing real good through these hard times, and that boy seems to take it all real serious. It would be a godsend to us,

Sooze, if we knew you was taken care of." He finished his cake and then laid his fork down on the table. "Besides, it'd be a big help to have another hardworkin' man around to help out during harvest season."

"I know it would, Daddy." I sighed, fidgeting in my chair. Knowing it's best just to come out and say what's on my mind, I said, "But I don't feel the love butterflies Mama talks about when she tells stories about meetin' you and fallin' in love. At least, I don't think I do." I waited for Mama's wise words, but instead, she reached into her apron pocket and pulled out a folded square of white cotton cloth. Pinned to it was a sewing needle strung with red embroidery thread. Without a word, she smoothed the cloth, then began her nightly stitching.

"Fairy tales," Daddy said. "You've been readin' too many stories, Sooze. Long as you got love waitin' inside you, that's all you need in these hard times." His tone deepened. "Lord knows, your mama and me already talked about not pushin' you into matrimony at sixteen, but we got faith knowin' you'll do the right thing."

Mama's slow, even stitches were as quiet as she was, and when no sound came from her, I heard my own voice saying, "I just feel like there's supposed to be more."

CHAPTER 3

Morning rose over the Arkansas hillside, shining its light in my eyes and waking me. Sharing a bed with Cora hadn't always been a chore, but since she'd turned twelve, she'd had her nose in everybody's business. If I'd had my druthers, I'd be sleeping in the hayloft by myself, but frankly, Henry was better suited for the barn than me.

Hoping for a minute more of peace, I didn't stretch a muscle, but when Cora rolled over and stared at me with those big brown eyes, I knew my peace was done.

"Do you think Henry's gonna ditch school again today?"

Cora always had Henry on her mind. From the time she was little, just learning to walk and talk, they'd been in each other's pocket. Henry had taken her under his wing like a mama dog takes a pup. He'd never let anyone, even our cousin Zane, pick on her. She'd grown up idolizing Henry. Their whole attachment riled me more than it should, but Cora made no bones about it—Henry was her favorite. Not that I cared, but it just wasn't fair. It was me who helped with her homework and taught her to read proper. And I was the one who helped Mama sew dresses for her, and it was me who put ribbons in her coppery-red hair so she didn't look like a boy. It was hard to do anything at all with it cut so short, but a hair ribbon surely helped.

"He *has* to go to school," I whispered. Bedroom doors stayed open overnight, so the heat downstairs could rise and warm us, which meant talking quiet was necessary, or the person asleep in the next room would hear us. In our case, that meant Henry. "The twelfth-grade study guide is bein' handed out today. Henry has to collect his to know what to study for on his exam."

I got out of bed, drawing the top blanket off with me, and wrapped myself in it like it was a long shawl. Shivering, I stretched the gray wool socks I'd slept in up to my knees and walked to the closet we shared. "Finals are less than a week away."

Inside our closet hung school dresses for the two of us. I skimmed through before pulling the yellow gingham off its hanger. Dropping the blanket, I took off my flannel night-gown and then poked my arms through the puffed dress sleeves. I drew it over my head and smoothed the gingham fabric to my knees. "Cora," I called with my back turned to the bed. "Can you button me up?"

Cora got out of bed with a huff, stomping across the floorboards. "You're always makin' me get up too early!"

"It's time to get ready for school anyhow. You always stay in bed too long."

As Cora buttoned, I brushed my hair, but when she stomped back across the room toward the bed, I grabbed my brown-and-white oxfords and headed for the stairs.

The scent of fresh, perked chicory coffee and cinnamon biscuits hit my nose. That was a sure sign Mama and Daddy were up, waiting in the kitchen for us.

"Mornin', Sooze," Mama said as I sat down at the table. She held six-week-old Grace in one arm while cooking a pan of eggs with the other. "You're up early."

"Anxious for school, I expect," Daddy said. "Only child I know who can't wait for learnin' to start."

"Oh, Daddy," I said, pretending to hide my pride about the truth. "Don't tease."

Mama poured me half a cup of coffee, which was as much as she ever allowed me to drink, and then topped it off with cream. After setting it down in front of me, she and Daddy picked up their hog-selling talk as if I wasn't there. I listened close, not just because I wanted to learn all the things they already knew, but because I wanted to know how to be a good partner to my future husband if I ever got one. Mama and Daddy had each other's heart—it was plain to see by the way they smiled and held hands—but they had something else, too. I was looking closely, trying to find it, when Henry and Cora came bounding down the stairs. They raced into the kitchen with Henry edging ahead of Cora. He lunged toward a kitchen chair, nearly knocking it over, seating himself in it before she could.

"You cheated, Henry Aaron!" Cora shouted with a stomp of her foot. "You're always shovin' me out of the way, and it ain't fair!"

"That's 'cause you're too skinny to hold your own." Henry laughed. "You gotta get tough, Cora. Otherwise, somebody'll be shovin' you around your whole life."

"Settle down," Mama scolded as she handed me the baby. "Cora, take the other seat."

Using a spoon, Mama scooped a ball of freshly churned butter onto a glass saucer and put it in the center of the table near the biscuits. Beside it, she set a big bowl of scrambled eggs. Our white porcelain pitcher of sweet milk was on the sideboard. Daddy had hoped our two-year-old heifer, Bluebell, would birth a calf, but we hadn't seen any signs of motherhood yet.

Reaching for the milk pitcher, Henry said, "Benny's goin' to the Friday night dance over in Bates tonight." He poured himself a glass of milk. Without looking up, he buttered his biscuit. "I was thinkin' about goin' over with him."

Daddy's head popped up to stare at Henry. "If I told you once, I told you a hundred times. Stay away from the

Simmons boy. He ain't right in the head, Henry. Both him and his mama are a bad bunch."

"What's wrong with Benny?" Cora asked. "I like him."

"See there?" Henry said. "Most everybody thinks Benny is fine. It's just his mama who causes folks to cross the street."

In a mutter, Mama said, "Men cross a different way than women." Then she gave us her *I expect you to mind me* glare. "You kids ain't to go nowhere near that hussy of a woman."

"We won't, Mama," I promised. Then to Henry, I said, "And it ain't true that most folks like Benny, and you know it. Everybody knows he's a thief, stealin' things right and left. He even drinks and smokes right out in public!"

"Shut up, Sooze!" Henry shouted as he stood up out of his chair. "Benny's never done nothin' to you." He gulped down his milk. Holding his biscuit in one hand, he grabbed his red flannel shirt off the row of hanging nails. "How come you always side with Mama and Daddy, Miss Goody Two-Shoes? Just 'cause you're marryin' a rich boy don't mean you're better than me—not better than Benny neither."

"I never said I was marryin' anybody!"

Henry slammed the front door on his way out. He never cared that it was more than two miles to school. He liked to walk it so that Daddy wouldn't know about his cigarettes.

Daddy shook his head and sighed. Standing up out of his chair, he said, "Come on, girls. I'm headed to Uncle Ray's new place to help dig a root cellar. We need to get goin' without any dawdlin'. You can ride with me as far as his farm, but you'll have to walk the rest of the way to school from there."

Cora stood. "When are we gonna get an automobile so's we can drive to town like other folks?"

Daddy patted her like a pup. "We got to watch our pennies, baby girl. You never know what's down the road, and automobiles and gasoline are just too expensive. We got to conserve." He pulled his favorite gray-and-black checkered flannel off the nail and put it on over his white under-shirt. "Horses are cheaper and just as good." He fit his worn felt fedora on his head. "I'll be outside hitchin' Frenchy to the wagon."

Before long, we heard a horse whinny, then Daddy yelled, "Come on, girls!"

I grabbed my homework off the writing desk. With the papers folded, I slid them into my sweater pocket.

"Go on. Get goin', girls," Mama urged. "Your daddy's already cross with your brother. He ain't in no mood to wait on you two this morning."

Almost an afterthought, I turned and gave Mama a peck on the cheek and then leaned to kiss the baby's forehead. "Bye-bye, Grace. I'll see you after school."

I followed Cora out the front door.

Frenchy, our ten-year-old mare, pulled us in our high-sided Springfield wagon down the hardpan road. As we neared Whitaker's low-lying meadow, a sweet floral fragrance rose from the earth. Newly bloomed wildflowers delicately scented the air as bees buzzed, bouncing flower top to flower. The next batch of honey was sure to be good.

Mother Nature had breathed life into the land for spring.

Creeping Jenny vines with whitish-purple trumpet flowers lined the road. Lovely as they were, the taller wild-flowers sang to my heart and whispered to my soul. Pale purple coneflowers, larkspur with reddish-blue, blue, and pink blooms, yellow yarrow, field poppies, and milkweed erupted in the meadow. A broad white swathe of Queen Anne's lace weaved through the meadow like a river. And on the outskirts, a field of oxeye—the daisy Mama calls the "She loves me, she loves me not" flower, grew in abundance.

Blossoms were best in May when the weather warmed, so Mama called them all mayflowers. I asked Daddy if we could stop and pick a handful for our teacher, but he was never very obliging when he was worried about Henry, and I could tell by his familiar frown that he was as worried as could be.

As we neared Uncle Ray and Aunt Lissie's farmhouse, our front left wheel, which was already wapper-jawed, hit a pothole. *Smack!* The bolster clapped against the wood under our feet, and Cora nearly flew off the wagon seat. I caught her by the brown puffed sleeve of her dress and pulled her back, holding tight. With a hard hand on the reins, Daddy stopped the wagon. We could hear Uncle Ray yelling.

"You get off my land, and you stay off, you no-good little thief!"

Busting out the hen house door, Henry's friend Benny was running like a wild man. His black hair was whipping across his face like strings from a wet mop, and he had his dirty white T-shirt pulled up like a hammock at his belly. It was filled with eggs.

"Go on, *scram!*" Uncle Ray came out the hen house door, swinging a leather strap. "If I catch you here again, I'll beat the tar out of you, boy!"

Benny was in a dead run. As he skidded around the back of our wagon headed for town, I saw a red welt the size of Uncle Ray's leather strap across his cheek.

"What'd he get from you, Ray?" Daddy called.

"He stole my whole batch of eggs!" Uncle Ray walked toward us with one shoulder of his blue bib overalls hanging. He wasn't wearing a shirt underneath to hide his big belly or a hat to cover his balding head. "I knew movin' in this close to town would just invite the hoboes and hooligans." He stopped at the wagon, reaching up to help Cora down off the seat, and kept right on talking. "But that boy—that loony little two-bit thief—he's the worst of 'em all. If he was stealin' so's he could feed his family, I might look the other way once in a while. But when I get to town later, I'll bet I see a fresh batch of brown eggs for sale at Huckabee's. All that boy does is sell what he steals from me so's he can gamble and booze."

"It ain't right," Daddy agreed, shaking his head. "It just ain't right. You want me to be an eyewitness and file a complaint with the sheriff?"

"Won't do no good," Uncle Ray said. "With only one lawman in town, the sheriff said I needed to catch that boy red-handed myself and hand him over. But who can catch him? Did you see the way he lit out of here runnin' like a jackrabbit?"

Daddy leaned down and kissed the top of Cora's red hair, then kissed my cheek. "You two get on to school now. I'll see you at home tonight."

"Thanks for the ride, Daddy," I said, and then I turned to Uncle Ray. "I'm sure sorry about your eggs."

With a pat on my shoulder, Uncle Ray nodded.

"Tell Henry I want him home right after school," Daddy said with a hard look. "We got some serious talkin' to do."

I nodded as me and Cora set off walking the rest of the way. When we rounded the last turn into Coaldale, the morning bell clanged.

Bugscuffle School stood halfway between the Coaldale cemetery and Huckabee's General Store. It had more than thirty pupils last year, but more than half pulled out when the coal mine shut down. Only fourteen kids, ranging in age from seven to eighteen years, still attended. Miss Stewart promised she would stay on as our teacher until no more pupils remained. Teaching was a profession near to her heart, she said, because she was helping shape young lives.

Like every school morning, I hurried to my double-seated hardwood desk, but Leona's empty seat next to mine reminded me how much times were changing. Without a tick of time passing, I heard Cora lift her rusty-hinged desktop and gather her papers and pencil. She moved everything right over into Leona's desk. Side by side, we sat together. From my seat, I was able to look out the window and see Huckabee's General Store. I was thinking about David when Cora's whisper broke my thoughts.

"Daddy said you'd better come home right after school." She was talking to Henry across the aisle, who'd slid into his seat without me noticing. "He was sure mad when you left the house."

"So let him be mad," Henry said. "I'm eighteen now. Too old to have my daddy bossing me."

"He's just worried about you," I whispered, too, not wanting the other kids to hear Henry's business.

"Are you comin' home?" Cora asked. "Like Daddy said?"

"Don't know yet." Henry slid back in his seat, pushing his legs out into the aisle.

I opened my mouth to remind Henry about the consequences of disobeying Daddy when Miss Stewart stepped to the front of the classroom with an armload of books. Her light brown hair was in a bun, and her plain tan dress hung almost to her ankles.

"Good morning, class." Miss Stewart set the books on her desk. She pointed at each pupil in the one-room schoolhouse, taking a headcount. When her gaze settled on Henry, she said, "It's nice to see you here today, Henry. Why weren't you in class yesterday?"

"Family business," Henry answered. "I was needed at home."

Henry often made excuses without a trace of truth to them, but it bothered me when he chose to lie about our family.

I glared at Henry as I handed him a folded paper where I'd written, "Did you spend the whole day gambling with Benny near Sugar Creek?"

The bank repossessed the Worster cabin at Sugar Creek more than two years ago, but Sid Worster's kin still frequented the empty old place for gambling. I knew that had to be where Henry got the pocketful of money he'd tried to hide.

Henry crumpled my note when Miss Stewart asked, "And Mr. Simmons, were you also needed at home yesterday?"

I turned to see Benny walking through the doorway. He was headed to his seat in the back of the classroom with his head hung down, cocked to the right, hiding the red welt stretched across his cheek.

"Yup," he answered without looking up.

Benny's white T-shirt sleeves were rolled armband-tight so his pack of cigarettes would stay put, and his coal-black hair, slicked back like he'd just crawled out of a swimming hole, curled around his ears. His chocolate-brown eyes darted from one staring student to another. There might have been handsome features to his face, but it was sure hard to tell. I could never look past the sight of his awful teeth colored part yellow, part snuff-brown, and as crooked as gnarled old kindling wood.

Benny was an only child, and no one, not even his mother, Paulette Simmons, knew who his daddy was. Some said he was a drifter passing through on his way to New York, while others claimed it was Winston Hicks, a quiet Negro from the Ozarks. I'd seen the stranger in town with Benny once, but Benny'd gone crazy, threatening to kill him if he ever set foot in Coaldale again. That was almost two years ago, and I hadn't seen Winston Hicks since.

Miss Simmons worked double shifts at the speakeasy across the tracks, so lots of men I didn't know came to town to see her. She dressed fancy, so I guessed she made good money, but she never spent any on shoes or clothes or a barbershop haircut for Benny, but he'd never held her accountable. He claimed other folks caused his hardships. Once, I'd been with Henry when Benny'd come bragging about stealing a pack of cigarettes. I threatened to turn him in if he didn't give it back, but he'd said, "It was owed me." When I asked him how, he'd said, "I don't answer to nobody —not you, not the law, not nobody." But just like Uncle Ray said—even though Benny had never been caught red-handed —Coaldale merchants talked, and I'd heard them whisper Benny's name when the talk of thievery came up. I hated that Henry was his friend.

"Sorry I'm late, Miss Stewart." David Huckabee's voice swept the one-room schoolhouse like a man in charge. "I got back from Waldron at midnight and then overslept this morning." He smiled at me. His perfect white teeth gave a glint of confidence to his stature.

David was surely a handsome boy. Well, not really a *boy*. He had deep blue eyes and mink-brown hair, styled slick with coconut pomade. He was two years older than me and the same age as Henry, but somehow he seemed a whole lot older than us.

"Sooze," David whispered to me. "I got something to ask you after school." The tone of his voice told me it was likely another marriage proposal, sweetened with a new scarf or a bottle of violet scent. I couldn't figure out why he kept proposing to me when I kept turning him down.

I felt just like Jo March in *Little Women*. Laurie was the perfect man—handsome, smart, and wealthy like David. Men who loved with a true heart, falling for women who couldn't make themselves love them back. And like Jo, as much as I tried, I couldn't change my feelings.

David first proposed when I was in second grade. He had offered me his hard tack candy as an enticement. Every year after that, he'd proposed again with special sweets or shiny trinkets. He had planned our whole lives. After marriage, he promised to open a second store in Waldron, thirty miles away. It would be *our* store, he'd said. In all those years, no matter who tried to woo him, David remained true to me, whether I wanted him to be or not. I'd been truthful, too, and told him I could never love him like he wanted. Not like the love I saw in Mama's eyes when she looked at Daddy. But he hadn't been discouraged.

"Who else can give you as much as I can?" he'd asked. That was truer now, more than ever, but I had a hard time settling myself among the Huckabees. They had a funny way of measuring folk. Once, after David learned Daddy had never finished sixth grade, he told me I needed to look harder at a future dependent upon him. He said Daddy was nothing but an ignorant, uneducated farmer who I shouldn't be admiring, but I'd sent him swimming in the Poteau River with one big shove, and he'd never said it again. He wasn't so careful spouting off about Henry and Cora. "Henry's a thug," he'd say. "And Cora's a spoiled-rotten brat with bad manners." For me, he had kinder words. "You're the only one worth a nickel out of your whole family. That's why you belong to me."

Call me stubborn, but I didn't like the thought of *belonging* to anyone.

CHAPTER 4

Huckabee's was a two-story building. The general store was downstairs, with the living quarters upstairs. Newly painted beige and blue, it was the only two-tone building in town. Come to think of it, Huckabee's was the *only* painted building in town. The filling station was a stone building, and both the sheriff's office and The Muddy Diamond Coal and Coke Company were brick. Most other places used raw lumber from the sawmill, and of those wood buildings, only half were white-washed. That limewash surely didn't give off the same sheen as real paint.

David held my hand as we walked toward the store, swinging it back and forth. I knew him well enough to know that his tight-lipped grin held back a secret.

Holding hands with David used to give me butterfly flitters, but the feeling had faded. I might as well wear winter mittens or hold hands with Cora for all I felt now, but I tried not to ponder it much. Instead, I set my thoughts on admiring the pink crabapple blossoms that filled the air with scents of gardenia and rose.

"I had lots of time to think about us on my trip to Waldron, Sooze." David tightened his fingers around my hand. "You're going to be surprised to see what I brought back."

We climbed the store steps, then David pulled open the front door. The new paint smell masked the store's usual coffee, grain, and perfume scent. The far counter held over-sized glass jars filled with colorful hard tack candy. Stacked on the floor were unopened boxes and bags. David's mother stood near the supplies with paper and pencil, taking inventory. She had her light brown hair styled in a loose topknot held together with red-beaded combs. Loose strands of curled hair trailed down her neck, making her look like an elegant lady headed to a ball rather than a shopkeeper ending her workday.

"Good afternoon, Sooze," Amelia Huckabee greeted. "How's your mama and daddy these days? I haven't seen them in the store for more than three weeks now."

"They're fine, ma'am," I said. "I'll tell them you asked after them."

"You might also mention a payment on their account would be appreciated."

"Mother!" David scolded. "Don't embarrass Sooze with the neglect of her father's charges."

"That's all right, David," I said, and then facing Mrs. Huckabee, I added, "I'll tell my father you mentioned it."

Fact is, I had no intention of speaking to Daddy about such things, but I did intend to talk to Henry. The gambling money he'd tried to hide was more than enough to pay the entire bill at the store. And since Mama and Daddy didn't have more than six dollars in their money jar, Henry was our best hope.

"Sooze and I will be upstairs in the parlor," David said. "Keep Owen and Lillie away, please?" He led me by the hand to the inside stairs at the back of the store.

"They're busy with chores out back," his mother said with disinterest. "And Lauralee stayed after school to help Miss Stewart."

David's surprise should have been at the forefront of my

mind, but I couldn't help but wonder what Lauralee could be helping Miss Stewart with that she hadn't asked me to do?

As we stepped into the parlor, the unmistakable stench of cedar-scented polish saturated my nostrils. It glistened off their dark wood furniture. David went to the window and raised it until fully opened. With a breeze blowing, the odorous air became bearable.

White lace curtains barely softened the sunlight, glinting off gold-framed photographs that hung like trophies.

The wall-mounted mirrored box shelf, displaying Lauralee's porcelain figurines, drew me closer. Like so many times before, I stood studying the fine statuettes. The women wore brightly colored gowns, and the men donned tuxedos and top hats. In dancing, twirling stances, they reached, fingers almost touching, forever motionless. But the figurine on the bottom shelf always drew me to her. She was different from the others—so out of place in her pink pinafore dress, sitting beneath an umbrella tree on a tuft of green grass. In her hands, she held an open book. The girl was alone except for a bluebird on the branch above and a rabbit on the ground. Although I wanted to believe that one day I could be like one of those beautiful dancing ladies, in my heart I knew I was that lonely country girl instead.

"Sweet tea?" David asked as he led me to the leather davenport.

I shook my head. "No, but thank you. What is it you wanted to ask me, David?"

"On my way to Waldron yesterday, I was thinking about how grand life would be if you'd just say yes to my proposal, Sooze." He sat beside me. "I couldn't imagine what your hesitation might be until—like a brick against my head—the answer came to me." David scooted off the davenport onto one knee, and then he reached into his shirt pocket and pulled out a red velvet pouch. He opened its drawstring. "I never bought you an engagement ring. I don't know how I could be so stupid!" He took a gold ring out of the pouch and held it for me to see. Embedded in its upraised center was a diamond the size of a mustard seed. I'd never seen a diamond up close, so I had a hard time taking my eyes off it.

"Will you be my wife, Sooze?" He slipped the ring onto my finger.

Suddenly queasy, I said, "Oh, David, it's beautiful, but..."

David sprang up. "No *buts*, Sooze!" He started pacing back and forth. "What do you want from me?" Then he stopped and stared at me. "What else, Sooze? Should I erase your father's bad debt? *Done!* What about an automobile for your family, a shiny new Model A?" He drew me to my feet as his voice quieted into a plea. "I'll buy it first thing tomorrow morning." Pulling me to him, he held me close, whispering, "Tell me, what more must I do for you to marry me?"

I withdrew from him, studying his eyes, looking for the love he had that I didn't. "Do you love me that much?"

"Sooze, I love you more than anything. I've dreamed of you being my wife for so long."

My heart ached, but not from love. The pull between doing what was right and doing what was best was too much. My thoughts swirled in confusion. I needed a reason to believe that I'd be doing the right thing by marrying him. I knew David meant every word of what he'd said, but I'd never ask him to pay our debts or buy such luxuries as an automobile. Such gifts would bring dishonor to Daddy. He'd always taken care of his family without any help from handouts. I knew him well enough to know he'd just as soon lie down and die than accept charity, and I wouldn't be the one to bring shame to him.

If I said yes and married David, a job working in the Huckabee store would pay wages. His folks had offered five dollars a week if I was engaged to David. Five dollars! Maybe more once we married. I'd be earning my own money. I could give it all to Mama and Daddy, so they could buy feed and seed for the farm and food for the family. And if David's plans worked out, he'd be opening his own store next year. Maybe there would be enough money to send Cora to college someday. No one in our family had ever done that.

I'd been David's girlfriend since childhood. I suppose God meant for me to be with him forever. Maybe no one loved like my heart believed. What if Daddy was right? Maybe I was dreaming fairy tales.

But it sure felt wrong when I heard myself answer, "Yes, David. I'll marry you."

David jumped into the air, yelling, "Wah-hoo!" and then came down hard, falling into a tumble. In a flash, he was back on his feet. Grinning wide, he came to me breathless. Taking me in his arms, he pulled me close. I wanted so much to feel true love. I closed my eyes, hoping the love butterflies would swoop in and capture my heart, but as his lips, full and soft, pressed to mine, all I felt was my clenched fists knotting his shirt. His manhood told me he had mistaken my hard grasp as wifely passion. Only my heart knew the truth of the stifling sadness running through me.

Mrs. Huckabee dashed into the parlor, panic splashed across her face. "What's happened? I heard a shout, and then something crashed to the floor! Is everything all right?"

"Better than all right, Mother!" David let go of me and pulled his mother into a bear hug. Picking her straight up off the floor, he held tight and twirled her around.

"David! Put me down!"

Laughing, David stopped and lowered her. "I'm sorry, Mother!" Struggling to catch his breath, he said, "Sooze has agreed to be my wife." He reached for my hand. "Show Mother the ring, Sooze."

I held out my left hand.

"Oh," Mrs. Huckabee declared, one hand shielding her heart while the other reached for my fingers. "It's lovely." Her eyes darted to mine, searching for a glimmer of worthiness. When it seemed she found none, she turned to David. "This must have cost a fortune."

"Who cares, Mother? Sooze has agreed to be my wife!"

Turning to me in hesitance, his mother posed a smile, then lightly embraced me with a pat on the back. After a moment, she said, "Oh, for goodness sakes!" She pulled me into a hug. "Congratulations!"

Mrs. Huckabee twirled to face David. "I was surprised by the diamond on this ring." Skirts lifted, she hurried to the door. "Let's tell your father the news. Owen and Lillie, too. We'll tell Lauralee when she gets home." But before setting foot on the first stair step, she stopped and turned back to me. "Remember, Sooze. You can start training to work in the store this summer. Five dollars a week, just like I promised." Then she went down the stairs without waiting.

"Sooze, we need to tell your folks. Right now. Even though we've already decided, asking your father for his blessing is the right thing to do." He leaned close and took my chin gently in his hand. Raising my head, he kissed me again. His lips were full and moist and felt filled with love. "I want everything done proper before you change your mind."

Outside on the steps, thirteen-year-old Owen rounded the corner, skidding to a stop in a cloud of dust. "Marryin' her, huh?"

"Yep," David told him. "You're gonna have another sister, Owen."

Before we got much farther, Sam Huckabee stopped us. He wore his white storekeeper's apron over his beige shirt and tan pants, and he smelled of clove-spiced cologne.

After giving me a hug, he shook David's hand. "Congratulations, you two. Amelia's out tellin' the world about your engagement." He pointed to David's mother, who stood between the store and the jail next door. She was talking to Willa Wingate, the sheriff's wife.

As we stood talking, an unfamiliar automobile pulled up to the front of the store. Both doors opened, and two men got out. The driver, an older gray-haired man, wore faded jeans, a black, threadbare shirt, and work boots, while the younger man, probably a bit older than Henry, wore a darker pair of jeans with a buckskin-colored shirt. His golden, wheat-colored hair was glorious in the fading light of day.

"Afternoon." The older man tipped his black fedora as they walked past us into the store. When Mrs. Huckabee saw them, she hurried up the steps, following them inside.

"Who are those men, Father?" David asked.

Sam Huckabee, his voice low, had started his answer when nine-year-old Lillie ran to me, flinging her arms around my waist.

"Oh, Sooze! We're going to be sisters!" Lillie shouted. "I always wanted a new sister!"

I tried to be polite, but I was curious about the strangers who purposely came to Coaldale when everybody else seemed to be leaving. Giving an effort to listen, I realized it was impossible to hear their low talk over Lillie's giggles and bouncy hugs, so I gave in, laughing at her delight. Kneeling, I wrapped my arms around her.

"Me, too, Lillie."

"Are you sure we shouldn't stay with Mother 'til they're gone?" David asked his father. "We were headed out to talk to Sooze folks, but I don't care much for outsiders these days, even if they are kin to somebody we know."

"No, it's all right," his father said. "You two go on and see the folks. I'll finish up here, and then I'll see if your mother needs help. Go on now." Sam Huckabee ushered us toward his pride and joy—a 1932 Ford Town Sedan. It was burgundy with black fenders and had orange striping to match the wheel color.

David spent most of the drive talking about their new automobile, and although I'd ridden in it the first week of March, I had not had a need to ride in it again. In fact, it was just the fifth or sixth time I'd ridden in any automobile at all. While David sped down the road, he bragged about the smooth and quiet engine and complained about the factory discontinuing the model. But most of my listening time was spent holding on to the seat so I wouldn't fly off onto the floorboard.

As we neared my family's farm, I surely wanted something else to talk about other than the sedan, but not a thought popped into my head other than the burden of being a storekeeper and a wife. What was this sad and lonely feeling? I wished Leona hadn't gone off to California so I'd have someone to talk to about it all.

When we rounded a stand of tall pines, I asked, "Who did your daddy say those men were at the store, David?"

"Father says they're kin to Earl and Pauline Kittridge. Names are Donald Kittridge and his son, Thomas. They fell on hard times in Chicago. Lost their jobs, bank took their house, all they had left was their automobile and the clothes on their backs." David looked at me. "Not everyone is as fortunate as us, Sooze. They had nowhere else to go, so they came here to live with Earl and Pauline. Father says Earl is too sickly to work his farm without help anyway. He's letting his kin take over. That way, they'll be helping each other." Glancing at me again, David said, "Cancer, you know? Doc Farrell says Earl is all eaten up with it."

A sorrowful sigh blew out of me, pulling my heartstrings with it. "I didn't know." Pauline Kittridge had paid me ten cents a batch the past two summers to help her with her canning. She'd taught me how to make blackberry jam from beginning to end. "Pauline never said a word about Earl."

As David pulled up to the front of the house, Cora pushed open the screened front door, carrying baby Grace. I heard yelling inside.

"Cora?" I called through my rolled-down window as I pushed open the heavy automobile door. "What's going on? Didn't Henry come home after school like Daddy said?"

"He did," Cora said. "But they're in the middle of a hollerin' match anyway."

"Maybe I should go in first, David," I suggested. "To let them know you're here."

"We're practically married, Sooze. You don't have to hide your family shame from me anymore."

On a normal day, I would have set David straight right away. I'd never been ashamed of my family, and I sure wasn't ashamed of them now. It was just an argument, and frankly, I'd had the same-sounding argument with Henry myself.

I closed the Ford's door and walked up the steps to our front porch. Opening the screen door, I stepped inside with both Cora and David behind me.

Before I could say a word, David spoke. "Sorry to interrupt this family discussion, but I got something important to say. I'd like to speak to you, Mr. Williams."

Quickly ending the conversation, Henry pushed past me, splitting David and Cora on his way outside with nary a hello.

Daddy sighed with a shake of his head at Henry. "Come on in, David," he invited. "I'm sure sorry about this." He motioned toward the front porch where the cigarette scent of Henry lingered. "Just came at a bad time, I guess." Daddy walked to the couch and sat down on a tattered spot, hiding it. "Come in here, Emma," he called. When she did, he patted a spot on the couch next to him. "Sit here by me. David's got somethin' to say."

"Cora, honey," Mama said. "Take the baby outside and sit with Henry."

I sat on the other side of Daddy, hiding my ring finger behind me to keep the diamond out of sight. After all, if David was going to the trouble of asking my folks for their blessing, he deserved the right to make the announcement, too.

"Mr. and Mrs. Williams." David's voice was shaky as he nodded at them. "I've come here to tell you I'm in love with Sooze, and she loves me, too." He shifted his feet. "Even though I've been sayin' that for a long time, things are different now. I've been working alongside Mother and Father in the store most all my life, and with a little more hard work and some luck, I intend to open my own store in Waldron next year. So, you see," he looked them in the eyes, "I have big plans, and that's why I've come here today." David glanced at me and smiled. "I've asked Sooze to be my wife. I'd like your blessing."

He held his hand out to me, so I stood to be beside him. "Sooze has already agreed."

Daddy jumped up off the couch and reached for David's hand. "Well, I think that's dandy, David! Course you got our blessing, right Emma?"

I couldn't help but wonder, did anyone *care* that I wasn't in love with David?

Almost as if reading my mind, a soft voice came from Mama. "I don't want to go against nobody, but is this what you really want, Sooze? Are you sure you're ready to get married? You just turned sixteen and ain't seen much of the world yet."

Mama understood.

But truth be told, with the state of things, it was awfully hard to feed and clothe us all. If Henry stuck to his secret plan, he'd be on a train to Chicago soon. Daddy would need help paying the bills and buying seed and feed for the farm. Harvesting the corn in a few months would require extra hands, too, and a man can't butcher a hog alone. Without Henry, the work would be near impossible. We couldn't lose Granddaddy's farm. Marrying David meant we'd be a team like Mama and Daddy had been to each other. I'd be able to send money home from the wages I drew at the store, and David and me would be able to help out come harvesting time. Plain and simple, I saw no other way.

Forcing a smile, I said, "Yes, Mama. It's the right thing."

CHAPTER 5

S unday mornings were special to Mama. Spending time with the Lord was important to her. I watched as she pulled the Holy Bible off a shelf near the fireplace, wrapping it in her white crocheted shawl like a precious pearl. With her free hand, she picked up the woven wood basket packed with our midday meal.

"John, can you get the baby? My hands are full with the Lord and lunch."

Daddy picked up Grace, all bundled in blankets and sleeping. "Cora, it's still a bit chilly outside. Hand me my flannel, baby girl."

When Cora handed Daddy his gray-and-black checkered shirt, I put on my tan sweater.

"You'll get to see the wildflowers today, Mama," I said. "They're all scattered about near the road to town this week. It's like somebody took a paintbrush to the fields."

Mama smiled. "God is here on earth today. I feel Him strong as I ever have." She stepped onto the porch. "Maybe He painted them just for you in celebration of your engagement."

Me and David. It never took long before a reminder was handed to me.

Our ride into town was spent listening to Henry and

Cora pick at each other. From the back of the wagon came the rumbling sounds of a wild wrestling match. I knew there was no use saying anything to them. They never listened anyway.

Daddy pulled the wagon back behind the schoolhouse, which was also the church on Sundays. As he pushed the brake bar forward, Henry jumped to the ground and hitched the horse to a low-growing tree. Walking together, we made our way to the front while the heavenly voices of the welcoming choir sang. Their sweet voices drifted on the breeze as easy as apple blossoms.

"Look, Mama," I said as we turned the corner. "The sermon is outside today near the crabapple tree!"

Split logs, still rounded on the bottom but flat on top, had been dragged in and set up as benches for the outdoor church. Our new preacher, Hockney Payne, stood at the wooden lectern, slowly waving his open hand in even pace to the singing of "Nearer My God to Thee."

At the front of the gathering, near the preacher, stood Amelia Huckabee, Willa Wingate, and Pauline Kittridge. Their mouths opened wide in rejoicing song as folks seated themselves.

> Nearer, my God, to thee, nearer to thee!
> E'en though it be a cross that raiseth me,
> still all my song shall be,
> nearer, my God, to thee...

I'd never been to a sermon outdoors, so I knew it must have been the new preacher's idea. I liked it quite a lot.

Log benches lined side by side with an aisle between slowly filled as more wagons and automobiles arrived. Folks from all over came to Sunday sermon. I watched Mama smile as she greeted her lady friends, passing the baby proudly. It's lonely being so far from town with no one but us to talk to every day.

As the preacher *tap, tap, tapped* his choir stick on the

wooden lectern, Henry and Cora raced down the aisle way, pushing and shoving.

"Settle down now!" Mama scolded. "Find you a seat!" Cora tried to run past, but Mama caught her arm and pulled her down onto the bench beside her.

Sputtering a laugh, Henry said, "I'm sittin' back here next to Uncle Ray." He slipped into the last row right behind Cora, then edged past Benny before plopping himself down. It seemed worrisome to me that Benny sat on the same log as Uncle Ray, especially with the red welt still marked across his face, so I thought it was good when Henry sat between them.

I seated myself beside Cora. Even though Daddy was on the far side of the log, I could still see him turn to look at Henry with one of his *I'll whup you if you don't settle down* looks. I noticed Henry had wiped the smile right off his face.

When the preacher bellowed his greeting to the congregation, baby Grace whimpered, squeezing out a scowl. Not wanting our day of worship ruined, I took the baby from Mama's arms and retreated to a spot under the crabapple tree behind Henry. I stood swaying back and forth like a cradle until Grace fell back to sleep in my arms.

"Hey, Henry!" Benny said loud. "How ya doin'?"

I watched Uncle Ray lean forward, eyeing Benny. "*Shhhh!* Preacher's talkin'."

Whispering, Henry said, "I'll talk to ya after church, Benny."

"Naw, it's all right," Benny nearly shouted. "Who cares what these peckerwoods think?"

Uncle Ray scooted sideways on the bench. Calm but serious, he leaned forward with his eyes fixated on Benny. "I asked you to be quiet, boy."

Henry scooted closer to Benny. Quiet-like, he said, "Come on, Benny. Don't egg him on."

"I got just as much right to be here as he does, and just as much right to talk, too!"

Daddy turned around and put his finger to his lips with a stern look toward Henry.

"I know, I know," Henry said to Benny. "But just be quiet, will ya?"

The preacher cleared his throat louder than needed. I knew it was his way of saying *quiet down* to the back-row talkers. But Benny paid no mind to the preacher. He tucked his hands into his armpits, then waved them up and down, flapping like wings. "*Bock, bock, bock!* You're a chicken, Henry Williams."

Standing straight up at his full 5'10" height, Uncle Ray turned around, facing me, then spit a mouthful of tobacco juice onto the ground before looking back at Benny. "I've had just about enough outta you, boy!"

Uncle Ray's back was to the preacher and congregation as he sidled across in front of Henry and Benny. Standing directly in front of them, he faced both boys and me. I watched as his face turned red as a cock's comb. He grabbed a fistful of their shirtfronts and lifted them both straight up onto their feet. With his hands knotted in their shirts, Henry and Benny were shoulder to shoulder, facing Uncle Ray.

"He spit on the church floor!" Benny yelled loud as Uncle Ray pulled tighter. "Did everyone see that? He spit right there...right on God's own ground!"

As the congregation shushed his outburst, Benny pulled his fist out of the pocket closest to Henry. I saw a silver knife blade spring open with a glint, then it disappeared with a jab into Uncle Ray's belly. I gasped, sucking in a scream, as I watched Benny jerk the blade upwards. Uncle Ray's eyes grew wide. His grip held tight to Henry as they both fell together, crashing against the split log bench where Mama, Daddy, and Cora sat. All three went flying forward, hitting the log pews in front of them before landing in the dirt.

"No!" I screamed as another shriek echoed mine. *Was it Aunt Lissie?*

"Uncle Ray!" Henry shouted as he pushed himself up off the body beneath him. He was on his knees when he reached for the knife lodged center point below Uncle Ray's ribs. He pulled it out, dropping it to the ground, then he used both hands, trying to close the gaping foot-long wound, but Uncle Ray's insides swelled up through the knife-slit like a sack filled too full with grain. His guts pushed up and out, one long intestine falling like a hair curl onto the ground. Henry reached and picked it up and then tried to push it back inside the bulging hole. He pressed down hard, holding it in with one hand while using his other to pick off the dried leaves and dirt sticking to the bloody innards. His hands and white shirt were blood soaked.

Again, I screamed, squeezing Grace harder than intended. She screamed, too, as shrills from the crowd pierced the air amid gasps and cries.

"You shouldn't have done it, Henry!" Benny shouted, dancing away, his white T-shirt red with blood. "You shouldn't a stabbed him!"

The knife—looking just like Henry's knife—lay open and bloody near my brother.

"You done kilt him, Henry!" Benny shouted with a slight laugh. "You done it now!"

Uncle Ray's eyelids flickered in sporadic blinks, holding Henry's focus. "It'll be okay, Uncle Ray." Henry's voice cracked and cried all at the same time. "It'll all be okay…"

Daddy scrambled to his feet as I clambered over the back bench, holding tight to the baby.

When I looked up, I saw folks moving away, scattering to the outskirts instead of rushing to help. Clustered together, women squished their children's faces to their dress skirts, trying to hide their innocent eyes from the frightful sight. Then a man pointed to the ground near Henry. He shouted, "He's got a knife!" With fearful faces, folks scaled back farther.

Mama was pulling Cora up off the ground when Uncle

Ray stopped blinking. I stood there staring as a long, low breath pushed out of his lungs. His dark blue eyes turned crystalline blue like sparkling glass marbles. They were the most beautiful eyes I'd ever seen. Mesmerized by their odd clarity and penetrating blue, I held tight to Grace as scream after scream blew past me.

Was it Aunt Lissie screaming? Why doesn't someone stop her? Uncle Ray is dead. She can clearly see he's dead. My focus fixed on his face. His bright, stunning eyes frozen wide open as his head lay cocked to the right, staring at Aunt Lissie. *Dead eyes...staring at Aunt Lissie.* She screamed again.

"Henry, close his eyes!" I yelled, but Sheriff Wingate and another man grabbed Henry, pulling him backward away from Uncle Ray.

Aunt Lissie screamed again. And again. She had both hands clamped to her cheekbones.

My feet were moving before my brain knew. I shoved the baby into Cora's arms, feeling her startled jolt, then dropping to the ground near Uncle Ray, I reached, a sob bursting out of me, and closed his eyes. When I looked up into Aunt Lissie's pleading gaze, I heard myself choke out the words, "He's gone, Aunt Lissie. We can't help him no more."

As if I'd just quoted God, Aunt Lissie stopped screaming. A deafening calm came over her as a hollow gray settled in her eyes. Ten-year-old Arnold clung to her skirt, sobbing.

I stood and moved away as Daddy and Doc Farrell knelt beside Uncle Ray. The new preacher came closer, his hands trembling as he held the Good Book and spoke words only meant for the dead.

Helping Mama, I moved Aunt Lissie back, off the blood-soaked ground. I held tight to her until Aunt Rose took my place. When they headed toward the schoolhouse, I turned, looking for Cora and Grace, but instead spotted Benny tearing down the main road in a dead run. He was headed out of town.

That's when I heard Daddy.

"I don't believe my boy did this, Sheriff. He was just in the wrong place at the wrong time."

Appalled, Sheriff Wingate said, "John, he admits to the knife bein' his, and it was layin' not more than six inches from his hand!" He pointed to the body. "I watched the boy pull the knife out of Ray myself."

"Daddy!" Henry cried as he struggled to free his arms from the lawman's grip. He sounded just like a little boy again. Where had that near grown man gone? "Daddy, tell 'em I didn't do it!"

But they dragged Henry away anyway.

"Sooze, tell your mama I'm headed to the jail with Henry."

I stood and stared as Henry kept looking back over his shoulder at Daddy. He had tears running from his eyes and was shouting, "I didn't do it!"

"*Sooze!*" Daddy screamed. "Pay attention to me, girl. Go find Cora and go inside the schoolhouse with your mama. Tell her I'm goin' to the jail with Henry. Do you understand?"

"Ye-yes," I stammered. "Yes, Daddy. I'll get Cora. Go. Help Henry, Daddy." Then, to make sure he understood, I said, "Henry didn't do it, Daddy. Benny killed Uncle Ray."

"Did you see Benny do it, Sooze?"

"I saw it, Daddy. I saw Benny pull Henry's knife from his pocket and stab it in Uncle Ray's belly." I swallowed hard. "It was Benny, Daddy. I was standin' right behind 'em."

CHAPTER 6

Inside the schoolhouse, I walked the creaky floorboards with Cora to the bench where Mama sat with Aunt Rose and Aunt Lissie. I shook my head, trying to keep my mind's eye from seeing what I'd just seen. Uncle Ray's lifeless body. His bright but dead eyes. His last breath as it pushed out of him. Again, I shook my head, hoping to shake the haunting memory.

Cora handed the baby to Mama. "Can I go with Daddy to the jail?"

Mama eyed me with a furrowed brow. Her face said, "Handle the younger ones."

"Cora," I said. "Go sit with Zane and comfort Arnold, so's I can help Mama."

"You go sit with them!" Cora snapped. "I want to go with Daddy to help Henry!"

"Daddy told us to stay here." I put my hand on her shoulder as if to say, "It's all right. Daddy will take care of Henry." But Cora jerked away. With stomping steps, she clomped to the double-desk where Arnold and Zane sat. She stood with her back to me.

Not knowing what else I needed to do, I stayed by Mama.

Aunt Lissie sat straight as a board on the wooden bench,

staring out the window. It was the first time I'd seen a person be so still and soundless. Not a whimper or a cry, her breath so shallow it left no tracks. It seemed all emotion had drained right out of her, leaving her empty.

Then, quiet and without expression, Aunt Lissie turned to Mama. "God took Ray today," she said. "Why didn't I know today was *his* day? I always thought I'd know…"

"The Good Lord had bigger plans for Ray." Mama's words were meant to comfort. "He needed a good man like him in heaven, and He don't always tell us why."

"God forgive me!" Aunt Lissie slumped into a limp curl, crying, "But I *hate* Him for takin' Ray! He had no right. No right at all!"

Arnold stood up—his face red from bawling. "God didn't take Daddy!" He yelled, "It was Henry who killed him! I saw the sheriff draggin' him off. *Hate Henry!*"

"You take that back, Arnold Garren!" Cora started yelling. "Henry didn't kill nobody!"

Arnold stepped back from the desk. In a dogged stance, he shouted, "You go to the devil, Cora Mae!" Then he spit on her shoes. "You and your brother, too!"

Cora tackled Arnold, knocking him to the floor. She had hold of both his wrists and was lying on top of him as he kicked and hollered, trying to scoot free.

"Cora!" I shouted. I ran to them and grabbed Cora by the back of her white flowery dress and tried to pull her off Arnold, but she had him held down, her knees clamped at his waist. She was yelling, and I was pulling. "Get off him, Cora!"

Arnold's legs flung up in a kick with one foot hitting me square in the face. My head flew back, and when it dropped forward again, blood spattered Cora's dress and Arnold's shirt, too.

"My nose!" I shouted, shielding it with both hands. "You broke my nose!"

Then I felt myself being pulled backward. When I looked up, I recognized the golden-haired boy as the one I'd seen walking with his Daddy into Huckabee's store on my engagement day.

"*Yah!*" Thomas Kittridge yelled. He grabbed the back of Cora's dress and snatched her straight up in one swoop, but she was wild with fight and kept clawing the air, trying to get at Arnold. Holding her kicking and screaming, he reached down with his other hand and pulled Arnold to his feet. He had a grip on both, keeping them apart like two scrapping dogs. "Stop it now! This ain't no time for fightin'!"

Mama had hold of me right away. She tilted my head upwards. With my jawbone and cheeks cupped in her hands, she inspected my nose.

"Somebody go get Doc Farrell and tell him we need him," Mama said to no one in particular.

"I think the doc has his hands full right now," Thomas answered. After settling Cora and Arnold, he loosened his grip.

With one of her *use the good sense God gave you* looks, Mama glared at him. "I don't suppose he's busy anymore, do you?"

I guess Mama was right. You can't do nothing to help a dead man, no matter how good a doctor you are.

"Yes, ma'am," Thomas stammered. He was out the door quick.

"Keep your head tilted up and back, Sooze." Mama gently pushed my chin up until I was looking at the ceiling. "Cora, find me some rag towels so's we can clean up this splattered blood. I need a nice clean one for your sister's nose, too."

I could hear Cora rummaging through Miss Stewart's rag box. Before long, Mama had a cloth pressed against my nose.

"Noses tend to bleed like a stuck hog, don't they?" Mama asked, but it wasn't really a question. I reckon she was just trying to tell me I wasn't dying. "Lord knows, we've seen a lot of blood today. Some worse than others."

Doc Farrell came through the open door with his black bag. Thomas was walking with him.

"Let me take a look." Doc took Mama's place in front of me. He pulled the cloth off my nose and said, "Well, looky there. Your pretty little nose sure got banged up, Sooze."

"Is it broke?" Mama asked.

Without answering, Doc put a finger on each side of my nose. "Sooze, I'm gonna have to examine you." He wiggled my nose a bit and warned, "This might hurt some."

Before I could say anything at all, he pinched the bridge of my nose and pulled down hard.

"Ouch!" I yelled. Tears ran down my face as if each eye was pouring its own bucket of water.

"There we go," Doc told Mama. "She'll be fine now. She might look like a prizefighter for a few days, though."

I could still feel the blood running down over my lips, so I grabbed the rag and held it under my nose again.

"Up, Sooze. You gotta keep your head tilted up toward the sky 'til the bleedin' stops," Doc Farrell told me. Then before picking up his black bag, he said, "I'm headed to a birthing. Sounds like a breach, but I should be back before nightfall. If the bleeding doesn't stop, come and see me." Then he lifted my chin higher, so my head leaned way back.

That's when I realized just how tall Thomas Kittridge was. He stood near me, and all he had to do was look down for me to gaze up into his eyes. No doubt about it, he was a handsome man. Long blond strands swept low across his right brow, barely brushing the lashes of his gentle green eyes. When he smiled at me, I couldn't help but smile back.

"Hi," I said to him. "Thanks for helpin' with Cora and Arnold."

"Wish I'd gotten here sooner." He nodded in a single motion toward my face. "I might have been able to save your nose."

"It wasn't a very pretty nose anyway," Cora butted in. "Mama always said she had Grandpa Garren's nose. Maybe it'll look better now, Sooze."

"I was happy with the nose I had, Cora." I lowered my head, pleased that a river of blood wasn't running down my chin anymore.

"Who are you anyway?" Cora asked Thomas. "I ain't never seen you before."

"I'm Thomas Kittridge," he told her. "Just moved to the area about a week ago."

"There's not usually this much commotion around here," I told him.

Daddy and Uncle Will showed up just then—without Henry—and walked straight to Mama and Aunt Rose, who were back tending to Aunt Lissie.

"It don't look good, Emma," Daddy told Mama. "The sheriff went and picked up Benny, but he claims it was Henry who done the stabbin', so the sheriff let the boy go." He looked at me. "What in the world happened to you, Sooze?"

"I got kicked in the face, but I'm all right."

Without a word to me, Daddy turned back to Mama. "The sheriff saw Henry pull the knife out of Ray..." Glancing at Aunt Lissie as if he'd spoken hurtful words, he said, "Well, anyway, it was Henry's knife, Emma. He said he'd lent it to Benny for skinnin' a rabbit he'd caught for dinner a few nights ago. Henry was proud of the edge he'd given it and wanted Benny to be impressed."

"Did you tell the sheriff I saw it all, Daddy?" I asked.

"Yeah, Sooze, but he thinks you're just protectin' Henry." Then Daddy spoke to Aunt Lissie. "I'm sure sorry 'bout Ray," he told her. "He was a good man, and this never should have happened."

"Can I go see Henry?" Cora asked.

"No, your brother's got some talkin' to do with the law. Sheriff Wingate is with him."

"What do we need to do to help him?" Mama asked.

"We been talkin' about that," Daddy said and nodded toward Uncle Will. "We might need a lawyer to defend the boy."

The room was quiet.

"We ain't got the money, Emma," Daddy admitted.

Mama pulled away from Aunt Lissie and stood up chest-to-chest against Daddy. She stared up into his eyes like coals were smoldering in her belly. "Well, we'll just have to sell somethin' to get the money then, won't we? I ain't gonna let Henry get sold down the river without doin' all I can to help him."

Before Daddy could answer, David opened the schoolhouse door. Without a care about the conversation at hand, he interrupted, "Sooze, what happened to you?"

"It was an accident," I said. I was still talking as David came toward me. "Doc says I'm gonna look like a prize-fighter for a while."

David whined, "My beautiful Sooze." He held my face between his hands. "Good thing our big day isn't upon us yet. Don't want my bride posing for a wedding photograph looking like this!"

Thomas stepped back. "Oh, you two fixin' to get married, are you?"

"Sure are!" David reached for my hand like I was a prize. "She's wearing a ring to prove it!" He grinned as if it were any ordinary day. "The date isn't set yet, but we want it to be soon, don't we, Sooze?"

The words stuck in my throat like a spoonful of molasses —too much to swallow and too much to spit out. "Ye-Yes." My head nodded with a power all its own, then the words, "That's right," skidded out of my mouth.

"Congratulations," Thomas mumbled. Turning toward the door, he said, "I should be gettin' back outside to my family. I only came in to see if I could help."

"You helped plenty," I said. As much as I wanted to sound prim and proper, my voice clogged up inside my nose like a train stuck in a mud hole. Sounding as if I had a terrible head cold, I finished by saying, "We thank you kindly, Mr. Kittridge."

"It's *Thomas*," he said as if he hadn't noticed my nasal

plug. "*Mr. Kittridge* is my father and my granddad. I've still got a bit of growin' to do before I earn the title of mister."

Then Thomas gave us a nod. Wearing worn, dark-leather work boots, he walked across the floorboards of the schoolhouse in even strides, his long legs straight and sturdy inside his faded blue jeans.

"David," Daddy called as if he were his son already. "I'll be needin' you to take Emma and the young'uns home so's I can stay here with Henry for a while longer. Can you do that for me?"

"Yes, of course," David said, putting his arm around me.

"Will and Rose are gonna take Lissie and Arnold home with them," Daddy told Mama as Uncle Will helped raise Aunt Lissie to her feet. With Arnold and Zane trailing behind, they all headed toward the door.

Turning back to Daddy, Uncle Will said, "We'll check soon to see how Henry's doin'."

Then everybody was gone from the schoolhouse except David and us.

"I'll run get Father's sedan," David told Daddy. He hurried out the door with nary a look back toward me.

"Daddy, why can't I stay with Henry?" Cora asked. "I sure hate to leave him here all by his self."

"Henry's locked up in a jail cage, Cora, and that ain't no place for you," Daddy told her.

"Somebody else had to see what I saw," I offered. "There must be more witnesses who can prove Henry didn't do it so's they can let him out of jail."

"You was the only one standin' behind the boys, Sooze. No one could see nothin' with your uncle turned around backward like he was. We talked to pert'near everybody, and all they saw was the backside of Ray. You and the two boys were the only ones facing him—you're the only three who could see straight on what happened."

Mama had a puzzled expression. "How can the sheriff believe my Henry stabbed Ray? How can anybody believe that? He's never hurt a livin' thing, 'cept when puttin' food on the table."

"You know as well as I do, Emma, the boy made a choice in choosing Benny as his friend, and soon as Henry got known for runnin' around with the worst boy in the county, people started believin' the worst about him, too. It's hard for folks to separate the two."

Daddy put his arm around Mama's shoulders and then leaned down to kiss baby Grace, who lay swaddled in her arms. He had worry in his eyes when he rose to kiss Mama's forehead. With one hand, he affectionately patted the back of her head as he leaned to see out the window.

"Get to movin', girls." Daddy shooed us toward the door. "David's got the sedan to drive you home."

Hearing dirt clods crunch under the tires, I knew David would be in to gather us, so I grabbed up the rag towels used for my nosebleed and poured some water from Miss Stewart's half-filled bucket onto the floor. Using the rags, I mopped up the red splatters. I was rolling the damp rags into a ball before stuffing them into the dirty rag bin when David stepped back inside the schoolhouse.

"Ready?" David asked us all.

"They're ready," Daddy answered.

"The lunch basket is still in the wagon," Mama reminded Daddy. "Take it to the jail and make sure Henry gets somethin' to eat."

Daddy nodded, then walked with us as we filed out the door and down the wooden steps. He pulled open the back sedan door, helped Cora inside first, then motioned for me. I slid in, but Cora was so busy rubbing her hand back and forth across the plush gray mohair seat, she didn't even notice me.

Holding the baby with one arm, Daddy helped Mama into the front seat and then handed her Grace before closing the door.

"Drive careful, David." Daddy leaned in through the open passenger window, his hand outstretched for a shake.

Looking into Mama's eyes, Daddy said, "I'll be home soon as I can, Emma. I'm gonna try to help Henry sort out this mess."

Then Daddy patted the outside of the door before stepping back, away from the sedan, as David's acceleration caused the automobile to lurch forward. The propelling engine *whirred* with a ticking as it carried us down the dusty road and out of town.

"I sure hope Daddy can help Henry," I said to no one in particular. It seemed strange when Mama didn't answer, but when I peered over the seatback to see if she'd heard me, I saw her pull the baby up close to her face and wipe her eyes against the swaddling blanket.

Mama wasn't one to cry easily, so I couldn't help but wonder whether she was crying for the loss of her brother that day or whether she might be crying for the loss of a son. I sure hated to see her cry at all, but I hoped she was crying for Uncle Ray.

CHAPTER 7

D avid parked the automobile near our front porch and shut off the engine. His confident glance said he was expecting me to invite him in, but truth be known, I needed time alone with my family. Mama's face was red and worn. I knew she didn't need anyone around who wasn't blood.

"Thank you for driving us home, David." I got out, holding the door for Cora, then I went to Mama's door and opened it. I took the baby from her and stepped aside so she could get out of the sedan, too.

Cradling Grace, I followed Mama and Cora, but I turned back to David before going up the porch steps. "We sure appreciate you drivin' us home." He closed his door and walked toward me. "David, we have family matters that need sortin' out, and it's best if we handle them alone if you don't mind."

He stopped. Confused, he said, "Sooze, you're soon to be my wife, so you and me—we're family now, too."

"I know, and I appreciate your concern. I surely do. But not now, David. This situation is a little deeper. You understand, don't you?"

David's face turned the color of a hot coal ember. His body tensed up straight. "What I understand is that you haven't yet learned it's the man who runs the family, and you're my family now, Sooze."

Remembering what Henry told Cora, *"You gotta get tough, otherwise somebody'll be shoving you around your whole life,"* I felt the defense of my family rising like the tide. My body pushed itself forward, and my foot stepped closer to David. I knew my face was red from the heat it carried inside. "Not yet, I ain't," I said. I didn't mean any disrespect, but I didn't intend to be bullied neither. "You go on home now."

David's shoulders slumped. He shoved his hands inside his pant pockets and head down, he turned and walked back to his father's sedan. He pulled open its door before turning around to face me again. "When are we gonna set a wedding date, Sooze?"

"We're surely not worrying about that tonight, are we?"

"I suppose not." David's head hung all sad and droopy, like a kicked coon dog. He got into the sedan and closed its door. Through the open window, he said, "I love you, Sooze."

But the words swelled in my throat like a ball of Mama's paraffin wax, and I couldn't find a way to say it back. "Good night, David." Then I hurried up the front porch steps. After closing the door, I leaned with my back against it and gazed down at the sweet baby asleep in my arms. I stayed there with my head down until I heard the sedan drive away.

"How long you think you can hold out before tellin' your intended you're at least a little fond of him?" Mama was standing right in front of me with a perplexed look. "What's keepin' the words stuck in your craw like that?"

"I don't know, Mama," I answered.

"You *do* love him, don't you, Sooze?" Mama asked. "I mean, you been boyfriend and girlfriend most all your life, and you agreed to marry the boy. He's a good, hardworking' man—the best one of marryin' age in Coaldale. Now that he's made the formal proposal with a ring and all, I'd think love would be pourin' out of you."

I looked at her. "Marrying into the Huckabee family, with

their money and all, would surely be a help to us, wouldn't it?"

But Mama stood staring at me with the same strange look she'd given Daddy when she'd told him she wasn't about to let Henry get sold down the river. Is that what she was thinking? That I was headed down the river, too?

"You don't marry for money, Sooze. You marry for love. If you don't, you'll spend your whole life earning every penny." Mama shook her head with a terrible look of disappointment.

Feeling tears coming on, I turned my face away—pretending to adjust the swaddling blanket around Grace—but when the baby started to cough from my jostling, Mama came and took her from my arms. Patting her gently, Mama laid Grace in the cradle and then covered her with another blanket. Whispering to me, Mama finished by saying, "I don't need to be worrying about you when I'm already overflowin' with worry about your brother."

She was right. I had no cause to be worrying Mama now. She needed to concentrate on Henry. We all did.

Just then, Cora came down the stairs carrying one of Mama's canning jars. Through its clear-blue tint, I saw coins.

"Land sakes, child," Mama said. "Where did you get all that money?"

"I been savin' for a long time," Cora answered. "Henry give most of it to me his self. I ain't never asked him where he got it." She carried the jar to the dining table and pulled out a chair for herself. She set the jar down with a *thunk* and then unscrewed its zinc lid. Turning it onto its side, she gently spilled the coins out onto the table, spreading them in a single layer. One by one, she began separating them into piles of nickels, dimes, pennies, and quarters.

"What are you planning to do with all this money, Cora?" I asked.

"I'm givin' it to Daddy so's he can buy a lawyer for Henry."

Mama's eyes lit up. We both hurried to the table, each pulling a chair for ourselves.

"We'll help you count it, Cora."

"Here, Sooze." Cora used her hands like a field plow and pushed a pile of coins across the table. "You take the nickels. Of the silver coins, nickels is what I got the most of, and you're a better counter than me. Henry only likes the silver ones, 'cept he never did like the nickels. He said they took up too much room in his pocket without being worth much. He liked the big silver coins best. That's why we don't have many quarters—Henry kept most of them."

"I can count the dimes," Mama offered. "We'll leave the pennies for last since they ain't worth as much."

"Mama, pennies is what Henry give me the most of." Cora pushed the copper coins into a bigger pile. "We got more of them than all the silver coins put together." Her voice had a tone of disappointment.

"That's all right," Mama said, patting the back of Cora's hand. "Every penny counts."

Dozens of stacks, all two knuckles high, set upright in the middle of the table when we finished.

"All told, it's $21.13!" Mama counted a second time before grinning at Cora, but fast as lightning, she said, "Now, I wouldn't be teachin' you a thing if I didn't first tell you that you shouldn't of been hidin' money from the family. What you bring into this house is for all of us. This could have bought your Daddy more seed at plantin' time or bought necessities like flour and sugar. It would have bought an awful lot of salt for this table." Then standing up and walking to Cora, Mama leaned down and hugged her. "But I'm mighty proud of you for savin' it."

"Do you think it's enough to buy a lawyer?" Cora asked.

"I don't rightly know, child." A worried look flooded Mama's face again. "Sooze, do you know how much a lawyer costs?"

"No, ma'am." I shook my head. "But I know it costs an

awful lot of money to go to a school of law, so it must cost a lot to buy one afterward."

Mama nodded, then got up from the table. She walked to the cookstove and tied on her apron. "Sooze, light a fire and let's get this house warmed up before your Daddy gets home. He'll be chilled to the bone coming home in this spring air after dark." She was looking out the kitchen window while dusting her biscuit-rolling cloth with flour. "With the sun done set, I'd expect your Daddy's wagon to be coming down the road, but I don't see it yet. I hope his time in town helped Henry. Maybe they'll both be home soon."

Cora picked up stack after stack of coins and dropped them back inside the canning jar while I loaded sticks of pecan wood inside our blackened hearth.

The woody scent of nuts and vanilla reminded me that the pecan wood wouldn't heat the house like post oak, so I added one more log before wedging a kindling stick soaked in coal oil in between. I struck a wooden match and lit the fire. Slowly, at first, flickering tines lapped at the wood before spreading out across the bottom layer. I found myself staring at the newborn flames as if our answers were hidden somewhere inside. Flaring off a thin line, the fiery reddish orange stretched the length of a log then drew back to its center, only to expand again—a taunting vein hinting it had more to come. I studied it, listening to its *pops* and *cracks* as if they were words. Maybe it was trying to tell me that Henry would be all right. Maybe it was saying my decision to marry David was the right one. But the harder I listened, the clearer I heard the sweet sound of Thomas Kittridge reciting his name. *My name is Thomas Kittridge. Name is Thomas Kittridge. Thomas Kittridge.* When he'd said it, he sounded proud. The memory of him sparked a lightning bolt that buried itself deep inside the hollow of my belly.

"Mama," Cora asked as she set the coin-filled jar on the sideboard. "What'll happen to Aunt Lissie and Cousin

Arnold now that Uncle Ray is dead? Who's going to take care of them?"

I came to the kitchen, so I could hear Mama's answer, too.

Without turning around, Mama said, "I don't rightly know."

"Maybe Aunt Lissie can get a job," I offered, thinking of my own opportunity.

Turning like she'd been bit, Mama glared at me. "There's no *jobs*, child! Why do you think your daddy is so thankful the Huckabee boy asked you to marry him? You're gettin' a rich husband and maybe a chance to run a business next year." Lowering her head, she wiped her hands on her apron. When she looked again, I saw tears glistening in her eyes. "I'm sorry for snappin' at you, Sooze, but I gotta know, are you marrying David for love or for money?"

"I'm tryin' to do the right thing, Mama." I lowered my head then admitted, "I'm just not sure what the right thing is."

"I would sooner have you hate me for tellin' you the truth than love me for tellin' you lies, so if you're searching for an answer, let me help you out. You got to love him, Sooze. Marriage is a promise meant to last forever—and forever is a long time—so anyone who's marryin' for money ain't building any sort of life for themselves." Mama came to me and put her arms around me. With my head against her shoulder, she whispered into my ear, "I love your Daddy with all my heart. It don't matter whether we have food or a farm as long as we got each other. That's what love feels like, Sooze. So if you're not feeling that, then it ain't love."

Mama held my face in her hands while she kissed my cheek, then she turned back to the countertop. I knew Mama well enough to know she was holding back tears. Pulling a drinking glass off the shelf, she turned it upside down and pressed its rim into the dough she'd rolled out. One by one, she cut out biscuit after biscuit and placed each round on a baking sheet. Her silence was cut short by a sniff. Clearing her throat but not turning around, she said, "You know I only want what's best for you."

Mama used her quilted potholder to open the door of the cast-iron stove then pushed the biscuit pan inside, closing the door.

"Yes, Mama," I told her. "I know." But the truth was, Mama didn't have all the facts. She didn't know Henry was leaving right after graduation, and she didn't know about the five dollars a week I would earn working in the store. I'd spent a lot of time talking to myself the past year, and I'd learned a lot by listening to the voice inside me. And there was one thing I knew for sure. This decision needed to be made by my head—not by my heart.

"I hear Daddy's wagon!" Cora ran to the front door and opened it wide. I matched her step-for-step.

Daddy pulled the wagon up close to the porch, then without unhitching Frenchy, he jumped to the ground and headed up the porch steps.

"Where's Henry? Didn't you bring him home with you?" I asked.

Daddy shook his head as he walked through the front door. He stopped at the hanging nails without a word before pulling off his flannel jacket and his hat. He hung them back where they belonged, then used one hand to push his hair straight back off his forehead.

Before I knew it, Mama was standing beside Cora and me. She had the hem of her apron all balled up in her hands, and she was twisting it tight.

"Where's Henry?" Mama asked. "You brought him home with you, didn't you?"

Daddy shook his head. "Henry's stayin' in town tonight."

Before Daddy could say more, the baby began to cough and cry. Mama hurried to the cradle near the fireplace and picked her up. She held Grace up to her shoulder and patted hard while bouncing back and forth in her "quiet down" dance.

"What's wrong with the baby?" Daddy asked, his voice sounding tired and aggravated.

"It's feedin' time, that's all. And she just don't want to eat tonight," Mama said. "But you need to go on and tell us what's happened to Henry."

Daddy went to his favorite armchair between the fireplace and the stairs and sat down. Cora and me hurried to his side, intending to hear every word.

"Given the circumstances, the sheriff won't release Henry, but he's agreed to pick up Benny again and hold both boys until he can sort out what happened today." Daddy looked up at Cora, who was hanging on his every word. "Get me a cup of coffee, will you, baby girl?"

Cora turned and ran to the kitchen. I could hear her pulling Daddy's cup off the shelf. She came walking back in quick but careful steps, trying not to spill a drop of the too-full cup. Its steam swirled up and out.

"Thank you," Daddy said as he took the cup from Cora's hands. Then patting her arm with his free hand, he said, "Henry said to tell you he has something hidden in his secret place, and he wants you to get it."

Turning toward the stairs, Cora took a giant leap and landed on the bottom step headed up.

"Whoa, now!" Daddy yelled to her. "I only intend to tell this story once, so if you want to hear what I've got to say, you'd better get on back here."

"But Daddy!" Cora's tone sounded desperate, but with her head hanging, she returned.

After a sip of coffee, his shoulders relaxed. He started his story again.

"Henry's stayin' in jail until the sheriff gets Benny back in to question him. The problem is that it's Henry's knife, and Henry was just as close to Ray as Benny. It's Henry's word against Benny's as to who had the knife and who done the stabbin', and with the sheriff seein' Henry pull the knife out of Ray, he says it's common sense that the boy put it in, too. Benny's good-for-nothin' mama showed up and told the sheriff Benny was awful upset about watchin' Henry stab a man to death. She said Benny'd gone off to be by his self for a while."

"But they're gonna go find him, aren't they?" I asked.

"Got to, Sooze. Benny's the key to clearin' up this mess."

"Did Henry eat supper?" Mama asked, cocking her head a bit as if she couldn't quite see the whole story through Daddy's eyes. "Did you give him a bacon sandwich from our lunch basket? Did you give him a pickle, too?"

"I did, Emma," Daddy told her. "I made sure the boy had a full stomach before I left this evening. He was mighty appreciative."

"Can I go upstairs now?" Cora asked.

With a nod of Daddy's head, Cora took off, running for the stairs. Even though the baby had started to cry again, I followed Cora, leaving Mama to quiet Grace instead of staying with her to finish fixing supper.

As I got to Henry's open bedroom door, I saw Cora lying on her stomach on the floor, lifting a loose floorboard under Henry's bed. When she got the board up, she turned to me with eyes wide as china saucers.

"Lord, Almighty," Cora said. "What's Henry gone and done now?"

CHAPTER 8

There, under Henry's bed, were three thick folds of money. It was more than I'd seen my whole life.

"There must be a thousand dollars here, Sooze," Cora whispered as she crunched upward onto her knees. She stood up, holding the folded money.

"Can't be," I said, my voice quivering. "But it's a few hundred maybe."

"Let's count it!" Cora plopped onto Henry's unmade bed. With her legs crossed, the skirt of her dress sunk down inside the hollow between her knees. She dropped the greenbacks inside like it was a salad. After handing me one of the folded bundles, Cora began separating her own wad of paper.

In a quiet mumble, we each counted the currency.

"I got $115, Cora. How much do you have?"

"I think $117, but we still got one more stack." Cora reached for the last folded bundle and began to count. She separated the ones, fives, tens, and the single twenty into stacks on top of the other bills as she counted. The quilted bedspread looked like someone's cashiering drawer. When Cora was finished, she turned her eyes to me. "There's $119 in this stack! How much does it all come to, Sooze?"

It took me a minute to add it twice in my head. I wanted to be sure.

"Cora, there's $351 lying here on this bed. Can you believe it? Henry could live for a whole year on this money."

"You don't think he stole it, do you?"

"No, I think he won it in the gamblin' games down at Sugar Creek." I rubbed the tips of my fingers over the green ink on the backside of a twenty-dollar bill. "We can surely buy him a lawyer now."

Grabbing the stacks of money and bundling them together, Cora jumped off the bed. "Let's go tell Mama and Daddy!"

I was behind Cora as we walked into the living room. She fanned the paper money in front of them. Even from the backside of her head, I could tell she was grinning.

Mama was rocking the baby, but like a stone had rolled underneath, she stopped mid-rock. Her mouth fell open like she wanted to say something, but no words came. That's when Cora folded up the paper money and handed it to Daddy.

"Cora, what in the world?" He stood up out of his chair.

"There's $351 here," Cora said. "Do you think it's enough to buy a lawyer for Henry?"

Daddy's face turned white as a bleached bedsheet. Without a word, he turned and sat back down in the chair. He gulped coffee from his cup until it was empty.

"What's wrong, Daddy?" I asked, perplexed. I knelt beside him, putting my hand on his. "Don't you want the money?"

"I ain't takin' anything stole from somebody else."

Then words started flowing from Mama's mouth like a flood.

"What makes you think our boy stole that money?" Mama stood, and even though the baby was finally nursing, it didn't stop her none. "Maybe he earned it... Maybe he earned it workin' hard so's he could hand it over to you to help pay these bills?" Her eyes had a glare. "Henry's a good boy—he's always been a good boy—a good hardworkin' boy, and you got no right to accuse him of bein' a thief!"

Daddy stood up mad. "And when do you think Henry was out doin' this work, Emma? The boy goes to school every day and comes home every night."

"He don't go to school every day." Cora was trying to help defend Henry, but Daddy turned on her like a wildcat.

"What did you say?" His tone had already found fault. "What else do you know about your brother that you should have been tellin' me?" He stared at Cora with fire in his eyes. "If he ain't been goin' to school, where's he been goin' all day? Why ain't he been here workin' this farm with me?"

"Daddy," I said. "Henry frequents Sid Worster's old cabin down by the spillway at Sugar Creek. He plays gamblin' games with Benny and the other men who come from across the tracks. He's been carryin' money for a while, but I never had no idea he had this much." Daddy's stare turned on me. With every word, a sorrowful sadness was replacing his anger. Disappointment seeped right out of him, but it wasn't for Henry—it was for me because I had hidden this information from him. I had chosen to protect Henry's secret rather than trust Daddy. "I should have told you. I'm sorry."

I glanced at Mama. She had her chin raised high and was nodding her head.

Staring straight at him, Mama said, "John Williams, you should be ashamed of yourself believin' such things about your own blood—our boy is not a thief!" She pulled the baby from her breast and held her against her shoulder, patting her for a burp. With her voice steady, she said, "Henry's an honest boy—the roots of his raisin' run deep. He don't take things that don't belong to him. You know better than that."

"Sorry, Emma." He walked to Mama and slid his arm around her shoulders. "I'm not sure bein' a gambler is much better, but bein' a thief would be a shaming thing. Better a gambler than a two-bit thief."

Turning to Cora and me, Daddy said, "Girls, thank you for tellin' me about your brother, and thank you for bringin' the money to us." He took the money Cora was offering. "How much did you say it was?"

"It's $351, Daddy," I said. "Can you believe it?"

"And I got another $21.13 myself!" Cora told him, but Mama jumped in quick when Daddy's brow lifted.

"Cora's been savin' the money as a surprise, John," Mama said. "We already discussed the situation, and I'm mighty proud of this little girl for knowin' how to save."

His face eased. With a nod, he said, "Seems we're one of the richest families in Scott County tonight."

After pulling the biscuits out of the oven, Mama cooked strips of salt pork and made milk gravy for dinner. Daddy's blessing asked for God's mercy if Henry was guilty and God's help if he wasn't.

After tossing and turning in a night of fitful, nightmarish sleep, I rose with the morning. I tried to be quiet while looking through my closet for a dress. Being the last week of school, two of my five dresses were threadbare, and all had fading colors. It was clear Mama and me would need to sew one or two new dresses for me before the start of the next school year. I inspected the ones hanging up, realizing most were too tattered to be handed down to Cora. We'd need to sew her a new dress or two, too. Maybe she was finally old enough to practice sewing for herself.

I picked my navy blue dress with white piping and slid it over my head. It used to be my fancy dress, but looking in the mirror, all I saw looking back was a plain-Jane girl with shoulder-length blonde hair that needed trimming, wearing an old dress with piping missing on one collar. Even its blue was faded from too many washings and too much wearing.

"Sooze, why do we have to go to school today?" Cora was sitting up in bed, rubbing sleep from her eyes. "Can't we go to the jail so's I can talk to Henry?"

"We've got less than a week of school left, Cora," I reminded. "And we've got tests to pass so we can move up a grade next year. You know how strict Miss Stewart is about attendin' class—we can't start missin' school now."

"What about Henry's test?" Cora's face turned into a frown. "How's he supposed to pass if he's locked up in a jail cage?"

The graduation exam was set in two parts, one Tuesday morning and one Wednesday morning, and I knew if Henry couldn't get to school for the test, he'd have no hope of graduating on Thursday. But there was no use in worrying Cora with more burdens than she already had.

"Let's just hope he gets out real soon," I said.

Crawling off the bed, Cora was quiet as a mouse as she walked to the closet, pulling her brown cotton dress off its hanger.

After a hair brushing, I tied a thin white ribbon to a handful of bangs I'd pulled back off her face. I used my fingers to curl her short red hair around the backside of her ears. "You look pretty, Cora."

She smiled, but there wasn't any happiness coming from her grin.

Daddy took us to school in the wagon, saying, "I plan to check in on Henry, and I want to see if the sheriff has picked up Benny yet. I got a few questions for the boy myself."

We rode all the way to the schoolhouse in silence before he dropped us off, then without so much as a goodbye, he slapped the reins, and the wagon pulled away down the road to the red brick building holding Henry. We watched Daddy pass Huckabee's General Store and then stop at the sheriff's office. He jumped to the ground, tied the reins to the walkway railing, and then disappeared inside the jailhouse.

It seemed strange walking into the schoolhouse with everyone turned around backward, staring at us. Not a person said a word, not even Miss Stewart. You'd have thought we murdered someone ourselves the way everyone was glaring.

Loud, Cora shouted out, "What are you lookin' at? We ain't got the pox!"

I nudged her. "Go on, Cora," I whispered. "Let's just get to our desk."

We slid into our seats as Miss Stewart started talking. She held a stick of white chalk in her hand, and she was turned around, writing on the blackboard.

In her teaching tone, she said, "Roman numerals are used by some of the finest writers of our time to number chapters and other important writings, so part of the final twelfth-grade test will include it." Miss Stewart wrote *I*, *V*, and *X* on the board, with variations of each. "I suggest you spend some time in review today."

Nine-year-old Lillie raised her hand. Her long brown ringlets hung over her shoulders, making her look a bit like a child movie star. "Miss Stewart?"

The teacher turned and pointed to David's little sister. "Yes, Lillie?"

"What do the fifth graders need to study? My mother said to ask."

"Vowels will be a big part of the fifth and sixth-grade tests. You'll want to study your long and short sounds." Miss Stewart turned her back to us again and started writing on the blackboard. "Sounds as in, *a* hate, *e* eve, *i* pine, *o* no, *u* unicycle." Miss Stewart turned to the class and said, "Now that's a fun word, isn't it? Has anyone ever ridden a unicycle?"

Before anyone could answer, the schoolhouse door swung open, banging against the back wall, and in walked Paulette Simmons. She was wearing a "floozy dress" if I ever saw one. Her coal-black hair was pulled up above her ears, and she had on a red, wide-brimmed hat with a showy black feather. Her flimsy dress was red, too, with shoulder straps thin as a noodle. The dress didn't even hide her knees. She strode the aisle in high-heeled shoes no decent woman would wear, and she reeked with the pungent scent of sour rose water. With fingernails painted ruby red, she stopped right in front of Miss Stewart with her hand held out. "I'm here to pick up my Benny's twelfth-grade study guide."

Without batting an eye, Miss Stewart said, "And why isn't Benny here picking up the guide himself? Today is a school day, Miss Simmons."

"Look, I don't intend to listen to no back talk from you." Paulette put one hand on her hip and leaned in close to Miss Stewart with a finger pointed right at her. "This graduation certificate is the only chance my Benny's got to make something of his self in this rotten world, and I got no intention of lettin' you or anyone else take it away from him."

Miss Stewart held her poise. "You're right. A diploma is important. But need I remind you, Benny is still a student here, and he's expected to earn his certificate like everyone else. He needs to attend class until school is dismissed for the year." Miss Stewart never gave an inch, even though that finger with its long nail stayed pointed at her face. "He only has three more days of school, Miss Simmons, and he's already missed more than I should allow."

That's when Miss Simmons straightened up tall and took a step toward Miss Stewart. "Are you gonna get me that study guide so's I can take it to my Benny, or am I gonna have to find it myself?"

"C'mon, Cora," I whispered. "We've got to tell Daddy that Miss Simmons knows where to find Benny."

Both of us were up and out of our seats in a flash. We hurried down the aisle toward the door without a word to anyone. Dashing down the steps, we saw Daddy's wagon still hitched at the jailhouse. Running, we reached the door of the sheriff's office at the same time. Turning the knob, I pushed open the door. Daddy was standing at the jail cage talking to Henry while Sheriff Wingate sat at his desk reading the newspaper.

"Daddy!" I shouted.

The sheriff dropped the paper and sat up straight in his chair as Daddy turned.

"What's all the commotion?" Sheriff Wingate was

glaring at us. His thick, round eyeglasses magnified his brown eyes.

"We've got to see our daddy," Cora told him.

"What in the world are you two doing out of school?" Daddy asked.

"We came to tell you that Miss Simmons is at the school, and she knows where to find Benny," I told him.

Cora hurried to Henry, wrapping her hands around the jail bars in a mirror image of him. She started talking to Henry while I focused on Daddy.

"How do you know?" he asked me.

"Because she came to gather his study guide for the graduation exam and said she was gonna take it to him."

"Sheriff," Daddy said, his voice stern. "Do you need me to drag that woman in here so's you can question her about Benny's whereabouts, or are you goin' to get up out of that chair and do it yourself?"

"Now calm down, John," the sheriff said. "I'll talk to Paulette. She's a reasonable woman, and I expect she'll tell me what she knows without bein' dragged anywhere by you or anyone else."

The sheriff, wearing his official tan uniform and steel star badge, stood up and put on his brown felt fedora, covering his short-shaven hair before stepping out the door. Turning back, he said, "Mind you, don't try any funny business. Jailbreakin' is a crime not tolerated." I watched through the window as he walked down the road toward the schoolhouse.

"So, how's it feel to be behind these bars, Henry?" Cora asked.

"It's not a feelin' I'd like to have for too long," Henry answered. "Did you find the money, Cora?"

"I did, and I gave it to Daddy so's he could buy you a lawyer."

"Good girl." Henry reached his arm through the bars and patted Cora's head. He was still wearing his church clothes —blue jeans and a long-sleeved white shirt still spattered with Uncle Ray's blood. "You done real good. Did you count it? How much was there?"

I stepped up to the jail bars. "It was $351, Henry," I said. "That's more money than I ever thought I'd see."

"I had a run of good luck this year."

"Well, you're payin' for it now," Daddy told him. "Ain't nothin' in this world that comes without a price."

"Only thing we can't figure out is how much a lawyer costs," I added. "Do you know, Henry?"

"No, but I know where to find one."

"How do you know where to find a lawyer?" Daddy asked.

"I hear things down at Sugar Creek," Henry said, real serious. "A man from down Bates way told me gamblin' wasn't always a bad thing. He said sometimes when you use the money for good, the Lord forgives the sin."

We were all gathered at the bars of the jail cage, listening like it was a Christmas story.

"The man told me somethin' last year I ain't never forgot," Henry continued. "He said he was in charge of payroll at the sawmill, and he never saw any sense in letting all that money sit in a safe waitin' to be doled out on payday, so he used to borrow the money and gamble with it. Soon as he'd win, he'd skedaddle back to the sawmill and replace the borrowed cash, but he'd keep the winnings for himself. He told me he'd won enough money a few years back to send his son to a law school over in Oklahoma called Mills Law College. Last I heard, his son was about to graduate. Probably looking for work by now. Maybe we can get him cheap."

"Do you remember the boy's name?" Daddy asked.

"And how are we supposed to find him?" I wanted to know.

"The man's name was Henry, just like mine, but everybody called him Hank. His last name was Beegle. He lives just this side of Bates. He told me his son's name was

Cordie—Cordie Beegle. Ain't too hard a name to remember."

Just then, the door to the office opened, and in walked Paulette Simmons with the sheriff.

"Well, well," Paulette said. "Look who's causin' trouble now."

CHAPTER 9

Daddy moved away from Henry's jail cage, right toward Benny's mother.

"Miss Simmons," he said. "I don't think you should be comin' in here with an accusatory tone when we all know you got your boy holed up somewhere so's he don't have to answer for the killin' he's done."

"*My* accusatory tone?" Miss Simmons had both hands on her hips, and she was shouting. "*My* boy didn't kill nobody! And I got a good, solid witness to prove it."

I looked at Henry, and he looked back at me.

"She can't have no witness, 'cause I didn't kill Uncle Ray." Henry was talking in a serious whisper to Cora and me. "Daddy said you saw the whole thing, Sooze. Go on and tell her. Tell her I didn't do it. Tell her Benny done the stabbin'."

Henry was right. I was his only witness, and I had to defend him against his accusers.

"I saw the whole thing," I blurted out. Cora stood next to me, nodding like she'd been a witness herself. When everyone stopped shouting and started listening, I finished by saying, "I was standin' right behind Henry and Benny, Miss Simmons, and I saw Benny pull the knife and stab Uncle Ray."

Maybe she didn't know. Maybe Miss Simmons thought Benny was innocent. Lord knows, Mama and Daddy had trusted me sometimes without ever considering that I might have done something wrong. And sometimes, I wasn't innocent at all. Like the time Henry went running to Mama after I'd pushed him into the mud while he was wearing his Sunday best. He'd made me so mad, talking about me like I thought I was the Queen of Sheba. When I'd heard enough, I shoved him right into that mud puddle. When Mama came and asked me about it, I lied straight out. I said Henry had tripped over his own clumsy feet. Maybe Miss Simmons was trusting Benny like that, not even giving it a second thought.

"You wasn't the only one standin' behind 'em," Miss Simmons said, bobbing her head like a banty rooster. Her face contorted into a sneer, and she leaned in closer. "I got a witness, too."

"You ain't got no witness!" Cora shouted. "Pert'near everybody was talked to, and nobody saw what happened. No one 'cept Sooze." She looked at Daddy for reassurance. "Right, Daddy?"

"That's right, Cora."

Miss Simmons stepped forward and pointed her finger in Cora's face. "God'll strike you dead for lyin' little girl."

Cora's giant step forward was fast as lightning. She swung her leg hard, but Daddy curled his arm around her waist and pulled her up so her swinging leg couldn't kick Miss Simmons.

"Everybody settle down!" Sheriff Wingate yelled.

Taking Miss Simmons by the arm, the sheriff led her to a chair on the other side of the room. She sat down and crossed her long, thin legs before looking up at the sheriff and smiling. Sheriff Wingate smiled back then leaned in, putting one hand on the arm of the chair. In a sugary tone, he asked, "Who's your witness, Paulette?"

Smoothing her red dress against her legs like stroking invisible wrinkles, she sweetly said, "Dimple Dodds. He was standin' back behind the tree and saw the whole thing."

"Well, now, Paulette," Sheriff Wingate said. "I don't mean to doubt your word, but I've lived in Coaldale for over forty years, and I ain't never seen Dimple at a church service. What do you suppose made him decide to come to one yesterday?"

"He come lookin' for me, Sheriff," Miss Simmons said, grinning shyly at him. "You know how it is, sometimes a man's just like an old coon dog."

Daddy stepped forward. Unforgiving, he said, "I ain't never seen *you* at a church service either, Miss Simmons. Where was you sittin' yesterday?"

Miss Simmons batted her lashes and gave a sideways glance to the sheriff. "As I recall, I was sittin' right next to you after our early mornin' meetin', Sheriff. Isn't that right?"

"Er, well, yes." Sheriff Wingate cleared his throat, his face red. "I believe you were sittin' next to me."

Miss Simmons and the sheriff eyed each other like they shared a secret I doubted would be told.

In a defeated stance, Daddy's shoulders slumped. He lowered his head. Without a word, he walked back to Henry. "You say the Beegle boy lives in Bates?"

"Yes, sir. His daddy does," Henry said. "Hank Beegle. Go to the sawmill—that's where he works. He'll be able to tell you where to find Cordie."

Just then, a rock busted through the window of the sheriff's front door, shattering its glass. From outside, a voice yelled, "*Murderer*! I hope you *hang*, Henry Williams!"

I recognized Arnold's voice. We all rushed to the window to confirm the culprit with our own eyes. The boy running away sure looked like Arnold. Pointing, I said, "That's…"

But before I could finish, Daddy clamped a hand over my mouth. Whispering, he said, "Let it be, Sooze."

Rushing out the door, Sheriff Wingate stood on the

porch and shook his fist in the air. He yelled after the fleeing boy, "I'll find out who you are!"

Daddy turned me around and looked me square in the eyes. His voice was low. "Arnold's our kin, Sooze, and the boy's just lost his father. He's fightin' hard to hold on to his daddy's life, and throwin' stones is the only way he knows. He'll come to his senses. He'll realize soon enough that Henry didn't kill his daddy. Let it be."

Right then, I realized my daddy was the finest man who ever lived. There wasn't a fairer, kinder, or stronger man on earth. I knew why Mama loved him. I knew why I admired him. And I knew why Henry needed him.

The sheriff came back in, kicking at the broken glass scattered on the wood floor. "Looks like you got some enemies, Henry. If my new spectacles serve me right, I think the stone thrower might have been your cousin Arnold. Dead men tell no tales, but sometimes his kin sure does."

"I told you, Sheriff," Paulette said, standing at the window. She pointed to Henry. "He's a killer. Even his kinfolks know it."

Rock bottom—that's where Arnold's stone had put us.

"Sheriff," Daddy sounded mad, "are you gonna bring Benny in for questioning, or are you just plannin' to keep my boy locked up without investigation?"

"Sure I am, John. I got plans to question Benny soon as I find him," Sheriff Wingate told Daddy. "I intend to keep my word."

"Then get to it!" Daddy scolded. "My boy's been locked up long enough, and it don't seem like you're doing much about it."

Unaffected by Daddy's tone, the sheriff turned to Miss Simmons. "Now, where's Benny hiding out? You know I've got to enforce the law, and even if he ain't guilty, he's a witness who needs talkin' to in detail. Do you understand?"

"Of course, I understand," Miss Simmons said agreeably. "But Benny's not hidin', Sheriff. He's just doing what boys do, you know? He's out at the three-man pigeonhole near Bates No. 2 Mine. They haven't used it for about a year, so he's not bothering anyone. He's just thinkin' things through."

Paulette Simmons stood up, smoothing her red dress. "How about I bring Benny back so's you can talk to him, Sheriff?"

"Daddy," Henry said. "She's just goin' out there to forewarn Benny so's he can run."

Looking at Henry behind the jail bars, Daddy said, "You're right, son." He turned to the sheriff. "How about I go get the boy myself?"

"No," the sheriff said. "*I'll* go get Benny. I'm the sheriff, and I don't want no one sayin' I didn't do my duty." Then turning with a smile toward Miss Simmons, he sweetened his voice and asked, "Now, Paulette, what about Dimple? Do you think you can find him and get him to come in on his own to talk to me? I got some questions for him about this killin', too."

"Sheriff, I'm happy to do just anything you ask me to do," Miss Simmons said. She was already standing close to the sheriff, but she leaned in closer. "But then, you already know that, don't you?"

The sheriff cleared his throat. Tenderly, he said, "Go on now, Paulette." He ushered her toward the front door. "Find Dimple and bring him back." Everybody stared as Miss Simmons sashayed away, swinging her red silk purse like a cowbell.

"Sheriff, we'll be staying right here with Henry," Daddy told him. "I intend to be here when you get back with Benny. I got questions, too."

"Okay, John," the sheriff said. "I understand." Sheriff Wingate adjusted the black leather belt that held his holstered revolver, then put on his hat. "Paulette will bring Dimple back soon enough, and it won't take me long to pick up Benny. If I'm not back before Paulette, can you two be civil to one another?"

"Yeah," Daddy said, his head lowered as if he might not be telling the truth.

"All right then. I've got some coffee in the back room. You're welcome to it."

Daddy nodded.

On his way out, the sheriff stopped and pointed at the windowless door. "While you're back pouring yourselves coffee, you'll see a broom and dustpan. It wouldn't hurt your family name none if you was to clean up this broken glass while I was gone."

Sheriff Wingate pulled the door open and looked back at us just long enough to tip his hat before walking out.

"Daddy," Henry said, both hands gripping the jail bars. "Do you think there's a cup back there small enough to fit through these bars so's I can have some coffee? A hot cup of Joe would sure taste good."

"I'll get you a cup, Henry!" Cora hurried to the back room.

I followed, saying, "I'll get the broom." I figured we could use all the help we could get to make our name good again, even though sweeping the floor sounded like a silly way to do it.

The back room was long and narrow, with a counter and cabinets running half its length. In the far back corner near the potbellied stove, I saw the broom with its yellow straw bent and curled from too many sweepings under heavy hands and a black metal dustpan—dusty and dirty—hanging on a nearby nail.

"What about this one, Sooze?" Cora held up a tin cup by its handle. "It's small enough to fit through the jail bars, but it's all bent up."

"It's probably the one the sheriff uses for prisoners. I'll bet it's been squeezed back and forth through the bars a hundred times."

"A *prisoner*," Cora repeated. "Who'd ever thought Henry would be one of them people?"

"Come on, Cora," I urged her. "Don't think too long on

things like that, or the thoughts will stick like glue inside your brain. Pour Henry a cup of coffee while I sweep up the broken glass."

Daddy had pulled a chair up to the jail bars and was talking to Henry when Cora slid the cup through the bars to Henry's waiting hands.

"Thanks, Cora," Henry said, then louder, he asked, "Sooze, how come you got a bruised nose and two black eyes? Was you in a fight?"

"Yeah, but it wasn't *my* fight." I eyeballed Cora, but she paid me no mind. "Cora tussled with Arnold, and I got kicked in the face tryin' to pull 'em apart." I swept broken glass into the dustpan.

Cora's head was down. "Arnold said you killed Uncle Ray." Her tone was sorrowful. "I couldn't let him get away with saying that about you, Henry."

With a nod toward the shattered glass, Henry said, "Well, whup him again next time you see him for breaking that window and calling me a murderer in front of the sheriff."

Cora nodded as Daddy said, "Don't be egging your sister on. She can get into enough trouble *without* your help."

When the front door opened, I was stooped over picking up the full dustpan when I heard David's voice.

"I thought I'd find you here, Sooze." David closed the door. "What made you run out of the schoolhouse like your dress was on fire?"

I straightened up without looking at him and walked to the tin trashcan near the sheriff's desk. I emptied the glass shards into it. "We had news for Daddy."

Daddy stood with an outstretched hand. "Hello, David. Glad to see you."

David shook hands without ever taking his eyes off me.

"The sheriff went to pick up Benny," I explained. "We're waitin' here for him."

"We're waitin' so's we can take Henry home," Cora added.

David nodded, but the look on his face said, "That ain't gonna happen today." I stared right at him. He couldn't see the future any better than me, and I resented him acting like he could. I handed the broom and dustpan to Cora.

"Can we talk outside, David?" That was as much politeness as I could muster.

"Sure, Sooze." He smiled like he'd won a prize.

Outside on the wood-planked porch, I walked beside David to the building's corner edge for privacy. I stood with my arms crossed against the cool midmorning air, but I could feel the summertime approach. The breeze carried a warmth on its chill like the hot engine of an ice truck.

"I can't wait to take you away from this life, Sooze." David flicked his hand toward the jail, indicating *this* meant my family. With the look of a serious businessman, he said, "The whole county is talking about this shameful situation. Course, a few local folk have sided with Henry. They think Benny stabbed your uncle, but it don't matter 'cause shame is pouring down on your family name anyhow. That'll change soon enough, though. You'll be Mrs. David Huckabee before too long, and then you can shed the Williams name forever. In next to no time, folks won't even remember you came from this family."

"Not that I care what folks think," I told David. "But the locals are right. Henry didn't kill Uncle Ray." It was important he knew the truth. Being the man I was marrying, he needed to understand. "I was standing right there—right behind the two of them—and I saw Benny stab Uncle Ray."

"Well, Sooze," David said in a snigger. "If you were *behind* the two of them, how could you see it? I mean, you surely didn't have a clean view of it all. And it was Henry's knife. What would Benny be doin' with Henry's knife? No one's going to believe Henry, and they won't believe you either, Sooze. You're his sister. You're bound by blood to lie for him."

I was stunned. If David doubted my witnessing, then the sheriff, the judge, and the jury would doubt me, too. I had to do something. "David, we need to buy a lawyer for Henry, and I need your help."

I had a plan, and I couldn't waste time. With David by the hand, I pulled him back inside the jailhouse.

CHAPTER 10

"Daddy!" I hollered as I came through the sheriff's door, dragging David behind me.

"What are you yellin' about, Sooze?" Daddy's tone sounded almost mad.

"We got to buy Henry a lawyer *now*—right now—while Benny and Dimple Dodds are on their way here to converse about the story." It was clear as a bell. Turning to my brother, I said, "Henry, you got to say you ain't talkin' to nobody without a lawyer. You can't say a word until we find Cordie Beegle and bring him back here. Do you understand?"

Daddy's face twisted into a confused squint. "Now, don't jump the gun, Sooze." He stood up out of the chair. "Let's not be spending any money 'til Benny's had a chance to spill his story. He'll slip up and brag about the killin', and then the sheriff will have to let Henry go."

Cora nodded. "He'll see Henry's been tellin' the truth, Sooze. He'll unlock these bars, and Henry will walk clean out of here. He'll be home with us straight away." She grinned. "Won't Mama be surprised when we walk in the door today with Henry?"

Henry and his honey-brown eyes showed interest. "Sooze, what's in that head of yours?" Then he looked at

Daddy. "She's a smart girl, Daddy, I think Sooze might see somethin' we ain't seein'—she can figure things out better than anybody I ever knowed. I want to hear what's on her mind. Go on, Sooze. Finish what you got to say."

Henry had never called me *smart* before. He'd never given me credit for getting good marks in school or for knowing how to calculate measures for cooking. I couldn't help but be a bit proud about his words. When my lips broke into a smile my face couldn't hide, I said, "Thank you, Henry."

With a nod, Henry said, "What's your plan?"

"They ain't never gonna believe us, Henry, because you and me—we're tight-knit kin. Benny's gonna keep sayin' it's your knife, and he's innocent. He's gonna let you hang for this killin'. We can't take any chances of lettin' him ruin the truth." Still holding David's hand, I pulled him with me as I moved closer to Henry. "The only way anyone is goin' to listen is if we have a lawyer talking for us. They *have* to listen to a lawyer, Henry. You can't say nothin' until Cordie Beegle is standin' here talkin' for you. His words are the only words that matter now."

Henry straightened up. He took a step back. "Sooze is right, Daddy. I just got a bad gut feeling inside of me."

"Me and David can drive to Bates right now and find Cordie and bring him back. All you got to do is make sure the sheriff holds on to Benny and Dimple Dodds so the Beegle boy can break their story apart."

"Whoa," David said, letting loose of my hand. "I got to get back to school, and so do you, Sooze. Our finals start tomorrow morning. These are important days for us!"

My blood began to boil. I looked straight at him. "Henry's life is more important than a school final. More important than a graduation certificate, too." I was giving David a chance to do the right thing. To make the right decision.

"We can go Friday, after Thursday's graduation." David took a step back like I had a contagion. "But I ain't goin' today, Sooze. Mother and Father expect me to pass my final and graduate this week, and I don't intend to fail them. I'm makin' this decision for our future." He looked at Daddy and, with a single nod, said to him, "Surely you agree."

Daddy lowered his head. He was silent. Not a word came from him.

"You worthless piece of crap!" Henry was shouting mad. "You ain't good enough to marry my sister!"

"Calm down, Henry," Daddy said, composed but stern. Raising his head, he turned to David and me. "We're needin' your help, David. Now, I know your school finals start tomorrow, but tomorrow's tomorrow—it ain't today, and today is when we need you."

"We got our own money, David," I assured him, just in case that's what he was thinking. "And you know I ain't very good at handlin' Daddy's wagon with all them logging trucks running the road. I just need a ride from you in your automobile to get to the sawmill in Bates fast. Daddy needs to stay and help Henry. If I can find Cordie Beegle quick, you'll be back in class before the lunch bell sounds."

Shaking his head, David was backing away. "I ain't doin' it, Sooze, and you're soon to be my wife, so you need to come along and do as I say."

David turned and held open the door with a look that said he expected me to follow.

"No," I said, shaking my head. If my heart had been filled to overflow with love like Mama talked about, it would probably have been breaking. "I'm goin' to Bates, David, with or without you."

"I'll go with you, Sooze," Cora offered. "When we get to the bridge, I'll jump off and run to the other side so's I can stop the logging trucks from driving the bridge head-on toward the wagon."

David slammed the door shut behind him while Cora was still talking. I watched, but I never saw him look back.

My face felt flush. What had I done? The future of my family had just walked out the door. Pulling myself together, I knew I needed to focus on the task at hand.

"Daddy, how do I keep Frenchy calm crossing the bridge if a coal train comes blowin' through on its way down the tracks? I sure don't want her spooked while we're on a decrepit old bridge."

Serious, Daddy said, "You'll need to put blinders on her before the crossing, Sooze. She don't like that bridge." He leaned, looking out the sheriff's broken window. David was walking fast toward the schoolhouse. "Sure is a shame." He glanced at me. "You'll figure out a way to patch things up with him, Sooze. Let's just get Henry taken care of first."

"He ain't worth your time, Sooze," Henry said. "How long's it gonna take before you get that through your thick skull? I don't know what you see in him. Aside from all his money, he ain't never been worth a hill o' beans."

I wasn't mad at Henry—in fact, I wasn't mad at anybody —but my words came out in a shout anyway. "Henry Williams, if you was so good at knowin' things nobody else knows, you wouldn't be in this mess yourself, now would you?"

Henry's shoulders relaxed, and he laughed. "See there, Daddy?" he said. "She's a smart girl. She's got some spunk, too, don't she?"

"Yeah," Daddy said without even a hint of a smile. "No one in this family has ever been short on spunk."

"What about the money, Daddy?" I asked.

"Nobody's gettin' any money until they show up here agreeing to defend Henry." His tone was firm. "Do you hear me? You make sure they know, Sooze." Then Daddy walked to the door, pulling it open. "Cora, your sister's in charge. I don't want to hear about trouble from you."

"I know," Cora told him. "It's only seven miles to Sawmill Road. That's not enough time for *anybody* to get into trouble."

I could hear Henry shouting a reminder as me and Cora left the jailhouse. "Cordie Beegle! That's his name, Sooze!"

In the wagon, I released the brake bar, and with a rein in

each hand, I slapped the straps against Frenchy's black mane, and we moved off down the road.

Dozens of byroads branched off between Coaldale and Bates, with most leading to farms, some still producing, but most not. I knew when we neared another homestead because a long-ago planted japonica bush marked its approach.

Most homesteaders had been hardscrabble farmers who collapsed under times too tough to survive. Daddy said they went broke gradually. Things like that didn't happen fast. If they had any savings, they exhausted those first then had to use borrowings. Soon they used up the gas for tractoring and couldn't work no more. Then they exhausted themselves. Just about everybody had to pack up and leave. Most headed to California. I felt sad looking at the abandoned homes, knowing so many memories still lived inside. Every few miles, the maroon-green foliage of another japonica waited to welcome someone home. Seemed a shame, so many people needed a roof over their heads, yet all those houses stood empty. It's not like the bankers needed the home themselves, so I couldn't understand why those down-on-their-luck families were ordered out.

"Sooze, look," Cora said, pointing up ahead toward the turnoff to Smoot Haney's farm.

Four teenage boys were in the middle of the road next to a black automobile, and they were handing a clear bottle from one to the other, each one sipping before passing.

"Do you know them?" I asked her.

When Cora shook her head, I made my decision.

"We're goin' round 'em, Cora." My whisper was hard. "We're not stoppin'."

"What if they're broke down? What if they need a ride into town so's they can refill their gasoline? Mama says offerin' to help is the Christian thing to do. Shouldn't we be givin' 'em a ride?"

"We're not stoppin', do you hear me?" I tightened the left rein on Frenchy, and she veered off the road into the grass and kept moving. "The bottle they're passin' looks like rotgut, and even though we don't know those boys, we know they're feeling mean 'cause that's what rotgut does to a man."

I tried not to look at any of their faces as we maneuvered around them. I just kept slapping the reins to make sure Frenchy didn't stop.

"Looky here!" Wearing a flashy red-and-blue plaid shirt, the brown-haired boy pushed himself away from the automobile, moving toward our wagon.

"We're in a hurry!" I yelled out. "Sorry we can't help you." I slapped the reins again, holding tight to the leather as it burned into my palms. Frenchy whinnied but then jerked when the boys sprinted toward her.

Before we could pull back onto the road, they had hold of the bridle, yelling, "Whoa!"

"Let loose of my horse!" I was yelling loud and slapping the reins, urging Frenchy to yank free, but when Cora screamed, I turned my focus to her. Climbing her side of the wagon was a boy I hadn't seen. He grabbed her off the seat with one hand and slung her to the ground like a ragdoll. He was a big boy with a belly that hung low over his belt. In a stumble, he fell onto the wagon seat beside me, grabbing the reins. He pulled hard on Frenchy, causing her to rear back, scattering those who had hold of her. When she settled, the boys laughed, poking fun at one another.

But when Cora threw a rock, the laughing stopped. She hit the big boy seated beside me square on the head.

He shielded himself with his arm, yelling, "For cryin' out loud, Roy! Grab that girl and settle her down, will ya?"

I tried to jump off the wagon, but he grabbed me and pulled me down onto his fat lap. I was kicking and screaming as I saw another boy climb the side and jump flat-footed into the bed of the wagon. He grabbed me around the waist, pulling me over the seatback and slamming me onto the wagon's floorboards. I kept kicking and screaming—

splinters snagging my blue dress as he dragged me toward the end gate.

"Earl, I had her first!" The big boy climbed over the seat and jumped into the back, too. "You know I like blonde girls." He took a step forward, unbuttoning his jeans before grabbing hold of my ankles and pulling me back toward the front of the wagon.

"Horace, let go of her! She ain't a wishbone!"

When I heard Cora scream, I screamed louder. "Leave her alone! She's only twelve!"

With my free leg, I kicked Horace in the groin. He doubled over, and his face turned a light shade of blue, just like his shirt. Before I could get free, the boy named Earl, foul-smelling and grungy, crawled on top of me. He held me down, and with breath smelling of rusted metal and ethanol, he pressed his open mouth hard against mine. I struggled against him, shaking my head side-to-side, trying to kick my feet beneath his weight.

Then, with a hard bounce, big Horace fell face-first beside me. Before I knew it, Earl was yanked up and off me, leaving me lying there with my dress pulled up, staring skyward. That's when I saw a tall, blond boy with his hands clamped around Earl's legs. He dragged him back, dropping Earl's legs with a *thud*, and then he knelt and started punching. I scooted fast to the end gate and leaped off the wagon.

"Cora, where are you?" I yelled, running around in circles like a cat after a mouse.

"Sooze, here!" Cora's voice came from the other side of the wagon.

When I got to her, she was standing in knee-high grass. I grabbed her by the shoulders and turned her around and back again. "Are you all right?" I asked, brushing my hand through her short, red hair.

"Yeah," Cora said, pointing. "But tarnation! Those boys are sure gonna be sorry when they come to, ain't they?"

I turned quick and saw two boys lying in the road, and Earl was half hanging off the wagon's edge.

I knew big Horace was lying face down in the wagon, 'cause that was where I'd left him when I scooted out, but the blond boy was still standing with his back to us.

"Who is that, Cora? I thought there was only four boys."

"That's Thomas Kittridge," Cora said. "He come out of nowhere and just started plowing those boys down with his fists. Then he jumped into the wagon and knocked out that fat boy before grabbin' the other one." She grinned before spitting on the ground like she was carrying the victory prize. "He sure don't like other people fightin', does he?"

When Thomas turned, I saw blood trickling down his forehead.

"He's hurt!" I ran to the wagon and climbed up the wheel spokes to grab Daddy's grease rag from under the seat. With it crumpled in my hand, I jumped down. When Thomas had both feet on the ground, I stood on tiptoes and pressed the cleanest side of the rag to his cut. "Are you hurt anywhere else?"

"No, ma'am," Thomas said. "Are *you* hurt?" Then he stammered a bit before asking, "Did they…"

"No," I answered, knowing what he meant. "They didn't."

"Did they *what*?" Cora asked.

"Never you mind, Cora," I said. "We need to get on out of here before these boys come to—they'll be madder than hornets!"

"Yes, ma'am," Thomas agreed.

When Cora and me ran to the front of the wagon and climbed up onto the seat, Thomas pulled Earl off the wagon's edge, dropped him to the ground, then he hopped into the back and rolled Horace off like a fat hog. Finally, he climbed over the seat back and onto the seat with us.

He was breathing hard as he took hold of the reins. "Two pretty young girls shouldn't be out here alone without an escort."

"It wasn't by choice," I admitted. Then looking around, I asked, "Where's your automobile?"

"I'm on foot, walking to my new job at the sawmill. That's how I come upon you two."

"The sawmill? That's where we're headed, too." Warmth filled my belly, but I couldn't tell whether it was a happy warm or a scared warm. All I knew for sure was we needed to get out of there fast before those boys woke up.

"Good. I'll handle the wagon if you don't mind." Thomas slapped the reins. "There's a bridge up ahead that makes me awful nervous walkin' it, so I expect it'll be just as bad riding it."

"That's the Poteau River Bridge," Cora told him. "Boards been missing for years, and every time a big storm comes along, it seems like one more blows off."

"Frenchy doesn't like the bridge either," I told Thomas as he maneuvered the wagon back onto the road. "We have to put blinders on her before we cross."

"Hey," Cora said, "Are we just gonna leave those boys lyin' back there in the middle of the road?"

"Yep," Thomas said without looking back. "We sure are."

The wheels lurched as Frenchy's head bowed, and her sturdy body pulled forward.

The road twisted and turned through the tree-covered hills—its shadows allowing just glimpses of the Poteau River below. Dogwood blossoms and fresh sawn lumber saturated the air with scent. From above, the blue sky cast shafts of dust-flecked sunlight spiraling down through the limbs, streaking our roadway with lines of light and dark.

With birds chirping in the newly leafed-out trees, it felt more like a picnic day than a fighting and lawyering day, but no matter what we were doing with the day, we were still gonna have to cross that bridge.

When the sound of the roaring river grew louder, Thomas said, "You got them blinders?"

I reached down and pulled the black blinders out of the box Daddy kept under the seat and handed them to Thomas. Without a word, he halted the wagon and jumped down off the seat. He walked up to Frenchy, patting her haunches first, and then slowly rubbed his hand along her side until he got to her face. He whispered with a scratch behind her ear, then slipped the blinders on. Frenchy never flinched, just as if she trusted Thomas completely, even though they'd just met. He had a gentle touch and calm manner.

Thomas walked back to the wagon and climbed up. His legs were long and thin, and his arm muscles filled out the long sleeves of his blue chambray shirt. His golden wheat-colored hair was short at the neck but long on top, naturally parting, so it swept low over one brow. I knew I was staring, but I couldn't pull my eyes away.

"You all right?" Thomas asked. He put the back of his hand against my forehead and was looking at me like I had a fever.

"O-oh," I stammered, my eyes glued to his. "I didn't mean to gawk."

Thomas smiled. "I can't think of anyone I'd rather have lookin' at me than you."

"C'mon!" Cora was impatient. "Quit lookin' at each other. We got to find that lawyer for Henry."

CHAPTER 11

In the oak and loblolly pine branches overhead, meadowlarks and bluebirds chirped to the rhythm of a woodpecker, drumming his beat on a limb.

As we rounded the bend, the distant whistle of the Arkansas Western train blew, and there, just a few feet ahead, was the old truss bridge—an open box of corroded steel beams with splintered wood planks lying atop rusted girders.

Thomas pulled back on the reins. "Whoa, horse."

Cora jumped to the ground. "I'll go first and call out the loose boards, but some are just plumb missin', and if Frenchy steps through an open hole, she's liable to break a leg."

"That's good, Cora," Thomas agreed. "Stay far enough ahead so's you can wave down any logging trucks headed toward us, too. Only one of us is gonna fit."

"Be careful!" I called to Cora before she started across.

Thomas handed me the reins then climbed down the wagon spokes. He walked ahead, holding Frenchy's leather lead.

"I'll listen for the train," I reminded Thomas. "When it gets near the crossing below, it'll start blowin' its horn. The whistle spooked Frenchy so bad one time she almost run Daddy down as he was leading her across."

Thomas nodded as I clutched the reins.

With Frenchy's first step onto the wood planks, she whinnied and danced, pulling back in defiance, but Thomas had her lead rope wound around his hand and kept walking forward. She followed even though her head bobbed to the side, testing the seriousness of his grip.

I held tight to the leather straps and watched Cora wave her hand right, then left, then motion us forward, guiding us farther onto the bridge. Working in tandem, Thomas followed every direction Cora gave him.

Cautiously, Thomas stepped over a long, narrow gap in the bridge floor, then he watched to be sure Frenchy's hooves cleared the opening too. The wagon was halfway across the bridge when, off in the distance, the train whistle blew again. That time the sound was far away, so I knew we would not have to contend with meeting each other this crossing. I breathed a sigh of relief until I heard Cora shout, "Stop!"

I jerked the reins taut, then stood up in the wagon to get a better view of Cora. "What's wrong?"

"I hear the gears of a logging truck grindin' up the hill!" Cora pointed to the road on the other side of the bridge. "I gotta go stop 'em!"

Cora turned and ran across the bridge, hopping and jumping over each missing board. When she reached the other side, she stood in the middle of the road and started bouncing up and down, waving both arms.

"Stop! Stop!" Cora shouted with each hop. Wildly, she waved her arms back and forth above her head.

A big, red logging truck, its trailer loaded down with eight limbed and topped-out pine trunks, came through the trees. Each log was big enough to build half a cabin.

The thought came to me as Cora hopped up and down, shouting all the while, that she should have worn something other than her brown dress today. A yellow dress would surely have helped flag the truck down.

Instead of slowing, the logging truck barreled toward her.

"Cora!" I screamed. "They don't see you! Get off the road!"

Then Thomas joined me, shouting, "Get out of the way!"

Cora darted off into the roadside bushes but was back in the middle of the road in no time. I saw her draw her arm back and pitch a rock straight at the windshield of the big truck. With screeching brakes, the truck skidded to a stop with dust boiling up from under its tires.

The driver's door flew open, and a man climbed down out of the cab, yelling, "What in the Sam Hill are you doing in the middle of the road?" Then pointing at the cracked window, he shouted, "You broke my windshield!"

The dark-haired, middle-aged man was mad, and he was walking toward her.

Cora stood, hands on hips, shouting back at him. "You nearly run me down! If I hadn't thrown that rock, I'd probably be lying dead under your wheels!"

Then the conversation quieted, and I couldn't hear their words anymore. Soon, the man climbed back into the cab of his truck. The engine gears grinded as he shifted into reverse, and then he backed up until the logging truck was off the roadway. He held his arm out the open window and waved, motioning us to cross.

Cora ran back toward us. "Come on! He says there's two more logging trucks behind him!"

Thomas nodded my way, and I slapped the reins. Frenchy started pulling again, and before long, we were across that bridge.

"Thank you kindly," Thomas called to the man as we neared his truck. Painted in white block letters on his door were the words *FORRESTER LUMBER*.

Stopped next to the driver, Cora and Thomas climbed back onto the wagon and settled in the seat, one on each side of me. When the man waved, Thomas snapped the leather straps, and Frenchy moved forward, pulling our wagon down the earthen road.

"You did good, Cora," I said. "But you sure scared me when I thought the truck was goin' to run you over."

"I wasn't gonna let him run me over!" Cora said. "Who would help you find Cordie Beegle for Henry if I was dead?"

"Beegle?" Thomas asked with a curious head turn. "It was a man named Beegle who hired me to do clean-up work for him at the sawmill."

"Was it Hank Beegle?" I asked Thomas. "'Cause that's who we're headed to see. We're hoping he can tell us where to find Cordie."

"Who's Cordie?"

"He's the lawyer who's gonna free my brother," Cora said with a snap of confidence.

"You see," I said, wanting more than anything for Thomas to understand and believe me, "the sheriff is still holdin' our brother Henry for the murder of Uncle Ray, but Henry didn't kill him. It was his friend Benny that stabbed Uncle Ray." I scooted a bit on the single bench seat to see Thomas's face straight on. "But no one believes me. I'm afraid they'll convict Henry if we don't buy him a lawyer. We heard Cordie Beegle graduated from Mills Law College. We're hopin' his daddy—Hank Beegle—will know where we can find him."

"We got lots of money," Cora added. "But we're not sure if it's enough to buy a lawyer. We just got to find Cordie so's we can talk to him."

With warmth in his eyes, Thomas stared straight at me.

"Why would anyone not believe you, Sooze?" Thomas said. His voice was smooth as a polished river rock. "I can't imagine anyone doubtin' a single word comin' outta your mouth." Pointing, he said, "Sawmill Road is just up ahead. I've only worked for Mr. Beegle three days, but I'd be proud to introduce you."

During the next half mile, the other two logging trucks

the driver warned us about came speeding down the road, one right after the other. At first sight of them, Thomas steered Frenchy and the wagon off to the side, allowing them—without so much as a nod—to speed past, leaving us in a fog of dust. When the billowing grit settled, we started again.

Soon, a big wooden sign, painted red and white just like the doors on the lumber trucks, stood before us. A white arrow lined the bottom of the long sign, pointing the way to the sawmill entrance.

My nose wrinkled at the musky scent of sawn wood and pine resin.

Dozens of men in denim overalls—each wearing a hat of one type or another—milled around in wait of another felled tree.

With Frenchy hitched to the post near the sawmill office, Cora and me followed Thomas to the door. He turned the knob and pushed the door open. "Ladies first."

Inside, amid the smoke and smell of tobacco, four men stood studying a strange-looking paper map tacked to the back wall. Instead of roads and state lines, the map had circular sections of green, naming familiar forested land, including the biggest patch, Ouachita National Forest.

"Excuse me for interrupting," Thomas said. The men turned, looking at us. "Mr. Beegle, I was wonderin' if we could talk to you for a few minutes."

"Sure, Thomas." The dark-haired man wearing dunga-rees stepped toward us. His wire-framed spectacles slid down his nose. With one finger, he pushed them back up the bridge until they encircled his bluish-gray eyes again. "What can I do for you?"

"Mr. Beegle," I said without waiting for Thomas. "My name is Sooze Williams, and this is my sister Cora. We've come here looking for your son, Cordie."

Mr. Beegle straightened his posture and took a small step back. "What do you need with my boy?"

"We heard he graduated from Mills Law College," I said. "We're needin' to talk lawyerin' business with him."

It didn't help my confidence when the other men snickered. Business discussions were a man's place—not meant for a girl.

"Thomas," Mr. Beegle asked. "Are these girls kin to you?"

"No, sir. They're friends, though, and they've got some serious business." Thomas stood beside me without flinching. "They made the trip from Coaldale just to talk to you and your son today."

Mr. Beegle lowered his head before turning his eyes back to me. "I'm sure my boy will be happy to discuss business with your daddy, but he'll not be wasting his time talkin' to little girls about legal matters. He's a full-fledged lawyer now, and he don't talk for free. Now, why don't you run along home and come back with your daddy."

"But..." Thomas started, but I popped my arm out in front of him like a yardstick. I didn't mind him standing up for me when needed, but it wasn't his place to fight this battle.

"Mr. Beegle," I said, my face flush with embarrassment and growing hot with anger. "With due respect, you'll find I'm a determined, strong-willed woman, and you have no business treatin' me like a child, especially with me being here on legitimate business." Without intent, I found myself standing tall with my chin up, one hand on my hip. I wasn't trying to be snooty, but I wasn't going to be a pushover neither. Henry was depending on me. I couldn't let him down. "If you won't tell us where to find Cordie, then we'll head on into Bates to do some talkin' with the sheriff. I'm sure he can tell us where to find him."

I took Cora's hand, and even though she was tugging hard to stop me, I turned and headed toward the door. Before leaving, I stopped and wheeled around. Looking at Mr. Beegle, I said, "And I'll be sure to mention to the sheriff about the sawmill payroll money you used for gamblin' down at Sugar Creek. Must have been a tidy sum you won to pay for a lawyerin' college."

The blood drained right out of Mr. Beegle's face.

"What's she talkin' about, Hank?" One man asked the question, but all three stood up and stared straight at him. Now everyone was paying attention.

Mr. Beegle didn't answer. Instead, he hurried to Cora and me and took us both by the arm, steering us outside. Thomas followed.

"Now, let's not be hasty," Mr. Beegle said, his voice low. "I'm sure Cordie will be happy to talk to you just as soon as I tell him how important it is."

"I thought he might be," I said, crossing my arms.

Turning to Thomas, Mr. Beegle growled, "Thomas, are you here to work today, or are you just plannin' to spectate?"

"I'm here to work," Thomas told him. "I need the money. I don't intend to shirk my duties, Mr. Beegle. I was just tryin' to help these ladies, but they seem quite capable of taking things from here." Then facing me, he said, "Sooze, are you gonna be all right? I'll stay if you need me."

Whispering for privacy, I said, "Thomas, I don't want you losin' your job. We're mighty grateful to you, and we sure ain't tryin' to cause you no trouble."

Thomas smiled. "Ain't no trouble."

"What if we meet those same boys goin' home, Sooze?" Cora asked.

But no matter how hard I tried, I couldn't make my mouth move to answer her, and I couldn't pull my eyes off Thomas. I was attracted to him like a magnet to metal.

"With any luck," Thomas said, "this Cordie fella will be escortin' you back, Cora." Then he turned his attention to Mr. Beegle. "If no one is needin' me here anymore, I'll be gettin' out to the yard so I can get my work started."

"You go on, Thomas. We don't need any more people than we got. We're headed over to find Cordie right now." Mr. Beegle pointed the way to a small pine building with one door and a single window. "My boy is here looking over a lumber contract for Mr. Forrester. He was born to be a lawyer! Come on. We'll walk over and see if he's finished."

"Did you hear, Sooze? He's right here!" Cora's voice was full of excitement. "We ain't even gonna have to hunt him down."

Thomas nodded a single nod to me, then turned, walking one direction while we went the other.

"Cora," I whispered as we walked a few steps behind Mr. Beegle, stepping over broken twigs and scattered pine boughs. Leaning close, I reminded her, "Let me do the talkin'."

Without so much as a knock, Mr. Beegle opened the door to the small office and stepped inside, acting like the big pine desk with strewn papers belonged to him.

"Cordie," Mr. Beegle called. "Are you 'bout finished here?"

The man at the desk stood up. "Almost."

I was taken aback by his youthfulness. He was a green-eyed boy, tall and lanky with thick red hair combed straight-forward over his forehead. Pockmarks scarred his face. His nose, thin and pointy, wore a saddle of freckles, but it was his ears that caught my stare. Protruding from the sides of his head were the biggest ears I'd ever seen.

"This here is Sooze," Mr. Beegle introduced, then asked, "What's your last name again?"

"Williams," I answered. "My name is Sooze Williams, and this is my sister Cora."

I stepped forward and offered my hand in greeting. Without any hesitation at all, the young man took my hand and shook gently.

"Pleased to meet you. My name is Cordie."

With a nod, I said, "We've come here to ask your help in defending our brother, Henry."

Even though I'd made Cora promise not to jump in, she did anyway. "And we need you right away—right now, in fact. We're wastin' time standin' here talkin'."

"Cora!" I scolded. "I'm supposed to do the talkin' to Mister Cordie." Turning back to the younger Mr. Beegle, I sighed before saying, "Fact is, my sister's right. Henry is in the Coaldale jail, and the sheriff is due back soon. He'll be expectin' answers a lawyer should be handlin'."

"What's the charge?" Cordie asked.

I hesitated. "Murder." The word soured in my mouth. "Our brother is accused of murder."

Cordie's eyes widened, and his jaw dropped open. The room was quiet as a prayer meeting until Cordie busted out with, "Can you believe it, Daddy? I got a murder case just a week after passin' the bar exam!" Grabbing my hand and shaking it like a baby's rattle, Cordie said, "What are we waitin' for? Let's go!"

CHAPTER 12

On our way back to Coaldale, I listened as Cordie talked. I surmised he had no idea his daddy paid for his lawyer college with stolen money—no idea at all. Riding his chestnut gelding alongside our wagon, Cordie talked about being the thirty-fifth graduate from Mills admitted to the bar and how hard his daddy had worked to scrimp and save for his tuition. He was grateful, he said, for everything his folks had done for him. I didn't feel like I had any right to take those good feelings away from him. Besides, with him being so devoted to his family, he might feel kindly toward ours.

Finally, I summoned up the courage to ask, "How much do you cost?"

"What do you mean?" Cordie studied me, his eyebrows scrunched.

"What's it cost to hire you?"

"Yeah," Cora said. Turning her head, she spit off the side of the wagon. "We need to know if we got enough money or not."

"Well, I suppose one of us should have thought about that before leaving the sawmill." Cordie used one hand to rub his fingers back and forth across his chin, and he got real quiet for a time. He was staring straight ahead. "I know I'm supposed to have a retainer..." He was mumbling to himself, making it hard for me to hear.

"What kind of container?" Cora asked him.

Laughing, Cordie corrected her. "*Retainer*," he said. "Not *container*. It's money paid upfront to keep me working for you."

"*Humph!*" Cora crossed her arms. "If it holds you here so's you can keep talkin' for us, then it sounds like a container to me, no matter what you're callin' it."

With us almost to Coaldale and still not knowing Cordie's answer, I was getting more nervous with each roll of the wagon's wheels. The longer we rode in silence, the tighter I held the reins, and that just made my hands shake with worry. What if we didn't have enough money? What if we got to the jail and Cordie said he wasn't talkin' to nobody without his retainer? What if this had been for nothing?

Coming down the hill, I saw the familiar rooftops. "Have you decided on a price yet?" I spouted out. "We're comin' up on Coaldale, and I'd just as soon not ride into town with you gettin' everyone's hopes up just to have you ride back out again when we don't have enough money to pay you."

"I've been trying to work this out in my head." Cordie sounded sincere. He was rubbing the back of his neck like it was an answer book. "To tell you the truth, I'm not rightly sure I know how much I'm supposed to be chargin' you folks."

That was the most confusing thing I'd ever heard. "Well, I suppose you charge what you charge, ain't that right?"

"Not exactly," Cordie said. "You see, my license hangs in a law office in Fort Smith. I agreed to do my lawyerin' work for Virgil Deets. His firm sets the price, and since I never expected a murder case to be handed to me right out of law school, we never had reason to talk about it." Cordie's fingers randomly tapped the side of his face like he was counting pockmarks. "I reckon I'll have to make a stop at the Coaldale switchboard and ring him sometime today."

"What are we supposed to do in the meantime?" Cora sounded part mad and part worried.

Straightening his posture in the saddle, Cordie looked at us both. He nodded once before saying, "You'll just have to consider me your lawyer until I tell you otherwise."

A smile spread across his face, telling me we still had a chance.

When we pulled up in front of the sheriff's office, I saw lots of people inside. I tugged Frenchy's reins to halt her and then set the wagon's brake bar.

Although everyone was talking and arguing, the jabbering stopped when I opened the door.

"They're back!" Henry shouted. "And they brought somebody with 'em!"

"Hey, Henry," I greeted him, a smile on my face with a bit of pride about toting back a lawyer. To the people in the room, I announced, "This is Cordie Beegle—Henry's lawyer."

"You did it, Sooze," Daddy said, his voice sounding proud. "You found him."

I nodded as Cordie's eyes began scanning the room like he was taking inventory. Paulette Simmons stood beside Benny, and Daddy stood near Dimple Dodds, who was seated in a chair. Cordie's eyes didn't stop moving until he spotted Sheriff Wingate's steel badge. Then, just as if he'd done it a hundred times, Cordie said, "As counsel for the accused, I demand to know if my client has been officially charged with a crime?"

The room got as quiet as a graveyard.

Sheriff Wingate stepped in front of Miss Simmons and gently nudged Benny until he was almost hidden behind his mama. Dimple Dodds stayed seated, head down, bowler hat in hand. His brown hair was messy and oily and hung forward, hiding his eyes.

"No, Henry hasn't been officially charged yet, but I'm

holding him for questioning in the murder of Ray Garren."
Sheriff Wingate's eyes were glued to Cordie. His gaze
started at the top of Cordie's head, then moved all the way
down his legs to his shoes before starting back up again.
"I'm questioning Benny, too." The sheriff's finger was lazily
pointing in Benny's direction. "I don't believe I know you.
You're a bit young to be a lawyer, ain't you?"

"Clarence Darrow was younger than me when he passed
his bar exam, Sheriff, and Mr. Darrow is now one of the
greatest lawyers in the whole country." Cordie had his head
slightly tilted as if hiding a secret. "I intend to follow in Mr.
Darrow's footsteps." He pointed to Henry, whose forehead
was pressed against the iron cage with both of his hands
gripping the bars. "I think I'll start building my fame with
Henry, right here in Coaldale. What do you think about
that?"

Sheriff Wingate grumbled a by-God remark but stopped
short of finishing.

Taking a step closer to the jail cage, Cordie gave a single
nod to Henry. Then, raising his chin to the sheriff in a
defiant sort of way, he said, "Now, I believe you're obligated
to give my client his privacy while he talks to his lawyer. Do
you think you can find another place to hold this gathering
of yours?" Cordie waved his hand back and forth like
shooing flies in the direction of Daddy, Miss Simmons,
Benny, and Dimple Dodds. When the sheriff failed to
answer, Cordie said, "You do intend to offer that right to my
client, don't you, Sheriff?"

Sheriff Wingate—without a word to Cordie—turned, and
with arms out, said, "Come on, folks. Let's give Henry a
chance to talk to his *law-yer* in private." He ushered
everyone to the door. "We'll be outside. You got fifteen
minutes."

After the sheriff took Miss Simmons, Benny, and Dimple
Dodds outside, Cordie pointed to Daddy. "Do you have
business keeping you here, sir?"

"Oh!" I exclaimed. "That's our daddy! You can't be sendin' him away."

Cordie's pockmarked face blushed. "I'm sorry." He reached out and shook Daddy's hand. "I should have seen the resemblance."

"Nothin' to be sorry for," Daddy said. "You done good so far. I'm pleased to meet you."

"Hey!" Henry called from his cell. "Has anybody figured out how to get me outta here?"

Cordie stepped closer and held his right hand out to Henry. Reaching through the bars, Henry shook his hand.

"Pleased to know you," Henry said. "Are you gonna get me outta here or what?"

"First things first." Cordie pulled a wooden chair close to the bars. Sitting down, he said, "I expect I'll need to know what got you in here in the first place. How about you tell me what happened?"

Like he was telling the story for the first time, Henry motioned with his hand, wanting all of us to gather around him. Daddy and Cora both obeyed, getting close as if he was telling a story they'd never heard before. They leaned against the bars of the cage as Cordie sat between them—but me, I just couldn't bear to hear the story again. It seemed like all we ever talked about anymore was Henry. Uncle Ray hadn't even been buried yet, and everyone's attention was focused on my brother. "You can't help the dead," Mama had said. "So you might as well help the living."

When Henry started to retell his account, I wandered unnoticed to the window near the sheriff's desk and stood looking out at Heaven's Café across the street. Vera Lange was most likely back in the kitchen baking angel cake muffins or sweet potato pies for her patrons. She was the best baker in three counties, and folks traveling through Coaldale almost always stopped to eat at her café.

I was so tired of thinking about bad things. More than anything, I wanted to think about good things again. Happy things. Things like Miss Vera's summertime delights like strawberry shortcakes and apple dumplings. Even thinking about simple things like home gave me a happy flutter. Our cornfield was sprouting up green shoots, and our garden was ready and waiting to be planted. Soon we'd have plump, ripe tomatoes, snap beans, okra, and squash sprouting up out of the ground into a prize-winning field of food. It was a lot more than most folks had, and I'd have been perfectly content to stay forever on the land my granddaddy handed down to my daddy. It was our land, and not a penny was owed on it. No one would ever be able to take it away from us.

I wanted to think about graduation, too. I wanted to think about my wedding and the cake I would ask Miss Vera to bake for us. I tried hard to picture myself standing before the preacher, wearing a white dress, holding my bouquet. Mama, Cora, and me would pick handfuls of Queen Anne's lace, blue larkspur, and oxeye daisies with their white petals and bright yellow centers from Whitaker's Meadow. At home, we'd tie the stems together with one of Mama's white sewing ribbons, and I'd soon have a wedding bouquet. At the altar, I envisioned my future husband in a black suit and bowtie, wearing an oxeye boutonniere, but I was having a hard time focusing on his face like he was a mystery man. But shoot-fire, he wasn't a mystery! I'd known David all my life, and his face was as known to me as my own. Still, not being able to picture him clearly was fiercely bothersome to me. I wondered, was he still mad about me going to the sawmill to fetch Cordie?

"Sooze!" Daddy shouted to me.

I whirled around, surprised at how lost in thought I'd become while Henry was telling his story to Cordie Beegle.

"Yes, Daddy?"

"Pay attention here, girl," Daddy said. "Cordie is askin' you a question."

"I'm sorry. I guess I was daydreaming."

Cordie stood up and faced me straight on. "Both your

daddy and Henry say you saw the whole thing. Is that right?"

My mind was back on Henry quick as a wink. "Yes, I saw it," I said, nodding. "I was standin' back behind the congregation and watched Benny stab Uncle Ray clear as day. I'll never forget what I saw."

Cordie stood up and started for the door. "Then let's get the sheriff back in here so's we can clear this up."

"Cordie," I called. When he stopped and turned to look at me, I said, "That's the problem. That's why we need you. No one believes me. They think I'm just protectin' Henry."

Cordie tilted his head, staring at me like he was trying hard to understand the words coming from my mouth. "Well, *are* you? Are you just protecting your brother?"

"Of course not!" How could anyone think I was lying after all I'd been through just to get him back to Coaldale? "I don't tell lies!"

"Then what's the reason for folks believing you aren't truthful?" Cordie was still talking as he turned and walked back toward Henry. "Before you answer, let me tell you something I learned in law college. There are two sides to every story, but only one of them is telling the truth. That doesn't mean the truthful side wins. Fact is, the side that wins is the side that tells the best story." Cordie stopped and turned. He stared at me like I was on trial myself. "So go on. Let's hear your story so I can tell whether Henry's going to hang or walk out of here a free man."

I felt a lump the size of bread dough rising inside my stomach. It grew so fast I felt like I was tipping over sideways, fixing to spill out sour milk. Was it just me holding Henry's fate in my hands? What if I couldn't tell the story right? Then fact came settling in—my brother Henry needed me. I couldn't let weak knees topple me. With my stomach knotted, I straightened up tall on shaky legs and raised my chin with family pride. I started telling my story like it was the first time.

Almost five minutes ticked by before my retelling was

finished, and when I was done, Cordie didn't have a word to say. He just stood looking at the floor, nodding his head like he was solving a puzzle.

I looked around the room. Daddy was staring at Cordie, Henry was staring at Cordie, and Cora was staring at Cordie. Everybody was quiet.

"So," I said. "What's your plan? How are we gettin' Henry out of this jail cage?"

Raising his head, Cordie focused his green eyes right on me. Before saying anything, he used both hands to smooth his red hair flat against his forehead, and if anyone had asked me, I'd have said he looked a little nervous.

"Let's start by getting the sheriff back in here." Cordie walked to the doorway, twisted the knob, and pulled open the door. "Sheriff, you can come back in now."

Sheriff Wingate ushered Benny back inside with Paulette and Dimple Dodds scurrying in behind him.

"Now," Sheriff Wingate said smugly as he eyed Cordie Beegle. "You've had your fifteen minutes, so if you don't mind, I'd like to get on with my official questioning now." He faced Benny. "Why don't you have a seat, Benny, so's we can get through this quick."

Benny walked to the sheriff's desk, pulled out the chair, and sat right down in it as if he owned the seat himself. "Okay, shoot," Benny said, urging Sheriff Wingate to start his questions.

"Benny, was it you who stabbed Ray Garren?"

"What kind of question is that?" Henry shouted through the bars. "He ain't gonna admit it that easy!"

"Hold on, Henry." Cordie used his hand like he was pushing down air. "Let's hear his answer."

Ignoring Henry, the sheriff said, "Go on, Benny. Answer the question."

Benny shifted in the chair before plopping his feet on top of the desk. Leaning back, he put his hands behind his head like he was as relaxed as an old coon dog on a summer day.

"Course, I didn't kill him. You got Henry's knife, right?

And you said yourself you saw Henry with the knife in his hand when he pulled it out of the old man's gut. It's got blood all over it, too, don't it?"

"Benny, you just can't do this to me!" Henry yelled. "You got to tell 'em the truth now!"

Benny leaned forward, dropping his feet to the floor. "Henry Williams, I *am* tellin' the truth! It was you who stabbed your uncle. It weren't me! And who'd blame you? He was a mean old pig of a man, and he got what he deserved." Leaning back in the chair, his voice slowed. "He used that leather strap one too many times. Ain't that right, Henry?"

Henry began climbing those jail bars in a fit of rage and didn't stop until Sheriff Wingate yelled, "Settle down!" Daddy reached up and commenced patting Henry's white knuckles as they gripped the bars. He kept right on patting until Henry slowly slid back down. Daddy didn't stop until the blood flowed back into Henry's fingers and his feet were on the floor again. The sheriff turned back to Benny, but Daddy was already moving toward the desk. I could tell he was ready to set the record straight.

"Sheriff, me and the girls were at Ray's house just a day or two before the killin', and we saw Benny runnin' from Ray's chicken coop with a whole batch of eggs. Ray whipped that boy with a leather strap as he was runnin' away." Daddy pointed at Benny. "It's proof right there he had it in for Ray! Why else would he mention a leather strap like he did?"

"That's a good argument," Cordie agreed. "Sheriff, you got proof enough right now to hold Benny as a suspect. You need to release Henry. It's clear Benny needs to be the one locked up."

"Are they right, Benny?" The sheriff asked. "Is it true you had a tussle with Ray?"

"Yeah, it is. But that old man was crazy! He invited me in and offered me fresh morning eggs to take to Mama as a gift, then when he saw Henry's daddy pull up, he went loco and said he couldn't let them see he was givin' me them eggs. Said they'd know he was paying for favors, and he didn't want 'em knowin' about it, so he pulled out a strap and commenced to slappin' me with it." Benny pointed to the faded welt on his cheekbone. "See there? That's where he hit me and told me to start runnin', or he'd hit me again!"

"Well, what'd you do?" Sheriff Wingate asked.

"I started runnin'!" Benny rubbed his hand against the side of his face as if he could still feel the sting. "When I told Henry about it, he become mad as a wildcat. He said he wasn't goin' to let nobody beat me like that, then he said, 'I'll kill him!' Ain't that right, Henry?"

"No, that ain't right!" Henry shouted. "I never said nothin' about killin' nobody! And you never told me it was Uncle Ray that give you that red mark neither. You said one of your mama's boyfriends give that to you!"

"So I been sayin', Henry." Benny looked at his mama. "Right, Mama?"

"I'm sorry, Sheriff," Paulette Simmons said, a bashful hint to her voice. "I know you don't like to hear about men I date, but Ray did like my company quite a bit."

"That ain't true!" Even I was shouting now. "Uncle Ray wouldn't acquaint himself with the likes of you! He was a decent man."

"That's right, Sooze." Daddy shook his head, saying, "Not Ray."

Cordie stepped between the sheriff and us. He pointed to Dimple Dodds, who sat quiet as a midnight moon. "What about you, Mister? Have you got somethin' to say about all this?"

"What about it, Dimple?" Sheriff Wingate asked. "Which one of these boys did you see stab Ray Garren?"

"Well," Dimple started, then stopped. With a downward gaze, he stared at his hands as he fiddled with the brim of his hat. Finally, he said, "Looked to me like Henry Williams done the stabbing." Then raising his head slightly, he glanced at Benny's mother. "That's right, ain't it, Miss Paulette?"

"Yes, Dimple," Paulette said and smiled. "That's right."

Sheriff Wingate turned to Daddy. "John, I got no choice but to hold Henry. Benny's a close-up eyewitness, and you heard it yourself. Dimple says he saw it too. That's two eyewitnesses. By Henry's own admission, the knife that killed Ray was his. I saw your boy holding the weapon myself." Then talking directly to Cordie Beegle, the sheriff announced, "I guess you got yourself a murder trial. I'll notify Judge Poe in Waldron that we got a case to be tried."

It felt like somebody hit me with a two-by-four.

"But we got a lawyer!" I don't know what came over me. Words just gushed out of my mouth like a big hole had been poked in my voice box. I started getting louder, shouting at the sheriff. "And you got a *real* eyewitness—*me*! If that ain't enough, Daddy gave you an account of Benny's egg stealin'. You just got to let Henry go!"

"That's right, Sheriff," Daddy was talking loud, too. "Henry's a good, hardworking boy. He's never done nothin' more than shoot some rabbits and squirrels for supper, and other than butcherin' our hogs, he ain't never stabbed another living thing in his life! Sheriff, he ain't no murderer!"

Seemed everyone was in an uproar. Henry was yelling Benny had done it, and Cora was swearing and shouting things a little girl shouldn't be saying to Paulette Simmons. Cordie was up close arguing with the sheriff while Dimple Dodds moved closer to the door, the knob already in his hand.

It wasn't until Benny stood up, grinning with his stiffened fingers angled at his forehead like a soldier's salute, that everyone stopped bickering.

"See ya, Henry. Too bad Chicago ain't in your future." Benny did a hard-starched wave and headed for the door, which Dimple held open.

Henry grabbed hold of the jail cage. His face reddened as

he shook hard, trying to loosen the bars. When they wouldn't budge, he started yelling like a lunatic.

"Shove in your clutch, Simmons! Go on! *Scram!* Get out of here, you bum!"

Benny never looked back.

CHAPTER 13

"Lord, no!" Mama wailed when Daddy told her about Henry. She raised her face to the heavens, then lifted her fists. Talking directly to God, she hollered, "Where you been? We been waitin' for you to pull us through this!" Then Mama did something I never saw her do before. She dropped to her knees in a fit of crying. I didn't know if she was praying to the Lord or blaming Him for quitting on us. "We been waitin' for you..." she sobbed. "I been waitin' for you..."

"Come on, Emma." Daddy put his hands under Mama's arms and raised her up. Her ash-blonde hair had come unpinned and was hanging in thick strands. Daddy coiled one curl behind her ear then pulled her close. He held her head against his shoulder and patted it while she cried. "God didn't choose Henry's friends for him, so He ain't to blame for Henry's troubles."

Mama stepped back, using her hands to wipe the wetness from her face, and then looked him in the eyes. Serious, she said, "I offered Him all we had if he'd help Henry. I said I'd give whatever He asked. I offered our crops to Him for the poor. Our livestock, too. I offered Him a lifetime of service, John." Mama wiped new tears. "I even offered Him *me* in place of Henry."

"Mama," I said, and although I truly didn't know what to say to help her stop hurting, words flowed out of me, sounding like I'd already thought them through. "You're the one who taught us that we don't need to make deals with God. We're all His children, and He loves us. He's going to save Henry, Mama. I just know it. He helped us find Cordie today."

Mama nodded like she agreed, but her voice was discouraged. "Sounds like you done good following His directions, Sooze. Thank you for tryin' to help your brother."

For the first time, I lost sight of the fire inside Mama. When Grace started to cry, Mama didn't even hear her. She just kept wringing her hands as if she was washing off soap. She turned and headed for the kitchen, leaving Grace coughing and crying in her cradle.

"Cora," Daddy said. "Take care of the baby. Your mama needs to sort her thoughts, and she's got no room to do more right now."

"Okay," Cora told him. She pulled Grace out of the cradle and began bouncing her back and forth while patting her bottom.

"She probably needs a fresh diaper, Cora," I said. "Mama's got clean ones on the clothesline out back. I'll bring 'em inside."

I walked through the kitchen on my way to the back porch door, but Mama never noticed me. She just kept scrubbing our table with a washcloth like dirt was ground into its pinewood grain, even though it was clean.

Stepping out back, I noticed a light breeze rustling the catkins—small, yellowish, foul-smelling chinquapin flowers clustered into a spike. Looking up at the tall trees, I saw the limbs covered, meaning come October, we'd have a mountain of sweet-tasting nuts. I made my way across the yard to the white metal poles strung with a clothesline. I should have thought to bring the clothes basket so I could have taken down all the dry clothes and bedsheets, but I just had one thing on my mind. I walked to the far end, where the diapers hung flapping in the breeze. I pulled off the wooden clothespins and took all three soft, white cloth squares back into the house.

I folded one into a triangle and handed it to Cora, but she shook her head, asking me to hold on to it. She laid the baby in the cradle then raised the white eyelet gown. Cora unfastened both safety pins then pulled off the wet diaper, rolling it into a ball. Curling her fingers around the baby's ankles, she raised her up just the same as Mama, then she laid Grace on top of the diaper. Folding the corners in, she pushed the pin into the cloth.

"Careful, Cora," I said. "Remember, Mama said to slide your fingers between the baby's skin and the cloth so's you don't stick the baby with the pin."

"I suppose I know how to diaper a baby, Sooze."

A minute later, Cora was holding Grace against her shoulder and patting the clean, dry diaper with her hand. She was a natural at handling babies, and she didn't even know it yet. It made me a bit envious, but I knew I needed to be grateful that Cora could take care of the baby herself, so I could help Daddy figure out what to do next.

"Daddy," I said. "What's our plan?"

He was sitting in the armchair, writing numbers on a notepad with a pencil, but he put the pencil down when he heard my voice. "The sheriff will be takin' Henry to Waldron for holding 'til the trial, so first thing we need to do is to get him some clean clothes for traveling." Daddy raised one eyebrow as he glanced at me. "He sure don't need to be showin' up in Waldron with blood still splattered on him."

"I'll go upstairs and get some clean clothes for him," I offered.

"Get his best school clothes, Sooze. We want him to make a good impression on the judge."

The minute I opened Henry's door, the odor of dirty socks and tobacco hit me. Mama and Daddy would have to be senseless not to know about his bad habits with his room smelling like a charred curing barn. Like most things, it seemed boys got away with more—like they had a right to be bad sometimes.

Henry's room was painted green like a forest. For Christmas three years before, Mama had quilted him a spread using green and white squares. The quilt lay rumpled on his unmade bed, just like he'd left it Sunday morning.

Even though it was my job to do all the laundry, I knew by looking at the dirty clothes piled on the floor that I had neglected Henry's. Instead of picking them up and carrying them downstairs to the washtub, I used my foot to push the pile away from his closet door then opened it. He had four shirts left hanging inside, and none were respectable for meeting a judge. The best was a cream-colored shirt with sleeves he usually rolled above his elbows to hide the holes. It was the nicest one. I pulled it off the hanger, folded it neatly, and then laid it on his pillow before going to his dresser and pulling open the top drawer. Mama taught us to keep our underpants and socks together, so I knew right where to find his. It sure seemed funny picking out Henry's underwear for him. Then without looking too long, I grabbed a pair of white socks and a clean undershirt. With the top drawer still open, I leaned down and pulled open the bottom drawer. Problem was, all Henry's pants were pert'near worn out. He didn't have a single pair of nice slacks like David wore, so none were fit for meeting a judge.

"Sooze, what are you doing in Henry's private things?" Mama stood in the doorway with laundry from the clothesline.

"Daddy asked me to find Henry some clean clothes for his trip to Waldron, Mama." I was a bit embarrassed to be standing at Henry's undergarments drawer, so I reached over and slid it closed. Pointing to his open bottom drawer, I said, "But I can't find any pants for him that aren't worn clean out."

Mama sighed. "I know. I'm ashamed to say it, but since Henry don't never complain, I let him go without more than you girls." She carried the folded laundry into the bedroom, handing the small stack to me. "Put these away while I look through your daddy's closet for a decent pair of trousers that might fit Henry."

She left the room with her head dropped down like she was watching her feet walk. I'd never seen Mama so worried and sad, so it was hard to decide what needed to be done about it. I put the laundry away, then looked again at his patched and threadbare trousers. Did Henry have to wear scraps so Cora and me could have better? Mama's words stuck in me like a thorn. Why hadn't I ever noticed?

"Here we go, Sooze," Mama said as she came back into the room with a pair of dark brown pants. "Pull out them black pants so's I can measure the inseam and use them as a hemming guide. They fit him good as any. I'll cut and hem your Daddy's pants tonight for Henry so's you two can take them to him tomorrow mornin' early."

"That will look nice, Mama." I went to the bed pillow and held up the cream-colored shirt I'd chosen for Henry so she could see. "This shirt and those brown pants should look good, don't you think so?"

"It'll be a handsome set of clothes. See if you can find brown thread for my needle. I'll be downstairs in a few minutes."

When Mama sat down on the edge of Henry's bed with a glazed look, I left the room.

Stepping down the stairs, I spotted Cora in the rocking chair. She was holding the baby against her shoulder, singing the "Rock-a-bye Baby" song, but Grace wasn't sleeping. Grace was coughing and crying.

"Pat her on the back, Cora. Help her clear her lungs."

"I been doin' that, but it just don't help."

"Maybe she's hungry." I laid Henry's clean clothes on the arm of our gold-colored couch. It was still bright even though it was older than me, but it had a few tattered spots where its white sheet material showed through the worn-out fabric.

"Mama tried to feed her before she come upstairs with

the washing." When Grace started to squirm, Cora stood up, swaying side-to-side. "Did you find some clothes for Henry?"

I was nodding when Daddy came in from the kitchen. "Sooze, what are you doing with my brown trousers? Are you expectin' Henry to wear those? You know they ain't goin' to fit him—the legs are long, even for me."

"I know, Daddy. Mama asked me to thread her a needle." I held the trousers up against my chest, letting the bottoms drag the yellowed linoleum floor. "She's plannin' to cut some off the length and hem 'em up for Henry."

"Well," Daddy said, sighing as he studied his best trousers. "Get on with threadin' that needle then." He grabbed his brown hat and fitted it onto his head as he moved to the front door. "I'll be in the barn puttin' Frenchy up for the night. Come get me if your mama needs me."

When the door shut, I went to the sideboard and pulled open Mama's sewing drawer. A pincushion with straight pins and one needle, threaded with white thread, set beside the scissors. I cut the knot off the end of the thread and pulled it out of the needle's eye, then wrapped the long strand around my finger until I had a tight curl. I laid it inside for Mama to use again. She had fabric scraps, a measuring tape, and buttons inside, too, and a few colorful embroidery skeins, but not a single dark thread matching the trousers.

If Mama hemmed the pants using white thread, it would show like a sore thumb, and her embroidery skeins were red, yellow, green, and blue. The last thing I wanted was for Henry to look like a ragamuffin in front of the judge. He needed to look respectable and worthy of a second chance to say what he had to say. Then I saw the living room curtains like it was the first time I'd ever seen them. They were dark brown—and sewn with dark brown thread! I hurried to the window and pulled the floor-length panel of fabric out from the wall. I tugged and stretched the hem to test the strength of the thread and then dropped it, heading back to the open sewing drawer for the scissors.

"Sooze, what in tarnation are you doin'?" Cora asked.

"I'm unthreading the curtains so we can reuse the thread to hem these trousers for Henry. Do you think it will ruin them?"

"Who cares? Nobody but us lives here anyway." She was still holding Grace, who'd fallen back to sleep.

"Sometimes we have visitors."

"Like who? Aunt Rose and Uncle Will stops by, but they don't care whether our curtains are hemmed neither."

"David comes by," I reminded her.

"Ain't nothin' about us 'cept you that will ever be good enough for him, so he don't count."

Cora was right. I sat down on the floor, legs crossed, and began to snip at the thread ends. It took two or three tries before I freed the hemming knots, but as soon as I did, I reached for the other end and started snipping there, too. Before I knew it, I was carefully pulling out long sturdy strands of dark brown thread. It was more than enough to hem one leg, so I moved to the other curtain panel and repeated the steps. Before Mama came down the stairs, I had both pieces curled up around my fingers for her.

"I got thread, Mama."

"Thank you, Sooze. Will you thread it for me? My eyes don't see good enough anymore," Mama said without any expression. "I need you to fix supper, too. I'll sew 'til the baby wakes up, but soon as she does, I'll be wantin' to feed her. She just ain't been hungry."

"She's got a cough, too, Mama," Cora added.

"Seems everybody's got somethin' they're strugglin' with these days," Mama said, shaking her head. "I think maybe this dry spring air is causin' her to feel poorly."

Mama took Daddy's brown trousers and sat down. She let out one big sigh then propped her elbows on the table so her arms could hold up her crestfallen face. "Sooze, bring me that needle and thread. Scissors, too, please? I feel plumb tuckered out."

"Yes, Mama." I took the threaded needle, both wound-up thread circles, the scissors, and a measuring tape to Mama. I set them on the table for her, then went to the icebox and opened it. I saw a half-full bottle of milk, a pint of buttermilk, more than a dozen brown eggs, almost a full ball of butter, pork chops, a bowl of ground sausage, and way in the back, I saw a jar of fresh-made applesauce. "Mama, how does pork and mush sound for dinner? I can make some gravy, too, using the bacon drippings."

"That would be real nice, Sooze," Mama said, nodding with a slight smile. "You'll need a vegetable. What kind are you fixin' to go with it?"

Beside the icebox sat the vegetable bin with one sweet potato and some yellow onions. I reached in, looking for more.

"We got two big carrots in here, Mama. I can make candied carrots, can't I?"

"Ain't got no sugar. Used it all up on your birthday cake." Mama kept right on sewing without looking up at me. "Just slice and boil 'em. Drain 'em when they're done, and we'll put some butter on top. They'll be real good, Sooze."

A fresh loaf of baked bread was under a tea towel on the kitchen counter. Pointing to it, I said, "Bread, too?"

"None for me but give everybody else a slice."

"You gotta eat, too, Mama," I was trying to give her a kindly reminder. "You got a baby who needs your milk, so you need to keep up your strength."

Glancing up at me with tired eyes, Mama grumbled, "I birthed and raised three perfectly good kids already. I think I know what another one needs, don't you?"

"Yes, ma'am," I said. I knew better than to argue, so I set about to fixing supper.

By the time the pork patties were crisp and brown, Grace was awake. Mama put down her hemming and went to her.

Cora had the plates set when Daddy came in with straw

splinters on his shirt and dirt on his hands. He grabbed the water bucket and went straight to the sink for washing. "Supper smells good, Sooze."

"Thank you, Daddy. What time are we leavin' in the mornin' to take Henry's clothes to him? Cora and me missed the whole day of school today, and finals start tomorrow."

"Sheriff said he's taking Henry to Waldron early. I expect about eight o'clock, so we'll need to get there by seven, so we don't miss his leaving. Can you girls be ready?"

"Yes, sir, and that will give Cora and me plenty of time to say goodbye to Henry before school starts. Are you going to Waldron with him?"

"Can't," Daddy said and shook his head. "Cordie's staying at the boardinghouse tonight so he can go with Henry tomorrow. I'll make another trip into town in the afternoon and place a call to the jailhouse in Waldron for an update."

"That reminds me, Daddy. Cordie was goin' to call the law office he works for to ask how much we need to pay for a retainer. Did he say how much it's gonna cost?"

Daddy was drying his hands on a dishtowel and talking to me just like I was someone important. "I don't know nothin' about a retainer." He refolded the hand towel and set it on the counter to be used again. "Surely, we got enough. I'll get with Cordie tomorrow and find out."

So we still didn't know how much a lawyer cost. Surely it couldn't be that hard to figure out, could it?

CHAPTER 14

Morning brought the sounds of a baby crying, and Mama walking the hallway between the bedrooms with her hand *pat-pat-patting* Grace's bottom.

Slipping out of bed, I tiptoed in my flannel gown and gray wool sleeping socks to our bedroom door and quietly opened it so I wouldn't wake Cora. From the hallway, I heard the faint creak of rusty hinges. It took a minute before I realized it was the baby.

"Mama, Grace sounds bad. How long have you been up walkin' with her?"

Turning to see me, Mama said, "Most of the night. Her breathin' is so hard I can't seem to settle her down."

"Do you need me to hold her for a while?"

"Thank you, honey, but I know you got lots to do today. I been worrying about you and Cora not havin' any time to study last night."

"I'm bothered, too." I clamped my hand over my mouth. I knew better than to agree! Those words had just slipped right out over my lips. Knowing I'd just made Mama fret more, I quickly said, "It'll be all right. We're good test-takers." I tried to hide my worry before disappearing back into my room.

Pushing my arms through the short sleeves of my sky-blue dress, I called to Cora. "Wake up! We got no time for sleepin' in this morning." I grabbed her white dress dotted with pink and red flowers and threw it onto the bed for her.

Mama was still walking the floor with Grace when the three of us headed off to town.

Daddy was mostly quiet on the road, but Cora was talking nonstop. She always talked fast—or not at all—when she was scared and judging by the number of words coming out of her mouth, I guessed she was awfully scared about Henry.

At least twenty times, Daddy asked what clothes I'd brought. "Henry's cream-colored shirt, your brown trousers that Mama hemmed, an undershirt and underpants, and a pair of white socks. Should I have brought black socks instead? Henry don't have any brown ones."

"No, white'll do fine."

The wagon bumped and jostled its way into Coaldale. It had barely stopped moving when Cora jumped off and ran for the jailhouse. I hurried behind her, leaving Daddy to wrap Frenchy's reins around the railing.

"Hey, Henry!" Cora shouted as soon as she opened the door to the sheriff's office. She went running to the jail cage with one hand holding her big, white hair bow in place.

Sheriff Wingate sat at a desk not more than ten feet away, wearing his neatly pressed tan uniform and steel star badge. With his feet propped up on the corner of his desk, he held a wide-open newspaper in his hands while a smoking cigarette hung from one side of his mouth like it was glued there. "Mornin'," he said as he turned the newspaper's page.

"Hey, Cora," Henry said. "Hey, Sooze." He was standing at the cage door like he was waiting for us to open it. "Did you bring something to eat? This jailhouse will starve a man to death."

"Mama sent two biscuits with jam for you," I told him as I handed the bundled tea towel through the bars. Then looking at the sheriff with a scowl, I said, "Mama thought Mrs. Wingate would have made you something for breakfast, or else she would have sent more."

"My wife ain't hired to be a cook for lawbreakers and murderers." Sheriff Wingate went right on about his business reading the paper.

Daddy came in right after and set Henry's clean clothes on the corner of the desk, but he missed hearing the sheriff's words, or else I'm sure he would have set him straight about calling Henry a murderer.

When the door swung open again, in walked Cordie Beegle. "Morning!" He was smiling like it was his birthday. "I hope you're rested up, Henry. We've got a big day ahead of us."

"Speaking of that," Daddy said. "Sooze was tellin' me about needin' to pay you a retainer." He pulled his brown leather wallet out of his pocket and held it in his hands. "How much do we owe you?"

"I'm glad you brought it up, Mr. Williams." Cordie moseyed nearer to Daddy, his head looking down the whole way until he was standing right in front of him. "Virgil Deets says you'll be needin' to pay a retainer plus my expenses, so I told Lola Posey over at the boardinghouse you'd be by to pay her for my room today. Hope it's all right."

"Well, if that's the way it works, then I ain't got a choice, right?"

"Well, yes, sir, that's the way it works, I'm told." Cordie put his hands in his pant pockets and looked down, shuffling one of his feet back and forth on the floor like he was rolling a bone. "And since I'll be riding to Waldron with the sheriff, my horse will need boarding, so there'll be a bill for that, too."

I was getting nervous. Cordie hadn't mentioned anything at all about us paying expenses, but Daddy didn't bat an eye in answering him.

"We'll have Red Batson at the livery take care of your

horse. He ain't paid me for the troughs and the wagon ramp I built for him last summer, so by boarding your horse for free, it'll cut down on the money he owes me. Now, what about this retainer? How much is it?"

"For us to get started, Mr. Deets says you owe $250 upfront. If we go to trial, which I'm expecting we will, he said to tell you the cost can run anywhere between $1,000 to $1,500, depending on the length of the trial and how much investigating we need to do. It will include him coming to trial with me since I'm fresh out of law school, but he said you're gettin' a bargain on his services since I'll be the one running the defense."

A long, low whistle came out of Daddy's mouth. "How do you expect a man to get that kind of money in these hard times?"

"Mr. Deets says he checked around. He says he knows you got a free-and-clear farm. He says if you don't have the money right now, his bank in Fort Smith or the one in Waldron might be able to loan you some money, so long as they can put a mortgage on your farm, that is."

Daddy opened his wallet, counted out $250 in cash from Henry's gambling money, and then handed it to Cordie. We only had about $122 left, and we hadn't even paid for the night at the boardinghouse yet.

"I'm sure sorry about this, Daddy," Henry said. "You was right. You was right all along. Benny's a no-good, worthless liar. If I'd just listened to you, none of this would have happened. Uncle Ray wouldn't be dead. I wouldn't be in jail, and none of you would be going through this mess with me." Henry's voice stumbled, and crying sounds started grunting out like he was trying real hard to hold it in.

"Now, Henry," Daddy said, walking toward him. "Uncle Ray's dyin' ain't your fault. Benny and him got into it without you even bein' around. And when we got to church Sunday, Benny was already sittin' beside Ray. He had this killin' planned with or without you. It ain't your fault, son."

"Daddy's right, Henry," I said. "It ain't your fault at all."

Cora was standing next to Henry like she was never going to leave his side, but it was time for us to go. The school bell would be ringing soon. I got close to the jail bars and reached my arms through. Henry reached through, too, and we hugged.

"Take care of yourself, Henry. I'll be there when the trial starts. I ain't goin' to let you down." I stepped back when I felt tears welling up and turned toward the door. "Come on, Cora. We got to go."

"Bye, Henry," Cora said as she hugged him. "I'll be there, too, if Daddy will let me."

Hurrying past Huckabee's General Store, we saw David talking to his daddy near the coal and coke bin. They were having a serious discussion by the look on David's face, but when he saw Cora and me headed to the schoolhouse, he stopped talking and came running.

"Hi, Sooze," David called to me. When he caught up to us, we were almost to the schoolyard. "I thought you were comin' back to school yesterday afternoon. Why didn't you come back?"

"It took us a little longer to fetch Cordie Beegle back than I thought," I said. We kept right on walking toward the schoolhouse.

"Yeah," Cora spouted out. "It would have been a lot faster if you'd just driven us there in your daddy's automobile. A lot safer, too, since pretty young girls such as us shouldn't be out alone without an escort."

"Hush up, Cora," I snapped, recognizing those words. That was exactly what Thomas Kittridge told us after he fought off those rotgut-drinking boys. "No need to rehash our day yesterday. What's done is done."

"What's she blathering about, Sooze?"

"Never mind," I said as we started up the stair steps to the schoolhouse. "Cora and me need to stay focused on our finals, and we got some last-minute studyin' to do. We don't need any distractions, David." Once inside, I pointed to the blackboard where Miss Stewart stood with her back to us, writing the day's test rules. She wore a white calf-length dress with puffed eyelet sleeves. Whispering, I said, "I'll talk to Miss Stewart about us missing school yesterday, Cora. Why don't you get to your desk and start studyin' your vowels?"

At the sound of my voice, Miss Stewart turned. Even though the weather was warm enough not to need the coal stove, the embedded smell of soot and smoke lingered in the wood from bygone years.

"Good morning, girls. Hello, David. You're all here early today. I won't be ringing the bell for another fifteen minutes."

"I know, Miss Stewart," I said as I walked the aisle toward her. "But we wanted to tell you how sorry we are that we ran out of here yesterday and didn't come back."

"Sooze, I know you well enough to know you had something important to do. I've never seen you leave school like that before, and the fact you're both back today tells me everything must be all right now." Miss Stewart smiled and put her hand on my shoulder. "It's another day, and I'm glad to see you here."

I nodded, grateful, and then went back to my desk, lifting its lid. My books from the day before were still right there inside where I'd left them. I pulled out Milne's *Standard Arithmetic* book and turned to the chapter review for fractions and real variables. I knew I needed to look at those first, and then if I had enough time, I needed to review long division.

David stood looking out the window near my desk while Cora and me studied. I guess he was feeling good about his test because he didn't act worried at all. When Miss Stewart rang the morning bell, the room filled with our classmates.

On the way to her desk in front of me, Lauralee Huckabee was the first to ask, "How's Henry? I heard he's still in jail." She looked just like one of her china figurines—pretty and perfect—and probably no one but me heard the snide tone of her voice.

"Henry is just fine, Lauralee. Thank you for askin'." She was David's sister, so I was trying to be nice, but she was a snooty girl who didn't give a hoot about my family or me. "We got him a lawyer, so he should be home soon enough."

"That's not the way I hear it." Lauralee was at her desk, filing her fingernails with an emery board. "But I'll believe it if you say so."

"Well, you can believe it." I closed my book with a *slap*.

"Good morning, class," Miss Stewart greeted. "Today is the first day of your finals, and it's only a half day of school. You're welcome to stay here with me this afternoon and study for tomorrow's portion of your finals, if you've a mind to, or you can go home to study. I'll be here until at least two o'clock, grading today's tests."

The class was in a stir with most of the town kids wanting to stay and most of the country kids needing to go home and finish their planting. I'd rather have gone with Henry, but it wasn't an option. In fact, the sheriff was probably ready to leave with him by now. I looked out the window, straining to see if I could catch sight of the sheriff's automobile that would be carrying Henry to Waldron, but I couldn't see a thing except for Daddy's wagon.

"Do you see Henry, Sooze?" Cora stood up, stretching to look out over my head toward the jailhouse.

"No," I said. "You need to sit down so's you don't get in trouble."

"David," Miss Stewart said. "Looks like you'll be the only one taking the twelfth-grade test today since Henry and Benny are both absent. We may have a graduating class of one this Thursday."

Seemed silly to have a graduation ceremony at all if there was only one graduate. Still, I knew we would be expected to attend. The town kids would probably be there, too, since Mrs. Huckabee was bringing punch and cookies for the event.

"Hey, I'm right here!" Benny's voice sounded happy as a lark as he walked through the door and made his way to his desk. He had on another dirty white T-shirt. I could never tell whether it was the same one or not. "You didn't think I was goin' to let fancy-pants get all the attention, did you?"

David turned around in his seat and stared straight at Benny, saying, "I got a name, Benny. Try using it!"

But when Benny played like he was jumping out of his seat at David, David flinched and ducked, causing Benny and some of the younger boys to laugh.

"Class!" Miss Stewart shouted. "There will be no teasing or provoking in my class!" Staring at Benny, she said, "That's one mark against you today, Benny."

"I got three to use, though, right? So two more to go before you kick me out for the day?" Benny snorted a low laugh, then quietly said to David, "Come on back and sit next to me, fancy-pants. We can take the test together. I promise I won't cheat."

David's face turned red as an apple, but he never turned around.

"That's two, Benny," Miss Stewart said. "And we haven't even started the test yet. Would you like to go for three?"

"No, ma'am," Benny said, then snidely as if he were a scared little boy, he added, "I'll be good. I promise."

"I *hate* him so much, Cora," I whispered. Her nodding gave me some peace.

Miss Stewart talked about the rules written on the blackboard as she walked up and down the aisles, reminding each student to put books away. "There's no talking during the test. Keep your eyes on your own paper. If you have a question or need to sharpen your pencil, please raise your hand." Then she started handing out the test papers, turning each one face down on the desk. When she was done, she said, "Older pupils have been given a blank page reserved for a bonus question. If you answer it correctly, it can add extra points to your final score. You'll need to finish your main tests first, and then if enough time remains, you'll be allowed to answer—in essay form—the bonus question which I'll write on the blackboard. Is everyone ready?"

I leaned over to Cora and said, "Good luck. Just do the best you can, and don't rush through the answers."

Cora was still nodding when Miss Stewart said, "Begin!"

I flipped through the pages and saw the day's tests were math, science, and history with an extra paper titled "Bonus Question–Shakespeare." *Hamlet* or *Romeo and Juliet*, I wondered? She'd made us read both. If I'd had my way, I would rather read *Little Women* another ten times. It sure made more sense to me than anything Shakespeare ever wrote.

At exactly noon, Miss Stewart announced, "Stop! Please put down your pencils."

Cora was still writing as fast as she could, but when I nudged her, she stopped.

"I was almost done, Sooze!"

"If Miss Stewart catches you writing after the test ends, she'll throw your whole test out. Better to get one answer wrong than all of them."

"Sooze and Lauralee," Miss Stewart said. "Please help me by picking up all the tests." She tapped the corner of her desk. "You can lay them here for grading."

"Yes, ma'am," I said and stood. I started with mine and Cora's tests and then moved down the aisle. When I got to Benny's desk, I reached for his papers, but he pushed all eight pages off onto the floor.

"Oops," Benny said.

"Pick 'em up," I told him.

"It ain't *my* job to collect the test papers."

"Well, it ain't my job to pick 'em up off the floor. Miss Stewart asked me to gather them from the *desks*."

"Oh me, oh my." Benny slapped one hand against his cheek and sweetened his voice to sound as though he was truly stumped. "What to do, what to do..."

"For crying out loud, you heel!" I turned and bent down to pick up the papers, only to feel Benny's foot planted squarely on my bottom. With one big heave, he pushed hard, sending me sailing down the aisle like I was riding a sled on ice. The test papers I'd been holding flew everywhere.

My slide stopped at David's desk. From the floor, I shouted, "He pushed me!"

David jumped up from his seat, but instead of defending me against Benny, he reached down and pulled me up. "You slipped, Sooze. You just slipped."

I heard Benny laugh, followed by a *crash!*

By the time I got to my feet, Benny's desk was knocked over with him still in it, and Cora was punching him in the face like Thomas had done those rotgut drinkers.

"Cora!" I shouted as Miss Stewart rushed past me to grab her. She had Cora by the back of her flowery dress and was pulling her off Benny.

"Cora, stop it!" Miss Stewart shouted. When Cora was on her feet again, Miss Stewart stepped back from Benny's overturned desk and smoothed her dress. Pushing loose hair strands off her face, she said, "Cora, I'm sure you're just doing what all of us would like to do, but the classroom is no place for fighting." Miss Stewart's light brown hair had partially fallen out of its bun, and she was out of breath. "Please, go back to your seat, and let me handle this."

"She give me a bloody nose!" Benny shouted, still lying on the floor. "See this? It's *blood!*" He held out his upturned fingertips for Miss Stewart to see.

"Get up, Benny," Miss Stewart told him. "Get up and go home."

"I ain't done nothin' wrong!" Benny stood, then pointing to Cora and me, he said, "It's them two! They're as crazy as their brother!"

"Get out!" Miss Stewart shouted it loud. "You can come back tomorrow to finish your other tests. Then maybe I'll be rid of you for good." She stooped and picked up the test papers, then walked back to her desk.

As Benny was leaving, he glanced our way. Real low, I heard him say, "So long, girls. Be sure to lock your doors tonight, so the boogeyman don't get you."

CHAPTER 15

After school, Cora and me headed down the street toward Posey's Boardinghouse. We knew Daddy intended to go there to make his telephone call to Waldron, and we sure didn't want to miss out.

Walking along the wood-planked walkway, I was remembering Miss Stewart's teachings about the history of Coaldale. She said it was important for us to know where we came from because the past causes the present, which in turn causes the future. If that was true, I wanted to learn all I could so our future would be prosperous. One of her lessons taught us about the grand old Posey Boardinghouse. It had been built shortly after the Civil War—1865, she thought—and it had been in Miss Lola's family ever since. The top and bottom floor had a surrounding porch with a white railing around all four sides. American flags hung off each corner of the top floor veranda in the summer.

Miss Lola cooked three meals a day for her boarders, but she said they'd have to go next door to Heaven's Café if they wanted dessert. She wasn't bothering with pies or cakes as long as Miss Vera was open. She'd say, "Why would anybody want a dessert of mine after gettin' a whiff of what Vera's cooking?" And sure enough, she was right.

Then when the Bell Company offered the town of Coaldale a switchboard in 1920, Miss Lola jumped at the chance to have it installed at her boardinghouse. She cleared a corner of her parlor and had the Bell people install the tall, dark wood switchboard right there with all the long cords hanging underneath. She'd paid Mama seventy-five cents to sew a skirt for the switchboard made from brown and red-flowered fabric to hide the cords. The skirting nearly matched her curtains. I'd heard she brought in eighteen dollars a month operating the board. She would have earned more if folks had the money for telephone lines to be strung to their homes, but as it was, it was mostly Scott County businesses that used the telephones.

On our way to the boardinghouse, we had to pass by Heaven's Café. It was worth the walk just to smell that day's delights.

"Cora, look," I said. She was strolling the walkway, head down, but when I swung my arm out like a ticket taker, she stopped dead in her tracks. "Miss Vera has a red velvet cake with white frosting in the window." One slice was missing, showing its pure white layers. "And looky there." I pointed. "The red rose she's got lying on the cake plate is a real one, and it ain't even summer yet." We pushed up close to the display window, staring like two starving children.

"Maybe you can ask for a cake like that for your weddin', Sooze."

"No." My empty stomach growled as I shook my head. "A weddin' cake needs to be white, just like the dress, so the marriage can start pure."

"Then how come the groom doesn't have to wear white?"

I'd never thought about it. "Well, I don't rightly know, Cora."

"Hello, girls!" Vera stood in the doorway of the café and seemed genuinely happy to see us, even though we were standing there gawking at her window cake. She was almost forty years old, but not a wrinkle showed, and her dark brown locks were styled in a short bob—the cut and gentle waves made her look as beautiful as Gloria Swanson from the moving picture shows. Her big blue eyes had a sparkle. "I could sure use a favor from you both, if you have a few minutes, that is."

"Oh, yes, ma'am," I said. "We'd be glad to help." Seeing as Daddy's wagon wasn't next door yet, I knew we had time.

"Wonderful," Vera said as she held open the door for us.

A heavenly smell came from the kitchen. It was a zesty, crisp, and clean scent.

"Girls, I've made a new cake which I would never have thought of myself, but my sister came over from Heavener yesterday to share a batch of lemons with me, and we came up with a recipe for using them. I'm just afraid to serve it to my guests without having someone taste it for me first. Would you two mind trying a slice of my new lemon jelly cake?"

Lemons! My mouth started watering. I'd had a slice of lemon pie at a church social more than two years back, and my tongue was reminding my brain of its smooth, tangy flavor. We didn't see lemons every day in Coaldale, so it would surely be a treat, but then I remembered our empty pockets.

"I'm sorry, Miss Vera, but me and Cora aren't carrying any money, and even if we had any, we shouldn't be spending it on such luxuries. But I'm sure your cake will be tasty. You have that special baking touch Mama calls a gift."

"Oh, girls, no!" Miss Vera put a hand on each side of her cheeks. "I'm not trying to *sell* you a piece. I want to *give* a piece to you both, and in return, I'd like to have you tell me, with as much truth as you have, what you think of the cake. Won't you please help me out?"

Cora's grin stretched bigger than her starched hair ribbon. "Yes, ma'am!" She was nodding wildly. "We'd be glad to help! Won't we, Sooze?"

"We sure will!"

Miss Vera led us inside to a table near the front window

so we could keep watching for Daddy. Eight tables covered
in white cloths sat scattered about inside the café, but the
counter along the west wall had another eight stools for
customers. Her dining room was wallpapered in a cream-
colored paper with small yellow and pink peonies, and three
gold-framed, watercolor sketches of flowers hung on the
long east wall of the room. Miss Vera disappeared through
the curtained kitchen door but reappeared fast, carrying two
small plates, each with a wedge of the prettiest yellow cake
I'd ever seen. The yellow jelly frosting was smooth as glass
and as bright as a real lemon.

"I ain't never seen a cake like this before," Cora told her.
"I can pert'near see right through this yellow frosting!"

"It's not really a frosting, Cora. It's a delicate lemon
pudding," Miss Vera said. "That's why I'm as nervous as a
long-tailed cat in a room full of rockin' chairs! Go on, try it."

I pushed my fork straight down through the pointed tip
of the slice and held the bright yellow bite up to my mouth,
inhaling its scent. The lemony smell was so strong it tickled
my salivating glands, making me swallow hard before
opening my mouth. As soon as the morsel touched my
tongue, I knew it was the finest cake I'd ever tasted. The
yellow jelly was tart, but the moist, pale-colored cake
balanced out the taste with its sweet, mellow flavor.

Miss Vera was standing bent over at our table with her
hands on her knees, looking back and forth between us.
"Well? What do you think?"

"Miss Vera," I said. "I've never had a finer cake."

Cora's mouth was stuffed so full she had lemon jelly
squeezing out the corners of her lips, but her head was
nodding.

Miss Vera straightened up and put both hands on her
hips. "That warms my heart, girls! I can't thank you enough
for helping me out today." She waved her hand toward our
plates. "Go on, keep eating. I've got to get the rest of this
cake plated for my supper patrons." Her floor-length, pale
green skirt twirled its bottom ruffle as she hurried back to

the kitchen, leaving us all alone in the café to finish our cake.

I scraped the last bit of yellow jelly off my plate as I saw our wagon turn the corner into town. "There's Daddy, Cora. We need to thank Miss Vera for the cake again before we go." With Cora licking her plate clean, I headed for the kitchen. I pulled open the curtain and called, "Miss Vera?"

"Yes, Sooze?" she asked. "You didn't change your mind about the cake, did you?"

"Oh, no, ma'am! It's just that our daddy is almost here, and me and Cora wanted to thank you again."

Miss Vera came close, leaning so our cheeks touched. "You're welcome, Sooze. But you two helped me. Thank *you!* Come back soon, you hear?"

"Yes, ma'am," I said as I slipped myself back through the curtain.

Cora was already outside talking to Daddy. When I got close enough, I heard him saying Mama couldn't come. Grace's cough was worse, and Mama was worried the dust would be too hard on her lungs.

"Hi, Daddy," I greeted. "Should I go tell Doc Farrell we need him at the house?"

"We're running short on money, Sooze, and Doc don't work for free when he don't have to. I'm afraid we're goin' to need every penny, and more, just to pay Henry's lawyer. Let's let your mama do her doctorin' first." Daddy climbed down off the wagon. His work boots were dirty and worn much thinner than should be tolerated, but Daddy'd never been a complaining man. He walked up the two front steps of the Posey Boardinghouse with Cora and me right beside him.

Reaching the entrance ahead of Daddy, Cora pulled open the screen door. She knocked three times.

When it opened, Miss Lola was standing there with the same grin on her face that greeted every visitor. She had a plain look about her. Mama said it was a *homey* look like grandmothers have, but truth was, it was more of a *homely* look. She had long, graying hair—which strayed, making her look like a haggard eighty-year-old woman even though she was still in her sixties—and she had thick, low-riding cheekbones on which leathered skin hung. Her cloud-gray eyes were burdened with ripples of sagging skin, so it was like looking at marbles that had been dropped into two still ponds. But Miss Lola had always been nice. She had a sweet voice and was happy to see anyone who knocked on her door.

"Hello!" Miss Lola greeted. "What brings you to see me today?"

"Ma'am," Daddy said as he took his hat off and held it waist-high in his hands. "I'm here to pay the outstanding bill for Cordie Beegle's room, and I'm also needin' to make a call to the courthouse in Waldron, with your permission."

"Oh yes, that's right." Lola Posey had already opened the door wide and had stepped aside for us as if our visit wasn't truly a surprise. "Do come in."

We followed her through tall interior doorways, all painted a deep brown, to the dining room with what she called *fleur-de-lis* wallpaper. She said it was a design meant to look like a lily, though I didn't see a flower in it at all. Miss Lola had pride when she explained, "I got the decorating idea from a man named Frenchy who passed through here a few years back saying he was looking for a young prince called the Lost Dauphin of France. He was an odd man with a heavy French accent, but he carried a satchel with him everywhere, and it had a gold fleur-de-lis design all over it." Extending her hand like royalty was present, she said, "It's pretty, don't you think?"

"We have a horse named Frenchy!" Cora spouted out.

"I know," Miss Lola said with a nod. "You should ask your daddy about the name sometime."

Cora eyed Daddy like he'd been hiding a secret from her. And frankly, I thought he might have been, too.

Looking at Miss Lola as if he wasn't too pleased with her suggestion, Daddy said, "Ain't nothin' to tell, girls."

"Nothing except for saying your daddy bought that horse off a dead man."

"A dead man!" Cora shouted. Then looking at Daddy, she asked, "How can you buy somethin' from a dead man? Is that fair? How can you do that?"

Daddy took a deep breath, then sighed. "Dead men don't need horses." His tone said he didn't want to tell the story, but he went on anyway. "And we needed one somethin' fierce. After Johnnie shot him dead for asking too many questions," he smiled and teasingly pinched Cora's chin, "I slipped payment for the horse into his pocket, so when his belongings got shipped home to France, the money would be there. His family got paid fair and square for that horse."

"Is that why you named the horse Frenchy?" I asked.

Daddy nodded. "It was out of respect for the dead. He left us a horse, didn't he?"

Then, easy as could be, Daddy turned to Miss Lola and said, "How much do I owe you for Cordie's room?"

"Let's see," Miss Lola said as she hurried to her writing desk near the tall, polished wood switchboard. She opened a blue-gray ledger and drew her finger down the page until she said, "Here we are...Mr. Beegle's room was a small one —he said he was tryin' to conserve—and it was for one night only, ain't that right? He said he wasn't comin' back tonight."

"That's right," Daddy told her as he opened his wallet. "I owe you for one night." But while Daddy was nodding, she turned back to her book again, and on a paper pad beside it, she wrote $2.75.

"And he had laundry service on his shirt and socks. Do you know, he didn't bring an extra stitch of clothes with him?" Taking pencil to paper, she added another charge to the column. Mumbling, she said, "So add twenty-five cents for laundering. Oh," Miss Lola said, glancing at Daddy with an *I sure am sorry* look. "He made a telephone call, too. It was long-distance to Fort Smith, and he talked for almost ten minutes!" She flipped through a red-backed book with *BELL* scrawled across the front cover in black lettering until finding Cordie's name, then wrote down $3.45.

"Land sakes," I said out loud without intending. "How much does all that come to?"

Using her pencil, Miss Lola added up the numbers. "I'll be needin' $6.20 to settle his bill."

Daddy's face turned a pale red, but I wasn't sure if he was mad or if he was embarrassed about having to pay for another man's bedding and laundering. He counted out four nickels first, then pulled a five-dollar bill and a one-dollar bill out of his brown leather wallet and handed it all to her. "Now, we need to make a private call to the Waldron Courthouse where the jail is. Can you tell me the cost?"

"That's long-distance, too, John," Miss Lola told Daddy. "So, it's more expensive than if you wanted to call, say, the Huckabees."

Daddy looked at her, perplexed. "If I wanted to talk to the Huckabees, I could just walk across the street for free, now ain't that right?"

"Well, yes, John, I suppose you could. I was just tryin' to explain the cost." She lowered her head and opened the red book again. "A three-minute call to Waldron will be $1.80, then it'll be another fifteen cents for every minute after. Do you still want to make the call?"

"Ain't got much choice." Daddy was shaking his head as if he was being robbed. "Let's get on with it."

CHAPTER 16

M iss Lola pulled the chair out from the switchboard and sat down. "John, have a seat over there by the telephone." She pointed to a small table where a black telephone was located. "I heard the Bell people have a new Bakelite telephone now, but I don't know of a soul within fifty miles who's got one yet. No need to worry about this old one of mine, though. It still works fine most of the time. Let me know if you have trouble hearing on it when I connect."

"Do I pick up the receiver now?" Daddy asked.

"No, I'll tell you when. I need to connect first."

I watched with interest. The shiny, black telephone had a circular dial with holes just big enough for Daddy's fingertips. Beneath the holes were numbers painted white, but I guessed that he wouldn't need to dial since it was next to the switchboard.

Miss Lola fitted a band over her head. It had thick, round earmuffs looking hard as overcooked biscuits with a black candy-cane-shaped cone curling up to her mouth. She pulled out a long cord and plugged it into a hole in the switchboard before using a stand-up dial, then she twisted a black knob until its white line was on the word OPEN. "Hello, Clara!" She talked into the cone at her mouth. "Why, yes, I'm fine.

And thank you for sending the railroad man my way for boarding last week. He stayed five days!" She was grinning as if a long-lost friend had made a surprise visit. "Well, I'll be... When did that happen?"

"Ma'am," Daddy interrupted. "I'd sure like to get on with my call so's I can get back home with news about our Henry. Emma is waitin' to hear."

Clearing her throat, Miss Lola said, "Yes, of course, John." Speaking into the cone again, she said, "Clara, we seem to be in a bit of a hurry. Can you patch me through to the Waldron Courthouse?" Then Miss Lola lowered her voice to almost a whisper. "Clara, I need the *jail* line, please. I know, I know, but I can't say more right now."

Miss Lola glanced at Daddy and smiled as if she had no intent on gossiping.

"Go ahead, John, pick up the receiver now. The line is ringing."

"Hello?" Daddy said. He fidgeted in the chair before picking up a pencil lying on the table near the telephone. Looking at me, Daddy acted like he was writing something in midair.

"Miss Lola," I said. "My daddy needs some paper to write on."

"It's in the drawer, darlin'." Miss Lola pointed to a handle under the tabletop.

I pulled out the paper and laid it down for Daddy, staying close in case I could overhear the voices from Waldron. Cora leaned against me, trying to hear, too.

"Hello?" Daddy said again. He scooted back in the chair, saying, "Yes, my name is John Williams. I'm Henry Williams' father. Sheriff Wingate brought my boy in this morning along with his lawyer, Cordie Beegle." Daddy nodded. "That's right. And I'm trying to find out when my boy's trial is goin' to be held."

"Ask 'em if Henry's all right," Cora whispered, but Daddy just waved his hand, trying to quiet her.

"Just a week, huh?" Daddy wrote the date down on the

paper then wrote 10:00 a.m. "Jury selection on Friday," Daddy repeated as he wrote it down. "Do I need to be there?"

I overheard Cordie's name come through the telephone just as Daddy said, "Well, then is Cordie there? I'd like an answer, and if he's the only one who can give it to me, I'd sure like to talk to him." He had a disgruntled face. "I'll hold," he said into the telephone.

Low and quiet, I said, "I think we should be there when the jury is picked, Daddy."

"Why?"

"'Cause it'll be the first time those folks see Henry, and I think they need to see his family supportin' him." I wasn't trying to tell Daddy how to run things, but I sure didn't want us missing anything important.

"Hello, Cordie," Daddy said into the receiver. "This is John. They say the trial is set for next Monday at ten in the morning, but they said the jury is bein' picked on Friday. Is that right?" He nodded to Cora and me. "Now, Cordie, do we need to be there on Friday?"

I could hear the sound of Cordie's voice, but I couldn't quite make out his words. As I leaned in closer, I noticed Miss Lola still had her earmuffs on, and the switch was still pointed to the word OPEN. Not that anything being said was a secret, but it just riled me that she thought she had the right to listen in on Daddy's call.

I stood up and took the few steps to Miss Lola's chair and, as polite as I could, I said, "Miss Lola, I don't believe anything being said on this call is anyone's business, so if you don't mind, I'd like that knob turned the other way until it's pointin' to the word CLOSE."

"Well, *you're* listening!" Miss Lola raised her voice in a tone I hadn't heard from her before.

"He's my daddy. He'll tell me if he don't want me listening, but he's paying you good money for a private call."

Miss Lola huffed but turned the knob until its white

mark lined up with the word CLOSE. She stayed sitting in her chair like she was glued there.

"Thank you," I said before returning to Daddy's side.

"Well, Sooze thinks we need to be there for jury pickin' day." Daddy was quiet, then nodded again. "Oh, so you do, too? I see. Do we need to do anything? Well, all right then. Sooze and I will be there on Friday. You'll tell Henry for us, won't you?"

Daddy said goodbye, and then put the telephone receiver back in its cradle. Standing up, he asked Miss Lola, "How much do I owe you for the call?"

"It was under three minutes, so it comes to $1.80, John."

Daddy reached into his pocket again and pulled the money out, handing it to Miss Lola. "Thank you kindly," he said in a somber tone. "Let's go, girls."

~

Soon as we walked in the door, Mama was at Daddy's side, asking about Henry. "Well?"

"I had to talk on the telephone to the man at the jail desk first," he told Mama. "And then I talked to Cordie. He said Monday is the trial, but he's expectin' us to be in Waldron on Friday for jury pickin' day."

"Are we all goin', John?" Mama's eyes were worried. "For jury day and trial day?"

"Emma, you're welcome to come every trip with me if the baby's up to it. I'm planning on Sooze goin' with me, and I know Cora wants to go, too. Cordie said the more people we have there to support Henry, the better it'll look for him."

"Should I ride over to Uncle Will and Aunt Rose's place to see if they'll come too?" I asked.

"They'll be coming on trial day, Sooze. They'll be bringin' Aunt Lissie and Arnold," Daddy told us. Then in a quieter tone, he said, "Cordie says Lissie is bein' called to testify."

"That's good, ain't it, John?" Mama asked.

"Well, it ain't good if her or Arnold sets about to callin' Henry a killer again." Daddy took off his hat and flannel and hung them up. "Cordie said it ain't him who put her on the testify list. She was already on there. He said the prosecuting attorney, a man named Pigg, has her down as a witness for his side."

"What does that mean?" Cora came close, listening intently.

"I guess she'll be testifying against Henry."

"*Against* Henry!" Cora yelled so loud she woke up Grace, who started wailing. "You can't let her do that, Daddy!"

"It ain't up to me." When Mama moaned, Daddy went to her and held her close. He stood and rocked from one heel to another with her leaning into him. "It'll be all right, Emma."

I picked up Grace and began bouncing in Mama's "quiet down" dance until her raspy cry calmed, then I leaned my ear close, listening as she exhaled. Her infant lungs blew out a rattle of phlegm on a long, hollow breath. Pulling her close, I kissed her forehead. My lips absorbed her heat, and I knew she was hotter than a baby needed to be.

"Mama, I think Grace has a fever." I held the baby out to her.

Mama pulled free of Daddy's arms and came close to take the baby from me. She pulled back the blanket around Grace and kissed her head just like I'd done. "Sooze, warm some water for a bath and fill the sink with it. And remember to stick your elbow in the water to be sure it's room temperature before I take these clothes off this baby."

"Yes, Mama." I hurried to the kitchen for the well bucket. It was times like these when I wished we had running water inside the house. It seemed so easy at David's with water running right into the kitchen through indoor plumbing. Daddy said he wanted to try to plumb the kitchen next year, but we'd have to make do with our outhouse for a while.

At the well, I lowered the bucket on its rope until it filled to the top with water, then pulled it back up. I unhooked the rope and carried the full bucket through the back porch door and into the kitchen. The stove was already hot because Mama was cooking stew for supper, but Cora was adding another heap of coal to keep it burning. I set the bucket on the floor and pulled our big chicken-boiling pot out from the bottom shelf of the storage cabinet. I poured the pot full before setting it on the stovetop. With some water still left in the bucket, I put it back down onto the floor, then scooted it under the legs of our white-enameled sink so it would be out of the way.

"Grace's cry sounds funny," I told Cora while we waited for the water to heat. "And she's coughing a lot."

"I know, and she's feelin' light, Sooze, like she's not gainin' weight. What do you think is wrong with her?"

"I'm sure all babies get this way at one time or another," I said, trying not to scare Cora. Problem was, I never remembered Cora acting that way when she was a baby, but I wasn't about to worry her more, so I didn't tell her about it.

Coming through the kitchen door holding Grace, Mama said, "How are you coming with that water?"

"Good, Mama," I said. "We got the pot filled, and it's starting to warm. We're using the big pot, so it'll take some time."

Nodding in approval, Mama said, "Cora, clean out the sink so's it'll be ready when the water is. And get a cloth to dry the baby off with, too." Mama turned and carried Grace back to the living room where Daddy was lighting a fire.

Taking Mama's kitchen bar of lye soap, Cora started scrubbing the inside of the sink. When she had soap rubbed all over the white enamel, she put the stopper in the drain then used the water bucket underneath to pour some clean water in for rinsing.

"Here, Cora," I said as I handed her a dishtowel. "Get the towel wet, then rub the sides so's you can get the soap off better. Then I'll pour the extra water from the bucket around it for a good rinsing."

Grace was crying a hoarse, coughing cry the whole time Cora and me were working, so as soon as the water was warm, I went to get Mama. "The water can go in the sink now if you're ready."

"Been ready," she said. "I got a clean diaper and night-shirt for her, too."

Back in the kitchen, I lifted the heavy pot of warmed water by its side handles. Moving slowly so not to slosh, I walked to the clean sink. "Cora, put the stopper in, please?"

"Oh! Sorry, Sooze. I forgot!" Cora hurried and plugged the drain.

I poured the warmed water into the basin, then like Mama always did, I dipped my bare elbow into the water to test its heat.

"It's good, Mama. Do you want me to hold Grace so's you can check it?"

"It's not that I don't trust you, Sooze, but this baby is mine, so I got to take responsibility for everything that happens to her." Mama handed the baby to me before pushing her long, white sleeve halfway up her arm. She dipped her elbow in and let it stay for a minute before saying, "You girls done real good."

"Thanks, Mama," we said in unison.

"Will you put her dryin' cloth, clean diaper, and night-shirt on the table for me, please?" Mama asked as she was unwrapping Grace's blanket from around her. "Then you girls fill some bowls with potato stew and slice the loaf of bread on the counter. Start eatin' your supper so's you can get upstairs and start studyin' for your tests tomorrow."

With three bowls filled and a plate of fresh sliced bread, Daddy, Cora, and me sat in the living room so's not to bother Mama doing Grace's bath.

"Sooze, it's your turn to say the prayer tonight," Daddy said. Sitting in the rocker in front of the fireplace, he seemed worn out and tired. I supposed keeping up with the farm while taking care of Henry was too much for any man.

"Sure, Daddy," I said. Then, sitting side by side with Cora on the couch, I held my bowl on my lap. Lowering my head, I nudged Cora to do the same. "Lord, thank you for this food tonight, and even though I know it's askin' a lot, please look after Henry, and Mama and Daddy, too. And Lord, please help Grace to feel better soon. Amen."

"Daddy," Cora started talking right away. "Am I goin' to Waldron too?"

"As long as your mama don't need you to stay here, you're welcome to go."

"Mama's comin' with us, so there wouldn't be no reason for me to stay here."

Daddy was stirring his stew to let the cooling air into it. "If the baby's still sick, your mama will want to stay home with her. She won't be able to take her out traveling with us. If that happens, I'll need you to stay here and help while Sooze and me are gone."

"Aww, Daddy, but Henry needs me there with him!"

"What Henry needs is for his lawyer to prove he's innocent." Daddy tore a bite off his sliced bread and dipped it into his stew before eating it. "And unless Cordie can break Benny's story apart, that's goin' to be a hard thing to do."

CHAPTER 17

"Sooze?" Mama called. "Cora? You girls need to wake up for school."

I was so tired it seemed like Mama was talking to me in a dream. I rolled over and forced my eyes open only to see her standing in the doorway, holding Grace to her shoulder.

"How's the baby?"

"She's still got the fever," Mama said. "Daddy's out gettin' the wagon hitched so's we can go see Doc Farrell this morning. You girls might as well ride along with us. Get up and get dressed. We need to get goin' early."

Sitting right up in bed, I reached over and shook Cora's shoulder, trying to wake her as Mama left the room. "Cora, time to get up."

Cora jerked her shoulder free from my hand. "Stop waking me up so early, Sooze!"

"It ain't me," I said as I threw my covers off. "Mama and Daddy are takin' the baby to see Doc Farrell, and they're needin' to leave right away. We need to get dressed and get out the door with 'em." I was at the closet, pushing hangers down the rod to find a dress when Cora jumped out of bed.

"Is Grace still sick?"

"Mama says she's still got the fever."

Cora was beside me in a single leap. She pushed through into the closet and grabbed her blue-and-tan plaid dress off its hanger. "Where's my shoes?"

"You took 'em off after supper last night and set them by the fireplace, remember?"

Cora mumbled, "Oh, yeah." She slid the dress over her head, opened the top dresser drawer, and pulled out a clean pair of white socks. With the back of her dress still unbuttoned, she headed out the door. I heard her bare feet moving fast down the steps.

From the closet, I pulled my gray gunnysack dress off its hanger and slipped it over my head, struggling to button up the back. David hated the dress, so I tried not to wear it often. He said it made me look like a sharecropper, but fact was, it was one of those things I appreciated because it was useful beyond its means. After me, the dress would be handed down to Cora, and after she outgrew it, Mama would cut it up and use its pieces to make a quilt. Once the quilt wore out, it would be weaved into a rug. So worrying about what David thought about my dress was not my concern—getting to town as fast as we could was my only worry.

"I'm ready, Mama," I said from the living room. "Can I help carry things to the wagon?" Mama shook her head as Cora handed me my tan sweater.

Daddy helped Mama up into the seat as me and Cora climbed into the back. With Daddy aboard, he slapped Frenchy's reins with a determined snap, prodding her onward.

The earthy, coal-driven aroma of the Arkansas hillside dulled spring's fresh, crisp scent. I could see the larkspur poking up through all but the Queen Anne's lace in Whitaker's Meadow. Lots of wildflowers grew low, so the height of the two plants, one white and the other a bouquet of blue, yellow, and red, overshadowed the others. Had Grace not been crying the whole way, the colors in the meadow would have been especially peaceful.

At the schoolhouse, Daddy stopped the wagon. "Go on in early today, girls. We'll see you at home after school."

"We're more than thirty minutes early. Can't we come see Doc with you so's we can find out about Grace?" I asked.

Daddy turned around from his buckboard seat to meet me eye-to-eye. "Don't sass me this morning. I said for you girls to go in early. Now get on down."

The tone wasn't right in his voice, so I wasn't about to question him again. "Yes, Daddy." I stood up next to Cora. We climbed the end gate and then jumped to the ground. Daddy slapped Frenchy's reins, and they moved off down the road toward Doc Farrell's office.

All alone inside the schoolhouse, Cora and I went to our desks and pulled out a book. Even though both of us were looking at a page, I don't think either of us was studying.

"What do you think made Daddy cross with you this morning?" Cora was looking at me with a truly perplexed look. "You didn't have a sassy mouth."

"I think he's worried about the baby," I said. "Did you see her spit up on Mama's blouse? It had a red color to it."

"Yeah, I saw it." Cora's words were slow coming. "Do you think it was blood?"

"Don't know what else could be red, do you?"

Shaking her head, she lowered her eyes and turned another page in her book.

"Good morning, girls!" Miss Stewart sounded happy to see us as she walked down the aisle with her arms loaded full of books. She wore a long-sleeved, dark blue dress with white buttons down the front and a white collar and cuffs. It was my favorite dress of hers. I wondered if Mama and me could make one like it in the summer. It had a sophisticated style. "Summer means I can bring all these study books back until school starts again next year." Putting the books down on the edge of her desk, Miss Stewart's eyes grew bright with a gleam. "Girls, I've decided I am going to make a trip in June to visit the Fort

Smith Library. I'm just dying to read a new book called *The Good Earth*, and I'll bet you two can find a wonderful book for your summer reading, too. Would you like to go with me?"

My heart lit up like paper on fire. "Oh, yes, ma'am! I'd love to go to a real library!" I looked at Cora to see if her excitement came anywhere near matching mine, but all I saw was a shrug.

"I think I'll have chores all summer," Cora told her. "And soon as Henry comes home, he'll need lots of help with the things he does for Daddy, so I'd best stay close to home."

"Cora, I just don't understand you," I said. "How can you think there's anything better in this world than to go to a place where there's free books for reading?"

"Well," Cora said in a moan, trying to sound polite. "Maybe you could pick one out for me, Sooze."

Everybody knew a book had to call out to you before it was any good reading, so how was I supposed to pick one out for Cora? It was as if she never learned anything at all about books.

Studying for the day's final took up most of our time until Miss Stewart rang the bell to call all the pupils inside from the schoolyard. Everybody hurried in and took their seats, but no one seemed pleased about taking the final test; they were just excited about it being the last real day of school. The next day would be to hand out final test scores and see if we passed to the next grade level. The afternoon would be spent celebrating David and Benny's graduation. It sure wouldn't feel like a celebration without Henry, though.

"Hi, Sooze." David snuck in without me seeing him and was standing behind my desk.

"Hello, David," I said, trying to sound friendly even though I wasn't feeling that way at all. "Miss Stewart is about to hand out today's test. You should get to your seat before she starts."

"I was late because I was worried about you, Sooze. Mother said she saw your mama and daddy at Doc Farrell's office. I thought I should stop and check to be sure it wasn't you who was sick."

"Well, it's not," I told him. I should have felt glad about him worrying about me, but instead, it made me mad that his mother took such pride in spying on people. "Lots of folks go to see Doc Farrell, David. Does your mama tell everybody who comes into the store about who's seeing the doctor, or who's staying at the boardinghouse, or who's eating pie at Miss Vera's café?" That was a silly question, I thought—of course, she does. "As you can see, I'm feelin' just fine, but thank you for worryin' about me."

Miss Stewart tapped her pointer against the chalkboard before announcing, "Rules are the same today as yesterday. There will be no talking, no looking at each other's papers, and if you need to sharpen your pencils or use the toilet, be sure to raise your hand first." She had a handful of papers and was walking up and down the aisles. She laid the papers face down on the desks, but before she got to the last aisle, Benny slipped into his back-row seat.

From her desk at the front of the classroom, Miss Stewart announced, "You may begin."

I felt more confident when I knew what I was being tested on, so I checked through my tests right away. English, geography, Latin, and a combined test on biology and anatomy. The English test would be fast and easy since it was my favorite subject, and geography wasn't as hard as I expected, but I saw no use for Latin when I had no plans to learn doctoring or medicines, so I wasn't feeling very *fidens* about passing that test.

I was doing fine on biology until I got to the anatomy part—it started asking questions about the lungs. That was when I started thinking about Grace again. I couldn't concentrate on anything else. Doc Farrell's office was around the corner from the jailhouse, which blocked my view unless I stood up and leaned. I wished I'd known how long Mama and Daddy had to stay before going home. I hoped it wasn't too long. Mama had been awfully tired. Doc had a big medicine cabinet in his office, so I was hopeful Grace was already feeling better. How in the world do young babies get so sick anyway? And when they do get sick, how can their little body defend itself? I should have taken biology and anatomy more seriously, and then maybe I would understand.

"Stop!" Miss Stewart was standing at the front of the classroom. "Time is up. Please put your pencils down and turn your test papers over on your desk."

"Dang!" I whispered to Cora. "I was daydreamin' and didn't even finish my anatomy test!"

"I didn't finish penmanship either. How come we have to learn writin' anyway? Printing is just as good, and more people can read it."

"Cora," Miss Stewart called. "Did you have something to share with the class?"

"No, ma'am," Cora said as she slid down into her seat. "Sorry for talkin'."

"Today, I want everyone to pass their tests to the person in front of them until all the papers have reached the front row, then I will gather the tests myself."

As papers were passed forward to me, I saw Benny's crooked scrawl spelling his name. I wanted to *accidentally* lose his top test, but since it was his English paper, I figured there was a good chance he'd failed it anyway, so I added my test to the short stack and passed them up to the next desk.

"Well, class, I'm very proud of each of you!" Miss Stewart smiled as she gathered the tests from the front row desks. "I'll be here for several more hours today grading papers. Before leaving for home, I suggest you clean out your desks and take your personal belongings. Remember to stack your schoolbooks on the ledge along the west wall." She walked over, brushing her fingertips along the wide, wooden wall shelf. "Please place your books in the right stack, so all the math books are stacked together, all the English books are together, and so forth and so on."

"Miss Stewart," David said, his hand raised high. "What time is the ceremony tomorrow?"

"Graduation starts promptly at noon, David, so please be sure to let your mother know she should have the punch and cookies here no later than a quarter to noon. I'll have a table by the door ready for her."

Lauralee stood up from her desk in the middle of the classroom. "I'll be helping mother bake the cookies, Miss Stewart. We'll be making oatmeal cookies, gingersnaps, and washboard cookies made with coconut shipped all the way from an island in the Pacific Ocean!"

With all the "oohs" and "aahs," folks would have thought Lauralee herself was planning to swim to the island and back with the coconut. Never mind that Cora was one of the excited ones.

"Come on, Cora," I said as I slid out of the desk. "Let's get home so's we can find out what Doc Farrell said about Grace."

Together we stood up and started for the door, but we were stopped before getting far.

"Sooze!" David called after us. When I turned around, he was hurrying down the aisle toward us. "You're staying after for my graduation tomorrow, aren't you?"

"Of course, David. Mama and Daddy are comin', too." Feeling kindly, I said, "We're all proud of you for graduating. Not many boys get the chance to do that nowadays. We wouldn't miss your ceremony."

"I'm glad your ma is baking cookies!" Cora said. "I ain't never tasted a coconut before, have you, Sooze?"

"No, I don't recall ever having tasted one myself. It'll be a real treat, won't it, Cora?"

David grinned with pride. "Mother sure has gone to an awful lot of trouble for me. I'm glad you'll be here to share this important moment with us, Sooze."

I stood on my tiptoes and kissed his cheek, causing his grin to grow and his eyes to light up like fireflies. "We have things to do, so we'd best be going, David. We need to get home right away." Without another word, I took Cora's arm at the elbow and pulled her with me through the door and down the steps. When our feet hit the ground, we both ran for home. If we kept up the pace, we would be home in twenty minutes, but as we reached the end of the school road and started to turn toward home, I spotted Daddy's wagon still parked in front of Doc's office.

"Cora, wait!" I shouted. "Look." I pointed to the wagon. "Daddy's here in town. Maybe him and Mama had to come back." But then another thought settled. "Or maybe they never left."

We both stared at the wagon as if our eyes were telling lies.

"It's been more than four hours since they dropped us off, Sooze."

A sick feeling washed over me. "It must be the baby." Looking wide-eyed at Cora, I said, "Can't be no other reason."

"Maybe Doc Farrell was out on a call, and they been waiting for him to come back."

I straightened up tall and started walking for the wagon. "Come on, Cora. We got to find out about this."

CHAPTER 18

I was nervous knocking on Doc's door. Inside, I heard the faint sounds of a baby's cough. I stepped back as the door opened.

"Hello, Sooze. Hello, Cora." Doc Farrell's face didn't smile. "You looking for your mama and daddy?"

"Yes, sir, we surely are. Can we come in?" I asked.

"How about I get your daddy instead," Doc answered. "Stay here, and I'll be right back with him." The door closed right there in our faces.

Me and Cora looked at each other, quiet as two church mice.

When the door opened again, Daddy was there. He stepped out onto the porch and closed the door behind him.

"Is school out already?"

"Yes, sir. It was a half day. We were headed home when we saw the wagon here at Doc's office." I looked hard at his face, trying to see inside him. "How come you're still here?"

"Well, I'm glad you spotted the wagon. I meant to come get you girls myself soon as school was dismissed, but I guess I didn't keep up with the time too good."

Straight out, Cora asked, "What did Doc say was wrong with the baby?"

Daddy's face was drained of color as if he hadn't seen

the sun in a lifetime. He sat down on the pine bench by the door and started talking. "Doc says the baby's got the consumption. He's been trying a few things to see if he can help her."

"What's *consumption?*" Cora asked.

"It's a sickness..." I started talking like it was my turn. "That's why she's coughing, and feverish, and losing weight, right Daddy?"

"That's right, Sooze." Daddy looked at us as we stood there in front of him. "Doc says a body just wastes away once the consumption takes hold."

"How do we make it let go?" Cora was near tears.

"It's an infection from the lungs, and it don't usually take hold of babies," Daddy explained. "Doc says it likes old people best."

"Then what's it doin' with Grace?" I asked.

"We don't rightly know." Daddy stood up and kissed us each on the forehead. "Doc's got the baby in a special tent right now to see if it will help her breathe, but he says it's contagious, and he don't want you girls to catch it."

"But what about you and Mama?" My body started to tremble. "You said yourself, the consumption likes older folks, so you and Mama shouldn't be in there, Daddy!"

"Go get Mama, Daddy!" Cora started yelling. "I want Mama out here right now!"

"Cora, settle down." Daddy sounded mad. "You want your mama to leave that helpless baby in there all by herself?"

"She ain't in there by herself! She's in there with Doc! He's better at taking care of her while she's sick anyway, ain't he?"

"Cora," I said. "You know Mama's not goin' to leave the baby any more than she'd leave you or me if we were sick."

Cora burst into tears and went running off toward the schoolhouse.

"Cora!" I called loud. "Come back here!" But she kept right on running.

"Let her be, Sooze," Daddy said. Putting his hand on my shoulder, he said, "Maybe you girls should go on home and wait for us."

"I'm not leavin' you and Mama here," I told him. "I'll sit right here on this bench and wait until we're all ready to take Grace home." I sat down. "Right here...I'll be right here, Daddy."

"Suit yourself, Sooze. I'll come out and update you when I can." Then Daddy opened Doc's door, but before he went in, he said, "I just don't understand what's happenin' to us, Sooze. It's as if God turned his head another way."

I watched Daddy go back inside and close the door. If I'd known where the new preacher was staying, I'd have had a mind to go talk to him about the decisions God was making. Not that he'd have the answers, but maybe he would be able to shed light on it. After all, he was the one who had God's ear. And if it wasn't him, I sure wished somebody would tell me who did because it surely was not us who God was listening to anymore.

Far away, I spotted Cora. She was hard to see, sitting on the ground under a huge old oak at the turn in the road leading home. I felt better knowing where she'd gone. She probably needed time alone, so as long as she was in sight, I wasn't going to bother her.

Doc's porch had forty six-inch hardwood planks. Forty exactly. I knew because I counted each one more than a hundred times while pacing. I waited for Daddy to bring news, but he was slow in coming. I'd walked from one end of the porch to the other, looking through Doc's white lace curtains with each passing. I never saw anything that hinted at an answer, except a time or two I saw Doc retrieve a few square white cloths with long strings attached. He'd hold one up to his face covering his mouth and nose, before disappearing into the back room again.

For as long as I was on the porch, Cora waited under the faraway tree. I didn't know if she could see me or not, but I wished she'd come back. I was wanting someone to talk to about all this, but I suppose it didn't matter. The only one Cora ever wanted to talk to was Henry anyway.

"I saw your daddy's wagon was still here," David said as he stepped onto the porch and sat down on the bench beside me. "I thought you might be, too," He held a shirt-sized box tied with a white ribbon. "I bought a gift for my wife-to-be." He handed me the box. "Go on," he said. "Open it, Sooze."

"I'm not much in the mood for gifts today, David," I answered honestly. "Do you want to keep it until another day?"

"No," he said. "You go on and take it home. You can open it when you're feeling up to it."

David was being awfully nice, and it made me feel more kindly toward him. "Who's sick enough to be keeping your daddy here all day, Sooze?"

"It's Grace," I told him. "Doc says she's got the consumption. They been in there all day, David, and they won't let us inside. What could they be doin' in there this whole time?"

"The consumption, huh?" David slowly shook his head. "Do you remember me talking about my Uncle Charles from Saint Louis? He's the only one I've ever known who had the consumption, and he died from it last October. Aunt Mary said he withered away until he was nothing but a feverish, sputum-covered man who coughed himself to death." David took my folded hands from my lap and held them inside his.

"I forgot about your uncle dying. I'm sorry, David. I guess it means more when it hits your own family. Did your aunt Mary say what treatments they had in tryin' to cure him?"

"She told Mother the doctors tried lots of treatments, but the one Aunt Mary thought might work was when they stuck a needle in under his arm and punctured his diseased lung. They used the needle to draw all the bad air out. She said they told her it was his last hope, but he didn't live more than three days afterward."

"Ain't there some kind of medicine for it?"

"Aunt Mary said they're using something in England, but she couldn't get the medicine here, and Uncle Charles wouldn't have survived the long trip to go there. Besides, he wouldn't have been allowed to board a ship." David looked at me straight on and said, "It's contagious, you know?"

"What kind of medicine could they have in England that we don't have here?"

"I don't know the name. I just know it's something they squirt through a needle into your arm. The newspaper says they're having real good luck with it."

"There's just got to be somethin' we can do here for a cure!"

"Fresh air. That's what Mother said. She said some folks go to a hospital in Switzerland where they wheel you outside in a hospital bed a few times a day, so you can lay in the sunshine and breathe the freshest air anywhere."

"Switzerland?" I repeated. "Land sakes, David. They have to be real rich."

"And, like I said, I can't figure out how the sick people get aboard ships sailing across the ocean anyway. Look at all those folks who are quarantined before getting on and off a ship just because they have a cold or a sore throat, fearing they might have the influenza." David was shaking his head. "It don't matter for Grace, though, I guess. It's not like your mama and daddy could do anything for her anyway when they can't even pay their overdue bill at the store."

I stood up, not wanting to be near him at all anymore. "Why do you always have to say somethin' that makes me mad?" I started walking toward the steps down. "I'm goin' to check on Cora." Turning back with anger still rising in me, I told him, "And I don't need no company."

"Sooze!" David called after me. After a minute of silence, he hollered, "What did I say?"

There wasn't no use discussing it with him. His understanding of circumstances made me feel like I was walking through a dark train tunnel, except instead of seeing a glimmer of light at the end, there was only blackness.

"Sooze!" David called again. "Why can't I come with you?"

I kept right on walking. When Cora saw me coming, she stood up off the ground, brushing the dust from her dress.

"Did Daddy come out again?"

"No," I told her. "I just couldn't stand spendin' any more time with David."

"*Humph*," Cora grunted. "And you expect to do *what* after you're married to him?"

"I haven't figured that part out yet." I turned back to look at Doc's office, and there was David, standing on the porch, looking in our direction like we were trick ponies getting ready to perform. "He's a nice boy, but my heart-strings aren't pulling me any closer to him now than they did in fourth grade." I whirled around. "What's wrong with me, Cora?"

"Maybe you're just not in love, Sooze."

"Maybe not," I said, agreeing for the first time. "But Daddy said love's got nothing to do with marriage in these hard times. And when I marry David, I'll be able to make my own money and send it home to Daddy so he can pay the bills and buy the seed and feed he's needin' for the farm."

"When I meet a boy," Cora said, holding her hands on her hips. "I sure ain't plannin' to let him buy me like David's buyin' you."

"Cora! That's a mean thing to say!"

"It's true—mean or not." Cora cocked her head upward, looking at me like she was daring me to call her wrong.

"Who do you think is gonna help Daddy with the farm when Henry runs off to Chicago, huh, smarty-pants?"

"Henry ain't goin' to Chicago, Sooze!"

"What do you mean he ain't goin' to Chicago? He told me, straight out, himself."

"And who do you think he's plannin' to go with? Benny?" Cora was looking at me like I was a mouse caught in a trap. "When Henry gets out of jail, he'll be coming straight home to stay. When Benny done him wrong, it was clear he couldn't go runnin' off with him. He knows now he can't trust Benny no farther than he can throw him. And Henry ain't gonna go all by his self, Sooze. Did you ever think of that?"

"Why, no, Cora," I said in a near whisper. "I surely didn't. You're right—Henry wouldn't be goin' anywhere now that all this has happened between him and Benny."

"Right," Cora said. "So if you're usin' Henry as an excuse for feeling like you got no other choice but to marry David, your excuse ain't goin' to work no more."

Her words put all new thoughts into my head. Maybe the need to marry David *wasn't* so urgent. Of course, we still needed the money from my wages. Then it hit me. Looking at Cora, I said, "Henry's still got to be home and not in jail for this to work, Cora. Cordie Beegle has to be a good enough lawyer to get Henry freed."

Cora leaned forward and spit on the ground just like I'd seen Henry do a hundred times.

"Come on," I said. "Let's go back to Doc's office and knock on the door. Surely, we can get someone to open it and tell us what's happening to Grace."

When we reached Doc's porch, Daddy was already outside waiting for us with David.

"Hi, Daddy," I said, feeling nervous for some news. "How's Grace?"

"Doc said he's done all he can for her. Your mama's wrapping the blanket around her now for the trip home."

"Is she well already? Did Doc give her some medicine?" Cora asked.

"He give her what he could. All we can do now is take her home and do the best we can."

In a respectful tone, David asked, "What about taking her to the hospital over in Fort Smith?"

"No," Daddy said, shaking his head. "Go on, girls. Get in the wagon."

David set the gift box in the wagon bed as Cora and me climbed inside. When Doc came out, he had Mama beside him. She was carrying Grace all bundled in a big, blue blanket. Mama's face looked like a statue without any expression, and her stony eyes were cold like a winter mist had veiled her vision. She never saw us waiting there for her.

"John," Doc Farrell said. "I still say the girls shouldn't be staying in the house for a few days. Can't they stay at Will and Rose's place?"

"Why do we have to stay with Uncle Will and Aunt Rose?" I asked. "We want to go home with you and Mama."

"Hush, Sooze." Daddy's tone was stern. Then to the doctor, he said, "They can't stay with them, Doc. Lissie and Arnold are stayin' there until Ray's funeral tomorrow. There's already too many crowded into such a small house."

"Oh, that's right," Doc Farrell said, rubbing his chin as if he was out of ideas. "Well, I'm sure you know what you're doing, John." Turning back for his office, Doc mumbled something about coming out to the house tomorrow to check on Grace. When he closed his door behind him, Daddy reached for Mama and helped her into the wagon.

As Daddy was climbing up the wheel spokes to his seat, I turned to say a polite goodbye to David, but I couldn't find him anywhere. "David?" I called. "Where are you?"

"Here, Sooze," David called from around the corner of the building. He stuck his head out like he was playing hide-and-seek.

"What are you doing hiding behind Doc's office?" I asked him.

"I'm not hiding," he said without coming out. "I'm just being careful. Germs fly through the air, you know?" Then sticking his head out farther, he said, "Sooze, how 'bout I get you a room at the boardinghouse tonight, so you don't have to breathe the same air as Grace?"

"Grace is my sister, David," I told him. "Breathing the same air as her is like sharing the same blood. Ain't no choice."

"Then, without meaning to be rude, Sooze, I'll just say my goodbyes from here." David stayed around the corner. "Don't want to take a chance of me catching the consumption germ."

"I understand, David," I said calmly. Of course, I didn't *really* understand—it wasn't me who had the sickness! He was my husband-to-be and taking a risk with me shouldn't have scared him so. What was he planning on doing when I had his babies or when I grew old or sick and needed his care? Just the thought of telling my future husband to stay away if illness struck never entered my head. Wedding vows said in sickness *and* in health, didn't they? I wondered what David thought those words meant. Maybe I'd never understand. Maybe no wife ever truly understands her husband.

Looking over his shoulder at the gift box next to me, Daddy asked, "What's in the box?"

"Don't know yet," I told him.

Daddy never once addressed David. He just slapped Frenchy's reins and started for home.

On our way, Mama didn't have a thing to say, and neither did Daddy, so it was a mighty quiet ride.

Mama patted Grace, trying to comfort her, but with her voice hoarse and weak, she cried most of the ride home. Each time Grace coughed, she'd gag, spitting up bright red phlegm. I'd never seen Mama so quiet or so worried. I wanted to talk about Doc Farrell's diagnosis, but it seemed like Mama was barely holding things together for Grace. I didn't feel right about taking her focus away from where it needed to be, so I sat real quiet next to Cora. All the way home, I kept my eyes on Mama and Grace. It seemed weakness had grabbed hold and was shaking hard, determined not to let go.

CHAPTER 19

We traveled home as the sun was setting. From the wagon, I saw a red-tailed hawk spiral lower and lower, eyes preening the ground. I wondered if everything, including us, looked weak and defenseless from up there.

"Daddy," I said, pointing to the sky. "That hawk's been taggin' along the whole way. How come he picked us to follow?"

"Things ain't always what they seem, Sooze," Daddy said, talking loud so I could hear his voice over the rattling of our worn-out wagon. "Maybe it ain't interested in us at all. We likely stirred up a field mouse along the road, and it's followin' the mouse. A hawk can see those little varmints from a mile up. It'll dive right down on it whenever it has a mind to."

"But, Daddy," I said. "The hawk is up so high. A mouse has plenty of time to run. It can skedaddle before the bird ever gets close enough to snatch it, can't it?"

"A mouse is like lots of folks. It keeps its focus only on itself and what it wants. It don't even notice trouble on the horizon. By the time the shadow of the hawk falls, it's too late to run."

Swift as lightning, the red-tailed hawk swooped. It

touched the ground near the wagon, startling me. With wings flapping, it rose into the air before Frenchy could flinch. I saw the long tail of a field mouse hanging from its talons.

"Lord Almighty, Daddy!" I said. "I was busy talkin' and never saw it comin'!"

Glancing over his shoulder at us, Daddy said, "Once you learn to listen, nature will talk to you, but you got to step back and let it show you the big picture before you can understand what it's tryin' to teach."

By the time we got home, Daddy was ordering chores for us. "Cora, you need to find us somethin' for supper, so your Mama can stay upstairs with the baby in our room. Don't matter what you fix—we just need food. And Sooze, since I ain't been home all day, the hogs need to be fed and so do the chickens. Get to it while I unhitch the wagon and take care of Frenchy."

"Yes, Daddy," I told him. I jumped off the end gate while Daddy helped Mama and Grace down off the wagon. Mama still wasn't talking. I watched her hold the baby close and walk into the house without a word, closing the door behind her.

"Cora," Daddy said. "You stay downstairs. Don't want you gettin' near the baby."

"How am I supposed to get Mama's supper to her?"

"I'll take your mama's food upstairs to her when I'm finished with these outside chores." Then Daddy stopped midway through unhitching Frenchy and said, "Cora, it's important that you mind me. Do you understand?"

"All right, Daddy. I promise I won't go upstairs to see Mama."

"All right," he said as if they'd struck a bargain. Then turning to me, Daddy said, "Go on, Sooze. It's been a long day. Let's get these chores done. Start with the hogs."

"Here, Cora," I said, handing her the gift box. "Can you take this in the house for me?"

Grabbing the box, Cora turned and ran. There was

nothing I could do about saying, "Be careful, I don't even know what's in it yet!" because she was already gone and in the house with it.

Two days before, Mama had wrung a chicken's neck, planning to make fried chicken for Henry's graduation celebration, but since he wasn't coming home for it, Mama had boiled the hen, and after cooling, she'd put it in the icebox saying, "It'll keep." She'd set the chicken's head and legs aside for the hogs, so I tossed those in the feed bucket. I figured it was as good a night as any to feed it to them.

I climbed the pen's split-rail fence with the chicken parts in a bucketful of Daddy's special hog feed—a mixture of corn, acorns, and crabapples. They were hungry, so they pushed against the fence, snorting and growling while I emptied the bucket onto the ground for them.

After finishing with the hogs, I headed to the chicken coop, but it was getting too late to clean the dusty ammonia stench from their pen since they were already roosting.

We had a flock of black-and-white Plymouth Rock chickens, our best egg-layers, and a bigger flock of what Mama called White Wy hens. It was always them she'd catch when making a pot of chicken and dumplins, but we also had Rhode Island Reds. They were good for both laying and eating, but to catch one was a feat in itself. The meanest rooster alive we called Big Red, and he'd spur you as soon as look at you. There was not a possum or a fox that could outfight him.

I didn't think it was a good idea to feed the flock this late, especially knowing their food would just attract weasels and rats after dark. Not only would the filthy critters eat the chicken feed, but they'd sure as shootin' eat the chickens, too. I hated to go against Daddy's orders, but if I just didn't bring it up, I could get up before dawn and do it. Maybe Daddy wouldn't ask about it.

I went into the house through the utility porch at the back door to get the water bucket, and I saw Cora had a pot of water boiling on the stove. "What did you find to make for supper, Cora?"

"You know I can't cook, Sooze." Cora was tying Mama's apron around her waist, and she had tears in her eyes. Stomping her foot, she put her hands on her hips and said, "I can't cook, I can't sew, I can't do the vegetable canning, and I can't cure a ham. I can't do anything!"

I pulled the bucket out from under the sink, and holding its handle in my hand, I said, "We can work on learning those things this summer, Cora. Now ain't the time to be worryin' about it."

"But I want to be able to help Mama, and I'm ashamed to say I ain't listened to nothin' she's tried to teach me. There was always more important things to do."

"You take real good care of the henhouse, Cora. And you're good with the baby. You're better with Grace than I am."

Cora nodded, wiping her eyes as I headed for the back door. Stopping, I turned around and asked, "What are you boiling water for again?"

"Oatmeal," Cora said. "I'm making oatmeal with toast and jam for supper."

"That's real good, Cora. I like oatmeal." Then I left through the door and started walking for the well. The least I could do was give fresh water to the chickens and add some to the hog's trough, too. Before headin' back into the house, I filled the bucket with water again and carried it in with me.

When I came through the screened-in utility porch, carrying the bucket to the sink, I saw Daddy was already inside, sitting in his favorite chair by the fireplace. He held his cup of coffee with both hands and was staring into the flames. When he heard me, he called, "Sooze, did everything go all right?"

"Everything was fine, Daddy," I said, hoping he wouldn't ask for specifics. "I gave the hogs the chicken parts Mama had saved for 'em, too."

"Good girl," Daddy mumbled.

It was hard to tell that my brown-and-white oxfords were brown *and* white after working outside in them, so I sat down in a kitchen chair and pulled them off my feet. I took off my dirty socks, too, and dropped them to the floor. I took a clean, wet rag and picked up a shoe, ready to start scrubbing, when I saw my legs and feet were as dirty as a field farmer. Grabbing my shoes and the wet rag, I went outside and sat down on the back steps, and then used the rag to wash my legs and feet. One good thing about marrying David was I'd have indoor plumbing with a private bath. What a luxury! Turning on a faucet right there inside the house and having water run out of it instead of carting buckets back and forth from the well was like a fairy tale.

After washing myself, I used the same dirty rag on my shoes. I washed the dirt off, finally seeing their oxford colors again. I inspected the shoes. The stitching was a permanent dirt color, and there was hardly anything left of the laces— they had broken off almost down to the tongue and could barely be tied anymore. The soles were pitiful, too. Each shoe had two holes worn clean through under the balls of my feet. On hog-killing day the previous December, the cold pushed through those holes so bad it nearly froze my feet, so I used the cardboard from the old shoebox to cut replacement soles and had slipped them inside until we could buy new shoes. Knowing I still had a few months to go before the corn harvest money came in, I decided to make new cardboard soles again. I pulled the worn pieces out of my shoes, carried them across the yard to the oil drum trashcan, and tossed them in. I'd be glad when I could toss my used-up shoes right in alongside them someday.

"Sooze, come and get it!" Cora was hollering out the back door.

I hurried across the yard. The narrow, screened-in porch held our galvanized washtub, two big wash pots, the clothes hamper, and our soap-making utensils. Daddy had also built special shelving for Mama's canning jars. From the rafters, we hung herbs for drying. The smell of rosemary was my favorite, and I swear it grew all year—winter or summer made no difference to it. Mama had a bush planted at the back corner of the house, and it was bigger than the bramble bushes growing wild behind the trashcan.

Soon as I opened the door, I knew Cora over-toasted the bread because a charcoal smell filled the house.

"Is the toast too burnt to eat?" I asked as I walked to the sink. When she shook her head, I pushed the stopper into the basin hole and poured a bit of water into it, then I washed my hands using lye soap, leaving the water so Cora and Daddy could do the same if need be.

"You got Mama's bowl ready, Cora?" Daddy was standing in the doorway like it was a house somebody else lived in.

"Yes, sir," Cora said. She took hold of the bowl in one hand and a saucer with burnt toast in the other. "I already buttered Mama's toast for her."

"You done good, Cora." Daddy took the bowl and plate from her. "I'll be back for mine in a bit. You girls go on and eat without waiting for me."

Taking our bowls and toast to the table, me and Cora sat in opposite chairs, staring at each other. "You want to say grace tonight, Cora?"

"I never know what to say, Sooze. You do it."

Bowing our heads, I said, "Lord, thank you for this food. Amen." I couldn't think of a single thing worth thanking God for other than the food on our table.

"Sure is different at supper around here now," Cora said. "Used to be that all of us, Mama and Daddy, Henry, me and you, used to gather all together. There was more talking at our table than I'd hear all day otherwise, and now it's just you and me, Sooze. And you ain't got no more to say than I do."

"It'll be back to normal again once Henry is home and Grace is well. It's just a lot of worry on the family right now."

"Sure hope it's soon. I don't like the sound of silence."

After supper, I washed the dishes, and Cora dried them and then put them away in the cupboard. After taking Mama's food to her, Daddy never came back downstairs.

After cleaning up the kitchen, I sent Cora upstairs to our bedroom while I blew out the flame in our coal oil lamps.

Upstairs, I leaned my head against Mama and Daddy's door, but I didn't hear any sounds inside. I wanted to knock to see if everything was all right, or at least go in and say good night, but if they were already asleep, I sure didn't want to wake them. Their day had been hard, and while Grace was quiet, I knew they needed their rest. Instead of calling out to them, I turned and walked back down the hallway to the bedroom I shared with Cora.

"I think Mama and Daddy are already asleep," I told her.

Cora was in her long, white cotton nightshirt and socks. She jumped into bed, bouncing across on her knees to her side nearest the wall. She pushed her feet under the covers and pulled the quilt up to her chin while I put on my gray flannel gown. I stood looking out the window, brushing my hair.

"Sooze, read me some of that book you like tonight so's I don't have to think about Henry or Grace anymore. Thoughts about them is wearin' me out."

"You know, if you'd read some yourself, you'd learn to find peace. That's why I read, Cora. It's like goin' to another place in my mind. Instead of worrying about my own problems, I worry about theirs. Somebody else's problems are always easier to worry about than your own."

"I know. I just don't read as good as you." Cora turned onto her side and propped her head up on one arm. She stared right at me with her wide brown eyes. "Can you read some?"

It wasn't like she was twisting my arm. I couldn't think of anything I'd rather do than read pages from *Little Women*, whether it was to myself or to my family. I grinned at Cora as I got into bed beside her with the book. "Should I start from the beginning or from where we left off last time?"

"You ain't picked up that book in a month, Sooze. Start at the beginning again. I like that part best anyway."

"That's because you usually fall asleep by the time we get ten pages in," I reminded her. "The rest of the book is good, too, you know?"

"I know," Cora groaned.

Opening the book to its first page was like getting a candy cane at Christmastime. It was sweet and satisfying, and I hadn't even read a word from it yet that night. I scooted down under the quilt and fluffed my pillow to raise my head, and then began:

"*'Christmas won't be Christmas without any presents,'* grumbled Jo, lying on the rug.'"

"Sooze, I just don't understand that part. Why would she lay down on a floor rug, especially in winter?"

"Well," I said. "I suppose they have better rugs than we do. Maybe theirs is thick and soft like a sleeping pallet."

"I thought they was poor!" Cora sat up in bed like she'd had the shock of a lifetime.

"They are poor." I closed the book, keeping my finger inside to mark the page. From memory, I recited:

"*'It's so dreadful to be poor!' sighed Meg, looking down at her old dress.*"

"They're telling us right there that they're poor."

"Maybe they ain't never seen a poor person's rug." Cora pointed to the round, multi-colored rug Mama had braided for us years ago. "Ours ain't worth lyin' down on. Fact is, it's so thin and worn it's barely worth *standin'* on. Last winter, I felt the cold right through it as if I was standin' on a snowbank in bare feet."

"Are you goin' to listen to this story or not?"

"Yeah, I'm listenin'," Cora groaned. She lay back and pulled up the quilt again.

I opened the book and started reading.

"'I don't think it's fair for some girls to have plenty of pretty things, and other girls nothing at all.'"

Cora's eyes were closing by the second page, but I kept reading until I couldn't hold mine open either. Just after Jo proclaimed herself to be man of the family, I began to wonder, did I need to look at things like Jo had? Did I need to take on Henry's "oldest child" duties while he was gone? Even though Daddy was still there, I felt the burden of being next in line for the caring of the family. I was grateful for the peace when sleep finally overtook me.

Chapter 20

I t was four in the morning when Mama screamed. I was up out of bed and running for her room while my eyes were still half shut.

I opened her bedroom door without so much as a knock and saw her kneeling at Grace's cradle. Daddy was down on one knee beside her.

"Mama, what's wrong?" I was nearly shouting, but neither Mama nor Daddy answered. Behind me, Cora pressed herself close, almost pushing me through the doorway. Intending to hold her back, I reached behind but grabbed a fist full of nightshirt instead and just held on tight. "Is baby Grace all right?"

When Mama stood, I saw Grace cradled in her arms. Mama had buried her face in the baby's swaddling blanket, and she was crying like the night she'd heard about Henry.

"What's wrong, Mama?" Cora's scared whisper snuck out from behind my right elbow.

Standing up, Daddy turned to us. "The baby's gone, girls." A sobbing sound spurted out behind his words.

"How?" The word screamed out of my mouth.

"She just stopped breathing, Sooze." Daddy's voice quieted. "That's all. She just couldn't breathe no more."

Mama carried Grace in her arms to the bed and sat down

on the edge as Daddy struck a match to light the coal oil lamp. The shadows inside the bedroom were eerie as if Mama and Daddy were somewhere between life and death. Maybe it was the dark before dawn, but it seemed I could almost see through them. Daddy moved in flickered steps while Mama's cry sounded miles away. As I watched, a smoky haze formed as if a gray veil had fallen over the room, but it didn't scare me none. I knew I was watching something extraordinary. I'd never been nearby when a baby died. Maybe it was different for them. A newborn can't have no sin, so maybe the angels are softer when they come to get them.

I twisted my hand tighter into Cora's nightshirt. Her tears soaked through my gown, wetting my back.

Mama stood up, yelling, "I did this!" Another sob broke free. "It's *me*, John! I promised God he could have it all if he wouldn't take Henry—my only boy—away from me! I said I'd give Him whatever He wanted!" Mama was crying so hard her teardrops splatted the floor. She pulled the swaddled infant to her face. "I'm sorry, Grace." Then looking upward, Mama shouted, "I didn't mean you could have *my baby*! Oh God," she cried, her voice sinking into a whimper. "I didn't mean you could have Grace."

Mama crumpled, falling to the floor. Instinctively, Daddy grabbed Grace from her arms as she went down. I ran to help Mama, but when I got close enough to grab her, I saw Daddy's face. His green eyes had a sickly gaze, and he was white as a bedsheet. Wrinkles had plowed themselves deeper overnight. He turned to the cradle and gently laid Grace inside.

"I did this," Mama cried again. "*I did this!*"

Daddy pulled Mama up and held her. "Emma, this wasn't your doing. It's an illness, and it ain't choosy about who it takes hold of, and *it* chose Grace—not you and not God. Do you hear me?" He patted her. "Same as when Will and Rose's boy Jimmy died five summers ago. It wasn't their fault neither. His was a bad fall, and Grace's was a sickness. You didn't cause this, Emma."

As I stood there next to Mama and Daddy, I couldn't help but look down into the cradle. If I hadn't known better, I'd have sworn baby Grace was just sleeping. Her face was peaceful, with parched lips parted just a bit. Her eyes were closed. Then I saw a stillness I hadn't known before. It was a peace that told me I wasn't looking at a *person* anymore. I was staring at an empty shell, like an egg that had been cracked open and emptied out.

"Sooze," Cora cried from the doorway. "Are you lookin' at Grace?"

"Yeah," I said.

"Can I see, too?" Cora's tears were running down her cheeks, but she was trying to wipe them away with her hand.

"Daddy?" I asked. When he nodded, I motioned for Cora, putting a comforting arm around her shoulders when she came. The lamplight was so dim it was hard to see clearly, but it gave Grace a soft light for lying in repose. Cora stopped crying and was staring down into the cradle. Reaching in, she brushed a finger over the baby's cheek. Her touch was soft.

"I think we should cover her now," Daddy whispered to us. Cora nodded with quiet tears. He straightened the extra swaddling blanket then lay it over Grace, pulling it up, so it covered her face.

"Daddy," I said. "Should I ride into town and get Doc Farrell?"

"What for?" Daddy asked. "Doc can't do us no good now."

Using her hands to wipe her eyes, Mama said, "Doc told us he'd come out today anyway."

"What can I do to help, Mama?" I asked.

"Nothin' to do." Mama started to cry again. "Your daddy and me will do the cleansing, and I want to lay her out real nice."

"Ray's funeral is this afternoon, Emma." Daddy's voice was strong but gentle. "He's your brother, and we should be paying our last respects to him today, too."

"I'm not leavin' my baby, John. Ray would understand." She was looking at him as if he should have known the answer already. "I'm not leavin' Grace."

Daddy nodded. With his head still down, he said, "Sooze, I'm gonna have to ask you to attend your uncle Ray's services today and represent the family. I sure hate to send you along without us, honey, but I need to stay here at home and help your mama today."

"M-me?" I stuttered. "I want to stay here with you and Mama!"

"I know you do, but Uncle Ray was a big part of this family too, and there ain't nothing you can do here at home." Daddy stepped closer to me, whispering, "And your mama and me need some time alone with the baby to do what we need to do. Take Cora with you. Go get your grades, go to your intended's graduation, then get to Uncle Ray's funeral at the cemetery. It starts at one o'clock, Sooze. By the time you get home today, we'll have things settled here." Daddy put one hand on my shoulder. "Can you do that for us?"

"Yes," I agreed. I wasn't sure if I was feeling needed or feeling like I was being shuffled off so I wouldn't be in the way. It's a hard distinction sometimes.

"Come on, Cora." I took her by the hand, led her out of the bedroom, and down the hall to our room.

The sun was just peeking over the horizon when we crawled back into bed, both of us raising our knees until the sheet and quilt tented over them. We sat there together, not knowing what else to do.

"Sooze, why can't we stay home?" Cora whispered.

"'Cause," I said with resolve. "Daddy gave us a job to do, and it ain't our place to question him. Not today, anyway."

"What are we supposed to tell people about Grace?"

Now that was a question I hadn't thought to have an

answer for, but one thing I knew for sure—Henry deserved to know right away, and we sure didn't want word getting to him without family telling him first.

"Cora, do you still have coins in your money jar?"

"Yeah, I got all $21.13. Daddy asked me to hold it for him until he needed it. Why?"

"Well, count out about $3.00 for us to take today. We're goin' to call Henry on Miss Lola's telephone."

I got up and picked out my navy blue dress. I didn't have a black one, and even though I knew black was what I should wear for Uncle Ray's funeral and what I should have been wearing to mourn Grace, I hoped dark blue would show the intended respect. I handed Cora her gray dress with white pinstripes. It wasn't black either, but it was the most solemn color I could find.

In the kitchen, I fixed us each a peanut butter and jam sandwich for lunch. David's mother was baking cookies and serving punch, but it surely wasn't enough to hold us over until the cemetery services were done. I spread peanut butter on two extra pieces of bread and handed one slice to Cora.

"Breakfast," I told her. "Are you ready to go?"

"Yeah, I'm ready, but I sure ain't looking forward to seeing folks today."

"Neither am I, but there's no sense worrying about it now. We got a job to do, and Daddy and Mama need us to handle things proper for them."

Cora helped me feed the chickens—a chore that put us a little behind—but when we arrived at the schoolhouse, all the kids were still playing out front like it was a perfectly good day. Instead of staying outside with them, me and Cora went on in and waited for Miss Stewart to ring the last morning bell of the school year.

"Good morning, girls," Miss Stewart said. "You're here early again today. Is everything okay at home?"

I surely didn't want to lie to her, but I also didn't want to tell her the truth just yet. Come to think of it, how does a person say someone died anyway? Should I just come right out and say it? Do I just say *she's dead*? Or do I start bawling as hard as my heart wants until she guesses right?

"Everything is fine, ma'am." My throat squeezed out the words as I took my seat next to Cora.

Turning her attention back to the papers on her desk, Miss Stewart said, "I think your folks will be proud of you girls when they see your year-end report cards today. It was clear to me, after grading the tests, that you both studied hard this year."

"Does that mean we passed?" Cora asked.

"Yes, Cora," Miss Stewart said and smiled. "You passed to the next grade."

"Me, too?" I asked, feeling like I already knew the answer.

"Yes, of course, Sooze. You're my star pupil!"

Of all people, Miss Stewart deserved to know. Even though she was our teacher, she was as much a friend to me as anybody I'd ever known, other than Leona. In fact, with Leona gone to California, I didn't have a best friend anymore, but sometimes Miss Stewart felt like one. I got up from my seat and walked to her desk.

In a voice so low it was almost a whisper, I said, "Miss Stewart, we're not wanting to tell anyone yet—not 'til I can call Henry on the telephone, anyway—but I just can't help but tell you." Miss Stewart had her eyes on me like an eagle, and she was waiting for my next word.

"What is it, Sooze? Is something wrong?"

My eyes started watering before I could get out a word. "Our baby sister died." That was all I could say before I started crying.

"Sooze," Cora said from her seat. "I thought we wasn't goin' to say anything?"

"But we can tell Miss Stewart, Cora. She ain't gonna tell folks."

"Oh, girls!" Miss Stewart stood up and pulled me into

her arms. Her lilac perfume smelled soft and caring, just like her hug. "I'm sorry. What happened?"

"I'd just as soon not tell the whole story right now," I said as I tried to hold my voice steady. "But Cora and me would like to leave right after the grades are passed out so's we can go to the boardinghouse and use Miss Lola's telephone to call Henry. We want him to know about the baby right away, and we don't want him finding out from anybody but us. Is that all right?"

"Yes, of course, Sooze. Whenever you're ready, you girls just get on up out of your desks and go. You don't need to explain anything to anybody."

"Yes, ma'am." I wiped my cheeks dry as I returned to my desk, so nobody who came through the schoolhouse door would see that I'd been crying.

Miss Stewart went to the entryway and pulled the knotted rope, ringing the school bell. The pupils rushed in through the door as if a prize waited for them.

David came in last, surely wanting to make an entrance garnering him the attention he likely deserved being a graduate. He came straight to my desk.

"Mornin', Sooze. Today is an important day for us. My graduation marks the beginning of our new life together."

I didn't want to look up because I knew the redness in my eyes would show, so I smiled politely as I stared down at my hands folded in my lap. "Yes, it's an important day."

"Please take your seat, David," Miss Stewart said, and then, "I'm pleased to say each and every one of you has passed!"

The whole class broke out into handclapping and shouts of *Hooray*!

Sometime during the commotion, I heard David. "All except one, right, Miss Stewart?"

Confused, I turned to look at him.

"No, everyone passed," Miss Stewart assured him.

"Aren't you forgettin' about Henry?"

"Oh," Miss Stewart's voice lowered into a tone of regret.

Then, standing with a straight posture, she said, "I'll allow Henry to take his final test as soon as he's able to come back in to see me."

"You will?" Cora stood up, nearly shouting. "You're goin' to let Henry take his test even though school is out for the year?"

It felt like my heart skipped one beat for every two while I waited for her answer.

"Yes, Cora. Henry's absence wasn't by his choice, so I'll allow a makeup day for him this summer to take his final test. If he passes, as I'm sure he will," she said, "then I'll be proud to present him with a diploma. It's just a shame he'll miss today's ceremony."

"Oh, Miss Stewart," I said with an excitement I didn't expect to have that day. "Henry won't care about cookies and punch! He'll be very happy for the chance, and he'll be very grateful, too."

"Well, that ain't quite fair, Miss Stewart," David said. Then pointing to Benny in the back of the room, he added, "Benny and me had to be here for our tests. Seems only fair Henry should have to be here for his test, too."

I heard Benny snicker before saying, "Hey, fancy-pants, don't try to make me your friend. What I do, I do on my own."

David sat back down without another word.

CHAPTER 21

Miss Stewart started handing out report cards. When she gave me mine, she winked and started talking to the class about the next year's curriculum. I knew that meant it was as good a time as any for Cora and me to leave.

Slipping out of our seats, we headed toward the exit, stopping only to grab our sweaters. We were almost out the door when David shouted, "Sooze, where are you going? My graduation isn't 'til noon."

"*Our* graduation!" Benny reminded.

We kept walking, but David followed us out. My foot had just touched the bottom step when he called louder. "Sooze!"

Turning to him, I said, "We'll be back. We just have an errand that needs running."

"David?" Miss Stewart emerged from the classroom. "You need to come back inside so we can discuss today's graduation."

"Go on, David," I told him. "Me and Cora will be back by noon."

"What about your mama and daddy? They're supposed to come for the ceremony, too."

"I'm not sure they'll be able to come today."

"Sooze, Mother is expecting them!"

"David!" Miss Stewart shouted. "I need you back in this classroom right now!"

I was sure grateful I'd decided to tell Miss Stewart about Grace. She was helping us more than she knew. We took the opportunity to turn and run toward the boardinghouse, even though David was still yelling, "Sooze!"

We were breathing hard by the time we knocked on the door of Posey's Boardinghouse.

"What a nice surprise!" Miss Lola said after opening the door. "Gettin' to see you girls two days in a row is quite a pleasure. What can I do for you today?"

"We need to make another telephone call, ma'am, if it's all right with you."

"Well, sure it is," Miss Lola said with a smile. "Do you girls have money?"

"I brought $3.00 with me," Cora told her. "Daddy's call yesterday cost $1.80, so surely we got enough for a call today."

"Well, come on in!" Miss Lola seemed pleased as punch.

We went right to the dining room where the switchboard was, and Miss Lola motioned me to the chair by the black telephone that Daddy used yesterday.

"Sit down, sweet pea, and tell me who we're calling for you today."

"We want to call the same number you called for Daddy yesterday," Cora announced.

"We need the jail line in Waldron, Miss Lola," I explained. "We need to talk to Henry."

"Well, I'm not sure if they'll let you talk directly to a prisoner," Miss Lola told us. "But we can surely try." She turned in her seat to face the switchboard and put the headband with earmuffs attached over the top of her head, properly adjusting the earpieces. She positioned the candy-cane-shaped mouthpiece close to her lips. Pulling out one long cord, she plugged it into a hole on the shiny wood board and turned her black dial until the white line showed it was open. She dialed. "Clara? It's Lola." She was smiling again, just like the previous day. "Sugar pie, we need you to connect us to the jail number in Waldron again. Can you do that for us?" Miss Lola smiled and nodded at me.

"Should I pick up the receiver now?" I asked.

"In just a minute," Miss Lola told me. "Clara is connecting the call."

"Can I talk, too, Sooze?" Cora was standing in front of me. "Can I talk to Henry?"

"Don't know if we'll be able to talk to him, Cora," I reminded. "But I promise I'll let you talk, too, if we can get through to him."

"Thank you, Clara," Miss Lola said into her mouthpiece. "Hello, courthouse? This is the operator in Coaldale, and I have a personal call for Henry Williams...he's in your jail. Fine, I'm connecting you to his sister." Then pointing to the telephone, she said, "Pick up the receiver, Sooze. You'll have to do the talking from here on out."

I lifted the receiver. With one end against my ear and the other up to my mouth, I said, "Hello?" The man on the other end sounded gruff like maybe he'd smoked too many cigarettes in his lifetime. He told me right off he wasn't running a hotel and said I couldn't talk directly to a prisoner. "But it's an emergency!"

"Ask if Cordie's there, Sooze," Cora suggested.

I nodded. "Can you see if his lawyer is there this morning? His name is Cordie Beegle. I'll talk to him if I can." I don't know what made me think that would work. I just had a fierce need to tell Henry what had happened, and I didn't know how else to do it. When I glanced at Miss Lola, I saw she had the switchboard's black knob turned to OPEN again. But what was the use in telling her to turn it off? She was going to hear everything I had to say anyway.

Even though no one was talking directly to me, I could hear men chattering inside the receiver. Then a voice, sounding like Cordie, came closer. "Hello?"

"Cordie? Is that you?" I said into the receiver. "This is Sooze. I need to talk to Henry."

I stared at Cora while I put my hand over the mouthpiece, whispering, "Cordie's talking to a man about it."

"Yeah," I answered into the telephone. "It's an emergency." I heard Cordie relaying the message, then he told me to hold on.

"Sooze," Miss Lola said. "The timer keeps runnin' even though they ain't talkin' to you, and it's been over two minutes already. After three minutes, I'll have to charge you an extra fifteen cents a minute."

"Thank you, Miss Lola. I know the cost." I turned to Cora and, in a low voice, said, "Cora, try to keep track, so we don't spend more than we got."

Cora was nodding to me when Cordie came back on the line. "Sooze, they're going to transfer this call back to the desk near Henry's jail cell so I can pick it up there. It's more than two rooms away, so it will take me a minute to get in there. Then I'll stretch the cord far as I can for Henry. You'll have to hold on again, though, all right?"

"All right, but Cordie," I said, my voice sounding desperate. "I ain't got a lot of money with me to pay for this call, so, can you hurry?"

Without hearing him answer, the next clicking sound startled me. "Miss Lola, I think we got cutoff! Is it going to cost us another first-minute charge of $1.80 to call him back?" The look on my face must have scared Cora, too, because she started grabbing at her pocket of money, trying to empty it out for counting.

"Cora, honey," Miss Lola said, reaching her hand out to stop Cora. "The telephone didn't disconnect. Listen, Sooze, you'll hear another click soon, and then they'll start talking again. We're still connected, I promise."

And just as she finished, the telephone clicked again, and then again, and then I heard Cordie saying, "Sooze, are you still there?"

"Yes!" I nearly shouted into the receiver. "I'm still here, Cordie!"

"Good. I'm at a desk outside Henry's cell. I'm goin' to pull this long cord to see how close I can get to him. With any luck, it'll reach."

I waited, listening to Henry's voice in the background. It gradually got louder until Henry's voice was on the other end, coming through the receiver loud and clear.

"Sooze?" Henry said. "Are you there, Sooze?"

"I'm here, Henry! Can you hear me?"

"I can hear you. Cordie says you got an emergency. What is it?"

"Henry," I said, trying to calm my voice down. "I wanted you to know straight from your family first before you heard it from somebody else."

"Heard what, Sooze? What's wrong? Is everybody all right? Spit it out!"

"It's Grace, Henry," I told him.

His voice got real quiet before saying, "What about Grace?"

"She got real sick, Henry," I told him. "And Henry," I swallowed hard and tried to keep my voice from cracking wide open, "she...what I mean to say is..."

"Spit it out, Sooze!" Henry was yelling at me like he usually did when he was scared.

"Grace died this morning."

Everyone, except Miss Lola, was silent. From her came a throat-clenching gasp.

"God Almighty," Henry muttered the words into the telephone. "How? Sooze, what happened?"

"She died of the consumption."

"Where's Mama and Daddy?"

"They're both home with the baby. Daddy's helping Mama with the cleansing and laying out. Doc Farrell is goin' out there this morning. I'm hopin' he can give Mama somethin' to help her hold up through all this."

"God Almighty," Henry repeated.

"Sooze, let me talk to him! We're gonna run out of money!" Cora reminded.

"Henry, Cora needs to talk, but we're almost out of money, so it's got to be fast," I told him. "And Henry?" My voice choked up. "We miss you, and we sure could use you at home with us."

I heard him say, "Miss you too," as Cora pulled the receiver out of my hand.

"Henry? It's me, Cora. How are you?" Cora had her head down, and she was pushing the receiver so hard against her ear I couldn't hear a word Henry was saying to her. After a few seconds, Cora told him, "Henry, Mama thinks she's the cause of Grace's dying. She said she'd promised God he could have whatever he wanted if he'd just give you back to her. She said it wasn't fair of him to take her only boy. So, I was thinkin'," Cora said. "Maybe you could talk to God, too. Maybe you can make a deal with him..."

"Cora!" I shouted and grabbed the telephone receiver out of her hand. "Henry—you ain't makin' no deals with God! Do you hear me?"

"I hear you, Sooze." Henry's voice was low and filled with guilt.

"I mean it, Henry Williams! You ain't done nothin' wrong, and if God don't know it by now, then we don't need His kind of help no more!"

Miss Lola gasped again, nearly falling out of her chair.

"We got to go, Henry," I said, taking notice of Miss Lola. "You take care of yourself, and we'll be coming to see you tomorrow for jury pickin' day."

After saying goodbye to Henry, I placed the receiver back into its cradle. "How much do we owe you for the call, Miss Lola?"

But Miss Lola was adding up the charges even before I asked. I knew she was thinking me a heathen for saying we didn't need God's help, but she could think whatever she wanted. I was tired of worrying about what other people thought of us.

"It was a twelve-minute call, Sooze, so you're owing $3.15." Miss Lola stood. "Now, I would have stopped you at $3.00, but to tell you the truth, your blasphemy shocked me right out of my head!"

Knowing we didn't need no more debt, I made a man-of-the-house decision. I took the handful of coins from Cora, and I laid them down on the switchboard desktop. "We ain't goin' to charge you for listenin' in on our private conversation." I pointed to the black knob as proof that I knew she'd been listening to both sides of the call. "I'm sure the Bell people would agree it's worth a fifteen-cent discount for us not to raise a ruckus about your eavesdropping." Grabbing Cora's arm, I started for the door. "Thank you for the use of your telephone today." We walked right out as if our debt was paid in full. And frankly, as far as I was concerned, our debt there *was* paid in full.

Walking back toward the schoolhouse, I spotted Thomas Kittridge coming out of Huckabee's General Store. He was loading supplies into his father's automobile. After emptying an armful of groceries onto the seat, he turned and went back inside.

My stomach started doing flip-flops, and the front of my neck had a funny tingling as if the air I was breathing had been soaked in camphor oil. "Cora, I'm goin' across the road. Do you want to come with me so's we can say hello to Thomas?"

When Cora nodded, I pulled her out into the road with me. I couldn't tell whether my heartbeat or my footsteps were faster, but either way, my plan was to get there quick, looking like I was just passing by nice and easy. I sure didn't want him thinking I was anxious.

CHAPTER 22

We crossed the road to where the Kittridge automobile was waiting. Thomas was still inside the store and hadn't seen us yet, and since I didn't want to go into the store after him, I decided we'd wait outside.

"Why can't we just go inside and say hi to him?" Cora asked.

"Because I don't want to talk to him with Mrs. Huckabee listenin' to every word."

"Well, hello!" Thomas called to us as he pushed open the store door. He stepped down the wooden porch steps, carrying another armload of supplies. "Would you mind opening the automobile door so I can set this purchase inside?"

"Oh, yes, of course!" I hurried to the same side where Thomas was standing. I grasped the door handle and pulled it open. Thomas leaned inside, putting his supplies on the floorboard.

Pulling himself back out of the automobile, Thomas stood up smiling. "Thank you," he said, adjusting his loose-fitting, belted jeans. "It's mighty nice to see you again."

"Are you in town for the graduation ceremony?" Cora

asked him. "It starts at noon, and Mrs. Huckabee is serving free punch and cookies at the schoolhouse."

"Are you graduating today, Sooze?"

I was embarrassed to admit that I wasn't old enough, so I knew my cheeks were flushing red. "No, I still got two more years before I graduate."

"David is graduating today," Cora explained. "He's Sooze intended. You can come with us if you want."

Thomas dropped his sight to my ring finger. "I should be getting back home with these supplies. Granny's wantin' to make a poultice for Granddad. He's been feelin' a bit poorly."

"You should remind Pauline—I mean your granny—that a spoonful or two of her blackberry jam always brightens Earl's day." A smile came. "I helped her make that batch last summer and it's the best I ever tasted."

"So you're the one who helps Granny with her summer jams?"

"It's a treat for me," I said, wanting to show my appreciation. "She's been teaching me jam and jelly makin' for two summers. She pays me to help, but all I really do is pick and clean the berries and learn canning."

"Granny says her helper does a lot more than pick and clean."

"She's a sweet lady," I said. Feeling I needed to say more, I figured it was as good a day as any to offer sympathies. "I'm sorry to hear about Earl. I'm sure Pauline is glad to have you and your daddy there to help."

With lowered head, Thomas nodded before glancing back up at me. His kind, green eyes had compassion. "It's what families do, and Granny and Granddad are helping us way more than we're helping them."

"How are they doing that?" Cora asked.

Without a bit of hesitation or aggravation at Cora's question, Thomas answered just as if she was a grown-up deserving an answer. "We were living in a nice house in Chicago. Seemed like we had everything going for us. Then

Mama got the influenza. Two months later, we were burying her. Things just kept going downhill from there. Daddy and me both had good jobs at the candy factory until times got so bad folks couldn't afford to buy chocolate bars anymore. The factory laid off more than a hundred people last October. That's almost *half* the employees. Can you believe it? A company doing so well just hitting rock bottom? We kept thinking the success of their new candy bar would revive the factory, and then they would be able to hire us back, but we couldn't hold out long enough. We stopped making payments on the house just so's we could buy food and keep the place heated for winter. The bank finally auctioned it off last month, and we had nowhere to go." Thomas closed the automobile door and stepped back. "Granny and Granddad needed us as much as we needed them."

"You got any brothers or sisters?" Cora asked.

"Nope. It's just Dad and me."

"I'm sorry about your mama, Thomas," I told him. "Losing a mama is probably worse than losing anybody else in your family, includin' a baby sister."

"Losing *any* family is hard." Thomas had pure sincerity in his voice. "Come to think of it, Sooze, I don't think I ever told you I was sorry about your uncle dying."

I whispered, "thank you," knowing tears were welling up inside my eyes again, but in all fairness, it wasn't Uncle Ray I was crying for—it was Grace. Trying to stifle the sad wanting to pour out of me, I said, "Uncle Ray's funeral is today, right after the graduation. He's being buried in the Coaldale Cemetery right up behind the schoolhouse."

"There's a cemetery behind the school?"

"It's sort of hidden by all the trees," I told him.

"You'd never know it was there unless you was from around here," Cora added. "Do you want to come with us to watch Uncle Ray get buried?"

"We'd be pleased to have you with us," I offered.

Thomas peered through the window to the inside of the

automobile. "Maybe I can stay in town for a while. Not one perishable in the whole purchase."

"That would be fine, Thomas!" I spoke with more excitement than intended.

"I still need to load seed, so how about I meet you when I'm done?" Thomas glanced at his wristwatch. "That'll give me another thirty minutes to finish my business."

"Daddy was right," Cora said to him. "Sometimes a wagon is better. There ain't much room in this automobile for totin' supplies. Where are you supposed to stack the seed?"

Thomas gave a pat to the automobile. "This is Daddy's Model T Coupe, Cora. It looks nice, but you're right—it don't have room for much of anything. Stacking proper is the key."

"Does it have one of them rumble seats?" Cora asked.

"Nope, but it's got a turtleback trunk. Course not much fits in there either, but it's a help. I only got a few bags to pick up. It'll fit."

I was startled by the store's front door swinging open. Mrs. Huckabee stepped out onto the porch. "Sooze, what in the world are you doing out of school?"

But it wasn't me David's mother was staring at—it was Thomas. Her eyes looked him up and down from head to toe and back again as if he had no right talking to me.

"Hello, Mrs. Huckabee," I said, nudging Cora with my elbow before whispering, "Say hello."

"Oh, uh...hi," Cora stammered.

"Well?" David's mother wanted an answer. "What are you two doing out of school? It's almost noon, so you need to be getting ready for the festivities."

"Yeah," Cora said louder. "That's why we're here. We wanted to help carry the cookies and punch. We ran into Thomas as he was comin' out of the store." No one could accuse Cora of being a slow thinker.

I mouthed a silent "bye" to Thomas, then turned to see Mrs. Huckabee's face go from a suspicious frown to a smile.

"Well, aren't you girls thoughtful!" Waving a hand to us, she said, "Come on, I have two platters of cookies and four pitchers of punch that need carryin' to the schoolhouse." She hurried into the store with us following her, calling, "Sam! Hurry up! We need to get these pitchers and cups to the schoolhouse right away. Sooze and her sister are here to carry the cookies." She disappeared into the back but kept right on shouting orders to Mr. Huckabee, even though I couldn't see him anywhere. "We need those paper napkins I special ordered, too!"

Before long, Mr. Huckabee lumbered in behind the store counter like I imagined the hunchback of Notre Dame might walk. He was bent over with one shoulder hanging lower than the other.

"Mr. Huckabee," I said. "Are you all right?"

"Oh yes. I'm pulling a child's wagon loaded down with punch, cups, and paper napkins. If I had to carry all this to the schoolhouse without something to haul it in, I'd have to make at least four trips! Mrs. Huckabee is on her way to the school to set up a table with her lace tablecloth for us."

Sure enough, when he came around the counter, he was pulling a small, red wagon.

"Oh, how darling!" I spouted out.

Mr. Huckabee straightened up into a standing position. "Maybe you girls could save up and buy one of these dandy little wagons for Grace this Christmas. You want me to put an order in for you? It's $3.00 if you buy it now, and by Christmas, you'll have a family discount, Sooze."

That sure put a damper on things. "No, thank you. I don't think we'll be needing one."

"Sure, you will! Grace will just be getting to the right age for riding in a wagon like this one. You'll be able to pull her to the barn and back in a snap."

"She said no!" Cora shouted. "Didn't you hear her?"

Mr. Huckabee raised halting hands. "All right, Cora. I didn't mean any harm in making the suggestion. I know times are hard."

I felt good about him thinking this was a money issue. I sure didn't want to be the one to break the news about Grace. We didn't need any gossip spreading, especially with Henry in jail and Uncle Ray about to be buried.

"It was a kind suggestion. Cora's just a little on edge today. She didn't mean to bark at you, did you, Cora?"

"That's right. I didn't mean to bark."

"No harm done." Mr. Huckabee smiled. "Go on upstairs and grab the cookie trays off the kitchen counter. I've got to pull this wagon through the side door, so I can use the delivery ramp to roll it down to the street."

I led Cora up the stairs, where she blew an admiring whistle. "I ain't never seen a kitchen like this one, Sooze."

"I told you it was pretty, huh?" The tri-colored zigzag design on the linoleum floor was in yellow, beige, and dark brown, and the cupboards and drawers were painted butter-scotch yellow. The kitchen smelled of sugar cookies, but not a speck of leftover flour or sugar was anywhere. It was clean as a whistle. On the countertop near the built-in sink were two big platters of cookies. "There they are, Cora." Beside them laid solid white tea towels. I shook out the folds and spread one of the thin towels over each platter. "Here, Cora. You take this one and follow me."

Walking to school with the platters was easy enough until we got to the schoolhouse door.

Before we ever entered, I heard Mrs. Huckabee ordering people around. "Lauralee, straighten up the cloth, and Lillie, bring me a chair, won't you, please?"

As we came through the door with the cookie platters, I saw David jump to his feet and hurry toward us. The whole room was filled with commotion and year-end excitement. Counting Cora and me, thirteen pupils were up and out of their seats in a happy muddle. Not a single seat was being used.

"Hi, Sooze!" David said. "Mother said she was sure surprised when you came by to pick up the cookies for us. That was mighty nice of you." Looking down at Cora,

David's smile disappeared. "You too, Cora." Using his arm, he pushed her aside then edged in front.

"Yeah, sure," Cora answered, sliding the platter onto the table. Poking a finger into each cheek, she twisted, denting in dimples, and then curtsied. Sweetly, she said, "My pleasure!" But when she turned to walk away, she muttered, "Dumbbell."

"Did you hear her, Mother?" David raised his voice, pointing to Cora. "She's incorrigible, just like her brother!"

Mrs. Huckabee hurried to David. She placed her hands softly on his cheeks. "I know, my darling boy. Pay her no mind. You're a graduate today, and not many boys can say that now, can they?"

"I can say it," Benny said as he wandered tableside. He pulled the tea towel off Cora's platter and tossed it aside. "Mm-mm! Look at them cookies." He grabbed an oatmeal cookie and stuffed the entire round into his mouth, with no one but me noticing.

Amelia Huckabee fanned out the paper napkins and then set them on the table, which prompted me to set my platter down beside Cora's. She moved to the punch bowl and began to fill the empty cups, setting them aside for easy pickings once the line formed.

"Class." Miss Stewart was standing at the front of the room, clapping her hands together for attention. "Please take your seats! It's almost time for the graduation to begin."

That was when Paulette Simmons walked through the door. She wore a knee-length white chiffon dress, haltered at the neck and shamelessly backless, with a white, wide-brimmed hat flaunting a deep blue ostrich feather. She looked around the room for Benny. When she spotted him, her bright red painted lips turned into a smile, and her eyes —heavily defined with feathery black eyeliner and drawn-on eyebrows—shined with pride. She raised her right hand, waving at him. On her finger was a ring with a blue gemstone as big as a nickel, and her perfume smelled fresh, as though she'd just bathed and dabbed fresh violet scent behind her ears.

"Well, Miss Simmons," Amelia Huckabee chided. "I'm surprised to see you out and about during daylight hours."

Without a hint of annoyance, Miss Simmons said, "Today, my Benny is graduating. It's an occasion worth attending, even if it is in the company of chin-waggers and holier-than-thou townsfolk like you."

A gasp came first, then Mrs. Huckabee firmed her stance. "My David is graduating today, too, Miss Simmons. It's just a shame he has to stand beside common thugs."

Miss Simmons stepped closer to the refreshments table. "There ain't nothin' common about my Benny." She put both hands on the tabletop and leaned across with her face inches from David's mother. "And I dare you to say another mean word about my boy."

Mrs. Huckabee pulled back, taking hold of her husband and shaking his arm, but Sam Huckabee was busy greeting the reverend, who'd just arrived, causing him to miss the whole incident.

"Everyone take a seat, please?" Miss Stewart was trying to settle the guests. "You'll all be able to get punch and cookies after the ceremony today."

Me and Cora were already on our way to our desk when Miss Stewart pointed to a line of six ladder-back chairs lined up against the wall. She directed the preacher, Hockney Payne, to the first chair before saying, "Mr. and Mrs. Huckabee and Miss Simmons, won't you please have a seat so we can begin?"

The adults walked to the front of the classroom as if it was their own special day—slow and proud as if all eyes were on them instead of their sons. There were still two empty chairs, but soon enough, I realized those chairs had been meant for Mama and Daddy.

Miss Stewart walked to each person in the room and handed out a sheet of thick cardstock paper. It was a cream-colored page with words printed in black ink on both sides. At the top was:

Graduation Ceremony
May 26, 1932
Coaldale, Arkansas

And then a verse filled the rest of the page. Flipping it over, I saw the names of all the pupils who were advancing to the next grade—which were all of us—and in bolded lettering at the bottom were the names David Huckabee and Benny Simmons, both listed as the 1932 Coaldale graduates. I wished Henry's name had been there, too.

When she was finished handing out the graduation announcements, Miss Stewart said, "Reverend Payne, would you give the invocation, please?"

The preacher, dressed in tan pants and a button-up white shirt, stood and walked to the front of the room, holding his black leather Bible. He said, "Thank you, Miss Stewart." Then turning to the classroom, he said, "Please bow your heads and pray with me." When the room was quiet, he prayed, "Dear Lord, today is a special day in Coaldale. We ask you to bless the future of our graduates, David Huckabee and Benny Simmons, so that they may go out into the world and do good with the knowledge they have acquired. We thank you for guiding them down this righteous path and ask that you continue to lead them all the days of their lives. Amen."

"Thank you, Reverend Payne," Miss Stewart said. Reaching for a white scroll tied with a red ribbon, Miss Stewart called, "David Huckabee, can you come to the front, please?"

David stood up so fast he almost knocked over his desk. Most children giggled, causing David's face to turn red as he walked to the front of the class. He stood before her as if waiting for a baptism.

Miss Stewart announced, "David, you have been a

shining example of a perfect pupil, and I am proud to award this graduation certificate to you!" She handed him the scroll. David took it from her hand then hurried to the chairs, hugging his mother and shaking hands with his father. As he returned to his seat, he locked eyes with me and held up the scroll in victory.

"Next," Miss Stewart said. "I'd like to call Benny Simmons, our final graduate this year."

Benny got up out of his seat and sauntered down the aisle toward Miss Stewart.

When he reached the front, she said, "Benny..." But instead of waiting, Benny snatched the certificate from her and turned to walk back to his desk. He held up the scroll for his mother to see, smiling with every crooked tooth showing.

"Well," Miss Stewart said in a fluster. "Let's just give both boys a round of applause."

The class clapped for David and Benny until Miss Stewart quieted them by saying, "To end our ceremony today, we have refreshments courtesy of Mr. and Mrs. Huckabee. Enjoy your cookies and punch, and please remember to thank them. School is dismissed!"

CHAPTER 23

D avid was edging through the crowd on his way to me, but I kept my focus on the door. When we passed the refreshments table, Cora grabbed a cup of punch and drank it down before taking two cookies from the nearest platter. "Here, Sooze," Cora said as she handed one to me. "It's the one with coconut."

I took the washboard cookie from her, appreciative to have it. "Ask if we can have another, Cora."

But instead of asking, Cora just picked two more cookies. She wrapped them inside the fancy white paper napkin before putting them in her pocket. "Let's go," she whispered.

David closed in behind us. "Sooze, can you come to my house for a real celebration after we're finished here? Mother will be making a pot roast with potatoes. It's time you watched so you can learn how to make my favorite meal."

"David," I said as we were stepping down the stairs. "Today is Uncle Ray's funeral." I continued off the last step before turning to look at him. "Surely you're planning to come, aren't you?"

"Oh," he said, slumping his shoulders. "Is that *today*?"

I would never understand why David couldn't remember

anything important to me but expected me to remember every little thing for him. "Yes, David," I said, my tone scolding. Then turning to Cora, I took her hand and started toward the hilly dirt road leading up to the cemetery. "We're going there now, even though we'll probably be early."

"I'll be along in a bit, Sooze. I'm going to see Mother and Father again for a few minutes. This is a big day for me!" David ran back up the stairs, disappearing inside the schoolhouse.

We ate our peanut butter sandwiches and washboard cookies on the way up the hill, but before the cemetery, I heard voices.

Standing together at Grandpa Garren's headstone were Aunt Rose and Uncle Will. They were with Aunt Lissie, who was dressed in a solid black, ankle-length dress. She was wearing a black lace veil over her face, and she was holding a white handkerchief.

It's not that me and Cora were trying to be quiet, but with the new spring grass, the sound of our approaching footsteps was almost silent. Our aunts and uncle jumped when I said hello, startled by our hushed arrival.

"I'm sorry!" I said. "I didn't mean to scare you." I looked around, but other than seeing our cousins Zane and Arnold at the far end of the cemetery where the oldest stones stood, we were the only ones there. Behind Grandpa Garren's headstone was a deep, rectangular hole in the ground. "Where's Uncle Ray's coffin?"

"He'll be in a casket, Sooze. A coffin uses more wood and costs more than we got," Uncle Will explained. "And the undertaker ain't brought it yet, but he'll be along soon. Are your mama and daddy on their way?"

"No, sir," I answered, feeling awkward. "We had some trouble at home. They sent Cora and me to represent the family today."

"What kind of trouble?" Uncle Will's chest puffed out as he stretched his shoulders back, pulling his black suit jacket so tight his button barely held the front closed. In case there was a fight brewing, it was clear Uncle Will was on our side.

"It's something Mama and Daddy ought to say." I wanted to change the subject, so I moved closer, standing next to Aunt Lissie. "Are you doing all right, Aunt Lissie?"

Looking down at me through her black lace veil, Aunt Lissie took her dark gloved hand and rubbed it under my chin like she was stroking a kitten. "Fine as can be expected, Sooze. I hope your mama and daddy ain't stayin' away today because of us." Her focus was on me at first, but then it switched to Cora. "I know Arnold's been awful mad and has been saying bad things about your brother, but I want you girls to know, I don't believe any of it and never did. Henry had nothing to do with Ray's killin'. Why him and Ray were like two peas in a pod. Henry wouldn't never do nothin' to hurt his uncle, and I know it."

I wanted to run home right that minute to tell Mama and Daddy what Aunt Lissie said, but I knew it wouldn't be long before we'd be able to tell them. I knew they'd be real happy, but then I was confused again. Why was Aunt Lissie plannin' to be a witness against Henry if she believed he was innocent?

"Sooze?" The sweet voice of Thomas Kittridge came from behind me. I whirled around, and as sad a day as it was, I couldn't help but smile.

"Hi, Thomas," I said to him.

Uncle Will gave us a serious look. "Who's this, Sooze?" Without waiting for my answer, he said, "And where's David? I'd expect your intended to be beside you today, considerin' it's your uncle who's bein' buried."

"David should be here soon," I told him. Then holding out my hand in introduction, I said, "This here is Thomas Kittridge. He's Earl and Pauline's grandson. He's come here all the way from Chicago."

"Well, then…" Uncle Will's tone changed. He reached out his hand to Thomas. "I been knowing your grandfolks for as many years as I been here. Fine folks," he said, shaking hands in as friendly a shake as I'd ever seen. "Nice to meet ya, boy."

"Thank you, sir," Thomas said with a smile.

At the bottom of the hill, a group of friends and neighbors, dressed in somber-colored clothes, turned uphill, holding hands and walking side by side toward the cemetery. There must have been ten or twelve people headed toward us, including the preacher and Miss Stewart.

Before I could say more to Thomas, Cora tugged on my dress sleeve and then pointed to the black horse and wagon, making its turn up the cemetery hill. It was carrying Uncle Ray's casket.

Harold Arthur, the undertaker, was sitting tall and somber in the wagon's seat. He was dressed all in black and wore a stovepipe top hat that looked like it once belonged to Abraham Lincoln. He was slowly working the wagon up the hillside. Everybody got real quiet, but they started pushing closer together as he neared, gathering around the gravesite. When the wagon stopped, the pallbearers joined at its tailgate and started pulling Uncle Ray's pine casket off the back. Using the four black handles hammered to the sides, they carried the pine box to the heap of freshly dug dirt and waited for the preacher.

Seemed odd to me that a preacher could preach the holy word to us on Sunday, then show up to speak the invocation at graduation, and in less than half an hour, be with us at the cemetery, fixing to say final words over Uncle Ray. I never knew a preacher's role was so diverse, but I guess a man of God is expected to do whatever's needed, whenever it's needed. I couldn't help but wonder, though, how Reverend Hockney Payne could deliver God's hellfire and brimstone on Sundays while calling us all sinners and then turn around saying we're all God's children and ask the Lord to bless us and keep us. Worse yet, like at graduation, how could he ask God to bless Benny—the boy who murdered Uncle Ray? None of it made any sense to me anymore.

By the determined way the preacher walked up the hill,

with one arm swinging free and the other clutching the Bible, I sensed he was ready to ask the Lord to let Uncle Ray into heaven without any condemnation of the soul who killed him. Maybe preachers got their commands all wrong. Or maybe words just came easier to a man of God. Maybe they don't have to mean what they really mean, and maybe that makes it easier to say the words. I sure hoped so because I supposed he'd be speaking the words over Grace soon, too, and I'd sure hate to have Mama judged for letting God take what was offered to Him, even though it was offered in haste and fear. If God knows all things, He should've known it wasn't Grace Mama was offering.

Reverend Payne stood at the head of the casket, waiting as Aunt Lissie laid a single red rose on top. She stepped back, using her handkerchief to wipe her tears, and then she reached down for Arnold's hand on one side before grasping Aunt Rose's hand on the other. Without a word to the preacher, Aunt Lissie nodded, and he began.

Spring carried with it a clean scent—an almost eye-watering sweetness that was surely an offering of hope. I knew it was a sign because an odd faith washed over me while I listened to Uncle Ray's eulogy. Holding Cora's hand, I closed my eyes and listened as the sound of tears and sadness faded. Behind the darkness in my eyes, I saw a shadow of myself standing alone in a meadow. I was wearing a long, white dress, and my hair wasn't in a pony-tail anymore. It was wild and free, just like my soul felt. In the distance was a man. He walked slowly toward me, his legs brushing through the wildflowers, which sent whispers to me. His blond hair—baby-fine, clean, and longer than most men's hair—was blowing lightly in the breeze. Without a word, I knew he'd been looking for me. My heart warmed, and in a gentle flutter, my smile blossomed, and it was returned.

Sooze… My name came in a whisper. I felt joy like I'd never known.

"Hey!" Cora was squeezing my hand. In a hard but quiet

tone, she called, "Sooze!" Shaking my hand like a pup wagging its tail, she asked, "What's wrong with you?"

I opened my eyes slowly as if waking from a dream. The preacher was still talking but standing beside me now with my other hand in his was Thomas Kittridge. "Are you all right, Sooze?"

"Oh," I said, embarrassed. So as not to disturb the eulogy, I whispered, "I'm sorry. I didn't hear you callin' me." Having my hand in his caused my heart to flutter like hummingbird wings. I was sure he could feel the beats right through my fingers, so I eased my hand out of his.

"You weren't hearin' nothin'," Cora said out loud.

"Shhh..." Uncle Will had his first finger to his lips so we'd know to be quiet.

"Sorry," I mouthed to him.

Hockney Payne's voice came in clear again. "Shortly, we will spend a few moments in silence so you can each remember Ray Garren in your own special way. Perhaps during this quiet time, you can spare a special thought and offer your sympathy, your love, and your support to Ray's family, his wife Lissie, and his son, Arnold. But first, as the casket is lowered, I'd like to recite the Lord's Prayer." The preacher motioned to the pallbearers that it was time to lower Uncle Ray into his final resting place, but putting their hands on the casket caused Aunt Lissie to cry again.

As the men struggled to lower the heavy box, the preacher raised his voice and lifted his face to the sky. He spoke the Lord's Prayer, but my focus strayed until I heard, *Amen.*

The preacher reached down and took a handful of loose soil, tossing it in on top of Uncle Ray's casket. Aunt Lissie and Arnold did the same, then Aunt Rose and all the others. I fell into the rhythm and emptied my hands of dirt, too. It wasn't until I looked again at the folks gathered here that I sensed the utter despair. Not just about Uncle Ray's death, but the desperation in their lives. It was suffocating. I wanted to run from it all. I wanted to be back in the meadow. I wanted to bring Cora and Henry, and Mama and Daddy with me. And frankly, I wanted Thomas there, too.

As the last handful of dirt fell, I caught sight of David. He was running up the hill toward us. By the time he reached me, he was out of breath.

"Did I miss it?"

Looking at him, a feeling of despair settled on me, too. My gloom had never been so strong. Maybe being boyfriend and girlfriend for such a long time made the need to be together seem right. But since our engagement, my gloominess had grown. My feelings felt more serious. I knew Mama was right when she'd said, *"You gotta love him. Marriage is a commitment meant to last forever, and forever is a long time."* I looked at David on my right side and then glanced at Thomas on my left. David felt as natural as a good-fitting glove, but different feelings stirred when my eyes settled on Thomas. One of those feelings was *happy*.

"Yeah," I said to David. "You missed the services, but you can still pay your respects to Aunt Lissie."

"Naw, it's all right. Are you ready to come back with me yet? I told Mother you wanted to learn how to make my favorite roast. A wife should be able to do that, Sooze."

I'd never said I wanted to learn his mama's cooking. That was *his* thought, not mine. But it seemed my words never mattered anyway. "No, we're going home, David." My eyes hunted for Cora, spotting her talking to Arnold and Zane. "Cora?" I called. When she turned to look at me, I was waving my hand so she'd know it was time to head home, and that was when I spotted Benny across the cemetery, peeking out from behind the trunk of a shortleaf pine. He was far away, but I couldn't mistake his grease-soaked black hair. Besides, he was wearing the same red-and-black plaid lumberjack shirt with the torn pocket he'd worn to school that day.

"But I already told Mother you were coming!" David had a mad tone in his voice. "What am I supposed to tell her now?"

"Tell her you was wrong." I reached for Cora's hand when she got close enough. "Come on, Cora."

As we turned, Thomas said, "I'd offer you a ride home, but my automobile is loaded full of supplies, and I got no room for anybody to sit." Then looking me straight in the eyes, he said, "Will you be all right gettin' home by yourselves?"

"Why wouldn't they be all right?" David asked him. "They do it every day, don't they?"

"Well, I wouldn't know about that," Thomas said with a shake of his head. "And Sooze..." I stood still, wanting to hear what he had to say to me. "It was nice to see you again."

"You, too, Thomas." Then almost as an afterthought, I said, "Thank you for coming to Uncle Ray's funeral today."

When he smiled and nodded, me and Cora started down the hill. When we got to the turn in the road, I glanced back over my shoulder and saw Thomas and David standing face-to-face talking. I wondered what the two of them could possibly have in common worth discussing with one another.

_____

CHAPTER 24

W hen we got home, Doc Farrell was in the kitchen with Mama and Daddy. They were all standing at the table together with a bundled sheet.

"Hi, Doc," I said, curious about their gathering. "Have you been here all day with Mama and Daddy?"

Doc glanced at me. "No, Sooze." His hands kept working. "I been up most all night and all day treating a bushel of consumption cases in the country folk. They been too sick to come see me, so I've been making rounds going house to house. I didn't get here 'til about a half hour ago."

"Did you go to Uncle Ray's funeral?" Daddy asked us.

"Yes, sir," Cora told him. "We did just like you said."

"Daddy," I said, not being able to contain my story. "Aunt Lissie ain't blamin' Henry for Uncle Ray's death. She says she knows he didn't do it." I smiled. "Ain't that good news?"

Neither Daddy nor Mama turned to look at me, but Daddy answered anyway. "Yeah, it's real good news, Sooze."

On the windowsill, lavender candles burned bright, filling the room with a cleansing scent.

"What are you all doin'?" Cora asked as she approached the table. When she gasped, I hurried to the table, too.

There, bundled in the white sheet, was baby Grace. Her eyes were closed like she was asleep, and Doc was trying to put her stiffened little arms through the sleeves of a christening gown.

I couldn't take my eyes off her. For the first time in my life, I realized that the body was nothing more than a casing meant to hold the human spirit. Her soul was elsewhere. There was no sadness in her, no regret, no feeling at all coming from her wee body. My heart felt hollow, knowing this little body was nothing more than the shell that used to hold a sweet, innocent life.

"Why's she here on the table?" I asked, not caring who might answer, but the longer their silence, the faster unease swelled inside me. "What's wrong with all of you?"

"Sooze..." Daddy faced me. "Calm down." He put his arm around my shoulders and then pulled Cora close, too. "We got to lay out the dead so's the family can watch over the body 'til a casket is ready."

Cora was sobbing. "Why can't Uncle Will and Aunt Rose do that? Why does Mama have to do it?"

"Did you girls tell 'em about Grace while you were at the funeral?"

"Sooze only told Miss Stewart," Cora cried. "We didn't tell no one else."

I tried to explain. "I thought it should be yours and Mama's place to tell the rest of the folks, Daddy, but we used Miss Lola's switchboard again and we called Henry. I thought he needed to know."

"That was a good grown-up decision, Sooze. You did real good." Daddy leaned to kiss Mama's forehead, but her attention wasn't on him. When Doc finished, she straightened Grace's white gown as if she was the only person in the room.

"I'll stop by Will and Rose's place on my way home and tell them about Grace," Doc said. "You want me to send the undertaker out tomorrow, Emma?" When Mama shook her head, Doc turned to Daddy. "Are you planning to bury Grace here on your land or in the cemetery?"

Daddy looked out the kitchen window above where Grace lay. He pointed to our biggest white oak, fifty feet or so from the house. "We'll be burying Grace beside my mama and daddy in the family plot, just the other side of the oak. I'm trying to finish the casket today, but it looks like I won't be able to dig the grave until me and Sooze get back from Waldron tomorrow."

"Me too, Daddy." Cora's face was still wet from crying. "I'm goin' with you to see Henry tomorrow, remember?"

"I'm sorry, baby girl. Your mama needs you here with her. Sometimes the family's got to split up to get everything done."

"No! I ain't staying here all day with a dead baby!"

That brought Mama to life. She took two steps toward Cora and then slapped her face.

"You don't *never* talk such disrespect again!" Mama's eyes blared.

"Emma!" Daddy took Mama by the shoulders and turned her around. "Cora didn't mean no disrespect. She's wantin' to help Henry, that's all."

Cora's hand flew up, covering her cheek, and her eyes welled with tears again, spilling down her face. I knew Cora good enough to know she wasn't crying from the sting of the slap; she was crying from being mad.

"You can't make me stay here!" Cora shouted at Mama. Then quieter, she repeated, "You can't make me..." Her voice trailed off as she ran, her hand shielding her slapped-red cheek.

Mama pulled out of Daddy's grasp and went back to Grace's side. I knew she'd just lost a baby and knowing how much it hurt me with Grace just being my sister, I couldn't imagine how hard it was for her. But still, Mama was acting as if nothing else in the world mattered. It scared me. I wondered if Mama would ever be the same again. When

Doc Farrell picked up his black doctoring bag and headed for the door, I followed him outside.

Doc set his bag on the buckboard seat and then turned around. "Sooze, you ain't never followed me out to my hitch before. What's on your mind?"

"Doc, why ain't we buryin' Grace? Why's she layin' on the kitchen table? Until recent, there ain't been a lot of folks dying in our family, so I can't say I've had a lot of experience with death, but this just don't seem right."

"Your mama follows the old ways, Sooze. To honor the dead, they have a laying out of the body where it's washed with oil and lavender so's to cleanse away all the earthly impurities. The burial is held two days after death, but the body can't be left alone until then. Don't want no evil spirits takin' up residence, so loved ones got to stand watch. On buryin' day, the family lays their dead to rest in a casket made by their own hands. Your daddy said he was working on a box for Grace earlier today with lumber he had stored from a loblolly pine. He was measuring pieces when I got here." Doc climbed onto his wagon's seat and took the reins in his weathered hands. "I know it's hard, Sooze, but the best thing is just to let your folks do what needs doin'. Now, you be a good girl and do what your mama and daddy ask of you."

Doc slapped the reins, and I watched his horse move away, turning the wagon completely around until it was headed in the opposite direction. With another slap of the reins, the horse jerked into a gallop headed back toward Coaldale.

I was on my way back inside when Daddy came through the door.

"I got to get back out to the barn and finish the baby's casket, Sooze. I had a few extra boards leftover from when I built the table for your mama. They're sure comin' in handy now." Daddy was putting on his plowing gloves. "I need you to find me some material to line the casket with and make it something pretty so your mama will feel at ease about it. Can you do that for me?"

"Yes, Daddy. I'll see what I can find."

"Just bring it out to me." He put his head down and headed for the barn.

I went inside the house and stood in the living room, watching Cora load our big rock fireplace with wood. "I'm sorry about you not bein' able to go tomorrow, Cora," I told her. And I really was sorry. I knew how important it was to her, but I'd also come to realize how much I'd grown to depend on her being by my side.

"You tell Henry why I'm not there, Sooze." Cora kept adding more kindling sticks to the firewood in the hearth. "You tell him, all right?"

"Of course, I will. He'll understand."

Without looking at me at all, she said, "I sure hate to stay here."

"I know, but Mama needs you. Besides, we should be back by supper tomorrow." There just wasn't anything that seemed right anymore, so I turned and headed up the stairs.

On the edge of our bed, I sat thinking. We didn't have anything pretty enough for a casket lining. But then again, nothing could ever be good enough for Grace. She'd been a sweet little baby, and she deserved better than to die at just seven weeks old. I felt tears filling up inside me again, but I fought to hold them back. Crying wasn't going to do nobody any good, and I had an important job to do. I fingered the blankets on our bed. We didn't have an extra one in the whole house, and we already slept cold, so I went to the closet instead. I started looking through our dresses for favorable material. Not a one of them wasn't already worn to threads and no good to reuse. I wanted so badly to find something soft and warm and beautiful for Grace. I walked into Henry's room and started looking through his closet. I could have cut up his black-and-gray flannel shirt; it was soft and warm, but it'd surely have made Grace's casket look like a boy was put to rest in it. I pulled it out anyway and laid it on Henry's bed. It was the best, so far. I went on down the hallway and stood in Mama and Daddy's bedroom doorway, but I felt funny invading their privacy. I thought maybe if I just opened their closet door, I could look inside without disturbing anything. Then if I saw something worthwhile, I could go ask Mama. But standing there inside their closet doorway, the best I saw was Mama's red winter sweater, and not only was it ragged and worn, but what would Mama wear come wintertime?

Feeling discouraged, I wandered back to my room and sat down on the edge of the bed again. That was when I saw the gift box Cora had tossed onto the floor by the door. I walked to it and bent to pick it up, hoping I wouldn't hear the sounds of broken glass rattling inside. I shook lightly but didn't hear much of a sound inside at all. I pulled the gift card out of its envelope and read: "To my sweet Sooze, A gift to wear to our engagement party. With love always, David."

I had to have an engagement party? No one had said anything about that. I took the box back to the bed and untied the white ribbon. After pulling off the lid, my jaw dropped. Inside was a purple-velvet evening jacket, more luxurious than anything I'd ever seen. I held it up. It had a long, rounded, shawl-like collar, and its sleeves puffed out mid-arm, elbow to wrist. I slipped my arms into the jacket sleeves and then pulled it up around my shoulders. Oh, how luxurious its satin lilac lining felt! The front hung hip-length, but the back was longer, fanning out, almost touching the backside of my knees. It was more beautiful than anything from a catalog! I hugged it close, feeling the soft crush of its purple velvet beneath my hands, and then twirled, imagining myself dancing at a fancy ball.

Then like a stone caught in a grinder wheel, I stopped twirling. Quiet, I contemplated. Knowing what I had to do, I took off the jacket.

Downstairs, I got Mama's sewing scissors out of the drawer and went back upstairs. I laid the jacket flat on the bed. I cut straight up the underarm seam without stopping. I did this on both sides, snipping all the way around the shoulder seams, removing the sleeves. I left the back and oversized collar of the jacket in one long piece. It would work! I just knew it would. With black thread, I stitched up the sides. When I was done, I turned it inside out again. It was the perfect velvet lining with a rounded flare for our baby's head. On my way out to the barn, I grabbed an old baby blanket, thin and faded, from the cradle.

"Look, Daddy!" I nearly shouted. "Is this enough for the lining?"

Daddy put down his sandpaper. "Where in the world did you get that?"

"It don't matter, Daddy," I said. "Can we see if it fits?"

"Sure we can!"

Daddy was as excited about the purple velvet as I was, and that made me happier than I'd been in a long time. It felt good to contribute something important to the family.

I folded the blanket and laid it in the box, then draped the velvet over it inside the casket. Working together, we curled the collar around the upper end, so it would look like an elegant fan above Grace's head. The material was too long for the little casket, so we crumpled it up, making it look extra soft. Daddy used his hammer and nails to tack the velvet inside of the box.

"It's beautiful, Daddy," I said.

"Sooze, you did a mighty fine job for your sister's burial. Your mama will be pleased."

It was almost eight o'clock in the evening before Daddy finished. I helped him sand the lid so it would be smooth and without splinters. We didn't have any pretty handles to put on it like Uncle Ray's box had, so we just left it plain. It wasn't like baby Grace would be heavy to carry anyway.

While Daddy was busy with the finishing touches, I went to the house and made jam sandwiches for supper. I was taking his sandwich to the barn for him when I heard the pinging sound of an automobile engine coming down our road. Through the trees, I saw the headlights.

"Daddy, somebody's comin'!"

Daddy walked out into the yard and waited with me as the automobile pulled up close to the house. Uncle Will and Aunt Rose got out.

"Good to see you." Daddy walked to shake Uncle Will's hand. "I was sure hoping you'd bring Rose tonight. The girls have been a big help, but you know how it is—sometimes a grieving woman just needs another woman."

Uncle Will pointed to the backside of Aunt Rose, who was hurrying into the house. "Rose brought some extra lace and her lavender candles. She's plannin' to spell Emma. Lord knows the two of you are probably needin' some rest."

"Rose is a good woman. Emma will appreciate havin' her here."

I thought they'd both be ready to come in after Daddy showed the casket to Uncle Will, but instead, they'd each picked up a shovel and an ax.

"Sooze, you go on in the house. I need you to get some rest so's at least one of us will be fresh for Henry's jury pickin' tomorrow." Daddy turned back to Uncle Will and said, "Do you think your sedan is big enough for me and Sooze to ride with you to Waldron tomorrow? Cora ain't goin' with us. I have her stayin' here with Emma for the day."

"Well, sure it is," Uncle Will told him. "Arnold and Zane ain't goin' neither, so it will be just the five of us."

"That's good to hear, 'cause if you wasn't driving, me and Sooze would have to leave out of here at sunrise to get us there by ten o'clock."

Uncle Will put a respectful hand on Daddy's shoulder. "John, you need to buy an automobile. Using a horse and wagon in this day and age just ain't practical."

"Can't," Daddy replied as they walked away toward the family plot. "Can't afford what we got now."

Back at the house, I found Cora sitting in the rocker,

staring at the flames from the pecan logs while Aunt Rose and Mama sat in the kitchen with Grace.

"Girls," Aunt Rose called to us. "Why don't you go on upstairs and find you some clean clothes for tomorrow, then go on to bed and get some rest. This family's had some hard hours today." She smiled and came to us with a hug. "I'm stayin' with your mama, so don't you worry none."

"All right, Aunt Rose," I said. "But you'll call if Mama needs us, won't you?"

"Yes, child. You'll be the first."

I nodded, suddenly realizing how weary I was. "Come on, Cora. I'll read some from *Little Women* tonight." I climbed the stairs feeling like my tired legs were full of lead.

When Cora opened our bedroom door, she found the velvet remnants still on the bed.

"What's this?" She held up an arm piece, rubbing the material between her fingers. "I ain't never seen anything like it, Sooze."

I sat down on the bed. "Remember the gift box David gave to me?"

"The box with the white ribbon?"

I nodded and picked up the other sleeve, smoothing its short, dense pile. "This was the finest evening coat you ever did see. More beautiful than anything in a catalog or magazine."

"What happened to it?" she asked.

I pressed the soft velvet to my cheek. "Grace needed a lining for her casket," I told her. "And our baby deserves the best. We didn't have anything else I could use, Cora."

"So you cut up the jacket David gave you?"

With my chin held high, I said, "Yes, I did. I surely did."

"Tarnation, Sooze! David will be mad as a hornet." Then Cora wrapped her arms around me and hugged. "But baby Grace will sleep like a princess for eternity because of it."

CHAPTER 25

I woke to the smell of coffee and voices from downstairs. Men's voices.

"Cora," I whispered. "Wake up. I think Uncle Will is here."

Sitting up, Cora rubbed both eyes with her fists. Then, cocking an ear to listen, she said, "That ain't Uncle Will."

She was right. I threw back the quilts and tiptoed to the open bedroom doorway. Leaning out, I peeked down the stairs. Stifling a gasp, I jerked my head back inside and closed our door.

"It's Thomas and his granddad—right here in our house, Cora!" I flew across the room to the closet. I needed to get dressed and run a comb through my hair. Heaven knows I couldn't go downstairs looking like I'd just crawled out of bed!

Still sitting up, Cora had the top quilt pulled up to her chin, and she was laughing at me.

"What's so funny?"

"I ain't never seen you act this way when it's David who's come around."

"Well, there might be a lot you ain't seen from me yet, Cora Mae." Her tone made me mad as can be, but I couldn't waste time arguing when I needed to get myself downstairs.

Wearing my yellow gingham, I brushed my blonde hair, letting it part naturally on the left, and then with a yellow ribbon, I drew my hair up high above my right ear and tied a tiny bow to hold the strands in place. I put on my oxfords, then stood, smoothing down my dress. "How do I look, Cora?"

She smiled. "You look like one of them pretty catalog models."

Sometimes Cora's words warmed my heart like no other, but then other times her words cut me to the quick.

Walking with as much poise as I could muster, I descended the stairs, aware that Thomas was watching my every step. At the bottom, I said, "Oh! I didn't know we had company." I hoped God wouldn't hold that little lie against me, but in my estimation, it was worth the risk.

"Morning, Sooze." Thomas greeted me with a smile. "You sure do look pretty today."

"Thank you, Thomas." Dressed in a starched, mustard-colored shirt and wearing denim jeans sewn with grain-colored thread, he looked like he'd stepped right out of a clothing catalog himself. And surely, his blond hair was squeaky clean. I knew because his left-side part had no natural oil holding it down. Wisps strayed across what had probably been a perfectly straight line at day's beginning. "It's nice to see you."

"Granny and Granddad heard about your baby sister and insisted I bring 'em right over. Granny's in the kitchen with your mama."

"I'll go in and say hello." I walked away, knowing Thomas's eyes were following me the whole way. In the kitchen were Mama, Aunt Rose, Aunt Lissie, and Pauline Kittridge, all standing over Grace, admiring the velvet-lined casket holding her little body. She wasn't wrapped in a sheet anymore; instead, she wore a white crocheted cap with her baptismal gown. With the purple-velvet lining, she looked like an angel on her way to God, special delivery.

"Morning," I said, forcing myself not to stare at Grace. I

knew my tears would let loose if I did, and I wasn't sure I'd be able to stop them. I turned my back and hugged Mama. Her eyes were alive like she'd come back from the dead herself.

Mama laid the palm of her hand on my face and kissed my cheek. She didn't smile, but I could see in her eyes that her spirit had returned from wherever it'd gone, and she was going to be all right. I hugged her again. It seemed like it'd been a long time since I'd felt Mama's love.

"Hello, Pauline," I said and smiled. "Good morning, Aunt Rose and Aunt Lissie."

Pauline hugged me, going on and on about how sorry she was about us losing Grace, and Aunt Lissie reminded me Uncle Ray was probably waiting to carry her through heaven's gate. It somehow made me feel better, even though I'd just as soon she'd been left here on Earth for us to love and care for.

"Two good souls are gone from our family," Aunt Rose said.

With that, Mama came to me, a pleading look in her eyes. "I want you to go to Waldron, Sooze. Do whatever you got to do to make sure Henry don't join this band of dead marchin' through our family. I ain't about to lose another child to this hollow gray that's swallowin' us, but I've got to depend on you and Daddy to take my place. You got to save Henry for me, Sooze. Do you understand?"

"Yes, Mama, I understand." And I truly did. Life seems to get taken away before we even have a chance to fight for it, so I knew I needed to fight hard for Henry's life before it was too late. "Is there anything you want me to tell Henry for you today?"

"Yes. Tell him I love him," Mama said to me. "And tell him I need him here with me."

"I'll tell him, Mama. I promise."

Cora came into the kitchen, dressed in denim overalls and her old green gardening shirt.

"Land sakes, child," Mama said, looking her up and

down. "We got company. Couldn't you find a dress to wear?"

"It's summer now, Mama," Cora told her. "And you always let me wear my overalls after school is done."

"Mercy me," Mama said, looking from me to Cora. Her face told me she'd forgotten all about our school finals. "Did you pass? Are you both movin' up a grade?"

"Passing was easy, Mama," I told her.

Her focus turned to Cora. "You, too, Cora? Did you pass, too?"

"Yep!" Cora's pride turned into a smile.

Needing another look at Thomas, I walked back into the living room.

It hadn't seemed important before, but suddenly I regretted taking the brown thread out of the curtains to hem Henry's pants. They hung ragged at the seams, and I was a bit ashamed about their condition. And with no one on the couch, its threadbare spots were an embarrassment, too. I glanced at Thomas to see if he was staring at our worn furnishings, but he was looking at me. When our eyes met, he looked away as if he was in the middle of men's talk.

"Sooze, you ready?" Daddy asked.

When I nodded, he said, "Well, grab your sweater and let's get goin'."

Everyone except Mama and Pauline gathered at Uncle Will's sedan. Daddy was getting into the front seat, and Aunt Rose and Aunt Lissie were in the backseat, making room for me. Uncle Will was in the driver's seat, and Cora was at the window talking to Daddy—no doubt giving him instructions on how to take care of Henry in her absence— while Earl Kittridge stood on the other side, helping to close Aunt Rose's door.

Just as I was getting ready to slide in on my side of the automobile, Thomas took hold of my arm and gently pulled me back. In a quiet voice, he said, "I know I'm supposed to respect another man's claim, and I do," he stammered. "But Sooze, I just got to tell you...I think I'm falling for you, so if you got any doubts about the Huckabee boy, I want you to know you have other options." He put his head down and took a step back. "And I'm sorry if I've overstepped my bounds, but I needed to tell you how I'm feeling." Steadying his eyes on me again, he said, "I can't take the chance of waitin' too long."

I stood there dumbfounded. I knew how I was feeling about Thomas, but I hadn't been sure about how he was feeling about me until right that minute. Problem was, I wasn't sure how to handle the situation. I was promised to another man. I had his ring on my finger. But in all the things I was feeling, one that didn't mean a thing to me anymore was the Huckabee money. I didn't care if we never had another dime. Suddenly, everything was clear. Thoughts were so heavy inside my head that I turned, got into the automobile, and closed my door. Before I could say a word to Thomas, Uncle Will had his foot on the gas pedal, and we were headed to Waldron.

When I looked back, Thomas was still standing there like he was waiting to see if I would come back to him.

T he biggest structure in the town of Waldron was the combination courthouse and jail. It was a stand-alone two-story, built with white stones. Centered high atop it was a rounded white cupola like a watchtower, which lent a softness to the building's harsh, square cut. Two chimneys poked through its otherwise flat rooftop—one on the north side and one on the south—and a black wrought iron fence was planted around the whole building. Its white stones wore dirty-water blemishes near the ground, but it was well kept with trimmed shrubs, clean-swept steps, and near-spotless windows.

Uncle Will pulled in, then stopped the automobile near the walkway. Seemed everyone decided to quiet down as we got out of the sedan, acting just like we were late walking into a church sermon. Daddy opened one of the thick wooden entry doors, and we all filed through.

Inside the courthouse, the dark wood floors and wood railings stung with a varnish scent, and even though sunlight poured through the high windows giving a shine to the wood, overhead hanging lights were still lit.

"Which way, Daddy?"

"Judge Poe is handlin' the trial. Let's just start looking at these doors until we find the right one."

All in agreement, we started down the wide hallway. The first few doors had a top half made of glass, and on the windows were gold-painted letters spelling out each office: *PBX Operator*, *Court Clerk*, *File Clerk*, and *Records*. As we walked farther down the hall, the doors were solid wood with gold-colored nameplates: *Jury Room*, *Bailiff*, and *Depositions*, until we came to two sets of double doors, one on each side of the building. We stopped and stood in front of *Courtroom 1* with *Courtroom 2* behind us.

Daddy pulled open one of the double doors leading to Courtroom 1. When we poked our heads in, I spotted Cordie right away. He was standing at a table, shuffling through papers with his back to us. Next to him stood an older man dressed in a dark suit. No one else was in the big room.

"Cordie!" I said, excited to see him. When both men turned to look at us, I hurried toward him.

"Hi, Sooze," Cordie greeted, waving us in.

I stopped at a wooden, spindle-legged railing separating me from Cordie. "Is this where we're supposed to be?"

Cordie nodded. When Daddy caught up, he reached over the railing to shake hands with the men. Speaking to the older man, Cordie said, "This is Henry's family." Gesturing toward me, he said, "This is Sooze, Henry's sister—she's the one I told you about who came to the sawmill to find me. She's our star witness." Pointing to Daddy, he said, "And this is Henry's father, John Williams." Then Cordie held out a hand indicating the man beside him and said, "This is Virgil Deets, my boss and the owner of the law firm where my license hangs. He'll be helping me with Henry's case since this is my first trial."

"How do you do," Daddy said, shaking hands with the man.

Virgil Deets had black hair peppered with gray—healthy and shiny. It was cut short with a wavy flip curving up from his front hairline. By the tanned color of his skin, folks might have thought he'd been working out in the sun all day, every day, but after taking in the rest of him, I doubted he'd ever spent time outdoors unless it was for pleasure. His potbelly rounded out his tailored shirtfront, so he was eating better than most, too. Looking into his olive-green eyes, I felt uneasy—were they the eyes of a man we could trust? It was hard to tell who was on our side anymore.

"And who are these other folks?" Mr. Deets asked, looking at the pack standing behind us.

Daddy turned, ready to introduce our family. "This is our kin—Will and his wife, Rose." Then Daddy motioned to Aunt Lissie. "And this is Lissie, Henry's aunt and also the wife of Ray Garren, the man Henry's been accused of killin'." Daddy said it as if the world already knew it, and Aunt Lissie just nodded.

"Well," Mr. Deets said. "Pleased to meet you. All of you." Then he pointed to a side door where a pudgy man in a gray suit entered the courtroom. "Mrs. Garren," he said to Aunt Lissie, "I believe you're supposed to be on the other side with Dellar Pigg, the prosecuting attorney."

When Mr. Pigg heard his name, his head snapped up, and with brown eyes singing loud with confidence, he said, "Hello, Virgil. I'm surprised to see you here in Waldron again. Ain't Fort Smith got enough criminals to keep you busy?"

"We got plenty to keep us busy, Dellar," Mr. Deets told him. Then pointing to Cordie, he said, "This is my new law graduate, Cordie Beegle. He's a real go-getter! He represents

Henry Williams, but I came along to show the boy the ropes, you know?"

"Sure, sure," Mr. Pigg said as he set down his black leather case on the tabletop and stepped across the aisle to shake hands with Cordie. "Nice to meet you, young man."

Seemed funny how everyone was so happy and friendly to one another when the whole assemblage was about Henry being accused of murdering our Uncle Ray, who was already dead and buried. I guess it was better than having everyone clawing at each other, though.

"Is this where we're supposed to be, Cordie?" I asked again, watching as Aunt Lissie followed the prosecuting lawyer back to his table.

"Yes. The bailiff will bring the jury folks in from over there." Cordie pointed to a closed door behind the judge's big, polished mahogany desk. "The first twelve folks will sit in the jury box, and then the rest will sit in the other section behind Mr. Pigg, where they'll wait to see if their names are called as replacement jurors." Then motioning toward the chairs behind us, he said, "You'll want to sit in the first row to be near Henry, and so the jury can see you. It's important they know that Henry has support."

"All right," Daddy told him. "What about Will and Rose? Are they supposed to sit with Lissie or with us?" He pointed to Aunt Lissie, who stood all by herself, talking to Mr. Pigg.

"I'd prefer to have Henry's family sitting here on our side."

Daddy turned to Uncle Will and Aunt Rose. "What do you think, Will? Do you think you two can sit here next to Sooze and me?"

Aunt Rose took hold of Uncle Will's hand. In a low voice, she said, "Will, I sure hate to leave Lissie alone on a day like this. Do you think I can sit with her?"

"You go on," Uncle Will told her, nodding toward Aunt Lissie. "I'll sit here across the aisle from you so's you can be with Lissie, and I can be a support for Henry. That's fair, don't you think, John?"

"Yeah, sure," Daddy told him. "That's fair."

We picked our seats and sat down just as a younger man with dusky-brown hair holding a camera came through the double doors. He sat in the middle of a bench not more than six rows behind us.

"Hey," he called to us. "Are you kin to Henry Williams, the kid on trial?"

I looked back at him and nodded as Virgil Deets said, "Kenny, you know better than to engage my clients or their kin in conversation without my approval, now don't you?"

The young man sat back in his chair. "Yes, sir, Mr. Deets," he groaned. "How come you're here all the way from Fort Smith anyway?" Then nodding toward Cordie, he said, "And who's the sidekick?"

"This is Cordie Beegle," Mr. Deets explained. "That's C-o-r-d-i-e, then B-double-e-g-l-e. Make sure you spell his name right. You know how I hate it when your newspaper gets the facts wrong about my firm."

The young man had a notepad and a pencil in his hands, and he was writing. "Oh, I'll get it right."

I leaned close to Daddy's ear and whispered, "Do you think we'll get our pictures in the newspaper?"

"Sure hope not," Daddy whispered back. "This ain't somethin' I'm wantin' the whole county to know about, and newspapers got a way of telling a story all backward. I heard an innocent man up north was tried and convicted in the newspaper before the jury ever took a seat."

CHAPTER 26

A door on our side of the courtroom opened, and a man with black hair wearing a tan law uniform ushered Henry through the door—his hands locked together in handcuffs. He had on the cream-colored shirt and brown trousers, but they weren't ironed anymore. In fact, he'd probably slept in his clothes by the look of them.

"Henry!" I slid one leg, then the other, over the top of the railing that separated us, and I had my arms around him in a flash.

"Get back!"

It took a minute before I realized the lawman was yelling at me.

"Sooze!" Cordie called out before grabbing hold of my arm and pulling me toward him. "You can't make contact with Henry while he's in custody."

My face flushed with embarrassment. "I'm sorry. I didn't know."

Henry grinned at me. "Well, how would you know, Sooze? It ain't like you visit prisoners every day." Then he greeted Daddy as I swung my legs back over the balustrade. "I sure hated to hear about baby Grace, Daddy. How's

Mama?" His eyes searched the courtroom before he said, "And where's Cora? Is she all right?"

"Hello, son." Daddy nodded to Henry. "Your mama's doing as good as can be expected, what with losin' a baby and all. I asked Cora to stay with her today."

"Cora wanted to come real bad, Henry," I told him. "And Mama said to tell you she loves you, and she wants you to know she needs you home with her."

"That's the plan, Sooze. You tell Mama that's just my plan. And tell her I'm goin' to make things right again, too." Henry's face was serious. "You got that, Sooze? You tell her for me."

"I'll tell her, Henry. I promise I will."

Henry nodded, then sat down in front of me right between Mr. Deets and Cordie. I leaned forward to talk to him across the railing, but just as I did, the door to the jury room opened.

Cordie leaned his head between ours, whispering, "That's the bailiff." He was pointing to the lead man. The bailiff wore the same tan uniform Henry's guard wore, but his hair was as red as a cock's comb. "He'll bring the jurymen in next, and when it comes time for the judge to take the bench, he will be the one to announce him."

The lawman walked into the courtroom, followed by a line of men. One by one they filed in, filling the empty seats in the polished mahogany jury box on the other side of Mr. Pigg. When all the jury seats filled up, it left ten more men standing in line. Moving in front of them as if he was the leader, the bailiff directed the overflow to seats in the courtroom directly behind Aunt Lissie. With Mr. Pigg at the lawyer table near the jury box, it was easy for him to give a smile to the seated jury. It aggravated me when they smiled back. I never saw any of them smile at Cordie or Mr. Deets or Henry. Cordie said the jurymen were impartial citizens ready to hear the whole story. He said they'd decide who was telling the truth and who wasn't. But if Cordie was right, and they were truly impartial, why weren't any of them smiling at anyone on *our* side of the room?

The bailiff moved to stand in front of the judge's desk, and then facing the courtroom, he announced, "All rise for Judge Poe!"

Everyone in the room stood up while a middle-aged bald man, dressed in a long, black robe, entered the courtroom through a door marked *Judge's Chamber*. Without looking up at any of us, he walked behind a wooden chair with a heavy wood railing and sat down behind a solid mahogany desk. Cordie had called it a bench.

The judge barked, "Be seated!" But it wasn't until everybody sat that his gaze drifted to Henry. His hard blue eyes stared through a half squint at my brother as if a guilty verdict was already on his mind.

"Mr. Deets, who do you have seated next to you as your co-counsel? I don't recognize him as anyone I've seen in my court before."

Virgil Deets stood and reached across Henry, motioning for Cordie to stand up. "This is Cordie Beegle, Your Honor." Mr. Deets straightened up, sucking in his gut to fasten the middle button on his brown suit coat. "He's a bright young lawyer just out of Mills Law College." After a throat clearing, he said, "I'm here as *his* co-counsel today. This is Mr. Beegle's first courtroom appearance."

"Very well," Judge Poe grumbled, his voice deep and gravelly and humdrum. "I trust Mr. Beegle has been counseled on the rules of my court? This isn't a classroom, and as you know, Mr. Deets, I am not a patient man with young, inexperienced law students."

"Your Honor," Cordie spoke up as if he wasn't a bit afraid of the black-robed man. "I know the rules of your court, and with all due respect, I am not a student anymore. I am a full-fledged attorney, licensed by the state of Arkansas, and I do not expect any special treatment by this court."

"Well, that's good," Judge Poe said, straightening

himself in his chair. "Because I do not intend to give you any." Turning his attention to the other table, he said, "Good morning, Mr. Pigg. Are you ready to begin today's jury selection?"

"Yes, Judge, the prosecution is ready."

"Well, get on with it then."

I had never been in a courtroom before, so I wasn't sure what I expected to see, but jury picking was surely an odd ritual. The twelve men sitting in the mahogany box were each dressed in their everyday clothes—some in field-planting overalls, some in store-clerking clothes, while others wore their Sunday best. But one man with chestnut-colored hair was different from the others. He sat in a front row jury seat and was dressed in an expensive, speckled gray, double-breasted suit with broad lapels. His eyes focused on Henry while his hands held the short brim of a gray hat, turning it round and round. I suspected the scent of sweet, spicy-smelling cloves was his cologne. With bright brown, puppy-dog eyes, he broke his focus to study each person in the courtroom as if taking stock. If I'd had a mind to bet, I'd have wagered he had money in the bank and was college educated.

"Mr. Beau Cassidy," Mr. Pigg called. He stood in front of the jury box facing the man with chestnut-colored hair. "How do you feel about an eighteen-year-old bein' tried for murder?"

Still turning his hat round and round, Mr. Cassidy eyed Mr. Pigg. "Same as I'd feel about an eighty-year-old bein' accused of murder, I suppose."

"What I mean, sir, is do you believe a young man still in school is *capable* of murder?"

"I think any man is capable of murder, dependin' on the situation."

"Are you sayin' there are some killings you'd approve of?"

"I'll tell you the truth—I don't condone the crime, but I am slow to condemn the man, having witnessed for myself the length a man must go to survive in today's hard world."

"So, in plain language, Mr. Cassidy," Mr. Pigg's voice had a frustrated grumble to it as he pointed straight to Henry. "Would you, or would you not, have trouble handing out a guilty verdict on this man-murderin' boy?"

"Objection, Your Honor!" Cordie was on his feet, talking loudly. "This juror is not on trial, and my client has not been proven guilty! Mr. Pigg is making it sound like a conviction has already been made."

Judge Poe hit a wooden mallet against his desk—once, twice, three times—because Mr. Pigg was shouting back just as loud at Cordie. "Gentlemen! Settle down! We aren't even to trial yet, and you're already at each other's throat." When the shouting stopped, Judge Poe said, "Now, Mr. Pigg, I agree with the young Mr. Beegle. Your questioning has a tone insinuating the defendant has already been tried and convicted, and you and I both know that won't happen 'til next week. You're gettin' way ahead of yourself."

"Your Honor!" Cordie shouted again. "Who's to say my client will be convicted next week? You're making the same kind of statements Mr. Pigg is making!"

I wasn't sure whether it was the yelling giving me a headache or whether it was the accusing, but my head was suddenly pounding. Was all that shouting and arguing going to happen again when it came time for me to tell my story to the jury? I felt vomit rising in my throat. I jumped up, running down the aisle, then pushed out through the double doors. Once I was outside in the long hallway, I spotted a door with a hanging sign above it that read, *Women*. I ran to it and pushed open the door. I barely made it to the white porcelain commode before throwing up.

"Sooze?" I could hear Daddy's voice outside the door. "Sooze, are you all right?"

I stood up and walked to the sink. "Just a minute, Daddy," I called. I turned the four-pronged faucet handle and leaned down, sucking water into my mouth. I swished and spit. My head was beating like a drum.

I opened the door to find Daddy standing right there. His scrunched eyebrows squeezed his worry to the middle of his face. "Sooze, you're not looking so good. What's wrong with you?"

"I think all that shouting and yelling gave me a sick headache." I stood, using my fingers to comb my hair back into a ponytail before realizing I didn't have a rubber band. "Daddy, what if they all start yellin' at each other when it's my turn to tell the story? What if they start rattlin' me like they're doing in there to each other right now? What am I supposed to do?"

Before Daddy could answer, a lady in her late thirties wearing a cornflower-blue dress came hurrying toward us. Her square-heeled black shoes clacked against the wood floors.

"Hello," she said. Her honey-brown hair, which she'd curled into a loose topknot, bounced as she came to a standstill in front of us. "Are you all right, sweet thing? I saw you runnin' to the ladies' room, and you're white as a bedsheet."

"Yes," I said. "Thank you. I've got a bad headache, that's all."

The lady studied Daddy before saying, "I work in the file department. Why don't you let me take this girl to my office—I've got a bottle of cola and some aspirin at my desk. I think it might help her feel better." She looked at me. "Will it be okay with you?" Before I could answer, she patted my back and said, "I'll bet I have a rubber band for your pretty blonde hair, too."

"Will it be all right if I go, Daddy?"

"Yeah, sure, Sooze," Daddy said, nodding. By the frown on his face, I could tell he was considering what I'd said. "You come back soon as you're feelin' better, though, all right?"

"Yes, sir," I promised. I watched Daddy turn and walk back to the courtroom.

"Come on, now," the lady said, taking my arm. She led me down the hallway toward the front of the building, stopping when we came to a door marked *File Clerk* whose top half was glass. Inside was a wall of cabinets and a scratched-up hardwood desk with a typewriter. She pulled out her chair and sat, then opened the bottom desk drawer. I saw two bottles—one filled with pink liquid and the other with white pills—then I saw a brown paper lunch bag. Beside her black purse was the cola. She took the aspirin bottle and poured two white tablets into my hand.

When she picked up the bottle of cola, I said, "Oh, no, ma'am." I backed away. "That's your lunch. I don't want to be takin' your drink."

"Nonsense!" the lady said. "And please, call me Trudy." She walked a few steps to a steel opener bolted to the wall above a trashcan. She tilted the contoured bottle, leveraging the metal cap inside the jaws of the opener, popping off the cap. It fell with a *clink* into the can below. She handed me the cola. "Have a seat, dear, and drink up. My mama gets real bad headaches, and this seems to help her. Maybe it'll help you, too."

"Thank you," I said. Several ladder-backed chairs lined the wall, so I sat down with the drink. We rarely had money for treats, so this would have been a nice luxury had my head not been pounding. I tipped the bottle back and sipped the sweet, brown liquid. Its syrupy-sweet fizz was bubbling inside my mouth when I glanced through the window in Trudy's door. A woman who looked a lot like Miss Simmons was hurrying down the courthouse hall. Even though her wide-brimmed hat mostly hid her face, I was sure it was her. I stood up to get a better look, but she passed by and was gone too quickly. I sat back down. Maybe this headache was making me see things.

Trudy typed paper after paper as if the comings and goings of people in the courthouse mattered little to none at all.

With the rhythmic *click-click-clack* of the typewriter keys and the sweetness of my cola, I began feeling better. I stood up and walked to Trudy's desk. "Thank you for your hospitality, but I should be gettin' back to the courtroom now." I handed her my empty bottle.

"Oh, sugar, you're welcome." Trudy stood up then opened a thin desk drawer, pulling out a green rubber band. She handed it to me with a smile. "For your ponytail."

"Thank you." I gathered my hair, wrapped the rubber band around it, and opened the office door. "You've been mighty kind."

Trudy smiled and winked without ever picking up her fingertips off the typewriter keys.

In the hallway, the juror named Beau Cassidy walked past me with his head down. He was headed for the front door.

When I got back to the courtroom, Cordie was standing at his lawyering table, addressing Judge Poe. Reading from an open book cradled in his hands, he said, "According to Arkansas Code, qualifications of jurors prescribed by statute clearly state—and I quote, Your Honor:

'The jury commission shall place on the jury roll and in the jury box the names of all male citizens of the county who are generally reputed to be honest and intelligent men, and who are esteemed in the community for their integrity, good character, and sound judgment, but no man shall be selected who is under twenty-one or over sixty-five years of age or, who is a habitual drunkard, or who, being afflicted with any permanent disease or physical weakness is unfit to discharge the duties of a juror, or who cannot read English, or who has ever been convicted of any offense involving moral turpitude'."

Cordie slammed the book shut. "*Moral turpitude!*" he shouted. "Judge, it is well-known that this replacement juror has a close relationship with a Coaldale woman whose conduct is regarded as immoral, proving moral turpitude!"

Pointing at the man, Cordie demanded, "You *must* dismiss this new juror!"

"Judge," Mr. Pigg objected. "To quote Mr. Beegle's own reading of the statutes, any man 'who has ever been *convicted*' of moral turpitude shall not be considered fit to serve as a juror. Need I remind the defense that this replacement juror has never been *convicted* of anything?"

"Mr. Pigg has a lawful objection, Mr. Beegle," Judge Poe said. "Unless you have a *valid* complaint, this juror shall remain on the jury."

Cordie leaned across Henry and was whispering fast to Mr. Deets.

"You okay, Sooze?" Henry had turned around to talk to me. I nodded as Mr. Deets shushed him.

The replacement juror was a fiftyish man, wearing a tweed suit like traveling salesmen wore. His face showed a few wrinkles, but none that smacked of hard work. He had one walleye which turned outward from his nose, and his other eye had a sad and lonely look to it. Even though seated, I could tell his posture was bent as if he'd driven a wagon too many miles.

Cordie straightened up tall after conversing with Mr. Deets. Both him and Mr. Pigg stood still and quiet as Judge Poe talked in low tones to the bailiff.

Banging his gavel, Judge Poe announced, "Jury selection has concluded." Swiveling his chair to face the jury box, he said, "Court will resume at ten o'clock Monday morning. All twelve jurors, and the two alternate jurors, should be here no later than nine o'clock Monday." He again banged his gavel against his desktop. "Jury is dismissed today."

When the judge stood, the bailiff bellowed, "All rise!"

We all stood and watched the judge leave the courtroom.

The bustle of jurors, led out by the bailiff, made me forget they'd be taking Henry away, too. He was up out of his chair before I could say my goodbyes.

Daddy called, "We'll be back Monday morning, Henry. Won't be long now, son."

But the lawman had already pushed Henry through the exit door.

"How do you think it went today, Cordie?" Daddy asked.

"To be honest, Mr. Williams," Cordie said as he laid his brown leather satchel—worn and aged as if it'd been handed down a hundred times already—on the tabletop. "There are two or three jurors that concern us." He nodded to Virgil Deets, who never raised his eyes to either of us. "Especially the replacement juror. How well do you know that man?"

"Not at all," Daddy answered. "But then I don't run in the same circles as Miss Simmons and her clientele. Only reason I was able to tell you about him at all is 'cause I recognize his walleye as one belongin' to a man who follows Paulette Simmons around town like a wandering dog lookin' for his next meal."

"Well, I thank you for giving me the information today, even though I couldn't make it work for us. I sure hated to lose that Cassidy fellow." Cordie had his head down, straightening his loose papers. "We'll do our best to deal with the adversity of having her *friends* on the jury by convincing them to do the right thing or not let the trial get that far."

Across the aisle, Mr. Pigg opened a polished, black leather case and packed a small stack of papers and pencils inside. He had a thin, green book he slid inside, too, but his other book was thick—too big to fit inside. He placed it in the crook of his left elbow and pulled it up close to his suit jacket. Turning around, he said to Aunt Lissie, "Be here Monday morning. You'll be taking the witness stand by midday."

"That was pretty slick, Dellar," Virgil Deets interrupted, talking to Mr. Pigg as he was leaving his lawyering table. "Gettin' that Drew Boyle fellow seated as a replacement juror for your side. Who you got secretly working jury selection?"

Cordie's eyes got big and were round as saucers—they darted back and forth between Mr. Pigg and Mr. Deets.

"Now you know better than that, Virgil," Mr. Pigg said with a grin. "I'm the most honest lawyer you'll ever know!"

"Ain't no such thing," Mr. Deets said, then pointing to Cordie, he added, "Even my new, inexperienced lawyer knows better."

Smiling, Mr. Pigg picked up his black leather case. "See you Monday morning, boys." He walked down the aisle and out the door without another word.

Turning to Mr. Deets with a look of disbelief, Cordie said, "So you think he manipulated jury selection? Is that the reason he excused himself for five minutes? Why didn't you object?"

"Sure do," Mr. Deets confirmed. "Dellar Pigg is a respected attorney in Scott County, and most folks will believe him without battin' an eye. Objecting any more than you did would have only hurt your case with the judge and jury because you have no way to prove any wrongdoing. But you managed to put a doubt in the minds of the other jurors when you brought up the issue of moral turpitude, and that's all you can do for now. We'll have to work around it."

"Is that why Paulette Simmons was here this morning?" I asked them.

"Here?" Daddy asked. "In the courthouse?"

"Yes, sir," I said. "At least, I think it was her."

"That's the problem, young lady," Virgil Deets said. "In a court of law, *thinkin'* ain't good enough." He squeezed between Cordie's chair and the balustrade separating us, then he walked down the aisle and out the door.

CHAPTER 27

It was after dark before we got home. I headed for the house while Daddy discussed tomorrow's funeral plans with Uncle Will.

The flame of the lavender candle in the kitchen window lighted the shadow of Pauline Kittridge. She had her head down in prayer, still holding vigil over baby Grace. I was quiet when I opened the door. Mama was asleep in the armchair near the fireplace. In her hand was a white cotton gown belonging to Grace. She had a peaceful face, so I tiptoed inside and quietly stole up the stairs.

Opening my bedroom door, I saw Cora sitting cross-legged on our bed. She had the book *Little Women* open on her lap.

"Which part are you reading?" I asked.

Surprised, Cora jerked her head up to see me, then said, "'Castles in the Air.' Laurie's layin' in a hammock, and it says the hot weather has made him 'indolent'...what's *indolent*, Sooze?"

"It means lazy," I told her. I was glad she cared enough to ask.

Cora closed the book and slid off the bed. "How's Henry? How did jury pickin' go? Did he ask about me?"

"Yeah, Henry asked about you right off. He was worried

'cause you weren't there today, but Daddy explained why you had to stay home. I told him you wanted to be there with him."

"Is he all right?"

"They had him in handcuffs, Cora, and they won't let us touch him, but other than that, he looks all right."

I recounted the whole day, and even after Daddy came into the house, I didn't budge from my storytelling spot on the bed. I couldn't bear to go downstairs another night with a dead baby, even if it was Grace. Hushed voices lasted only a minute before we saw Daddy in the hallway carrying Mama, still sound asleep, into their bedroom. He didn't come out again, so Cora and me curled up in our bed and talked until we fell asleep.

At sunup, I woke to the smell of coffee and voices downstairs. Throwing back the cover, I got out of bed and went to peek over the stair railing. Daddy was talking to Earl Kittridge, but I didn't see anyone else or hear any other voices, certainly no one who sounded like Thomas. Maybe Earl had driven himself here to pick up Pauline. Maybe Thomas didn't want to come after I run out on him like I did. Or maybe folks were growing tired of all the problems God had handed us.

The navy blue dress I'd worn to Uncle Ray's funeral was the only proper funeral dress I owned, but I sure hated to wear it again. Being a baby's funeral, I thought maybe I could wear something with more color and still have it be respectable, but after looking through my closet again, I realized no dress was worthy of wearing to a funeral for Grace anyway, so I slipped the navy blue dress on over my head.

"Cora, wake up," I said quietly while nudging her shoulder. "Soon as I get my shoes on, I'm going downstairs." I sat on the edge of the bed, pulled my white socks onto my feet, and then pushed them into my oxfords. By the time I finished brushing my hair, she had started to stir, so I headed for the stairs.

"Good morning," I said, stepping into the living room.

"Mornin', Sooze," Daddy said. He was standing next to Earl and Pauline Kittridge.

"Mornin'," Pauline greeted. She looked plumb worn out after being here all night. "Your mama's with the baby. You should be gettin' in there to spell her so's she can get ready for the day."

"Yes, ma'am," I told her as I started for the kitchen.

Mama was standing over Grace. In a state of trance, she stared out the window. She held a cup of steaming coffee in her hands. I walked straight to the stove and poured myself half a cup, then opened the icebox, pulling out the cream pitcher. I poured until my cup was full and then stirred. "Are you doing all right, Mama?"

Startled, Mama sloshed a few drops of hot coffee onto her hand. "Oh, Sooze," she said, brushing her hand down her flowered apron to dry it. "I didn't hear you come in. Where's Cora?"

"She's just wakin' up." I sipped my coffee near the kitchen's back door, not wanting to get anywhere near the table where baby Grace lay in state. The smell of death had overtaken the calming scent of lavender candles. "Should I stay here with Grace while you get washed up and dressed, Mama?"

She nodded and then left the room. I stood there alone, staring at the casket from across the room. I would sure be glad when this was over and done.

By the time Mama came back downstairs in her black dress, folks had started arriving for the burial services. Automobiles were pulling up in front of our house like we lived on the main street of a busy town. I guess folks felt more kindly toward a baby's soul.

Looking out through the kitchen window, I spotted Reverend Payne, Miss Stewart, Doc Farrell, the whole Huckabee family, Aunt Rose and Aunt Lissie, and Uncle Will was trailing behind them, spurring Zane and Arnold along after their mothers. They were pushing and shoving each other like cousins do. I saw Sheriff Wingate and his wife, Willa, with Miss Lola and Miss Vera. It seemed everyone had dressed in their Sunday best for Grace. Then I saw Thomas. He had on his blue jeans and was wearing a long-sleeved white shirt with a dark-colored tie. He was standing beside his daddy and granddad when Pauline stepped outside to greet folks.

"Hi, Sooze." David surprised me, coming in through the kitchen doorway. "We brought flowers for the grave, but I saved a rose for you." He handed me a long-stemmed red rose.

Instinctively, I held it to my nose and sniffed its sweet fragrance. "It's beautiful, David. Thank you. And thank you for coming today." I slipped the long stem of the flower through the blue belt around my waist.

"Hey!" David said, pointing to the open casket. "That lining looks just like the velvet jacket I gave you."

"It *is* the jacket you gave me, David."

"What do you mean?" David's face furled into an angry squint. "Do you mean to tell me you're *buryin'* it with the baby?"

"It makes her look like an angel already, don't it?"

"Well, you can't do that, Sooze! That jacket cost a lot of money, and I already bragged to Mother about it!"

"I'm sorry, David," I said. "I truly am, but I did what I had to do. We needed to send baby Grace to heaven with the best we had, and I'd like to think you were part of that."

"Not by my choice, I wasn't!" David was shouting. He walked to the table. "Help me pull this jacket out of the casket."

"Don't you dare touch that!" I ran to stand between him and Grace. "You gave that jacket to me as a gift, so it's mine to do with as I please!" I felt as if all the goodness had gone out of the world. "Besides, I had to cut it up so's it'd fit."

Before more words were thrown, Daddy and Uncle Will came into the kitchen, paying no attention to us at all. At the table, Daddy picked up the casket lid and handed it to

David, asking him to carry it to the gravesite. Then Daddy and Uncle Will picked up Grace's pine box and started out of the house with it.

With the lid tucked under one arm like a load of schoolbooks, David reached out with his other and grabbed my hand, jerking me toward him. "We ain't done talking about this yet." His whisper was harsh. "But I got enough class not to make a scene about it today." Pulling me into a stumble after him, we followed Grace to her final resting place beneath the white oak.

As we approached, I loosed myself from David's hand, then moved to the front, squeezing in beside Cora, Mama, and Daddy. Grace's open casket lay before us. It was barely tilted on the mounded dirt from the hole dug by Daddy and Uncle Will.

David laid down the lid and stepped back, wedging himself between me and his mother who, though nary a word had been spoken yet, already had a handkerchief held to her crying eyes. I glanced the other way, looking at Mama to see if she was crying, too, but found her standing tall, staring straight ahead, showing remarkable strength. It filled me with pride.

"Do you need a handkerchief for cryin' into?" David was holding a hankie he'd pulled out of his suit jacket pocket.

I shook my head. "I'd just be cryin' tears for us, and there's no sense in that." David gave a perplexed look, staring at me like I was an oddity. "Grace is already headed for Heaven, David, and our tears won't help her on her way." When Mama overheard, she turned and nodded to me and then reached past Cora, taking my hand and squeezing it tight before letting go.

"It still makes me sad," Cora whispered.

"I'm sad, too, Cora," I whispered back. "I miss our baby so much I feel like I can't breathe, but it won't help nobody for us to cry and carry on. We got to have strength today to help Mama hold up."

Cora's head lowered when the preacher started talking.

It all sounded to me like a repeat of the sermon over Uncle Ray—so much so, in fact, the words became a muddled jumble of verse.

It wasn't until Thomas stepped up to stand beside the preacher that I snapped back. He held a guitar.

"Thomas Kittridge has offered to sing and play for these services today," Reverend Payne announced. "Thomas, which hymn have you chosen?"

"Amazing Grace," Thomas answered. The reverend nodded and stepped back, leaving room for him to slip his guitar's red-and-brown shoulder strap over his head. Talk about music had never come up in our conversations, so I was taken aback by this surprise.

With strumming fingers, Thomas opened his mouth in song, and out came the voice of an angel. The gathering was silent, except for sniffles and throat clearings.

When the song ended, Reverend Payne said, "Thank you, Thomas." Then he faced the gathering again. "Please bow your heads and join me in a final prayer."

In silence, all heads bowed.

"Dear Father, we send this baby to you today so she may live in love and comfort within Your Great Kingdom. Her mother, father, and sisters—and her brother, too, who could not be here with us today—and all the others who have gathered, ask that you cradle little Grace in the palm of Your hand. Lord, we also ask You to guide and lead this family through these troubled times. Speak to their hearts. Make them sensitive to Your promptings and what is happening around them. Let them surrender fully to You and teach them to trust You in all things. Amen."

"Amen," we said in unison.

Daddy stepped up and put the lid on Grace's casket, and then Uncle Will nailed it shut. When Mama's throat gave a stammer, I took her hand in mine, but I knew I couldn't look at her or I'd start bawling myself. I just squeezed and held on tight. Daddy and Uncle Will slid the little casket gently into the hole dug for it, and when Daddy stood up again, he had a handful of soil. He tossed it in on top of the closed casket and then reached out for Mama. She stepped forward then kneeled beside the grave. With both hands on the ground, she balled up her fists in the loose dirt and squeezed hard. After a minute, she tossed her handfuls in and then rose off her knees. She put her arms around Daddy's waist while Cora and me picked up a handful of dirt. We tossed it in, then almost as an afterthought, I dropped in my red rose.

One by one, folks tossed handfuls of soil into the grave, covering Grace's casket. When everyone was finished, Uncle Will and Thomas took the spades and started shoveling soil into the grave until it mounded. Using the back of his shovel, Thomas patted the loose dirt and then laid the Huckabee flowers on top of the grave.

I walked to Thomas.

"Thank you for everything you did for my family today," I said. "Your song was like a last lullaby. I felt Grace was floating up to Heaven on a ribbon of song."

"Before my mama died," Thomas said, "she used to say I had a gift from God, but I always felt it was a gift from her. She had a beautiful voice. Sometimes, I think it's what I miss most about her."

"Hey there!" David reached out to Thomas for a handshake.

"Hello again," Thomas said, his voice quiet.

With the mourners gathering at the house, I knew I should go help Mama and Daddy, but I wanted to stay with Thomas. I had things to say, and I was trying to find the right words, but my breath was stifled when David pushed in behind me and slipped his arms around my waist.

All I found myself saying was, "I should be tending to our guests." I pulled free of him, but then I squatted at Grace's grave before leaving. Laying my hand atop the freshly dug soil, I whispered, "Bye, bye, baby. We will always love you."

CHAPTER 28

With her white crocheted shawl wrapped around her shoulders, Mama sat next to me in the front row of the courtroom. She held my hand, squeezing tight to hide her nervous tremble.

"What's taking your daddy so long?"

"He'll be back soon, Mama." I patted her hand just like she'd done mine a hundred times when I'd needed reassurance. "They got Henry locked away upstairs, and Daddy said he'd have to be cleared to see him. I expect the law is probably looking over the clean clothes we brought Henry, too, to make sure we didn't hide any weapons inside."

Cora leaned forward, looking at me from across Mama's lap. "Why would they think we was bringing him weapons when we already spent most all our money to buy him a lawyer? Any dumbbell should know we wouldn't throw our money away if we was just gonna break him out of jail!"

Kenny, the newspaperman who'd gotten a warning from Mr. Deets on Friday, sputtered a laugh from behind us. Leaning forward, he asked, "What's your name, little girl?"

Cora turned, and with one leg curled up under her, she leaned sideways over the chair back. "My name's Cora— Cora Mae Williams. What's yours?"

"I'm Kenny Barton from *The Advanced Reporter*." He reached out his hand to Cora. "Pleased to meet you."

When Cora reached back, I cautioned her. "Don't be hobnobbing with a newspaperman. They ain't always on our side, and their words can cut a man's throat faster than a butcher knife."

Kenny sat back in his seat. "Aww, now, that just ain't fair! Newspapermen are strictly impartial. We just report the facts."

"Then the facts you need to start reportin' are about how my brother is innocent and how that lyin', cheatin' Benny Simmons tricked him into being accused of murder," I said.

"Is that a fact?" Kenny seemed especially interested, but when Cordie Beegle and Virgil Deets came through the side door together, everybody stopped talking.

"They're gettin' ready to bring Henry downstairs," Cordie told us as he leaned across the railing. "The jury will come in right after him, so be sure you present yourselves in a favorable light. We don't want them thinking negative things about Henry or his family, or it could play out bad for us come verdict time."

"What do you mean?" I asked.

"I mean no yelling, and no outbursts of any kind, no matter what happens," Cordie said. Then looking at Cora, he added, "And no name-calling or swearing or spitting either."

"I ain't gonna spit indoors!" Cora said as she straightened herself, crossing her arms tight against her chest.

"Sooze," Mama said to me. "Ask him where your daddy is."

But Cordie answered without me having to ask. "He's on his way down, Mrs. Williams. We were discussing business upstairs before the trial starts, and him and Henry still had some talking to do. Mr. Deets and myself came downstairs early to give them some privacy."

"Talking about what?" I asked, but instead of telling me, Cordie nodded toward Daddy as he entered the courtroom, hat in hand. He walked the aisle in silence, looking at all the strangers who'd filled the courtroom in his absence, stopping only once to shake hands with Doc Farrell. After Daddy came Sheriff Wingate, who held the door open for Dimple Dodds, Paulette Simmons, and Benny. They all took seats together at the back of the room. Even in a court of law, Miss Simmons was barely respectable in her skintight pink dress with black buttons and piping.

When Daddy slid in beside me, I asked, "Is everything all right?"

Leaning toward me, he whispered, "We need to go to the Waldron Bank first chance we get. We're goin' to owe a whole lot more money than we got, Sooze, but I had to promise Mr. Deets he'd get it right away or he was goin' to withdraw from Henry's case."

"Well, he can't do that!" I shouted. Then lowering my voice, I said, "I knew we shouldn't trust him."

"Shush," Daddy scolded. "We can't take no chance on the jury, or that newspaperman, thinkin' we're the kind of folks who can't hold our temper. That opinion would not be a help to Henry at all."

He was right, so I bit my tongue and nodded.

When the door opened again, David and his folks were entering the courtroom. When he saw me, he grinned and waved, then pointed to the empty seat on the other side of Daddy. The only other open seats, except a few single chairs, were in the back of the courtroom, so Sam and Amelia Huckabee took two together on our side of the room. As David got near, Daddy nudged me, wanting to trade seats so he'd be seated next to Mama, and I'd be next to David. I thought it was a fine idea until I saw Thomas Kittridge coming through the door. My eyes stuck to him like glue. He walked the aisle in a calm, easy manner, smiling at me the whole way until he got to the row behind us where the newspaperman sat. He squeezed in, taking the empty seat directly behind Daddy for himself. Chill bumps popped up, causing me to rub my arms for warmth even though I was wearing my tan sweater.

"When's it supposed to start, Sooze?" David asked.

"Should be a few more minutes," I whispered.

Uncle Will and Aunt Rose both sat beside Aunt Lissie across the aisle. There wasn't any newspaperman on their side of the room.

A lawman hastened Henry into the courtroom, but this time his hands were not cuffed. Dressed in the black trousers and long-sleeved, button-up white shirt we'd bought him, Henry looked like a respectable boy. Daddy had brought a comb, too, so his reddish-brown, collar-length hair had been combed straight back over his head, leaving his soft green eyes visibly shining with hope.

"Henry!" Mama's love stood her right up on her feet.

Daddy stood, placing one arm around Mama's shoulders. "Henry's got to stay there with his lawyers, and you got to stay here with us." He took her hand. "Let's sit down, Emma." They both sat, but Mama still leaned forward toward the balustrade.

"How are you, Henry?" Mama asked in a low voice.

"I'm doing all right, but I sure will be glad when this is all over." Smiling as if the mere sight of Mama calmed him, Henry said, "You look mighty nice today with your hair all done up."

Before Mama could say a word, the door to the jury room opened, and all eyes turned to watch the chosen jurors walk to their seats. When all twelve men and the two alternates were seated, the bailiff announced, "All rise for the Honorable Judge Arlen Poe!"

The judge opened his chamber door, and I could see floor-to-ceiling bookcases filled with colorful backed books in the room behind him. After stepping into the courtroom in his long, black robe, he closed the door and took his seat at the bench.

"Be seated," Judge Poe ordered. Turning his swivel chair to the side, he started talking to the jury as if they were the only people in the room. "Good morning," he said as he brushed his hand back over the top of his bald head. "Before we get started, I have a few things to say. When you were administered your juror's oath this morning, you swore to consider every question of fact in this case, no matter how big or small. I want to remind you that it is your duty to act fairly and impartially with regard to those facts. You are not to base your decision on feelings or emotions but on reason and judgment and according to the court's instruction. However, you are not expected to set aside your life experience and common sense. Remember, your task is to determine the true and correct facts in this case, making your service as a jury member very important. As long as you perform this duty to the best of your ability and make an honest, careful, and deliberate decision, the American system of justice will be served."

Then the judge turned, situating himself in his chair, so he faced forward. He nodded to the redheaded bailiff, who loudly said, "The State of Arkansas versus Henry Raymond Williams—court is now in session!" The judge banged his gavel on the desktop.

"Mr. Pigg, are you ready for your opening statement?" Judge Poe asked.

"Ready, Your Honor." Mr. Pigg stood and walked to a spot directly in front of the jury box. "Gentlemen of the jury, good morning."

It seemed every man on the jury smiled, nodded, and mumbled "good morning" to Mr. Pigg as if everybody was friends.

Standing mid-center of the jury box, halfway between the lawyer's table and the judge's bench, Mr. Pigg started talking. "Gentlemen," he said. "What you're going to hear today is a sad story about two people: Raymond Garren, the deceased, a hardworking husband and father, who'd just bought a piece of land right outside Coaldale, hoping to give his family a better life. And then the other..." Mr. Pigg turned, and with an outstretched arm, he pointed straight to Henry. "Well, the other is that boy sittin' right there at the defense table—Henry Williams, a young man whose brain is so racked with thoughts of runnin' away and gettin' himself free from the drudgery of being a sunup to sundown, hard-labor farmer that he snapped—just *snapped* —killin' Ray Garren for nothing more than a piddlin' fit of anger. You see, Henry and one of his lifelong pals were plannin' to pack up and sneak off to Chicago the day after they graduated without telling a soul, other than his friend's mama, where they were headed for fear of being stopped."

Mama stood straight up. "That ain't true!" she yelled, her white shawl falling to the floor, revealing a tatty gray dress. "Henry was planning to work our farm full-time!"

"Mrs. Williams!" Cordie was yelling while Daddy was trying to sit Mama back down. Judge Poe was banging his gavel when Cordie turned to him, saying, "Your Honor, we apologize for this outburst. You see, Mrs. Williams just lost her baby to the consumption. The funeral was Saturday, Judge, and well, she just ain't thinkin' straight yet."

"You tell 'em it ain't true!" Mama was still yelling, even though Daddy had put his hand to her mouth to stop her.

I stood, and leaning in, I whispered hard into her ear, "Mama, it *is* true. You got to quiet down, or the judge will throw you out of here!" When Mama heard me, she gripped her dress above her heart and, in disbelief, turned with wide eyes to Henry.

"I'm sorry, Mama." Henry's voice buckled like a dandelion trying to hold its own against the wind. "I don't want to go no more though."

Mama dropped her head into her hands, hiding her face, and she sank, sobbing, back into her chair.

Leaning in with a stern look, I heard Cordie whisper "be quiet" into Henry's ear as the judge said, "Proceed, Mr. Pigg."

"Now, that disruption right there tells you how despicable Henry Williams is, don't it? Why even his own mother is heartbroken now that she knows he intended to run out on his family."

"Objection, Your Honor!" Cordie shouted.

"Mr. Beegle, I can't allow you to object to an opening statement. However, Mr. Pigg, I do agree that you should not drag the frailties of this boy's family into court unless it specifically pertains to the facts of this case. Is that clear?"

"Yes, Judge. It is not my intent to put the boy's family on trial. I was just stating what seemed apparent."

"Very well then. Just get on with your statement."

"Now, let's see," Dellar Pigg said with a sly smile to the jury. "Where was I before the defendant's moving display of remorse?"

When the jury chuckled, the prosecuting lawyer grinned as if he'd won the first battle. Adjusting the belt holding up his trousers, he said, "Oh, yes, we were talking about Henry Williams runnin' away from home!" Walking back and forth in front of the jury box, the lawyer started in again. "Henry and his good friend, Benny Simmons, planned to skedaddle out of town with a bundle of money won from a year or more of illegal gamblin'."

"Objection!" Cordie was on his feet again.

"Your Honor," Dellar Pigg pleaded, "I'm only stating what I expect the evidence will prove."

"Mr. Beegle!" Judge Poe pounded his gavel on the desk. "I will not listen to objections during opening statements, and if I hear one more interruption from you, I'll hold you in contempt of court!"

Virgil Deets grabbed Cordie by one shoulder and pushed until he had him down into his seat.

"Proceed, Mr. Pigg," Judge Poe said.

"Thank you, Your Honor." Shaking his head as if Cordie didn't know how to play the game, Mr. Pigg took a deep breath, slowly exhaling, before beginning again. "I don't mean no disrespect to the dead, but what folks don't know is that Ray Garren had a secret relationship with a woman who was not his wife…" His voice had a wary tone as if telling a deep, dark secret.

Aunt Lissie cried out, hiding her face in her hands. Standing up, Aunt Rose pulled her to her feet. "Come on, Lissie. We ain't gonna sit here and listen to this!" Guiding her down the aisle, they both headed for the door.

"Truth is hard to hear sometimes," Mr. Pigg told the jury. He waited until the courtroom door closed behind them, then he turned to the jury and continued. "Ray Garren felt compelled to hide his promiscuous relationship by punishing the Simmons boy. Fact is, the evidence will show that it was Henry Williams who stabbed Mr. Garren to death in this senseless churchyard killing in retaliation for Ray leather-whipping his friend." Studying the jury, Mr. Pigg let the story settle. "And he killed him in the presence of God and his faithful parishioners." Before walking away, Mr. Pigg pursed his lips and shook his head, then slammed a startling fist down on the railing, causing the jurymen to jump with surprise right along with me. He shouted, "Henry Williams is as guilty as the sin he committed, and I intend to prove it!" He turned, and glaring at our side of the courtroom, he walked back to his lawyer's table and sat down.

It was just like Cordie said, way back that first day I'd met him. He'd said, *"There are two sides to every story, but only one of them is tellin' the truth. That don't mean the truthful side wins. Fact is, the side that wins is the side that tells the best story."* Until right that minute, I wasn't sure I understood what Cordie meant, but after hearing the prosecutor's speech to the jury, I understood it as plain as day. The best I could hope for was that Cordie had a better story.

CHAPTER 29

Cordie stood in front of the jury box with his hands in his pants pockets as if he was ready to discuss the weather.

"It's true that Henry Raymond Williams has been *accused* of the murder of Raymond Henry Garren." Cordie was talking slow, pacing back and forth in front of the jury. He didn't pay any attention to the confused faces of the jurors. "But I want to remind you, being *accused of murder* and being *guilty of murder* are often two different things, and I intend to prove Henry Williams is not guilty of this heinous crime."

Mr. Pigg and Mr. Deets were both dressed in well-to-do, successful lawyer clothes with their square-shouldered, double-breasted suits with sleeves tapered to their wrists, while Cordie was wearing a gray bowtie with a black, three-button suit which had a missing top button. What Cordie had that the other lawyers didn't, though, was an impressive swagger that nearly took the focus off his boyish, pock-marked face. He'd visited the barbershop since we'd seen him on Friday, too, and I was pleased to see the barber had kept his red hair long around his big, cup-shaped ears so that his hair puffed out on the sides like the cropped ears of a big tomcat instead of looking like two open jalopy doors.

Just like he was solving a riddle, Cordie moved closer to

the jury, and with his hands on the railing, he leaned over. "I saw the look of surprise on your faces at the similarity between the two names—Henry Raymond and Raymond Henry. The prosecuting attorney conveniently forgot to mention that strange similitude, didn't he? And certainly, no one else has told you why those names are so alike, have they?" Cordie gave a slap to the railing before taking one, then two, steps backward from the jury box. "Well, I'll tell you! I'll tell you, 'cause that's what you'll get from me during this trial—the *truth*!" Standing two feet from the jury box, Cordie quieted, letting a calm fall over the courtroom. He lowered his head for a moment. It was hard to tell whether he was saying a prayer or readying a confession, but when he raised his head again, his eyes shifted from Henry to the anxious faces of the jurymen. "Raymond Henry Garren—may he rest in peace—was Henry's beloved uncle." Cordie quieted while a few jurors sucked in a surprised breath, then he pointed to us. "Ray Garren was so loved by Henry's family that they named their only son after him."

The jury shifted uncomfortably in their chairs.

Cordie went on, sounding more like a preacher than a lawyer. "Is anything more terrible than to have a hard-working husband and father, a good, God-fearing man, stabbed to death as he attends church to worship with his family?"

I turned my head to glance at Mama and Daddy with the hopeful intent of being able to peek at Thomas in the seat behind, but instead, I caught Daddy wiping a tear off Mama's cheek with his thumb. As hard as recent circumstances had been, it was Mama who had suffered most. Her brother, Ray, was murdered, her son had been jailed for his killing, and her baby girl had died, all in the span of a few weeks. Mama was a strong woman, but that could beat down even the strongest.

Cordie walked back and forth in front of the jury box. He rubbed his chin as if deep in thought, then said, "Come to think of it, gentlemen, there *is* something just that bad." He stopped and faced the jurymen. Extending his arms wide as if waiting for a ray of sunshine, he leaned his head back and roared, "To be wrongfully accused of murdering your own uncle!" He tipped his head forward and planted a stare on the jury.

Pointing at Henry, Cordie said, "Henry Williams is *not* Ray Garren's murderer. Like lots of other young boys, Henry made some bad decisions—there's no denying it—but he did not kill his uncle, and I intend to prove it to you beyond all reasonable doubt. In fact," he told them, "I'll go one step further. Before this trial is over, I'm goin' to tell you who the *real* murderer is!"

Cordie smiled a smug, confident grin as the judge pounded his gavel. "Mr. Beegle! We'll only be tryin' one murder case here today, so I suggest you focus on defending the one you were hired for and stop tryin' to create another one!"

Cordie was still talking to the jury all the while, even though the judge kept banging his gavel. I couldn't hear a word he was saying over the judge's hammering, but I knew he was still talking because I could see his lips moving.

"Mr. Deets!" Judge Poe shouted. "Reel in your law student before I throw him in the county jail for contempt!"

Virgil Deets stood, but Cordie had already stopped talking and was walking back across the room. Halfway across, Cordie turned his head to look back to the jury and said, "Mark my words."

The judge pounded his gavel one last time before slamming it down. "Mr. Beegle, I will not be so understanding the next time you ignore me!"

"I apologize, Your Honor," Cordie said with a sound of regret to his voice, but when he sat down, he turned his head to Henry, and I saw him grin.

Judge Poe adjusted himself in his seat before saying, "Call your first witness, Mr. Pigg."

Turning to the courtroom, Mr. Pigg announced, "The

State of Arkansas calls Sheriff Byron Wingate."

Sheriff Wingate stood up from his seat next to Miss Simmons and walked toward the bailiff. He had his right hand raised for the oath before he ever got there, then started saying the words without any help from the bailiff at all. "I swear to tell the truth, the whole truth, and nothing but the truth, so help me, God." The sheriff moved right into the witness chair and sat down.

"Hello, Bud," Dellar Pigg greeted the sheriff. "Sure do appreciate you coming all the way from Coaldale today."

"Just one of the many job duties, Dellar."

"Sheriff, did you bring the murder weapon as evidence for us?"

"Yes." The sheriff reached into the deep pocket of his uniform jacket. When he withdrew his hand, he was holding a white cloth. He handed it to Mr. Pigg, saying, "This is the switchblade that was used to kill Ray Garren."

"Can you unwrap it for us, Sheriff, and describe what you've got?"

"Sure," Sheriff Wingate agreed. After unrolling the cloth, I saw Henry's knife in his hand.

"Doesn't look much like a murder weapon all cleaned up like that!" Mr. Pigg laughed.

"Well, Dellar, you didn't think I was goin' to carry a bloody knife around in my pocket, did you?" When a few of the jurymen chuckled, the sheriff turned to them, saying, "Common sense to wash the blood off, you know?"

Mr. Pigg grinned. With both hands clasped behind his back, he leaned forward as if inspecting the weapon and said, "How about you tell us 'bout this knife?"

Sheriff Wingate held up the closed knife as if displaying it for all to see. "This here is what's called a switchblade. It's got a jigged-bone stag handle with a four-inch stainless steel blade with strong action and a solid lockup. It's a deadly weapon. That's for sure."

"Can you show us the blade, Sheriff?" Mr. Pigg asked.

"Oh, you bet!" Holding the switchblade in his right

hand, the sheriff pushed a silver nub on the knife's handle and out popped the blade. "There you go. Locked into place like it was made that way."

"Whoa!" Mr. Pigg held both hands in surrender. "Yes, sir, it most surely is a deadly weapon!" He stepped back, lowering his hands, then said, "Sheriff, where did you find that knife?"

"It was laying in the dirt, right where Henry was kneeling."

"Do you know who owns the knife?"

"Yes, it belongs to Henry." The sheriff pointed to my brother.

"What makes you so sure?"

"'Cause he confessed to me when I took him in for questioning."

Mr. Pigg grinned when a few jurors shook their heads with looks of disgust toward Henry.

"No more questions, Your Honor," Mr. Pigg announced before walking back to his chair.

"Mr. Beegle," Judge Poe said. "Do you have any questions for this witness?"

"Yes, Your Honor, I do." Cordie walked to the sheriff, still seated in the witness chair. "Sheriff, when you told Mr. Pigg, 'Henry confessed,' you just used a poor choice of words, isn't that right?"

"What do you mean?"

"Well, you kind of made it sound like my client confessed to the killing, but that's not the case, is it? I think what you meant to say was, 'I asked Henry if this was his knife, and he said yes.' Isn't that more accurate, Sheriff?"

"Same thing," Sheriff Wingate said.

"No, I beg to differ with you," Cordie said. "By the way, were you a witness to the stabbing, Sheriff?"

"No, I was not. I was busy praising the good Lord when it happened!"

"Uh huh, uh huh." Cordie was nodding his head. "Well, then what made you decide to take Henry, and only Henry, in for questioning when you had *two* boys standin' side by side when the killing happened?"

"'Cause the congregation said Henry done it, and he was the one kneeling over Ray Garren's body pulling this knife out of him!"

"Oh, now, be careful, Sheriff," Cordie cautioned in a head-tilting glance. "If I recall, the only person who said Henry stabbed Ray Garren was the other boy named Benny Simmons. Isn't that closer to the truth?"

"Well, yes, come to think of it, I guess that's right."

Tapping his stiffened fingers on the edge of the judge's desk, Cordie said, "No more questions, but I'd like the chance to recall this witness if needed."

Judge Poe agreed and then leaned forward, speaking to Sheriff Wingate. "Sheriff, you can be recalled at any time for further testimony, so don't head on back to Coaldale yet."

The sheriff nodded then stepped down, making his way back to his seat.

"Next witness, please," the judge called.

Standing, Mr. Pigg said, "The State of Arkansas calls William Farrell to the stand."

I turned to watch Doc Farrell walk the aisle. He was a tall, thin man with extra-dark blond hair, wearing a gray wool suit. It seemed strange not to see him with his black doctoring bag. With his head down the whole way, Doc kept his long stride until he got to the witness chair railing where the bailiff was waiting with Bible in hand. He didn't wait to be asked, he just laid his left hand on the black leather Bible and raised his right hand.

"Do you swear to tell the truth, the whole truth, and nothing but the truth, so help you, God?"

"I do," Doc said.

"Please have a seat in the witness chair, Mr. Farrell," Judge Poe said.

But when Mr. Pigg approached, he said, "I believe your proper title is Doctor, am I right?"

"Yes," Doc Farrell answered in a somber tone. "I'm a

medical doctor. Most folks around the Coaldale area just call me Doc."

"Well, Doc, I just have a few questions for you today," Mr. Pigg said. "First, were you a witness to the murder?"

"No, I was too far away," Doc said as he shook his head. "I was up near the singing, and Ray was killed way in the back row."

"How many rows back would you say he was?"

"Oh, five or six benches, I'd guess."

"I see…" Mr. Pigg muttered as if thinking hard. "Did you try to help Ray when he was stabbed?"

Doc shook his head. "No, Ray was dead by the time I got to him. There wouldn't have been anything I could do for him anyway."

"What do you mean?"

"Well, like the sheriff said, the knife blade was four inches long. It entered Ray's sigmoid colon, ending up at his stomach. With the cut bein' so ragged, it cut through his large intestine all the way up 'til it tore through the bottom of his stomach. There was no way I could have saved him after a knifing like that."

Sounds of disgust traveled through the courtroom.

"Have you ever seen a knife cut like it before?"

"Not on a man, I haven't," Doc said.

"If not on a man, then what?"

"It looked to me like a sloppy, hog-butcherin' cut."

"Do you know anyone who knows how to butcher a hog, Doc?" Mr. Pigg asked.

"Lots of folks in the Poteau River Valley butcher hogs."

Mr. Pigg leaned closer to Doc, then asked, "Does Henry Williams butcher hogs?"

"Objection!" Cordie called out. "My client lives on a farm! Butcherin' hogs is part of farm life in these parts. Mr. Pigg is making it sound as if it's a rarity."

"Overruled," Judge Poe told Cordie. "Please answer the question, Doctor."

"Yes," Doc said. "Henry's one of the best in Scott

County at hog butcherin'.'"

"That's what I thought. Thank you, Doc," Mr. Pigg said. "No further questions."

"Your witness, Mr. Beegle," the judge said.

Cordie got right up out of his seat and was walking fast toward the witness chair. "Doc, did you say that cut on Ray Garren's belly was a ragged cut?"

"Yes, jagged, crooked, not a clean line at all."

"Wouldn't you think someone who's considered nearly an expert at hog butcherin' would have a skilled slice and not a sloppy, ragged cut?"

"Objection, Your Honor," Mr. Pigg said. "There's no way of knowing whether a man will react differently to slaughterin' a hog or guttin' a man! The fact that Henry Williams knows how to make the cut at all is the important fact."

"Sustained," Judge Poe agreed.

Cordie's face was an angry red. He walked a small circle in front of the witness stand before stopping in front of Doc again, saying, "Have you ever watched Henry butcher a hog?"

Doc started to answer but stopped when Mr. Pigg shouted, "Objection, Your Honor! This has no bearing!"

"Sustained."

Bent down face-to-face with Doc, Cordie asked anyway. "Have you, Doc? Have you seen Henry make that cut?"

Judge Poe beat his gavel against his desktop, barking, "Mr. Beegle! I said *sustained!*"

Doc spoke loudly so all could hear him over the gavel banging. "Henry makes a straight, clean cut with no ragged edges!"

"Strike that from the record!" the judge ordered, pounding his gavel.

"Thank you, Doc." Cordie smiled. Passing Mr. Pigg's table, Cordie said, "I know it has no bearing, Mr. Pigg, but I want to be sure you heard—Henry Williams makes straight, clean cuts when he uses a knife!"

The courtroom buzzed with chatter.

"Order in the court!" the judge was shouting. Slamming his gavel down on his desk, he stood up from his seat and yelled, "Court is in recess until one o'clock, and I want to see both counsels in my chambers right now!"

Judge Poe turned and headed for the room marked *Judge's Chamber* as the bailiff yelled, "All rise!"

Standing up between Daddy and David, I watched the lawman take custody of Henry, leading him through the side door. Cordie and Mr. Deets followed the judge and Mr. Pigg into chambers.

"Whew!" I said to anyone listening. "I thought the judge might have a stroke before Cordie stopped talkin'! Do you think Cordie's in trouble?"

"Well, any good lawyer knows you're supposed to do what the judge says," David told me. "I guess that's what happens when you hire an inexperienced lawyer."

"Sooze," Daddy whispered into my ear. "We need to find the Waldron Bank and get the money I was tellin' you about. I'm goin' to talk to your uncle Will to see if he'll drive us there."

"All right, Daddy," I said. When Daddy squeezed in front of me on his way to Uncle Will, I glanced back at Thomas. His blond hair had a clean glisten to it, and I liked the way he combed it to one side. His green eyes smiled at me before I ever noticed the corners of his mouth turning upwards. "Hi, Thomas. I didn't expect to see you here today."

"Your brother is on trial. It has to be one of the biggest things ever to happen to you. You didn't think I'd stay away, did you?"

"Hi, Thomas!" Cora had turned around backward in her chair and was shouting out her greeting. "Mama, look...it's Thomas Kittridge. He come here to be with us today."

Mama turned and smiled, but the words that came out were meant for me. "Sooze, when's Henry comin' back?"

"They won't bring him back 'til one o'clock, Mama."

"Do you think they're feedin' him lunch upstairs in the

jail?"

"Oh, yeah. I think so. This ain't like the Coaldale jail."

Mama was nodding her understanding as David said, "Sooze, we're happy to share a lunch table with your folks at the café across the street so they won't have to eat alone. I'll buy yours, of course, but they'll have to buy their own and Cora's, too. Mother wants to do some shopping at the mercantile a few blocks from the café after lunch." In a snide tone, David said, "Maybe I can find you something respectable to wear that you won't cut up and put in a casket."

"Thank you," I said, my tone fired with indignation. "But I don't need any gifts. Besides, I'm goin' with Daddy on an errand, and I think Mama and Cora will be having a picnic lunch in the park with Uncle Will, Aunt Rose, and Aunt Lissie."

"I ain't hungry, Sooze," Mama said as she patted Cora's hand. "And I think Cora will be fine stayin' here with me until Henry gets back."

"Aww, Mama!" Cora whined. "I don't hardly ever get to go anywhere, and since Henry ain't here, why do we have to stay?"

"Cora," I said. "You'll do whatever Mama wants. Do you hear me?"

Cora sat back with her arms crossed and her bottom lip sticking out like she'd been busted in the mouth.

"What kind of errand, Sooze?" David asked.

I had no intention of telling David about the money we needed, so I said, "It's just somethin' Daddy asked me to help him with. We'll be back by one o'clock."

But before David could put his foot down and demand I go with him, Daddy came walking back, saying, "Uncle Will's got to go find Rose and your aunt Lissie. He said they're not in the corridor outside, and Lissie's got to testify right after the lunch break."

"What are we gonna do, Daddy?" I asked.

Looking at David, Daddy said, "David, do you think you

could drive us down to the Waldron Bank?"

"The Waldron Bank?" David asked. "What for?"

"We got to make a withdrawal, David, and we sure could use your help." Daddy had his head down. I hadn't ever seen Daddy hang his head to nobody, so it caught me by surprise.

"Well, I'm sorry, but Mother and Father have their own plans today. We need the automobile ourselves."

"David," I said. "This is mighty important. Please ask your mama and daddy?"

"Sooze, I hate to disappoint Mother. She's been looking forward to this Waldron trip for days now."

"I thought she came for the trial, David. Not for shoppin'."

"Well, sure, Sooze, but there's nothing wrong with folks combining several activities into a single trip. That's being resourceful. Once we're married, you'll be learning all about being resourceful and practical. There's lots of things Mother plans to teach you, Sooze."

"Pardon me," Thomas interrupted. He was looking back and forth between Daddy and me. "I don't mean to be eavesdroppin', but I'd be happy to drive you to the Waldron Bank."

"Well, that'd be dandy!" Daddy said in relief. "What about it, Sooze?"

Nodding, I said, "We'd be much obliged."

"Well now, hold on, Sooze!" David was fidgeting. "Why do *you* have to go?" He was looking at Thomas like he had the plague.

I didn't want to discuss the situation with David, so I just excused myself while sliding between him and the railing. I made my way into the aisle where Thomas was waiting.

"Cora, stay with your mama, honey," Daddy told her. "Sooze and me will be back before you know it."

The three of us walked out through the courtroom door before David could say more.

CHAPTER 30

The black Model T Coupe was a tight fit for three people, but I could see neither Daddy nor Thomas wanted me to stay behind. I was pleased as punch to squeeze in between the two of them. Scooting to the middle to make room for Daddy, my hip touched Thomas, causing a pulse to run through me like pollywogs swimming down my insides. A smile pushed right out of me. When I glanced up at Thomas, he was smiling, too.

"Sure appreciate you driving us to the bank," Daddy said. "It's only a few blocks, but we need to get back quick before the trial starts up again, and I'm not sure how long this will take."

Thomas sat in the driver's seat with one hand positioned on a lever near the left of the steering column and one hand on a lever to the right. "Happy to help, sir."

"Call me John," Daddy said. "And I'm curious, what year is this model, and do you ever have to use the crank to start it?"

"Had to crank it up in Chicago," Thomas told him. "But haven't had to use it here hardly at all what with this nice Arkansas weather. My daddy bought this right off the assembly line in '26. Have you ever driven one?"

Daddy shook his head. "No, never drove one, but I

helped old Cecil repair his last summer. He had a little too much corn liquor one night and ran his coupe right down a hillside, puncturing the crankcase."

Since I'd never been in a coupe before and didn't know anything about crankcases, I focused my attention on Thomas. He adjusted the two levers, left side up and right side down, before reaching across me. As soon as he turned the key to BAT, I heard a swarm of angry bees coming through a hole near my knees! I screamed and pulled my legs up until my feet were on the seat with me, then threw my arms up over my head, covering my face. Daddy and Thomas both jumped like they'd already been stung.

It wasn't until they both started laughing that I realized the buzzing sound was coming from a box mounted under the dashboard. "What is that?" I asked. Flustered, I lowered my legs.

"It's the coil box, Sooze," Thomas told me. "It sounds like a mob of angry bees, don't it? I'm sure sorry it scared you."

Daddy was still chuckling, holding his hand to his mouth as he turned to look out the side window. Although I'd normally have been mad as a hornet about embarrassing myself, it did feel good to see Daddy laugh again. "I suppose I've never been this close to a coil box before. Does this automobile do any other things I should know about?"

"Not if it runs right," Thomas said with a grin. Setting his right foot down hard on the floorboard, the engine started right up. Adjusting the two levers again, Thomas put his hands on the steering wheel, and we started off for the bank.

Even though the automobile ran fine, I could tell by its tinny engine sound and worn gray upholstery that it was older than the Huckabee's Model A. The loud *tap, tap, tap, tap-tap, tap, tap-tap, tap* of the motor made the men talk louder, but when the sound of whirling iron grinded, Thomas would stop jabbering and start adjusting his levers again.

Leaning forward to look past me, Daddy told Thomas, "I want to thank you again for the beautiful song you sung at Grace's funeral."

"Good people pull together," was all Thomas said.

Moving the levers again, Thomas pressed the floor pedal, and the front wheels ground to a stop. When we all got out of the coupe, we were standing at the front door of Waldron Bank, a red brick, two-story building. It was the corner building, anchoring a whole block of stores and businesses lining both sides of the road.

"Look, Daddy," I said, pointing. "The theater sign says they got talking picture shows!"

"Well, sure, Sooze," Daddy said. "Waldron's got more than a thousand people living here. They got to have things like that in a big town."

"I'll wait outside for you," Thomas said. He leaned against the automobile with his legs stretched out, crossed at the ankles. "Take your time."

Daddy nodded, saying, "Come on, Sooze. Let's get this over with."

The bank had five customers, all standing in one line or another.

"I suppose we should just pick a line and wait 'til one of these bank people comes free," Daddy said. We walked across the marbled floor then stood halfway between two cashiering cages. Both tellers wore black suits, white shirts, and skinny black ties, and neither one looked very friendly.

"How about that one, Daddy," I said, pointing to the window with the youngest-looking teller. "The men in his line look like they're in a hurry, so maybe we'll get through faster."

"Good thinking." Daddy made a quick turn, and we walked straight to the farthest cashier window and stood behind two men. The first man was wearing a business suit, but the other one who stood directly in front of us wore bib overalls. He had a worn-out hat perched on his head. Daddy tapped him on the shoulder. "Excuse me, can I ask you a question?"

The man turned his upper body toward us without moving his feet at all. "Sure, what can I do for you?" He was holding a small, yellow paper in his hands.

"I'm looking to get a loan. Do you know who I should be talking to here at this bank?"

The man pointed to a door past the first cashier's cage. "Over yonder is the bank manager's office. His name is James, Duncan James. Just go knock on his door."

"Thank you kindly," Daddy said.

The bank manager's door had his name painted right on it in gold letters, so Daddy stepped right up and knocked. When the door pulled open, an older man wearing a black suit greeted us with a smile. "Hello, hello! Are you by chance John Williams from Coaldale?"

Both Daddy and me sucked in a surprised breath when this stranger knew his name. "Yes, I'm John Williams. How did you know?"

"Mr. Deets is a valued customer of our bank, and he called to say you were probably on your way. He asked me to do what I can to help you today." Opening the door wide, the balding, round-faced man held out his arm, inviting us inside. "Please come in and have a seat."

He had two brown leather chairs sitting in front of his big hardwood desk. When we sat down, Daddy started talking. "I own an eighty-acre farm just outside of Coaldale. It's been in my family for near-on fifty years, so it ain't never had a mortgage on it, but I sure need one today."

"Yes," Mr. James said. "That's what I hear. It's a shame about your boy, just a shame." He slowly shook his head back and forth while looking down at his desk.

"Well, we're not lookin' for pity, Mr. James," Daddy said. "What we need is $950."

I gasped! Flinging my arm across, I grabbed hold of Daddy. "That's...$950! Are you sure, Daddy? You already paid 'em a $250 retainer."

"Mr. Deets says we owe $1,200, Sooze. The retainer's deducted from the final amount due, so we still owe $950."

"Land sakes," I groaned.

"That's what Mr. Deets conveyed to me, as well," Mr. James told us. "But, Mr. Williams, he also said if your son is convicted, he'll have to appeal the case for you, and it will cost another $500 just for the filing and preparation of the appeal."

"Well, if Mr. Deets and Cordie does their job, we won't need an appeal, and Henry will walk free," Daddy said.

"True. However, I won't be able to make you a second loan within the year. Bank policy, you know? Think about it, Mr. Williams. I believe it would be in your best interest if we arranged a $1,500 loan for you, then if you need the appeal, you'll already have the money."

"Well, why can't we just go to another bank if we need more money since you say you can't make a second loan to us?" I asked him.

Mr. James leaned forward across his desk so his face was closer to mine. He pushed his black, wire-framed glasses farther up the bridge of his nose until the frames encircled his eyes again. "Because," he said, "I'll be holding the paper on your farm for this loan. You won't be able to offer it as security to anyone else. Do you have automobiles or farm equipment like tractors and trailers? You'll need worthy collateral for a second loan."

"What does he mean *collateral*, Daddy?"

"He means we can't get a loan twice for the same piece of land, and since we don't have any farm equipment or an automobile, I guess we'll be needing that $1,500 today."

Daddy's face was flush, and his head was hanging low. I couldn't tell if he felt defeated, embarrassed, or both.

"What do we need to do, Mr. James?" Daddy asked. "We need to be getting back quick to the courthouse with the money."

"Well, first of all, I need to be assured your farm is a

good producer. Do you expect any problems with making monthly loan payments to the bank?"

"No, sir," Daddy said. "Won't be no problem. Me and Henry plan to increase our hog production. You can ask anybody in the county—they all know we butcher quality hogs. And even though our crop of corn ain't barely sprouted yet, it'll come in fine like always."

"What happens if your son is convicted?" The banker was tapping his pen. "Then what?"

"Then I'll have a job!" I sat up straight in my chair, holding my folded hands in my lap. "I'll be making five dollars a week working for Huckabee's General Store."

Daddy turned to me to see if I was lying to the man or telling secrets. "Who says?"

"Mrs. Huckabee says, that's who," I told him. Then holding out my hand with the diamond ring, I explained to Mr. James. "You see, I'm engaged to David Huckabee, and being nearly family and all, his folks have agreed to pay me five dollars a week for working in their store, maybe more after the wedding. So you don't need to worry about Daddy paying you back, 'cause I'll be giving him my whole earnings."

"Well, that is good news!" Mr. James stood and reached across the desk to shake Daddy's hand. "It'll just take me a minute to draw up the papers." Then he was gone, leaving Daddy and me alone in the office.

"Sooze, why didn't you tell me?"

"Because, Daddy, every bad thing that has happened struck us right after my engagement. First Uncle Ray died, then Henry was accused of murderin' him, and then Grace died. Talkin' about my marriage and my job wasn't the right thing to do at the time."

Daddy nodded his head. Before I knew it, he'd straightened up, pulled my head close, and kissed me on the forehead. "Thank you, Sooze. Now, all we got to do is get Henry freed."

Mr. James opened the office door and came back to his

desk. He slid a fancy-looking long paper across the desk. "Now, Mr. Williams, all you need to do is fill in the right information on those blank lines—you know, address of the property, what the property is used for, any collateral you may have—then just sign and date the bottom for me. I'll sign it after you."

"You do it, Sooze," Daddy said as he slid it to me. "Your writin' is a whole lot better than mine." But Daddy stayed right there, reading over my shoulder the whole time.

After finishing the blanks, I handed the paper back to Mr. James. "Is this all right?"

Mr. James leaned over the paper, and I could see his eyes scanning each line. Finally, he said, "This looks fine, just fine." Smiling, he slid the paper across the desk to Daddy. Pointing to the last line, he said, "Sign right there, Mr. Williams. Your first monthly payment is due July first. That gives you more than thirty days."

Daddy didn't say a word, he just took the fountain pen and signed his name in black ink across the bottom line, then handed the paper back to Mr. James, who signed it, too.

"Now," the banker said as he stood up. "It'll take me a few minutes to get your money. Sit right here 'til I get back." He left the room again.

"Daddy, how are we gonna get the money for the first payment when the corn won't be ready for harvest 'til September, and we don't have a hog ready for butcher yet?"

"That was a ten-year note I signed, Sooze, and it said the monthly payments are goin' to be about $15. The way I figure it, after we pay Cordie and Mr. Deets that $950, we'll have $550 left. If we need the $500 for the appeal, it will still leave us $50 cash, which will give us three months' worth of bank payments. By then, our corn cutting will be done, and we'll be able to get some money comin' in."

I smiled. "You're so smart, Daddy."

"I wouldn't go so far as to say *smart*, but I do know how

to make ends meet. Most of the time, anyway," he said with a timid grin.

Mr. James seemed as happy as a cat in a saucer of milk when he came back. "Here we go!" He handed Daddy a stack of money. "Good luck with the trial, Mr. Williams. I'll expect to hear from you again on July first."

"Much obliged." I stood when Daddy did. He shook Mr. James' hand then slid the money inside the pocket of his gray-and-black plaid flannel shirt. "Come on, Sooze. We got to be gettin' back to the courthouse."

Once outside, Thomas straightened right up from his leaning pose when he saw us and said, "I was just about to come inside. It's past one o'clock already."

"I know," Daddy said. "Let's get!

CHAPTER 31

N one of us said a word to one another on the drive back to the courthouse until we pulled up and parked. Then, as we were getting out of the automobile, Daddy said, "Much obliged to you, Thomas. We won't forget the favor today."

"It's all right. Happy to help," Thomas told him.

When we opened the door to the courtroom, it seemed the whole room turned around to look at us. The judge was already in his chair, and Aunt Lissie was sitting up front in the witness chair. Mr. Pigg kept right on speaking to her.

"Now," Mr. Pigg was saying, "were you able to see Henry stab your husband?"

"Objection!" Cordie was standing and shouting.

"Objection sustained," Judge Poe said. "Mr. Pigg, you know better than that. I've got no patience for courtroom antics. You have not proven the defendant stabbed anybody yet, so you'll need to refrain from saying so."

"Yes, Your Honor," Mr. Pigg said. "I'll rephrase the question."

While Mr. Pigg was walking back and forth in front of the witness chair where Aunt Lissie sat, Daddy and me hurried to our seats. We settled in beside Mama and David. Reaching across the balustrade, Daddy handed a folded batch of paper money to Mr. Deets. That was when I turned to thank Thomas, but instead, I saw Cordie's daddy, Hank Beegle, seated where Thomas had been before the lunch break. I stood up, searching the filled room, finally spotting him in the back row. He was next to Sam and Amelia Huckabee.

I hated that he was so far away. I sat back down between Daddy and my intended as David leaned close and whispered, "What took so long?"

"More to do than we thought. That's all." It aggravated me when he didn't bother to ask if everything was all right.

Mr. Pigg stood rubbing his chin as if he was thinking hard. Suddenly he stopped, jerked his head up to look at Aunt Lissie, and said, "Did you see your husband fall backward after he was stabbed?"

"Yes," Aunt Lissie said. "It was awful. It was just awful!" Tears burst out of her as she buried her face in a white handkerchief.

The courtroom was silent, except for Mr. Pigg. "Who was holding the knife when your husband fell?"

Aunt Lissie raised her head to look at the prosecutor. Her eyes were red. Using the hankie, she wiped her nose, then said, "Well, I don't rightly know. I was lookin' at Ray."

"Well, if you had to guess, Mrs. Garren, who would you say it was?"

"Objection!" Cordie shouted, slamming his pencil down on the table. "I can't allow my client to be tried on the basis of *guessing*."

"Objection sustained," Judge Poe agreed.

"Your Honor, I'm just asking her opinion! Mrs. Garren was closer to the killing than anyone else!"

"Try again, Mr. Pigg," the judge advised.

With a sigh, Dellar Pigg said, "Mrs. Garren, if you were the person closest to your husband when he was stabbed, can you tell us how you missed seeing the whole thing?"

"I wasn't the closest," Aunt Lissie answered.

"You wasn't?" Mr. Pigg sounded baffled.

"No," Aunt Lissie said. "When Ray stood up, it put Henry closer to him than me, and Henry said Benny done the stabbin'."

Mama grinned big and wide and reached over to pat Henry's shoulder. When he turned to smile back, Mr. Pigg shouted, "Hold on now! Are you tryin' to tell us that the boy on trial for your husband's murder says somebody else did it?" Mr. Pigg roared with laughter. He leaned his arm on the corner of the judge's desk, and looking at the jury, he said, "Well, that'd be a first!" When the jury laughed, Mr. Pigg said to them, "Prisons are plumb full of innocent men, ain't that right?"

Judge Poe pounded his gavel. "Mr. Pigg, try to stay focused, please?"

Cordie was nodding to Henry, saying, "It's all right. It's going better than you think."

"What else did Henry Williams tell you, Mrs. Garren?" Mr. Pigg asked.

"Henry didn't tell me nothin', not directly anyway. I ain't had a chance to talk to Henry with him being locked up. Family talk is all I hear."

"Oh, I see." Mr. Pigg backed up from Aunt Lissie's chair. "So it's his mama, and his daddy, and his sisters who tell you everything, is that right?"

"Well, yes, and Henry's other aunt and uncle, too."

"So, it's the *whole* family?"

"Yes, I suppose it is," Aunt Lissie told him.

"Well, that makes a convincing case now, don't it?" Mr. Pigg was grinning at the jury. "Knowing that the boy's family says he's innocent."

When the jury laughed, Cordie stood. "Your Honor, what's the point in this line of questioning?"

"Yes, Mr. Pigg," Judge Poe said. "What is the point?"

"The point is, Mrs. Garren was standin' right next to the murdered man and never saw the stabbing. Now how, you might ask, can that be? With Your Honor's permission, I'll tell you how!" Mr. Pigg waited for the judge to nod before he walked to the jury box. Extending both arms forward, he leaned onto the railing, focused on the jurymen. "It's clear as day, and Mrs. Garren probably don't even recognize it herself, she's been so blinded by family lies."

Aunt Lissie had all her focus on Mr. Pigg as if he might have something to say which would explain it all.

Mr. Pigg stood up tall right in front of the jury and raised his left arm into the air, wiggling his hand. "If Mrs. Garren is standing over *here* on the left side of Henry," Mr. Pigg said before holding out his right arm, "and Henry stabs Ray Garren with *this*, his right hand, then Henry's body would have blocked her vision from seeing the knife, now wouldn't it?" Mr. Pigg lowered both hands and stood nodding at the jury. "If anyone else had done the stabbing, Mrs. Garren, or another witness across the aisle, would have been in a position to see it happen." When he turned to Aunt Lissie, her eyebrows were squeezed into a thinking wrinkle. "It's all right, Mrs. Garren. You aren't the first person to be misled by their family." Walking back to his table, he said, "I think I've proved my point. I'm finished with this witness, Your Honor."

"Mr. Beegle," Judge Poe announced. "It's your witness."

Cordie stood and walked to Aunt Lissie's witness chair. "Hello, Mrs. Garren." He spoke kindly to her as if she were his own aunt. "I'm sorry to put you through this today, but I just have a few questions for you. Will that be all right?"

"Yes," Aunt Lissie said. "That'll be fine."

"When your husband was stabbed, did anyone go help him?"

"Oh, yes, Henry helped him right off. I guess I was in shock, or I would've tried to help. I don't know why I didn't..."

"That's understandable, Mrs. Garren. You had a bad shock, and our brains don't always give us the direction we want, does it?"

"No," Aunt Lissie said. "It surely don't."

"So," Cordie said as he slid his hands inside his pants

pockets. "Henry was the only one who came to the aid of your husband?"

"And Sooze," Aunt Lissie said, pointing to me. "Sooze, too."

"Anyone else?"

"Well, John and Emma was tryin', but when Ray fell, he knocked over their bench, and they all tumbled to the ground. I saw John tryin' to help Emma up. Soon as he did, he come to be by Ray's side."

"Anyone else?"

"No, I don't believe so," Aunt Lissie told him. "Other than Doc and the preacher, I mean, but they was too late."

"Thank you, Mrs. Garren," Cordie said, nodding. "So, as I understand it, your husband grabbed hold of the shirt-fronts of both Henry *and* his friend Benny, is that right?"

"Yes, because Benny was actin' up, as usual, and Ray was mad."

"What was Ray mad about?"

"Oh, you know, Benny's egg stealin' and…"

"Objection!" Mr. Pigg shouted. "Who's on trial here, Judge?"

"Sustained," Judge Poe said. "Mrs. Garren, please limit your remarks so's not be accusatory toward anyone else."

"Your Honor," Cordie spoke up. "Mrs. Garren has to tell us why her husband grabbed those two boys, which eventually led to his murder!"

"I see your point, Mr. Beegle," Judge Poe said. "But I caution you not to be accusatory. Remember, you're here to defend Henry Williams, not to try a trial that don't exist."

Cordie nodded, then said, "Let's try this another way, Mrs. Garren. Can you tell me what caused your husband to get angry enough to pull Henry and his friend Benny to their feet on that Sunday morning?"

"He was fed up with Benny's mouth runnin' all the time."

"Well, what grudge did Ray have against Henry to cause him to grab him, too?"

"Oh, no grudge!" Aunt Lissie's voice gained strength. "He didn't have nothin' at all against Henry, other than he was mad that Henry was a friend to Benny."

I turned to look toward the back of the courtroom, where Benny and his mama sat. Benny had slumped down in his chair, making it hard for me to see him, but nonetheless, I spotted his hanging head, all covered in coal-black hair, looking like he was hiding behind the man seated in front of him. When I turned forward again, I saw the newspaperman craning his neck to see what I'd been looking at.

"Thank you," Cordie said. "No more questions, Judge." Cordie walked back to his table and sat down beside Henry.

"Mr. Pigg," the judge said. "Call your next witness."

Mr. Pigg stood again, calling, "The State of Arkansas wishes to call Delbert Dodds to the stand, Your Honor."

"Who?" I whispered to Daddy.

He leaned close to me and said, "Delbert is Dimple's God-given name."

I turned to watch Dimple walk the aisle to the witness chair. He'd had the good sense to wash his oily brown hair for the trial, but he still needed a trimming badly with his long, thinning strands hanging forward over his eyes. Considering his attire, I'd have said he'd just come from his job at the railway station. He was wearing a tan suit, so worn out he'd had both elbows patched, and he was carrying his round-topped derby in his hands.

When he started to sit, the bailiff said, "Hold on, there. I need to swear you in." He was holding out a Bible in front of Dimple. Dimple tossed his hat onto the witness chair then raised his right hand while laying his left on the Good Book. "Do you swear to tell the truth, the whole truth and nothing but the truth, so help you, God?"

"I do," Dimple said. He picked up his hat and sat down in the witness chair.

"Tell me, Delbert..." Mr. Pigg said.

"Dimple."

"What's that, you say?"

"Ever'body calls me Dimple 'cause of this here indentation I have in my chin." He used his finger to poke the deep, round dent.

"Oh, I'm sorry, Dimple," Mr. Pigg said. "Thank you for correcting me. We certainly want the folks to know who you are, don't we?"

"If you want the truth, I'd just as soon not be here at all."

"Well, of course, we want the truth! But it's a man's duty to come forward and tell what he knows."

Dimple looked down as if inspecting the hat in his hands.

"Can you tell the court where you were on the day Ray Garren was stabbed?"

"Back behind the apple tree," Dimple said, so quietly I could barely hear him.

"Say what again?" Mr. Pigg asked. "You'll need to speak up, Mr. Dodds."

Straightening himself in his chair so he sat taller, he glared at Mr. Pigg and repeated louder, "I was standing back behind the apple tree."

"Good, good," Mr. Pigg praised him. "Were you in a position to see the killin'?"

"Yes, I seen it. It was Henry Williams who stabbed that man."

"Well!" Mr. Pigg turned to face the jury. "That's pretty plain and simple—and you'll notice this testimony didn't come from one of the defendant's relatives!"

When the jury laughed, Mr. Pigg said, "No more questions, Your Honor."

"Mr. Beegle," Judge Poe said. "Your witness."

Cordie was walking toward Dimple Dodds, saying, "Now, Mr. Dodds, were you actually standing behind the apple tree, or in front of it?"

"What?" Dimple asked.

"Were you behind the tree or in front of the tree?"

"Like I said, I was behind the tree."

"Mr. Dodds, if you were behind the tree, how did you see the killing? Didn't that big 'ole tree get in your way?"

"Uh, I mean I was in front of it, I guess."

"You *guess?*" Cordie leaned forward with his question, turning his head to the side like he didn't quite hear him. "Mr. Dodds, one should remember whether they were hiding *behind* the apple tree or in *front* of the tree, wouldn't you agree?"

"I wasn't hidin'."

"Really? Because all but two or three people at the church service said you were never there at all!"

The jurymen's eyes grew big like they were waiting for a fight.

"Well, maybe I was behind the tree then!" Dimple had sweat beading on his forehead.

"So we're back to that big 'ole tree blocking your view, aren't we? Can you explain to this jury how you were able to see right through a tree trunk when none of the rest of us can?"

"I don't know where I was!" Dimple shouted and stood up out of his chair. "That's all I got to say!"

Judge Poe was pounding his gavel and ordering Dimple to sit back down. When the bailiff moved closer to him, Dimple lowered himself back into his chair.

"Your Honor," Mr. Pigg was shouting. "He's badgering the witness!"

"Overruled," the judge said without ever taking his eyes off Dimple.

"Now, come on, Dimple," Cordie said. "You know as well as I do, lying under oath can get you into a heap of trouble, and I don't think you want trouble, do you? You could lose your job, go to jail, be fined..."

"No, I don't need trouble." Dimple was shaking his head.

"Then why don't you tell us the truth?" Cordie looked at the judge. "I'll bet Judge Poe might forget all about those lies you just told so long as you tell the truth before being dismissed today."

Dimple glanced at the judge as if waiting for reassurance. When Judge Poe nodded, Dimple said, "All right, all right! I wasn't at the church service."

"Dimple Dodds!" Paulette Simmons popped up out of her seat, shouting from the back of the courtroom. The heads of everyone turned to stare at her. She had her hands on her hips with her coal-black hair curling down around her shoulders. "You lied to me!"

"Order in the court!" Judge Poe was beating his gavel against his desk. Standing up, he pointed to Miss Simmons and said, "I'll have you removed from this courtroom unless you take your seat!"

Sheriff Wingate stood and grabbed Paulette by the shoulders, then forced her down onto the seat next him.

Cordie turned to Dimple. "Who asked you to say you were there, Dimple? Who asked you to lie today?" With Dimple holding quiet, Cordie said, "You promised to tell the truth, so go on now. Tell us who it was."

With his head hanging, Dimple mumbled, "It was Miss Paulette."

"Who?" Judge Poe asked.

Cordie turned to the judge, saying, "Oh, I believe you've already made her acquaintance, Judge." Turning to face the courtroom, he pointed to Benny's mother. "Paulette Simmons—right there—she's the woman disrupting your court today, Your Honor."

"You lyin' little dog!" Paulette screeched as she stood again. Pointing at Dimple, she snarled, "Don't you dare come crawling back to me, you little weasel!"

Slamming his gavel, again and again, Judge Poe warned, "Miss Simmons, I will hold you in contempt of court if you do not settle down!"

Sheriff Wingate had his arm slung across Paulette's shoulder, trying to muscle her back into her seat, but she shrugged hard, knocking his arm away before sitting down of her own accord.

"Thank you, Dimple," Cordie said with a smile. "No more questions, Your Honor." Cordie returned to his seat, grinning big at Virgil Deets.

CHAPTER 32

"Mr. Dodds, you are excused," the judge said. Dimple stood, and with his head hung low, he used his hat to shield his face. When the newspaperman flashed his camera light, Dimple ran for the door. "Mr. Pigg, let's hope the prosecution's next testimony is more reliable. Please call your next witness."

Mr. Pigg let out a frustrated groan before standing to face the courtroom again. "The State of Arkansas calls Benny Simmons to the stand, Your Honor."

Heads of every person in the room turned to watch Benny walk up the aisle toward the witness chair. He had on black dress pants held up by a brown belt and a white, long-sleeved shirt. I'd hardly ever seen Benny wear anything other than his blue buckle-back jeans and a T-shirt and flannel, so I was staring more than most, I think. When he got almost even with Henry's chair, he glanced over at my brother and grinned. They might have dressed him in nice clothes, but his crooked teeth were still stained brown, and I doubted his hands had seen a bar of soap in days.

The bailiff stepped up, meeting Benny at the chair, and held out the Bible. With his left hand laid on top, Benny raised his right. The bailiff said, "Do you swear to tell the truth, the whole truth, and nothing but the truth, so help you, God?"

"Always do," Benny said with a rotten-toothed grin. He sat down as if he owned the seat.

"Good afternoon, Benny," Mr. Pigg said as he approached the witness chair. "Are you doing okay today?"

"Guess so," Benny said.

"Good, good," Mr. Pigg had one hand in his pocket, and he'd lowered his head, looking at Benny's dust-covered black shoes. Looking back up, he said, "Benny, where were you when Ray Garren was stabbed?"

"Well, I was standing right beside Henry." He pointed to the defense table as if Henry needed identifying.

"Did you see Henry stab the man?"

"Yup," Benny said, sliding back in his chair. "Sure did."

"What did he stab him with?"

"He used the switchblade the sheriff showed you," Benny spoke deliberately, gauging his words. "He'd worked real hard sharpenin' it on a whetstone a few days before the stabbin', too."

"How do you know?"

"'Cause he told me so!"

"Why do you think he worked so hard givin' it a razor edge? Had he been plannin' this stabbing?"

"Objection!" Cordie was calling out as he stood.

"Overruled," Judge Poe said. "Sit down, Mr. Beegle, I'd like to hear this story without you yelling objections every few minutes." Then, looking at Benny, the judge said, "Go on, son."

"Henry wasn't plannin' to stab nobody—not in plain sight anyway—but he was riled up after his uncle took a leather strap to me. Beat me like a dog, he did." Benny sat up straight and rubbed his hand against the spot where the red welt used to be. "When Henry heard about the beatin', his temper had him flyin' off the handle!" Benny laughed and began popping up and down in his chair like he couldn't hold himself still. "You should have seen him," he said.

"Henry says to me, 'I'll kill him for beatin' you like that! I'll kill him!'"

"When did he say that to you, Benny?" Mr. Pigg asked. "Do you remember the day?"

Choking back a giggle, Benny got serious again. "Yeah, it was on a Friday, 'cause I'd asked Henry to come with me to the Friday night dance over in Bates. Even though he asks pert'near every week, his daddy never does let him go. Henry come to tell me, so that's when I told him what his uncle had done."

"I see," said Mr. Pigg, now pacing back and forth in front of the jury box. "What I don't understand, Benny, is why Henry would get so mad about *you* gettin' whipped." Turning to face Benny, he said, "Why do you think he got mad enough to kill someone over it?"

"That's easy," Benny told him. "We was fixin' to ride the rails all the way to Chicago, and Henry knew my mama wasn't goin' to give me my travelin' money if I got into any trouble before graduation. That was our deal. Mama said, 'If you graduate with no trouble, you'll get the money I been saving for you.' I think she's got pert'near $500 saved up! But Henry—he wanted out real bad, you know? And he didn't want to go alone, so it scared him when I got that welt." Benny rubbed his hand against his face again. "I didn't think Henry'd really stab him, but he proved me wrong, didn't he? He said he didn't care none about graduatin' anyway, but he knew I had to or my mama wouldn't give me the money to leave Coaldale with him."

"Do you think Henry intended to kill Ray Garren?"

"Naw, I really don't." Benny had his head tilted upward into a cocked position as if he'd given this a lot of thought. "I think Henry was just trying to teach the old man a lesson, and then just like butcherin' a hog, the excitement got to him, and he kilt him."

Henry stood up quick, his face red as an apple with his mouth primed to shout, but before words came out, Mr.

Deets put a hand on his shoulder and settled him with a warning stare.

"Speculation, Your Honor!" Cordie shouted, pushing up out of his chair. "Unless my client divulged his thoughts to this witness—which he did not—then all this is pure hogwash!"

"Overruled, Mr. Beegle," the judge stated. "Please proceed, Mr. Pigg."

"Thank you, Your Honor," Mr. Pigg said. "But I believe we've got a clear picture now of what happened, so I got no more questions for this boy."

"Very well, then," the judge said. "Mr. Beegle, your witness."

Cordie sat silently in his chair for a minute, as if gathering his thoughts, then he took a breath and stood up. He walked over to Benny's witness chair, then calm and collected, he said, "Hello Benny."

Benny sat with his head cocked, staring at Cordie without a word.

"Something's been troubling me, Benny," Cordie said as he stood in front of the railing, separating him from the witness chair. His voice was calm. "After Ray Garren was stabbed, why didn't Henry run away? Seems to me he should be halfway to Chicago by now."

"Like I said, like I told that other lawyer, I don't think Henry meant to kill him. I think when he did, he was in shock or somethin' and stayed tryin' to fix it."

"Hmm," Cordie positioned one leg up on the platform where the railing was affixed, and he was staring at Benny. "Well, then, how come you ran away?"

"Wasn't you listenin'? I already told about how I needed to stay away from trouble, or my mama wouldn't give me my money."

"So you got scared and ran?"

"I wasn't scared. I just skedaddled to get away from what Henry'd done. It was a mess there, too." Benny was wiggling in his seat like it was suddenly hard for him to sit still when a nervous laugh popped out. "You should a seen it! There was a bucket of blood comin' out of his big gut."

"I see," Cordie said as he straightened up tall. "And that bothered you? That's why you ran away?"

"Yeah, that's why." Benny was serious again.

"How 'bout you, Benny? Are you good with a knife, too?"

"Objection!" Mr. Pigg was on his feet. "Whether the witness is good with a knife or not has no bearing, Your Honor."

"Mr. Beegle," the judge said. "Where are you going with this line of questioning?"

"Your Honor," Cordie's tone was defensive. "I'm simply trying to ascertain whether the witness has knowledge in the use of knives so I can ask some specific questions about the knifing. Benny was standing as close to the weapon that day as my client."

"I will not tolerate another circus show like we had before the lunch break, Mr. Beegle. Do I make myself clear?" the judge asked.

"Yes, Judge, but the question is fair, and I feel we have a right to hear his answer."

"I'll allow it one time, Mr. Beegle, but tread cautiously," the judge said. "Objection overruled."

"Thank you, Your Honor." Cordie turned his attention back to Benny. "Now, Benny, do you ever find an occasion to use a knife yourself?"

"Yeah, I got a pocketknife I use for skinnin' rabbits sometimes," Benny admitted.

"A pocketknife? And that's all?" Cordie asked.

"All I need, really," Benny told him.

"Have you ever borrowed Henry's switchblade?"

"Naw, Henry don't never loan it out. He won't even let folks open it up or nothin'."

"Is that right?" Cordie's voice was low and doubtful. "Didn't Henry lend his knife to you for rabbit skinnin' just a few days before Ray Garren was killed?"

"Like I said, Henry never loaned his knife to nobody, me included."

Cordie stood tall, staring at Benny. Shaking his head, he said, "So you've never borrowed Henry's knife?"

"Naw," Benny said, shaking his head.

Cordie put his hands on his hips and stood staring at Benny, speechless.

"Well, Mr. Beegle," Judge Poe said. "Are you waiting for the witness to question himself?"

"Uh no, Your Honor," Cordie said as he turned, looking back at Virgil Deets as if the answer he'd expected had just disappeared. "I have no more questions at this time, but I'd like permission to recall this witness again later, please?"

"Permission granted," Judge Poe told him, and then he dismissed Benny from the stand. "Mr. Pigg, do you have any other witnesses to call?"

"No, Your Honor," Dellar Pigg said as he raised halfway up out of his seat before sitting back down again. "The prosecution has proved its case."

"Mr. Beegle," the judge said. "As the defense, please call your first witness."

Cordie seemed nervous as he walked back across the courtroom. At the balustrade, he leaned over and whispered to me, "You're next, Sooze. Just be truthful, and don't leave no room for doubt. You saw what you saw, and don't let Mr. Pigg rattle you. Remember, you got to be forceful in your answers, Sooze."

A bucketful of butterflies emptied into my stomach. "Me? Already?"

"Yes, and I'm going to need you to help me prove Henry lent his knife to Benny. You got that?"

I was nodding when Henry turned around and said, "I'm countin' on you, Sooze. Don't let me down."

Cordie stood facing the judge, flipping through his notepapers. "The defense would like to call Sooze Williams to the stand, Your Honor."

I stood up, stepping between David and the balustrade. I

felt the eyes of the courtroom on me as I walked to the witness chair in my faded blue dress. My heart was pounding so hard I was sure the bailiff could hear it beating. Holding out the Bible, he said, "Place your left hand on the Bible and raise your right, please?" When I did, he said, "Do you swear to tell the truth, the whole truth and nothing but the truth, so help you, God?"

"I do," I said, intending to do exactly that.

"Please have a seat in the witness chair, young lady," Judge Poe said.

I stepped around the railing and sat down in the wooden chair, and waited.

In front of me, Cordie stood silent, rocking back and forth from heel to toe in his shiny black oxfords. Finally, he said, "Sooze, can you tell the court what your relationship is to the defendant, please?"

All I kept thinking about was Cordie's words to me, "be forceful in your answers."

"Henry's my brother," I said real loud, not knowing whether I was forceful enough or not.

"Your older brother?"

"That's right," I told him. My hands had started a tremble I couldn't stop, so I pushed them into my lap, hoping no one would notice.

"Now, Sooze, I need you to tell us, in your own words, exactly what happened at church on the morning of Sunday, May twenty-second."

The judge scooted sideways in his seat so he could look at me straight on, and all the faces in the courtroom locked on me like I was their supper hen.

"Well," I said, straightening up tall in the witness chair. "When we got to church Sunday mornin', we saw the services were bein' held outdoors. It'd never been that way before." I looked at Cordie to see if I was doing all right, but he just stared like he was waiting for the rest of the story. "They'd dragged in outdoor benches made by sawing logs lengthwise. We was all excited about the change."

"So being outside was unusual?" Cordie asked.

"Oh, yes, I'd never been to a church service outdoors before. I think the new preacher must have decided on it."

Cordie was standing close to the railing in front of my chair, and he was looking at me with a serious face. "Go on, Sooze. Tell us what happened next."

"Well, it was such a nice spring day that just about the whole countryside was there, so all the benches upfront was already taken. While the choir was singin' so pretty, we went toward the back rows to find ourselves seats." I shifted in my chair, feeling a strong start to my story. "I remember Henry sayin' he was goin' to sit by Uncle Ray, but the last bench only had a small sittin' space left open between Uncle Ray and Benny." I glanced at Cordie to see if he recognized what an odd thing that was, but he just kept looking at me like he was hearing my story for the first time.

"So anyway, Henry ran and plopped himself down in that little spot, so Mama and Daddy and Cora and me had to sit one bench up from him. Mama was holding the baby, tryin' to bounce her on her knees, but she was fussin' anyway, so I took Grace and I—"

"Grace is the baby?" Cordie asked.

"Was... Yes, Grace *was* our baby. She's up in heaven now." I heard Mama's breath stumble, but I put my head down, not wanting to look at her for fear I'd bust out crying again.

"I'm sorry, Sooze," Cordie said. "Just keep on goin' with your story, and I'll try not to interrupt again."

"It's all right," I told him. I used both of my hands to curl my loose blonde hair behind my ears, then clasped my hands in my lap again.

"After gettin' baby Grace, I went and stood back by the apple tree, right behind Henry and Benny. I was bouncing back and forth with the baby, trying to get her back to sleep while listening to the beautiful song bein' sung by our ladies' choir." I spotted Mrs. Huckabee smiling from the back of the courtroom, which drew my eyes to Thomas. He was sitting beside her, focused on me like I was the most important person in the room, flustering me and my story.

"Your Honor," Mr. Pigg stood up, saying. "While I'm sure the ladies choir was lovely, what does it have to do with the murder of Ray Garren?"

"Well, it sure sets the mood, don't it, Mr. Pigg?" Judge Poe laughed right out loud. "Now sit back down, and let's let this young lady tell the rest of her story."

Dellar Pigg sat down with a sigh so strong it rattled his papers.

"Go on, Sooze," Cordie encouraged. "We need you to tell us the rest of the story."

"I'm sorry to be taking so long," I said.

"It's quite all right, Sooze," the judge said in a kind voice. "You go right on."

I glanced at Mama and Daddy and saw Mama holding on to Daddy's arm. She grinned real proud like I was starring in a stage play, but when my eyes met Daddy's, he just nodded as if saying I needed to get going and finish my story.

"Like I was sayin'," I started off again, "I was bouncing the baby and listening to the song when things started gettin' quiet. I remember seeing the new preacher standing at the pulpit, opening the Good Book when Benny—right loud like—started talkin' to Henry."

"What did Henry do?" Cordie asked me.

"Henry asked Benny to quiet down, but not before Uncle Ray did. I could see plain as day Uncle Ray was mad, 'cause his face always turns a splotchy sort of red, and then he told Benny to be quiet 'cause the preacher was startin' the sermon."

"So did Benny quiet down?"

"No. Fact is, Benny got louder, and he says to Henry, 'Who cares what these…people…think.'"

"That's what Benny said? 'Who cares what these people think'?"

"Well, not exactly," I admitted. "He said somethin' worse."

"Sooze, you need to tell us *exactly* what you heard. Don't be shy, now," Cordie said.

I shifted in my chair. "Benny said, 'Who cares what these *peckerwoods* think.'"

I heard snickers and giggles from the courtroom, but I tried to stay focused.

"Uh huh, all right. That's good, Sooze. Now, what happened next?"

"That's when Uncle Ray got louder, sayin', 'I asked you to be quiet, boy!' Henry was still trying to get Benny to quiet down, but Benny was sayin' he had as much right to talk as anybody did. Then Uncle Ray got real mad and stood up. I remember thinkin' there was gonna be a whole lot of trouble now—Uncle Ray won't stand for rude behavior—so I stopped bouncing the baby and held on to her real tight. I was staring right at 'em when Uncle Ray turned around, facing Henry and Benny. He grabbed hold of their shirt-fronts and twisted his fists into the fabric, and used those knotted-up balls of shirt to lift Henry and Benny right to their feet."

"What did the boys do then?"

"Well, Henry was just standin' real still and straight, but I saw Benny pull back like he had a fist ready. I was wonderin' what in the world he was doin' trying to punch Uncle Ray in the stomach, but then I saw the glint from a knife blade. Before I could say a thing, Benny jabbed it in him. He started jerkin' that blade upwards, cuttin' right through Uncle Ray's belly."

"Objection, Your Honor!" Mr. Pigg was shouting.

"On what grounds?" Judge Poe asked.

"On the grounds that this is a *ridiculous* story! We've already established that the murder weapon belongs to Henry Williams. She's just protectin' her brother!"

"Overruled," the judge said to Mr. Pigg. Then looking at me, he said, "Go on, Sooze."

"Oh, but I didn't know it was Henry's knife right away."

"So, you thought Benny used his own knife?" Cordie asked.

"Objection! Mr. Beegle is leading the witness."

"Sustained," the judge agreed.

"I'll rephrase the question, Your Honor," Cordie promised. Standing still, I could see Cordie thinking hard. Finally, he asked, "Sooze, this knife you saw in Benny's hand, was it *Henry's* knife?"

"Well, it was Henry's knife that Henry pulled out of Uncle Ray."

"Your Honor," Mr. Pigg said. "I'd like the court to note that this eyewitness has positively identified that the knife which was used to murder Ray Garren was seen in Henry Williams's hand immediately after the stabbing."

"Point noted, Mr. Pigg," the judge said. Turning to the jury, he asked, "Does everyone on the jury understand Mr. Pigg's clarification?"

I looked at the jury, and seeing most everyone nod, I said, "But Henry didn't stab Uncle Ray—Benny did."

"Objection!" Mr. Pigg sounded mad.

"Sustained," Judge Poe said. "Mr. Beegle, see what you can do to move this along, please?"

"Sooze, could Benny have had Henry's knife that day?" Cordie asked.

"He did have it. I know because Henry lent his knife to him."

"How do you know?"

"'Cause after school on my birthday, Henry and me were talking at the firewood box. He was having a hard time fittin' more logs inside after the rope handle on its lid knotted up, so I said, 'Use your knife,' and Henry said, 'Can't, I lent my knife out.'"

"Objection!" Mr. Pigg said. "Irrelevant unless Miss Williams can give a clearer answer."

"Sustained." Leaning across his desk until he was closer to me, the judge asked, "Can you be more specific?"

I had no understanding at all as to what the judge wanted me to say.

"Sooze," Cordie said. "Did Henry say *who* he'd loaned his knife to?"

"He'd lent it to Benny but didn't say why. Later he told Daddy and the sheriff he'd lent it to Benny for skinnin' a rabbit."

"But did you hear Benny testify earlier saying Henry never lent his knife to anyone?"

"Yeah, but it ain't true. Henry'd loan you the shirt right off his back, if he thought you needed it more than him," I told Cordie. "Henry's been like that as long as I can remember."

"Can you name anybody else who Henry lent his knife to besides Benny, Sooze?"

"Let's see," I said, thinking back on times gone by. "Henry lets Daddy use it, and he's taught Cora how to open and close it, but that's not really lendin' it out, I guess. Uncle Will and Uncle Ray used it last December on hog-butcherin' day. I watched them sharpen the gambrel stick with it, and Henry also let 'em use it to cut a hog's throat because Henry was braggin' about how sharp the blade was." I looked at Henry, and he was nodding. "Henry's always been mighty proud of his knife. It belonged to Grandpa Garren, and Daddy says it's the only thing of value he left when he passed, other than my mama."

"Anyone else you can think of?"

"Not right off, except Benny, of course. He let Benny borrow the knife lots of times for skinnin' rabbits and squirrels, and who knows what else," I told him. "He used to get riled up because Benny'd keep it for too long. Henry would almost always have to ask for it back."

"How do you know, Sooze?"

"I've seen him with it," I said. "One time, Henry was walking home from school with Cora and me, and Benny snuck up on us and jumped out from behind an old hickory with the knife blade pointed at us like a robbery—only he got his foot caught in a bundle of vines, and he tripped and fell flat on his face. Me and Cora laughed, 'cause he looked so silly lying there in the dirt, but Henry commenced to yelling at him. He pulled him to his feet, saying he could've killed hisself with that knife! Henry was telling Benny that he needed to learn the basics of knife handlin' and said he'd teach him if he'd settle down long enough to learn. Then Henry took the knife away from him and closed it up, saying, 'That's probably why your mama won't let you have one of these for yourself.'"

"You're a liar!" Benny shouted from the back. "I know how to handle a knife good as Henry—good as anybody!"

Just as quick as Benny said it, Paulette slapped him across the back of his head. "Dummy up, you nitwit!"

The judge started banging his gavel, yelling, "Order in the court!"

That was when Cordie stood up straight and grinned at me, saying, "That's good, Sooze. That's real good." Then he announced, "No more questions, Your Honor."

Cordie was walking away before I realized it was Mr. Pigg's turn. I suddenly felt cold and pulled the front of my tan sweater tight around me.

CHAPTER 33

"Well, Miss Williams..." Mr. Pigg was standing in front of me, smiling, but it wasn't a friendly grin at all. He put one hand on the witness chair railing and leaned into it. "I think you and I should have a little talk, don't you?"

"Your Honor," Cordie was saying. "Mr. Pigg is trying to intimidate this witness."

"He hasn't even asked her a real question yet, Mr. Beegle," Judge Poe told him.

"But we can all hear the tone of his voice!"

"Sit down, Mr. Beegle!" The judge banged his gavel once before laying it down, which caused Cordie to drop back into his seat with an irritated look.

"You told some nice stories trying to protect your brother," Mr. Pigg said. "Truth is, you'd do just about anything to help Henry, wouldn't you?"

"Yes, I would," I said, lifting my chin proudly.

"You'd even lie for him, wouldn't you?"

"I would not!" I shouted. "I'm not here to tell lies!"

Straightening up, Mr. Pigg wasn't smiling anymore. "All right, Miss Williams. I'll play this little game." A doubting growl rumbled out as he looked at the jury.

"Objection, Your Honor!" Cordie shouted as he bounded out of his chair. "This is clearly intimidation!"

The judge banged his gavel again and, in a snooty tone, said, "I hear you, Mr. Beegle, but I do not see where Mr. Pigg is out of line. Now, if I promise to pay close attention, will you sit down, please?"

Cordie threw his hands up in the air and sat back down.

Mr. Pigg continued. "Let's examine your story, Miss Williams." The prosecutor walked to the jury box, and with his back to me, said, "Describe how Mr. Simmons supposedly got the knife in his hands."

I was as stumped as could be with Mr. Pigg's question. I glanced at Cordie and then Mr. Deets, but neither of them motioned a hint. "I don't know what you're askin' me."

"Well, it's a simple question." Mr. Pigg had raised his voice to an angry pitch, still facing the jury. "If your story is true, you should have seen Mr. Simmons get your brother's knife from somewhere!"

"Oh, well no, I only saw the knife in his hand when he jabbed it in Uncle Ray's belly."

"So, you never saw your brother hand over his knife?" Mr. Pigg turned to me.

"No, Henry never had the knife. Like I said, Benny's arm drew back—"

"Oh, that's when you thought Mr. Simmons was punching Ray in the stomach?"

"Yes, that's right."

"How do you know he wasn't?"

"How do I know he wasn't *what*?" I asked.

The prosecutor turned, staring daggers at me. "Punching Ray in the stomach? How do you know Benny wasn't punching Ray in the stomach when Henry decided to knife him?"

I sucked in a breath, but it came out a gasp.

"Oh, you hadn't thought of that, Miss Williams?"

"Objection!" Cordie was on his feet again. "Mr. Pigg is badgering the witness and—"

But before Cordie could finish, Judge Poe banged his gavel, saying, "Overruled!"

I straightened up again and scooted to the edge of my seat. "Oh, no, sir, that's not how it happened at all!"

"It *is* how it happened! Henry Williams stabbed Ray Garren to death with his switchblade knife!" Mr. Pigg was yelling, which started Cordie to hollering, too. The judge started shouting "Order in the court!" and pounding his gavel, but it was Mr. Pigg who outshouted them all by yelling, "No amount of lying will change the facts!"

The judge dropped his gavel when the head of it snapped right off.

With the whole courtroom in a frenzied buzz, I got scared, thinking maybe they were believing Mr. Pigg and Benny. With no more thought than that, I stood, shouting, "You got no right to steal the truth from Henry!" My heart was pounding like a gavel itself. "What you're doin' is just the same as robbery!" The courtroom got quiet as corn growing. Standing steadfast, I glared at Mr. Pigg. "Henry didn't kill Uncle Ray. No matter what lies you tell tryin' to convince folks otherwise, truth is truth! I know what I saw, and my brother is innocent!"

Using the flat of his hand, the judge slammed it down on his desk. "Sit down, young lady!"

I sat fast, watching Mr. Pigg stare a hole right through me. Standing halfway between his lawyer's table and me, he finally turned and walked away saying, "No more questions, Judge."

Judge Poe stood, saying to me, "You're dismissed for now, Sooze, but don't leave the courthouse until we know whether you'll be recalled." Then he announced to the room, "There'll be a fifteen-minute break, and bailiff, I need a new gavel!" Then he stepped down off the raised platform and disappeared into the judge's chambers.

As the bailiff escorted the jurymen out, I hurried back to my seat, but by the time I got there, the black-haired lawman in charge of Henry had taken him away, and David had moved to the back of the room. I saw him talking to his mama and daddy.

With the rest of the courtroom spectators emptying out into the hallway, Mama asked, "Why can't they leave Henry here so's we can talk to him instead of hiding him away behind that door?"

"Emma, the boy needs to use the facilities, too. He'll be back," Daddy told her.

Then seeing me beside her, Mama grinned big, saying, "Sooze, you done real good."

"I was so nervous, Mama, I had to hold my own hands still to keep 'em from shakin'!"

Daddy took hold of me and hugged. "By gum, Sooze! When you started yellin', I thought for sure the judge was goin' to throw you into jail with Henry."

"Well, Daddy," I said, pulling away, "it sounded like everyone was startin' to believe Henry done it, and I didn't know what else to say."

Mama patted my arm. "We're mighty proud."

With people milling around in the wide corridor outside the courtroom, I led Mama and Cora through the crowd to the toilet where I'd thrown up Friday. Mama didn't get to go too many places other than the stores in Coaldale and to school with us on special occasions, so venturing out to a big town should have been a fun experience had we not been there for such a worrisome reason. Still, it was nice to see her finding interest in things. She stood at the washbasin, turning the sink's four-pronged handle, watching the water pour out. Then she'd turn the handle the other way until the water shut off.

"It'll be nice when Daddy plumbs the house with running water, won't it, Mama?"

"It sure will, Sooze," Mama said without looking up. She was gliding her hand over the edge of the clean, white porcelain sink.

After a flush, Cora came walking out from the toilet, smoothing the back of her blue-and-tan plaid dress. "Come wash your hands, Cora," Mama told her. She turned the faucet handle for Cora until a good stream of water was flowing. "My, my..." was all Mama said.

"We should be gettin' back," I told them. "The judge will be coming back any minute."

When we walked into the courtroom, Daddy was standing up at his chair, looking for us.

"Here we are, Daddy!" Cora called out, waving her arm in the air. When he saw us, he waved, trying to hurry us up. It looked like we might be the last ones into the courtroom, except for the judge and jury and the lawyers and Henry.

"Do you have to go back up there and sit on the witness stand, Sooze?"

"I don't know, Daddy. The judge said I might, but I think I'm supposed to sit here for now and wait to see if he calls me again."

Just as we took our seats, David slid in beside me. Talking low near my ear, he said, "Sooze, I talked to Mother and Father, and they think you should be actin' more dignified and not standin' up yelling at these folks like you did."

"They do, do they?" I asked.

"Yes, and I think so, too," David whispered to keep the conversation private. "Besides, lots of these folks are goin' to be our customers when we open our store here next year, and we sure don't want them to have a bad impression of you. Folks remember these things."

"David, I'm tryin' to save my brother's life."

"Well, can you do it more ladylike, please?"

I wanted to push David right off his chair into the aisle so I wouldn't have to sit by him for the rest of the afternoon, but I knew it was not the time to cause a commotion.

When the side door opened, Henry hurried to sit down, turning himself around in his seat to face me. "Sooze, you done good! You stood right up there and told 'em all off! You're a star!"

"Shush, Henry," Cordie told him. Then turning to look back at me, he whispered, "He's right, you know?"

I felt relief running through me like a free-flowing river. I didn't know whether I'd truly done good on the witness stand or not, but I knew my family was proud of me for trying.

The jury room door opened, and all the men filed in, taking their seats in the jury box. When the judge entered, the bailiff said, "All rise!" We stood and waited while he took his seat.

"Mr. Beegle, let's get on with this, please? Call your next witness," Judge Poe told Cordie.

"Your Honor, I'd like to recall Benny Simmons to the stand, please?"

Benny stood up from his seat in the back and said, "I already been up there."

But Judge Poe was in a grumpy mood. He barked, "Well, you're coming up here again, Mr. Simmons! Now take the stand."

Benny made his way to the witness chair and stood, waiting for the bailiff to say the oath. Instead, the judge said, "You're still under oath, Mr. Simmons. Just sit down."

Cordie walked to the witness stand and stood in front of Benny.

"Help me out here, Benny," Cordie said, "I'm having trouble understanding exactly how all of this happened." Looking around the room, Cordie's eyes settled on Virgil Deets. "Your Honor, I'd like to know exactly what Benny saw that day so we can get the gist of how this knifing happened. To do that, I'd like to recreate the circumstances. May I ask Mr. Deets to assist me so Benny can demonstrate?"

"Objection, Your Honor!" Mr. Pigg was standing. "This courtroom is not a theater!"

"Now, hold on, Mr. Pigg," Judge Poe said. "I'd kind of like to see this myself. Objection overruled. Go on, Mr. Beegle."

Cordie waved Virgil Deets to come stand beside him in front of the witness stand. At his direction, Mr. Deets positioned himself so the judge could see Cordie clearly, just like we could.

"Good, thank you, Mr. Deets," Cordie said. "Now," he glanced at Benny, "let's pretend Mr. Deets here is Ray Garren. I'll be Henry." Mr. Deets stood quiet, facing Cordie straight on. "Benny, come on down here and show us where you were standing."

"Objection, Your Honor!" Mr. Pigg was on his feet again. "This is child's play!"

"Overruled. Now, why don't you just sit back down, and let's wait and see what this young attorney wants to show us?"

"Thank you, Your Honor." Turning back to Benny, Cordie said, "Come on, Benny. Come down here and show us what happened that day."

Benny stood up, then stepped down off the platform, walking around the witness chair railing. "So, what do you want me to do?" Benny asked. His brows scrunched together, bringing a confused squint to his eyes.

"I want us to be able to see what you saw, Benny. So, think of me as being Henry, and Mr. Deets here..." Cordie looked up, smiling at his stone-faced boss who stared straight ahead. "He's going to be Ray Garren. So, tell us, Benny, where were you standing?"

"This is stupid," Benny told Cordie.

"I know, I know," Cordie agreed. "Just humor me, all right?"

Benny stepped forward, shoulder to shoulder with Cordie. "Now what?"

"Is that about where you were standin', Benny?"

"Yeah, I reckon."

"So then, what happened next?"

"Henry stabbed him! What did you think happened?"

There was a chuckle, which ran through the courtroom and the jury box, pleasing Benny.

"Show me," Cordie urged. "Where was the knife?"

"Well," Benny said. Reaching his left hand into his pants

pocket, he began acting out his explanation for Cordie. "I guess he got the knife in his hand while it was still in his pocket, cause when his hand came out of the pocket, he had it."

Cordie glanced down at Benny's clenched fist. With his body still facing Mr. Deets, Cordie pointed to Benny's tightened hand. "So the knife blade was out and ready?"

"Well, no, he probably pushed the button so's the blade would pop open. *Snap!*" Benny grinned as if an adrenaline surge had been unleashed inside him. Bouncing back and forth on the balls of his feet, a little dance escaped.

"Oh," Cordie said with an understanding tone. Talking to Benny as if they were the only two people in the room, he said, "See, Benny, I've never used a switchblade, and I'm not very smart about knives, so I didn't quite understand the sheriff's explanation. It works different than a regular knife, huh?"

"Oh, yeah, yeah..." Benny settled himself, focusing on Cordie's interest. Pretending to hold the knife in his hand, he explained. "See, the blade is inside the handle, same as a pocketknife, except with a switchblade, you don't have to lift the blade out yourself. It's got a little silver button, and when you push it, the blade shoots out and locks in place. It's a one-handed knife."

"Is that right?" Cordie said with a look of amazement on his face. "And I didn't think you had much experience with a switchblade, Benny."

But Benny just stared at Cordie with a blank look.

"So," Cordie continued. "How did that work? I mean, if you were standing shoulder to shoulder with Henry, how was he able to maneuver the knife, so no one else saw it?"

"Oh, well, see..." Benny bent slightly into a crouch, looking like a cat ready to pounce. "Soon as Henry pulled the knife out of his pocket, all he had to do was push the silver button and out popped the blade!" Benny cackled as he moved into a reenactment.

I was glued to Benny. It was like watching the stabbing

all over again, except slower. The whole courtroom must have been glued, too, because the room was dead silent except for Benny and Cordie. Acting just like he had a knife in his hand, Benny jabbed at Mr. Deets, wrenching the pretend knife upward in a belly-gutting slice. When his clenched hand reached Mr. Deets' ribcage, Benny stopped, his eyes and ears recognizing the silence. He stood up and lowered his hands. He looked all around the room before his gaze came back to Cordie. "So, that's how Henry done it, I think. I couldn't see it all, though." Benny turned and, without any prompting, he walked back to the witness chair and sat down.

Nodding to Virgil Deets, Cordie said, "Thank you, Mr. Deets. I think we're finished here for now." As Mr. Deets walked back to his seat beside Henry, Cordie took his green-marbled fountain pen out of his pocket and turned it round and round in his hands. "I don't know why I didn't think of it, Benny, but we could have used this pen as the pretend knife." Cordie tossed the green cylinder to Benny.

Reaching up, Benny caught the pen with his left hand. "Don't matter none," he said as he tossed it right back to Cordie. "We're done anyway, ain't we?"

"Your Honor," Mr. Pigg intervened from his seat. "The witness has got to be tired from all the games he's had to play with the defense counsel here today, and it's too late in the day for any more of Mr. Beegle's shenanigans."

Before the judge could respond, Cordie said, "I'm almost finished, Your Honor. With the court's permission, I'd like to ask just a few more questions."

"Mr. Pigg," Judge Poe said. "I'm well aware how late it's getting, but I'd like to give Mr. Beegle a chance to finish this line of questioning. Do you think that'll be all right?" The judge had a shaming tone.

"Certainly, Judge," Mr. Pigg tried to explain. "I just thought…"

"When it concerns my courtroom, Mr. Pigg, I'll do the thinking. Is that understood?"

"Yes, sir," Mr. Pigg mumbled.

"Please continue, Mr. Beegle," the judge said.

Cordie held the green-capped fountain pen between two fingers, rocking it one way, then the other, as he focused on Benny in silence.

"Benny, are you left-handed or right-handed?"

"Why do you care?" Benny grumbled.

"Well, it's just that I noticed you caught my pen with your left hand. And when you demonstrated the knifing, you used your left hand. So, I'm just curious, do you do everything with your left hand?"

"I don't know," Benny said as he straightened himself in the chair.

"Do you write with your left hand?" Cordie asked him.

"Yeah," Benny said.

"Well, how about that?" Cordie sounded impressed as he turned to the courtroom. "I guess Benny is left-handed!"

"So what?" Benny had a cold, hard stare focused on the lawyer, but when Cordie held his pen like a knife and mimicked a low, left-handed jab, Benny's temper exploded. "I know what you're trying to do! You're trying to say I stabbed that old man—well, it ain't true! It was Henry who kilt him!"

"But I'll bet you wanted to kill him, didn't you, Benny? What with him beating you with a leather strap and all. Why wouldn't you want to kill a man who'd done that to you? Or were you just runnin' scared?"

"I ain't scared of nothin'!" Benny sat forward in his chair, shouting, "I could've kilt him if I wanted, but I didn't! You ain't gonna pin this murder on me."

Leaning close to the railing, Cordie said, "You're pretty tough, aren't you, Benny?"

"Yeah, I guess so. What's it to you?" Benny eyed Cordie.

"Aww, nothin', really," Cordie said. "I just can't figure out why a hard-boiled kid like you can let an innocent boy like Henry take the fall for you."

"Objection!" Mr. Pigg shouted, but Cordie had already

stepped back from the witness chair and was walking away toward his seat with his head down.

"Sustained," the judge said.

But before getting too far, Cordie turned back around, saying to Benny, "I always thought tough guys fought their own battles."

"Objection!" Mr. Pigg roared.

As the gavel banged, Benny shouted, "Are you sayin' I ain't tough? Is that what you're sayin'?" But when Cordie turned his back and started to walk away again, Benny yelled after him. "Come on back here, Gator-face! I'll show you who's a tough guy!"

Cordie turned for the challenge with a step toward Benny. "A coward only threatens when he feels safe, and you felt plenty safe that Sunday with Henry standing there beside you, didn't you?"

"Your Honor, this is absurd!" Mr. Pigg shouted.

Judge Poe was pounding his gavel again. "I'll not have this hostility in my courtroom!"

"Are you callin' me a coward?" Benny shouted. Clenching balled-up fists, he stood and yelled again. "Are you callin' *me* a coward!" In a flash, Benny leaped up onto the witness chair railing then jumped flatfooted to the floor. Landing in an ape-like crouch, he shouted, "I ain't no coward!"

"You're a coward right now by not ownin' up to this killing!" Cordie was standing firm with both feet planted, yelling back at Benny. "You're a coward, Benny! Do you hear me? A coward!"

Judge Poe shouted, "Order in the court!" as his gavel pounded, but instead of stopping, Benny dove forward, lunging at Cordie. Panicked, the bailiff sprang into action, grabbing hold of Benny from behind. With arms entwined, he held Benny restrained as both feet kicked out and up, fighting the air to get loose.

Yelling wildly, Benny screamed, "I'll kill you same as I kilt that old man! *I'll kill all of you!*" Benny's arm jerked free as the black-haired lawman, who'd been in charge of Henry, bolted forward to help. He grabbed Benny in a headlock, knocking him to the floor. Wrestling his arms behind him, the lawman pulled out a pair of handcuffs and snapped them around Benny's wrists. Thrashing about on the floor, Benny was writhing like a fish out of water. With a lawman each holding an arm, they pulled him to his feet.

Most all our row, me included, had crouched behind the safety of the balustrade spindles, listening as the judge continued to yell, "Order in this court!" But Daddy and Henry, and Cordie, too, were all standing ready in case Benny broke free again.

Paulette Simmons was yelling like a crazy woman from the back of the courtroom. "I told you to shut your mouth, you stupid little fool! Look what you've done now!" Benny's head was turned, looking back over his shoulder at his mother as the lawmen dragged him toward the door. "Don't you expect me to help you no more!"

"Get that boy out of my courtroom!" the judge was shouting to his bailiff. "Lock him in a holding cell until he's properly charged with the murder of Ray Garren!" The lawmen muscled Benny, kicking and screaming, out through the side door beside us. Standing with gavel in hand and sweat beading on his forehead, the judge declared, "Henry Williams, all charges against you are dropped! You're free to go." Turning to the jurymen, he added, "Jury is hereby released." Then banging his gavel one last time, Judge Poe shouted, "Court is dismissed!"

With Cora right beside me, we both flung our legs over the railing and jumped to hug Henry. We were holding on to him like he'd been away for a year or more.

"I'm free!" Henry was wailing.

When Mama came around the railing to grab hold of Henry, I stepped back to make room for her and found myself standing next to Cordie at the lawyer's table. He was looking down, stacking his papers neatly inside his brown leather satchel, and he was grinning.

"I want to thank you, Cordie," I said.

He looked at me with his green eyes sparkling. "Sooze, that was the most fun I've had since my first year in law school when all the seniors threw a freshman party, and we all ended up in the lake."

"Well, I don't know about bein' fun, but I can sure say your daddy was right about puttin' you through law school. You were born to be a lawyer," I told him.

"Thank you, Sooze. I'm indebted to you for believin' in me."

Amid all the courtroom commotion and chatter, Daddy scooted in close, saying thank you to Cordie, too, and shaking his hand. Then Henry squeezed in beside me. He laid his hand on Cordie's shoulder, saying, "I'm sure thankful for you gettin' me out of this hot water!" Henry grabbed his hand in a shake and then said, "Who'd ever thought we could win this fight pittin' a Beegle against a Pigg? I'll never forget what you done for me, Cordie."

David squeezed in close to stand beside me. "Well, what do you know, Sooze?" Shaking his head, he said, "It really was Benny who stabbed your uncle!"

"I told you it was Benny," I said. "I told you I'd seen the whole thing, David. Why didn't you believe me?"

"Surely you understand," David said. "Families are obligated to one another, and it was clear to me that you felt pressed to uphold your family name. I understand how it is, but I can't be expected to stand up for somethin' like that."

I pulled my sweater tight around me, trying to bind my anger. "No, I *don't* understand. I don't understand at all. How can you say you love me but not believe me? How can you say you love me but turn your back on me when I'm standin' there askin' for your help? How can you do that, David?"

"Come on now, Sooze. I got a family name, too, and mine is an important and respectable name. I can't be expected to risk my family's reputation by standing up for one like yours. It'll be different when we're married because then your name will be the same as mine, but it's not the same yet."

I stood there looking at David like he was a stranger, but in my heart, I knew he was the same man he had always been. The feelings I'd tried so hard to preserve had rotted inside me. Money wasn't important anymore. The job didn't matter either. Love and family—those were worth the fight.

"Here's your ring," I said as I pulled the diamond off my finger and handed it back. "Bein' engaged to you has been like standin' in a bucket, trying to lift myself up, and I can't spend my life doin' that, David."

"What do you mean?" David said, surprised.

But I'd said all I was gonna say. Expecting to have some explaining to do to my family for calling off the wedding, I turned to them, but they were all dutifully attending to Henry and hadn't heard a word.

Grabbing my arm, David pulled me back. "Sooze, we ain't done yet!" I jerked my arm, trying to free myself, but he held on tight. "You're comin' outside with me!"

That was when Thomas Kittridge stepped in. Reaching out with intent, he pressed his hand against David's shoulder. "I don't know whether I'm protecting Sooze from you or you from Sooze, but you best let go of her."

David's grasp melted. In a childish whine, he stayed focused on me, saying, "Sooze, you can't do this. What am I supposed to tell folks?"

Thomas reached down and folded his hand around mine. "Tell 'em Sooze is a strong-willed woman, and she's changed her mind." Thomas squeezed my hand just hard enough to release a bushel of butterflies into my belly. "That's what you tell 'em."

CHAPTER 34

H enry's homecoming should have been a celebration, but soon as we got home from Waldron, we gathered at Grace's grave for Henry to say goodbye. Mama cried when Henry did, but I think their tears were a mix of sadness for Grace and relief for Henry.

Kneeling with his arm around Cora, Daddy looked at his family like we were all that mattered to him. Even though Uncle Ray had died, and Grace was lying there in the family plot, it seemed the strain of unpaid bills and hard times had somehow softened.

So much had changed since the day I turned sixteen.

As we settled back inside the house, Mama said to me, "Sooze, why don't you make pork pancakes for supper so's I can talk to Henry a while longer." The sparkle in her eyes showed how glad she was to have her only boy home again, and Henry seemed just as pleased.

"All right, Mama," I told her.

Even though they all sat within earshot, I couldn't focus on their conversation one bit. In fact, I had not been able to think of anything but Thomas since leaving the courthouse.

With daydreams in my head, I started supper. I wondered if I felt about Thomas the same way Mama felt about Daddy. When I glanced into the living room, Mama had hold of Daddy's hand, and both of them were listening to Henry's jail stories with Cora.

Later, when we sat down to supper, Daddy bowed his head. "Dear Lord, we thank you for this food today, but most of all, we thank you for bringin' Henry home to us. Amen."

As the bowl of creamed corn passed from hand to hand around the table, Henry asked me, "Sooze, what was you and fancy-pants talking about so serious-like at the courthouse?"

I hadn't thought anyone had noticed. "If you mean David, I gave him his ring back."

"You did *what*?" Daddy asked.

Both Henry and Cora whooped with grins smeared across their faces.

Concerned, Mama asked, "Why, Sooze?"

I laid my fork down on the table and leaned back in my chair, trying to work my words out. "It's like you said, Mama," I started. "You told me I got to love the man I'm marrying—really love him like you love Daddy—because marriage is meant to last a lifetime." I scooted myself closer to the table's edge, and with Daddy at one end and Mama at the other, I found myself looking one way first then the other so I could address them both. "You said it don't matter whether you and Daddy have food or a farm as long as you got each other." Looking at Daddy, I asked, "That's right, isn't it?"

Daddy wiped his cloth napkin across his mouth. "Yeah, that's right, Sooze. What are you tryin' to tell us?"

"I don't love David," I said. "I guess I never did. I thought, by marrying him, I'd have a husband who would be here to help us through harvest season, and I'd be able to send money home from the job I'd have at the store so's you could pay the bills." I looked back and forth between Mama and Daddy, but neither one said a word. Seeing the strain of their hearts inside their eyes, I spoke louder, trying to show the importance. "I thought David would be a good husband, and I'd be a good, hardworking wife to him, but every time I needed him in the last few weeks, he wasn't willin' to help." With my voice starting to break, I raised it, saying, "I'm sorry if I'm disappointin' you, but I can't bind myself to a man I don't love, especially one who's quick to turn his back on us."

I'd said it, and even though it felt like a rake was scraping down my insides, I couldn't turn back.

Daddy leaned in, looking me right in the eyes, and with his voice soft, he said, "I'm sorry, Sooze. I had no idea you was plannin' to marry the boy for *us*. I would have stopped you straight away if I'd known."

"You done the right thing callin' it off, Sooze," Mama said as she got out of her chair and came to me with a hug. "You done the right thing."

"I never did like him anyway!" Henry said.

"Yeah, but you liked Benny," Cora told Henry. "So nobody would've listened to *you* anyway."

Henry jumped out of his chair after Cora as she flew from the table and hit the front door, running hard. They were both laughing like two little kids.

"What are we goin' to do about the mortgage payment now that I won't have a job at Huckabee's, Daddy? How are we supposed to pay the monthly bill?"

"We'll make do, Sooze," Daddy said. "We got Henry back now, so we'll figure it out. Besides, we still got our appeals money, remember?"

"What does that mean?" Mama asked. "*Appeals* money."

"We had to take out a bigger loan than we needed from the bank, Emma. We got more than $550 left. It's more than enough to pay our bills and plumb the house. Maybe we'll even find us a used automobile. It sure was hard bummin' rides back and forth to Waldron."

"Almighty, John," Mama said. "Maybe we should give the extra money back to the bank?"

"It don't matter," I told her. "We'd still have to make the

same payments to the bank for the money we already used on Henry's trial anyway."

"She's right, Emma," Daddy agreed.

Henry and Cora came back inside the house, both laughing and out of breath. "Sit back down here!" Mama scolded. "You two quit acting like a bunch of yahoos!"

"Sorry, Ma," Henry said as he settled himself back into his chair. He picked right back up, eating supper where he'd left off, just like he'd been at the table the whole time.

"Don't worry about David, Sooze," Daddy said. "If you ask me, I think that Thomas boy is sweet on you anyway."

I could feel the flush in my face. "I'm feeling the same about him, too, Daddy."

"Whoa, wait a minute," Henry said, focusing on our table talk. "I don't know nobody named Thomas."

"Oh, you'd like him real good, Henry!" Cora said with excitement.

"Who is he?" Henry asked. "I mean, one minute you're marryin' the Huckabee chump, and the next minute, you're sweet on a boy I ain't ever met!"

"You never met Thomas 'cause you got yourself locked up in jail, remember?" I said.

"Woo-wee!" Henry leaned back in his chair with an ornery grin. "I can't leave this house for a minute without everything gettin' turned upside down!"

It sure felt good having Henry home again.

With the rising of the morning sun came the comforting sounds of a home put back in order. From the kitchen downstairs, I smelled fresh perked coffee and bacon frying alongside the scent of Mama's cinnamon biscuits. Outside, the barn door banged shut in the still spring air, telling me Daddy and Henry were already slopping the hogs and tending the chickens. I stretched my arms over my head and yawned as I listened to our big Rhode Island Red rooster crowing out his lungs.

Summer was almost upon us, and I hadn't even planted the garden yet. What with Henry's trouble, lots of chores had gone undone.

I rolled over and slid out of bed quietly so as not to wake Cora. With school out, I felt more kindly toward her sleeping in. Besides, I was looking forward to being by myself in the garden soil. There was something healing about planting a crop, and I felt like I had lots of heart and soul that needed soothing.

Not wanting to wear my school dresses for digging in the dirt, I pulled out my old, short-sleeved blue chambray shirt. I'd already handed it down to Cora, but I slid it off its clothes hanger and slipped it on anyway. It was too small to wear anywhere other than the farm, but the garden bugs wouldn't give a hoot about what I was wearing. I buttoned most of it but had to stop just a little more than halfway up. My bosom had grown, and it was hard to keep those top two buttons fastened. To cover myself better, I went into Henry's room and opened the bottom drawer of his clothes dresser. I pulled out last year's denim overalls, pushed my legs through, then pulled the front flap up over my chest and hooked the shoulder straps. With wool socks on my feet, I went downstairs.

Mama and I had half a cup of coffee together, and I ate one strip of bacon and a biscuit with butter before setting out to gather the seedlings Mama started weeks ago. She went with me to the back porch, where the sprouts grew in planters alongside the west-facing window. She helped me carry them out the back door, where we set them on a big square of plywood. As soon as we had all the tomato, snap beans, zucchini, and okra plants loaded onto the board, we picked it up and headed out to the garden patch. Daddy and Henry always planted four rows of garden corn separate from the field corn, so that had been done in mid-April.

Those rows were already a good three feet high. We set the plywood down next to the stalks.

Pointing to a separate, cultivated square of ground closer to the oil drum trash can, Mama said, "Remember to get the sweet potato slips and the seeds for the butternut squash when you're finished here. Plant them a foot apart over there in the other garden patch. They need lots more room to grow than these seedlings, so don't get your patches mixed up."

"I won't, Mama," I promised.

When Mama walked back inside, I went to our wooden storage shed beside the outhouse and picked up a digging fork, hand hoe, and shovel. We'd grown the garden in the same spot for so many years, the rows never changed much. I knew to plant the beans next to the corn, the okra next to the beans, and then the tomatoes and zucchini. Daddy and Henry had already worked the land, fertilized it, and trenched the rows back when they planted the corn, so I just needed holes dug for the seeds and seedlings. Settling down on the ground, I worked until all the garden rows were planted, constantly curling my loose-hanging hair behind my ears. The earthy smell of our soil and the feel of dirt on my hands brought me peace. Daddy said it was proof I was born to be a farmer, but maybe it was just God's way of saying there was nothing better out there for me.

I was daydreaming when the *tap, tap, tap-tap* of an automobile motor crept into my wits. I stood, slapping the dirt off my overalls, as the sound disappeared behind the line of chinquapin trees. Turning back to my planting, I was bent over counting seedlings when Henry shouted for me. Straightening up again, I saw a Model T Coupe parked between the barn and the corncrib. It looked just like the Kittridge automobile. Walking closer for a better view, I spotted Daddy and Henry, and they were talking to Thomas! When Henry caught sight of me, he raised his arm straight up and waved like he was flagging down a lineman.

My eyes shot a glance downward, and I saw myself in

Henry's old overalls, wearing a shirt too small to button. Never mind the dark fertilized soil on my hands and the specks of dirt on my face and in my hair. Of all the times for a visit!

With Henry waving his arm like a lunatic, Thomas turned. Even though we were a good hundred yards from each other, I'd swear I could see his green eyes sparkle.

"Hey, Sooze!" Henry was yelling loud. "Look who's here to see you!"

Before I could make a dash for the house to change clothes, Thomas had started my way. He was walking fast like a man nervous or mad. I stood there dumbstruck, waiting for the humiliation.

"Hi, Sooze," Thomas said as he neared me. "We didn't get much chance to talk yesterday after the trial, and, well, I've got a few things I'd like to say if it's all right with you."

"O-oh, of course," I stammered, smoothing my hair. "I'm just a bit embarrassed about the way I'm lookin' right now." I lowered my head, adjusting the front flap of the overalls. "I wish I'd known you was comin' for a visit."

Thomas used his fingers to comb his blonde hair back over the crown of his head. Then a smile came. "There's not a more beautiful girl in the whole county than you, Sooze."

His green eyes sent tingles racing through my insides again.

"Thank you, Thomas." I couldn't stop my lips from smiling. "What was it you wanted to talk to me about?"

"Sooze," he said in a practiced tone. "The day you went to Waldron for the jury selection, I admitted to fallin' for you."

"I remember," I said.

"Well, you've never mentioned it, and I'm worried about waitin' too long before bringin' it up again."

My stomach was doing tumbles as I curled my hair behind my ears, hoping to hide the dirt darkening my blonde strands. "You go right on and say whatever you want to say."

Thomas took a breath, and then straightened himself into the stance of a serious man. "I know it's awfully soon after your breakup with Huckabee," he said. "But, Sooze, if you could just give me a chance, I'd like to prove myself worthy." With a throat clearing, he looked down, then shifted from one foot to the other before looking back at me again. "Now, I know you got better choices, but I want to say there's nothin' I wouldn't do for you. If you knew what was in my heart..." His affection took hold of my soul, filling me with so much love it came seeping out in tears. "Oh, no, don't cry, Sooze. I couldn't stand it if I made you cry."

Without taking our eyes off each other, we each took a step closer as if a magnet drew us together.

Using my garden-soiled hands, I wiped my tears. "I'm not cryin' out of sadness," I told him. "It's happiness that's leakin' out of me."

Thomas smiled then took my hand in his. "Does this mean you'll give me a chance?"

My heart was beating so wildly I was sure he could hear it, so I held my free hand to my chest, hoping to steady it. "I *have* to give you a chance, Thomas. You're the one who gave me a reason to believe."

He wrapped his arms around me, gently pressing his lips to mine. A flurry of love fluttered inside me like a collared dove caught in a cage.

After an extra-loud throat clearing, Daddy said, "Looks like you two found each other."

Thomas stepped back, nodding with a shy grin. "Yes, sir, we found each other."

"How long you been standin' there, Daddy?"

"Long enough for us to hear the news." Daddy's eyes had a twinkle as he motioned to the others.

I turned to see Mama, Henry, and Cora. Mama was wiping tears on the apron she'd pulled up to her eyes.

"Cora was right, Sooze," Henry said. "I sure like him better!"

"Told you!" Cora stuck her tongue out at Henry.

Reaching into her apron pocket, Mama pulled out the embroidery square she'd been working on for weeks and began smoothing it against herself. She held it up, looking at it with a satisfied smile before handing it to me. "I finished this for you, Sooze. I been plannin' to make it a gift, but when you called off your engagement, I didn't think you was ready for it yet. I guess I was wrong."

Holding up the white cotton square, I saw colorful wild-flowers just like those growing in Whitaker's Meadow embroidered along its edges. I smiled when I read the words stitched into its center: "Love is sweet when it's new, but sweeter yet when it's true."

If you like this, you may also enjoy: Hearts and Mountains

By Lynn Eldridge

A tale of feuding hearts amidst dangerous mountains...

Spicy McCoy is pilfering berries for her mountain medicine, when confronted by a foe claiming to own the West Virginia land she's on. Stealing could result in jail or worse, death. Strikingly handsome, the enemy is like none she's ever met. He says his name is Stone, he's a doctor and not out to hurt her. She can have the berries he says. Sure, for a price. He blocks her escape until she kicks his shin, flees and poles across the Tug Fork River. But when her patient worsens, she may risk her life to seek Stone's advice.

Stone Hatfield has come home to escort his mother and aunt to an election. Living in Philadelphia for the past twelve years, he's at his house on the hill when he spies a trespasser. Never in his wildest dreams did he expect to find a sexy river siren swiping his blueberries. She refuses to identify herself, but a man in the Kentucky woods calls out Spicy. The sassy name fits. Due to Tug Valley's dark and deadly history, Stone isn't surprised by her flight. Unable to get her out of his mind, he defies the feud to find her.

Clay McCoy, a murdering madman intent on marrying Spicy, is determined not to let anybody get in his way.

Vorticia Hatfield, a self-proclaimed witch plans to eliminate any threat to her squatting rights on the backside of the Stony Mountains.

Feuds from every emotional and physical angle erupt, threatening to destroy the good instead of the evil.

AVAILABLE NOW

ABOUT THE AUTHOR

Karen (K.S.) Jones comes to us from the beautiful Texas Hill Country where she writes Historical Fiction and Contemporary Western Romance. In 2014, *Southern Writers* magazine awarded Karen their grand prize for "Best Short Fiction" of the year, and soon after, her first two novels, *Shadow of the Hawk*, Historical Fiction, and *Black Lightning*, a middle-grade sci-fi/fantasy, saw publication. Her work has garnered numerous literary awards, including the coveted WILLA Award from Women Writing the West in 2016, as well as the 2015 and 2017 Literary Classics International Book Award, the 2015 Chaucer Award, and the 2016 RONE Award. Her newest novel, CHANGE OF FORTUNE, was released this past February and within hours it rose to #30 on Amazon's list of top 100 in American Historical Romances. The novel is already in its third printing.

www.ingramcontent.com/pod-product-compliance
Lightning Source LLC
Chambersburg PA
CBHW011422010726
47494CB00011B/2452